DIVERSE SIMILARITY

SHARON ROSE

Eternarose Publishing

To Laura:
Your joy and encouragement sweeten my life.

CONTENTS

PART ONE

Chapter 1	3
Chapter 2	11
Chapter 3	18
Chapter 4	29
Chapter 5	37
Chapter 6	50
Chapter 7	60
Chapter 8	65
Chapter 9	72
Chapter 10	80
Chapter 11	86
Chapter 12	93
Chapter 13	102
Chapter 14	110
Chapter 15	117
Chapter 16	125
Chapter 17	136
Chapter 18	144
Chapter 19	157
Chapter 20	167
Chapter 21	175
Chapter 22	183
Chapter 23	194
Chapter 24	199
Chapter 25	208
Chapter 26	218
Chapter 27	229
Chapter 28	237
Chapter 29	250

PART TWO

Chapter 30   261
Chapter 31   272
Chapter 32   281
Chapter 33   293
Chapter 34   304
Chapter 35   313
Chapter 36   322
Chapter 37   333
Chapter 38   341
Chapter 39   350
Chapter 40   359
Chapter 41   371
Chapter 42   382
Chapter 43   390
Chapter 44   400
Chapter 45   413
Chapter 46   424
Chapter 47   432
Chapter 48   440
Chapter 49   453

Cast of Characters   465
The Next Adventure   467
More From Sharon Rose   469
Acknowledgments   471
About the Author   473

PART ONE

CHAPTER ONE

K ena extended her awareness as she stepped into the astro observation room. As always, she identified the races first, not by sight, but by the feel of their emfrel —that faint mental energy all exuded but only Humans noticed. Prednian, Tenelli, and Dantokrellie. No Meklehon. Good. That meant Gordahl, chief of science fleet, wasn't here yet.

She could use a few minutes to study the astro display and find some hint of what lay behind this sudden meeting.

Gordahl's invitation—no, summons—puzzled her. True to Meklehon custom, he'd worded it as a courteous request, but she wasn't misled. Not with ten minutes' notice and no mention of purpose.

She walked toward the enormous three-dimensional viewing area, which dominated the center of the room. A Prednian member of the space station's staff operated the control console mounted in the wide railing that encircled the display. Locks of hair escaped his headband and divided around his circular ear. A dozen or so strangers stood around in small groups; gesturing, frowning, or questioning, depending on their race. All as puzzled as she, it seemed. Their multi-pitched voices reminded her of an

3

orchestra tuning instruments before a concert. She strolled between them, her attention fixed on the 3-D display.

Two rocky planets, each with a moon, spun before her. No unique traits gave a clue to their identities. She glanced at the star designation: SMG76428. SMG—a single yellow star, not unlike her own. Numbered rather than named, so the system was probably uninhabited. Kena checked its location—the far side of PitKreelaundun space and the nebula bordering it. Her brows shot up. *That* would allow no simple route for an Interstellar Collaborative ship.

A raspy voice to her right exclaimed, "Look! That must be a Human female."

Kena kept her gaze on the planets and her expression neutral. A Prednian, no doubt. Sharing knowledge trumped manners every time.

Someone gasped, and another muttered, "Brilliant observation."

The Tenelli standing nearest to Kena jerked his hand back as though he had touched something disgusting. "He's Prednian. With all their experience, you'd think he would know better than to blurt out something like that."

Kena smiled. Tenelli used such picturesque gestures. She whispered, "But you said it yourself. He's Prednian."

The man laughed, revealing the Tenelli smile that looked so Human. "I take it you're not bothered."

"I'm well aware that my figure is unusual to non-Humans," Kena said. "And this far from Earth, there aren't many of us." She waved a hand toward the display. "Do you know why we care about this?"

"Not yet." He turned fully to her. "I am Thrayl."

Before she could respond to his introduction, the door opened, and Gordahl entered. He bowed as he strode toward the display. Only a Meklehon could make that combination look graceful. Easy to believe that their spines contained more vertebrae than any other race.

4

DIVERSE SIMILARITY

"I thank you all for joining me with so little notice or explanation," Gordahl said. "The urgency cannot be overstated. You'll understand as soon as you see this progression." He nodded to his aide at the console.

The 3-D display zoomed out. The two planets took up positions in relation to their star, a small, glowing ball near the floor. Yellow and green lines marked half of their orbital paths, which arced above the star. Prednian symbols floated by the now tiny objects, revealing additional information. The outer planet just might be within the habitable zone. A little bigger than Earth, with a moon a bit smaller than Luna. The inner planet, about the size of Mars, with a tiny moon, was probably too near the star to support any form of life.

The planets neared alignment. Even the two moons joined the show, drawing between their host planets. They appeared too far apart to be tidally locked. This was a one-in-a-million alignment.

Gordahl's low, resonant voice filled the room. "The outer planet has an elliptical orbit. It's now at perihelion. We have some interesting tidal forces to consider. Anomalies have been noticed recently, but even still, these objects are too widely separated for gravitational disruption." He turned to his aide. "Zoom back in on the planets, please."

The display split in order to show planetary details. Although orbital motion was still revealed, the four objects appeared close together. The spheres aligned in elegant symmetry much like the hands of a huge clock approaching the top of the hour. Unique and serene beauty—it begged for musical accompaniment. But why were they watching this?

Then, the outer planet shattered. Kena jumped, sucking her breath in. Seconds later, the inner one broke apart. She staggered back a step.

Amidst the loud exclamations of those surrounding her, Kena breathed the words, "Oh...my...God." How could this happen?

A half-minute more, and the large moon fragmented. Such devastation—so rapid. She held her breath, as though the distant

5

shockwaves battered her and another was on the way. An awareness rose from deep within her. There was more to this—something of much greater significance than visible destruction.

Questions and speculations escalated throughout the room. Kena studied the display, listening with half an ear, filing away what little was known. No, there was no sign of collisions...The system had been under study because of gravitational anomalies...A bizarre energy reading preceded the events. Let them speculate. She needed to understand subsequent motion.

Gordahl's voice rose over the din. "Quiet, please. Analysis can wait. We are here to plan the science mission." He turned to the Prednian at the controls. "Speed up the progression to current position and then extrapolate."

The aide fulfilled his order.

"The mission is assigned to the *Ontrevay*," Gordahl said, "which is en route to this space station. It will be re-supplied and set out by 13:00 tomorrow. It will make use of a spatial rift to approach the nebula, and then travel along the PitKreelaundun border." He inclined his head as though acknowledging an objection. "Not a very desirable course, but it is the fastest. The debris cloud you see now is our projection for the *Ontrevay's* arrival time. If we opt for a slower route, the debris from the two planets will be mixed, which would present problems with both navigation and origin identification."

He went on to talk through decision timeframes and provisions that had been made for the hurried departure, all standard information. Kena studied the display until Gordahl came to her side.

"Kena Talgarth, it pleases me to meet you," he said.

She returned his bow and greeting with the polish of a Meklehon. Some believed members of each race should use only their own native courtesies. She was not among them. These simple observances had often tipped the scale in her favor when she encountered the critical stares of alien races. It worked again, lightening his formal expression.

Gordahl glanced around the room. "You may have already noticed that all of these are scientists. Their specialties were chosen for the mission, of course. Shall we step aside and let them immerse themselves in their passion?"

Those nearby took the hint, and Kena found herself in private conversation with one of the highest-ranking officers in the Collaborative. Not normal procedure for crew assignments!

"The *Ontrevay* is adequately staffed with navigators," Gordahl said, "but you have experience with the PitKreelaundun and a piloting record that no one can fault. To reach the level of senior navigator in only six years is no small accomplishment."

"Thank you, sir."

"Does the mission interest you?"

"Interest me? Indeed!"

"Forgive me if I misconstrue your tone," he said. "Does that mean you've already decided to join it?"

Why was he asking, when he'd given everyone three hours to respond? "I do rather like to see an offer before I accept it," she said. "There's more to consider than just the mission."

"The offer has been prepared. Feel free to download it—and the preparation files, as well."

He paused while she unclipped her private computer from her belt and pressed the re-form control. It extended and changed shape to accommodate finger input, which she used to access the waiting information. A voice, familiar and loving, spoke within her spirit. *Go with them.* His peace embraced her.

"Please do not feel that I'm pressuring you," Gordahl said. "You'll have the full time allowed, but there is one aspect of the decision, perhaps two, that I would like to discuss with you. What do you know of the *Ontrevay*?"

"It's one of the investigation ships commissioned by the Collaborative itself, rather than a member race," she said. "That means it has the latest technology and a multi-racial crew. Openings are rare and sought after, which speaks well of its leadership." Kena shrugged. "That's about it."

"All true. Eleven races at the moment. The largest percentage is Prednian, closely followed by Tenelli. They use the Prednian language exclusively, as we do here."

"Are any Humans among them?" she asked.

"No, you would be the first." He inclined his head again. "This was one of my concerns. I realize you may prefer to travel with other Humans, but at least I can assure you that Frethan, the chief navigation officer, is Tenelli. He has the reputation of being fair and well liked."

Stated with diplomacy, but he didn't pretend there were no issues. Her respect for him rose a notch. Traveling in the company of Humans wasn't as necessary to her as to some. Cultural issues were the real thorn.

Gordahl was likely old enough to remember when the Tenelli had first made contact with Humans and sponsored their entrance to the Collaborative. Whether it was a leftover from sponsorship, or simply their kind natures, the Tenelli still carried a protective attitude toward Humans. If a cultural issue turned nasty, she would have support.

Kena nodded. "It's always a pleasure to work with the Tenelli."

"I checked your emfrel acclimation records," he said. "Your broad travels have prepared you well. You've already been acclimated to ten of the races that make up the *Ontrevay's* crew. The other race is even less common than Humans on Collaborative ships. I must inform you that the captain, Ghent, is Plynteth."

"Oh..." She drew the word out. No point in hiding the obvious.

He nodded, compressing his lips. "It's commonly understood that Humans have difficulty with acclimation to Plynteth. Being Meklehon, I'm sure I don't comprehend just how bad it is. I checked with the station's chief medical officer." He hesitated. "She informs me that Human acclimation to Plynteth emfrel has the distinction of being the most traumatic anyone could experience. There is risk of short-term memory loss. She does not recommend it."

8

Gordahl paused a moment as if he felt that needed special emphasis. "So, even though we do want you to join this mission, I fully understand if you choose not to. There would be no negative reflection on you. If you do accept, Ghent asked me to convey his gratitude and to assure you that he will grant you all the time you need for full recovery. We're told to expect at least three days."

"Thank you for your concern," Kena said. "I heard similar warnings when I was acclimated to both Meklehon and Grfdn, but I lost no memory. Sooner or later, I'm bound to travel with Plynteth, so I'll need acclimation anyway." Her hair tickled her chin as she shook her head. "I'm not about to let it stand in the way of joining such an intriguing mission. The only problem is timing. I assume that's why you'd like an early decision. If I'm to be awake and functional by tomorrow morning, I should get on to medical immediately."

"No," he said. "That's what I expected you to do, but it's what I want to prevent." His brows pinched together. "We prefer that you allow the *Ontrevay's* doctor to perform the acclimation. Your recovery will not be interrupted, and you'll be cared for by the same doctor throughout. This also removes the need to rush your decision."

"I see."

"Good," he said. "You're off duty until morning, so take time to review the mission info. I've already authorized live communication for you—to Earth or wherever you like. It wouldn't hurt to record your conversations." He rested an arm on the display area's railing. "The *Ontrevay* will assign one of its small craft to you and have it waiting at the station by morning. You may depart as early as you choose. Any questions?"

She tilted her head. "No, not really, but you've gone to some trouble for me. I thank you, sir."

This drew a smile from him. "You are welcome, ma'am. May I ask you a personal question?"

"You may."

"I wondered when I saw your name," he said, "and even more

when I saw your eyes and heard you speak…Are you related to Andrew Talgarth?"

Kena smiled. It was a good thing she loved her dad, because their relationship couldn't be hidden. Not with the unusual mixture of green and blue in their eyes—or the tilted corners of the lower lids.

"Ah, these eyes," she said. "They're always announcing that I'm his daughter. Do you know him?"

"I heard him lecture a few times," he said, "but I only met him briefly. It must have been thirty years ago. I doubt he'll remember me, but please give him my regards when you talk with him next."

"I will." Kena inclined her upper body. "Thank you for offering me this opportunity."

Instead of returning the formality, he shifted his gaze to the display. The breakup and extrapolation sequence was repeating. Debris filled the gap between the two planets, and some fragments collided. His brow tightened. "I'm never sure how to respond to thanks for sending someone into danger." He bowed. "I wish you safe travels."

CHAPTER TWO

A tidal wave of alien emfrel crashed into Kena. It snuffed out physical awareness, suffocating her in a dark, silent void where time could not be measured. Only a presence existed: So unnatural, so foreign, she could not lay hold to push it away. The full power of an alien mind forced itself upon her.

As fast as the wave had struck, it was gone. Her floundering mind tried to grasp for identity. Who had attacked her so? But there was no one. Oh—artificial emfrel. It would return. She shuddered, and her heart pounded with painful intensity.

Kena arched her back and tried to kick free of whatever held her. A vain attempt. She lay in a full body restraint. Adrenaline pulsed through her. She took full advantage of it and threw all the strength of overcharged muscles into a desperate attempt to break away. Useless.

All at once, her shoulders and head broke free. She had no idea why, but tried to squirm her arms loose. Hands gripped her, and an unintelligible voice reached her ears. Why couldn't she see?

Someone was rubbing her shoulders. The hand brushed her hair out of her face. A low voice said her name and made a garbled demand. The darkness opened on a room she didn't recognize.

"Kena, look at me!"

Ah, the words weren't garbled; they were Prednian. Locating his face and focusing took way more effort than it should, but it didn't help. She had no idea who he was.

His frown eased when she made eye contact. "You'll be all right. Relax, now."

Oh, sure! Her entire body was vibrating.

"Start your relaxation technique," he said.

She tried to draw the first deep breath. It trembled and escaped as a sob.

"Rest," he said. "I'll help you. Try again."

Kena's shaking stopped, too abrupt to be natural. Indescribable feelings surged down her limbs. What was he doing to her? A drug? Or drugs? *No, no, no!*

"Take a deep breath," he said. "Think of gentle waves."

That was the beginning of her technique—How did he know? Had she told him? Did she know him?

Control. She had to get control. Her mind darted back and forth; one side convinced he was attacking her, the other asserting that she should do as he said. She had to find some rational way to make a decision. If she could just ask, just translate that simple question into Prednian and get her lips to utter it. After a failed attempt, she managed to whisper, "What's happening?"

"Acclimation to emfrel."

Could that be true? She'd never experienced anything this bad. "What race?"

"Plynteth," he said. "Don't talk yet. Rest. Gentle waves."

Perhaps that explained a little, but...so many questions. She drove her mind toward the first sensations of her technique: The sound of waves lapping at sand. Her body lying on an air mattress while a breeze pushed ripples beneath her floating bed. Sunlight warming her skin.

Symbolism triggered her memory. Draw on the light—the one true light that lived inside. *He's always with me. My protection when I'm weak.*

Her breath eased and steadied. She wrapped herself in her dear friend's comforting love. Distracting sensations passed through her mind and body, still so difficult to comprehend. But she was with her love, and he was drawing her deep into his stillness. She floated there.

Another wave of emfrel slapped into her mind.

This time, she recognized it. *Endure. Endure!* Darkness approached but didn't swallow her. She could still feel restraint against her tensed muscles. A strangled groan reached her ears.

Then, the emfrel was gone, and the groan ceased. Had that been her voice? Her breath panted, dashing to keep pace with her heart.

"Kena, do you know what's happening?"

"Yeah," she moaned.

"Tell me what it is."

He wanted her to talk? Maybe it was over. Maybe he'd let her sleep if she answered. She found the word and manage to get it out. "Acclimation."

"Rest again, Kena," he said.

The restraint dissolved as he spoke, taking her fear of a repeat away with it. She lay cushioned in a medical couch, which had formed to her body. Simple comfort. She sent her mind back to rocking waves and sunlight, hoping to still her trembling body before he could pump more drugs into it. Maybe she succeeded. She wasn't quite sure. Exhaustion swept her down, down toward sleep.

Again, emfrel smashed into her relaxed mind. She grasped it and thrust back. It felt so much like a person. As before, it evaporated—a sensation as disconcerting as slamming a fist into a shadow.

This could not go on! Through clenched teeth, she snapped, "Are you quite finished?"

"Yes. Calm yourself."

His voice, devoid of emotion, only stoked her fury. She fumbled for the couch control and brought it upright. She would have stood, but he pressed a hand to her chest and brought the couch back down to half recline.

"You will remain on the couch." His tone of authority was unmistakable.

Who was this guy? She'd just yelled at him. What if he was an officer? Kena studied him. Dantokrellie, of course. His fuzzy hair in varied shades of brown made that obvious, but she couldn't remember meeting him. "I suppose I should know this, but, uh, who are you?"

"Metchell, chief medical officer."

"Lovely!" she said. "I just shouted at an officer."

His strictly-business demeanor melted into laughter. "Extreme provocation. You get away with that one."

Maybe her world was normal, after all. He behaved true to form. A Dantokrellie would laugh at most any quip if one's tone was lowered. "Where am I?" she asked.

"You're on the *Ontrevay*, one of the Collaborative's investigation ships."

"Oh." A tingle surged through her chest as the realization hit her. "How much memory have I lost?"

"I don't know yet, but don't worry. We recorded memory tracing." He began removing an intravenous tube from her arm. "What was your last ship?"

"*Baktel*," she said.

"Mission?"

"Charting the latest spatial rift to be discovered." She dropped her tone. "A remarkably boring endeavor."

He held the laugh in, but his eyes crinkled. "Oh? Why was that?"

"The one and only unique feature of the rift was its uncharacteristic uniformity."

"So I heard," he said. "Not enough twists and eddies to amuse you, I suppose. Did you complete the mission?"

He continued prompting her forward through memories that coalesced as he questioned. She no longer doubted they had

14

conversed, though she couldn't yet remember it. He brought her up to the memory of shattered planets and her discussion with Gordahl. That conversation took on a whole new significance.

"Did you know in advance what we spoke of?" she asked.

He nodded. "We planned it that way, so you'd make your decision several hours before acclimation. Gordahl was convinced you would accept the mission." The corners of his mouth pinched.

"Did you try to talk me out of it?"

"Of course." He uttered a soft chuckle. "You were hard to persuade. What did you do after you met with Gordahl?"

"Um..."

His hand moved to his medical console. The memory crystalized.

"Oh," she said, "I talked with my family. You triggered that one?"

"I did. Did you record the transmission?"

"Yes."

"Be sure to listen to it again," he said. "What next?"

Her recollection from the rest of that evening remained fuzzy until he triggered the memories. The following morning had gaping holes even after he triggered. All she remembered was the space station's external operations command room. That and the cold or curious stares the support navigators had turned her way, plus an over-awed junior navigator. How annoying and how typical. One minute, she's treated with kindness, the next with disdain, and then someone's fawning over her like she's a hero because she knows her job.

That was the end of her recall. She didn't even remember which craft she'd piloted to the *Ontrevay*. "Can you trigger it again?" she asked, suppressing her third yawn.

"No," he said. "You're not going to be awake much longer. Do you want to sleep here or in your quarters?"

"My quarters."

"Then I'd better get you there now." Metchell hovered close as she stood and took a few steps.

Did he think she couldn't walk? She moved for the door but paused when he touched her arm.

He pointed to the counter. "Your computer."

Only now did she realize it wasn't clipped to her belt. She picked it up and stared at its display of the ship's layout. She must have used it to find the medical section. "You needn't escort me," she said. "This will guide me."

"You're more likely to get halfway there and lie down to sleep in the hallway."

She forced her sagging eyelids open. "That would be embarrassing."

Metchell shook his head. He took the device from her hands, closed it, and clipped it to her belt. Grasping her arm in a firm grip, he said, "Come."

By the time they reached her quarters, he'd wrapped an arm around her waist as well. When they stepped across the threshold, the lighting came on, and garish color assaulted her eyes; random splashes of intense scarlet, orange, and magenta. Streaks of chartreuse shot through the jumble of blinding color.

Kena gasped, covered her eyes, and staggered backward against the wall. "I can't sleep here."

Metchell chuckled and pulled her computer from her belt. "I hope you stored a décor scheme in this thing." He accessed the public controls. "Ah, yes. Dozens of them. Do you have a preference?"

"I don't care," she murmured.

"Then, we'll try this one named *Ocean*."

The device accessed the room controls, and the glowing colors beyond her lids dimmed.

"There," Metchell said. "It's now safe to open your eyes."

Kena peered through her fingers, then exhaled. The color scheme had changed to soothing hues of sea and sky, beach and driftwood. An audio accompaniment of waves on sand completed the effect.

Metchell glanced around. "Why is this called *Ocean?*" He

turned back to Kena. "Never mind." He drew her past the table and couch, then guided her to the bed in the adjacent room. "Sit," he said, pushing the blanket aside, "but don't lie down. I'm getting you some water."

The rising triple chime of a command tone sounded, and Kena groped for her computer.

"It's mine," Metchell said, taking a quick look down at the message.

He touched her shoulder, startling her. His intent gaze moved over her face as he offered her a cup. When had he gotten that? Was she asleep sitting up? Kena reached for it, sloshing water over the edge.

He kept his grip on the cup and guided it to her lips while supporting her. "Drink."

Kena gulped the water down with sudden awareness of her thirst. A need almost as strong as the sleepiness that engulfed her. She sagged under its weight, only half aware of Metchell easing her down onto her side and lifting her legs onto the bed. It didn't seem right that he was putting her to bed, particularly when a command tone had...

CHAPTER THREE

G hent tapped the annoying little computer clipped to his
belt. Its distractions had nearly driven him insane until
he taught his officers just what sort of messages
warranted immediate delivery.

Remlishos, chief engineering officer, stood next to him near the
sloped window of the external operations command room, which
overlooked the craft bay. One of the large modularized craft rested
below them with its hull open.

"Just performing routine maintenance," Remlishos said, "while
the craft are idle."

Ghent nodded and glanced at the message on his computer.
Metchell had responded to him by asking his location. Ghent
entered *ex op command*, then snapped it shut. "Are there any issues
with the *Ontrevay?*"

Remlishos uttered the standard systems report, though he
could have summarized it with two words: Everything works.

"Thank you," Ghent said. Among his own race, a quick nod
would have ended the conversation, but the Meklehon placed a
high value on such courtesies. Remlishos left him with a slight bow,
and Ghent moved nearer to Jorlit, the Tenelli navigator on duty

before the low-profile consoles at the window's edge. Ghent glanced over the schedule displayed on the console. "Not much for you to do."

Jorlit crimped his lips. "It is the boring part of the trip."

"Were there any issues when Kena came aboard?"

"Bringing a tiny craft into a wide-open bay?" Jorlit's pale, fuzzy hair shifted as he shook his head. "Not much possibility of anything going wrong. Nor any scope to showcase her skills."

"You've heard of her before?"

"Oh, yes! Bound to after her evasive maneuvers around that fractured asteroid, a PitKreelaundun fighter right on her tail. The way she darted within meters of the surface..." Words seemed to fail him.

Jorlit's excitement drew a smile from Ghent. "I suppose. That famed bit of flying has become something of a legend."

"I doubt anyone would fully believe it if it hadn't been recorded." Jorlit angled his head, eyes wide. "She used that asteroid almost like a shield, staying out of weapon range while leading her opponent in so close that he crashed trying to catch her."

"An impressive flight," Ghent said, keeping concerns to himself. Skill, he admired. Bravado? No.

The door opened, admitting Metchell, but Jorlit continued speaking. "Then, there's the time she rescued that injured navigator." He spread his hands. "Humans aren't even telepaths. I don't understand how she could have done it."

Metchell's step hesitated, and he stared.

"I've wondered that myself," Ghent said. "Metchell, maybe you can tell us; but first, how is Kena?"

"She is resting in her quarters. She's off duty until I let you know otherwise."

Ghent waited for more, then said, "That doesn't tell me much."

"Humans have some privacy restrictions, so I can't say more than necessary. Who was on duty when she arrived?"

"Just me," Jorlit said.

"She doesn't remember it. How much did she interact with you?"

Jorlit frowned and murmured, "That bad?" before answering. "We exchanged standard entrance communication. After she anchored her craft in the bay, she came up here, and we talked a few minutes. Then, she left for medical section."

"When she's awake and active, see if you can find a way to walk her through that. It might help her recover memory."

"I'd be glad to."

Metchell looked back at Ghent. "What were you talking about when I came in?"

"One of Kena's remarkable accomplishments," Ghent said. "She remote-piloted a craft via a telepathic link."

Metchell's brow creased. "How can navigation have anything—anything at all—to do with telepathy?"

Ghent adapted, for the doctor knew little of navigation. "To be more precise, she telepathically linked with the injured navigator who could do nothing more than look at his environment. Remote piloting is just a form of robotics, using a communication beam to send commands to the craft. The problem is feedback. The result of actions and changes in the environment must be perceived instantly, but that's too much data for a comm beam. Hence the need for telepathy."

Metchell stared for a moment. "Is that actually taught in navigator training?"

Ghent let a grin show. He never had to worry about offending Metchell. "Not that I've ever heard of. The first time it happened was between a Meklehon couple. They were already linked when the accident occurred, and the wife continued to use their existing link. And saved her husband's life thereby."

Metchell's expression finally relaxed. "Ah!"

"It got a lot of attention at the time," Jorlit said, "in navigation circles, anyway. The technique has been used in several rescues since then." A voice came over the comm channel, and Jorlit turned away to respond.

"The strange thing is," Ghent said, "the only successful attempts have been between members of the same race, and only for races that do not need a tactile cue to link. How could Kena—not even a natural telepath—have initiated contact?"

"Ah!" Metchell's brow knit. "What race was the navigator she linked with?"

"Meklehon."

"I suppose," he said, stretching his words, "she could have given an audible cue over the comm system."

Ghent shook his head. "He was deaf."

"Deaf? What happened?"

"The hull ruptured."

Metchell made a sound in his throat and grimaced.

"The emergency shield deployed, and the craft re-pressurized within seconds," Ghent said. "I'm not sure why, but his shoulders dislocated."

"Another vulnerable area for that race." Metchell rolled his shoulders and swept a hand to one ear "As for hearing, his entire ear would implode in a vacuum. Excruciating."

Ghent watched Jorlit operate one of the robotic lifts, moving equipment in the bay. "Despite that," Ghent said, "Kena established a link, endured the distraction of his pain, and brought him into range for recovery. Her skills explain part of that, but I cannot fathom how she initiated the link."

"It's hard to be certain, Ghent. Meklehon are strong telepaths. He must have reached out for help."

"I am equally strong, and I've linked with Remlishos countless times. But if he experienced the same thing, I doubt I could establish a link with him. And Humans aren't even natural telepaths!"

"That very lack could be the key," Metchell said.

Jorlit straightened and turned their way again. "What do you mean?"

"Perhaps, since Humans are unable to establish links as we do, they use a method that would never occur to us. I've seen a hint of this already." He glanced between their faces. "I recorded her memory tracing before acclimating her. When I asked what cue she wanted to link with the recorder, she said, 'Humans don't use a cue. Just turn it on.' She linked almost instantly."

"But..." Jorlit shook his head. "She linked to a device...with no identifying cue?"

Metchell nodded, his pinched lips revealing how thoroughly he identified with Jorlit's amazement.

"I so look forward to linking with her," Ghent said.

Metchell's lips parted. A shift along his throat preceeded a rising tonal change. "I need to talk with you in private."

Ghent turned for the door. "My consult room, then." The door to ex op command slid open, then shut behind them. "Before you get too irate with me, let me assure you that I don't intend to link with her immediately."

Metchell expelled a controlled breath as they strode through the hallway. "That was going to be my first warning. We'll skip the reason why for now and move on to public information. If you telepathically link with her, it is necessary—absolutely crucial— that you allow her to control the link."

"Metchell, do you seriously believe I haven't read—no, studied —the Human racial profile?"

"If you have, you ought to forgive me for belaboring this point."

Ghent chuckled. "I suppose I shouldn't be surprised. The profile did emphasize that it's fatal to any non-Human who takes control. I cannot imagine why, but I do acknowledge it. So let me assure you, I'll permit Kena to control if she is willing to link with me."

"You have me puzzled, Ghent. It appears you've selected a navigator—a Human navigator, no less—for her telepathic skills."

"Not at all. You simply walked in while we discussed an unusual event. Kena's telepathy is a small bonus, which we may never need. Her navigation skills are another matter. I could tell you of flight after flight where she accomplished near impossibilities." Ghent dropped his tone. "I'll spare you, though. I know you wouldn't appreciate them as they deserve."

Metchell laughed. They walked in silence for a moment, and the humor faded from Metchell's face. "I hope her Human nervous system is adequate justification for what she endured."

Ghent's shoulders tightened. Had acclimation been worse than expected? He couldn't ask in the hallway. "Don't assume her skills are limited to the proverbial Human quickness. She is much more than that. Decision-making. Training skills. Leadership under pressure. I could go on, but it will all point to one thing. Kena Talgarth is not an average navigator. And if you think I praise her highly, you should have heard Frethan when we discovered she was available."

"I'm sure the two of you can judge her skills far better than I." Metchell's brow creased "Talgarth. Her family name strikes me as familiar."

"It should. Andrew Talgarth is a highly respected culturalist, although not as public as he used to be."

"Is Kena related to him?"

"It's hard to know. Humans reuse names." Ghent touched his four long fingers to the access panel beside the door of his consult room, causing it to slide open.

They seemed to step from a spaceship onto a Plynteth balcony. Three walls displayed a panoramic view of a canyon from Ghent's home-world. Ghent skirted the granite, half-moon table and lowered himself into his traditional chair behind the table's straight edge, while Metchell took one of the re-formable chairs along the its curve.

Ghent took a deep breath and savored the change. This was one place where he could be fully comfortable. His chair was as stable as the rock wall behind him, unlike the swiveling, sliding chairs that others preferred. Better yet, its back was no higher than the armrests, so it never rubbed his fur in a contrary direction. He settled himself and rested his forearms on the table. "What's the problem, Metchell?"

"As far as the crew is concerned, Kena is simply off duty. But for you, don't go anywhere near her."

What was this? "Are you saying that she cannot acclimate to Plynteth?"

"It's not that bad. With the Human privacy restrictions, I can't go into details without reason. Jorlit was present, and anyone could have walked in."

"Ah. As captain, I require an explanation of Kena's condition."

"Trauma was severe. I had to use three bursts, which completely exhausted her." Metchell's voice ground. He shook his head as though the motion were necessary to bring his changeable tone back to a neutral pitch. "Progress is adequate for her to finish unassisted, but she's now highly sensitive to Plynteth emfrel. She's going to find your presence extremely distracting for a while."

Even Metchell's neutral tone sounded tense to Ghent. Was *severe* an understatement? "I wish I could comprehend this better. It's hard to empathize when I've never been disturbed by an acclimation."

"That's because Plynteth emfrel is so complex," Metchell said, "almost as though it combines energy patterns from other races. Alien emfrel may feel odd to you, but there's always some nuance you can identify. Humans have faint, simple emfrel. They weren't even aware it existed until they met the Tenelli. Alien emfrel comes right through their shields into their minds. They can't recognize it unless it's concentrated. To a Human, acclimation feels like an invasion." He dramatized, sweeping his fingers up to his head, then jerking back as though assaulted. "Like a powerful being entering the mind without warning or permission."

The fur on Ghent's forehead puckered. "That must be appalling for a non-telepathic race. Why three bursts?"

"The first is too—*incomprehensible* may be the best word. The shield doesn't get much chance to identify and adjust."

"Why is it so much worse for Humans then other races?" Ghent asked, leaning back in his broad chair. "Is it because they're not natural telepaths?"

"Spoken like a telepath." A trace of disbelief lifted Metchell's voice, but he leveled it again. "Every race has emfrel. It's the excess life energy that is *not* used. That's why it gets vented and affects others. Telepathy requires specific, focused energy, which is not vented. Whether a person is a telepath has nothing to do with how emfrel affects them."

"Then why," Ghent asked, "are Humans so traumatized?"

"Acclimation creates a disorienting form of shock in Humans, which shuts down sensory perception." Metchell glanced around. "Imagine you're standing by that railing over there, and suddenly the room goes dark and silent as the void. Vertigo hits, so you try to grab the railing—but you can't feel it. You don't even know whether you're floating up from the balcony or plunging into the canyon."

Metchell's gaze followed his movements. Ghent realized he was gripping his table and forced his hands to relax.

"Exactly," Metchell said. "To make matters worse, their stress hormones are hyper-activated. One hormone in particular—adrenaline—makes it impossible to relax. Of course, relaxation is necessary for effective acclimation, so neutralizing drugs are required, which adds another twist of unreality."

"That sounds like a hormone they could do without."

"Better hold the criticism," Metchell said, his voice grinding again. "It's also the hormone that enables their incredibly fast reflexes under pressure. I hope Human reflexes are adequate reason for putting her through this."

"Calm down, my friend," Ghent said. "Do you really thing I'm criticizing her? Or that I'm careless of any crewmember's wellbeing?"

Metchell drew a deep, audible breath and measured it out before he answered. "Sorry. Patients are supposed to leave my care in better condition than they arrived. Today, I received a healthy, pleasant woman and then put her through such torment it incapacitated her." He drew another breath. "And yes, I know she requested it." His lips twitched. "And yes, I know it's not actually your fault."

Ghent grinned and dropped his tone. "Well, not entirely, anyway."

Metchell huffed a laugh and shifted in his chair as if to loosen tense muscles.

Ghent asked, "Can you give me a guess on Kena's recovery time?"

"She was lucid for a while before exhaustion took her," Metchell said. "I expect she'll be reasonably capable when she finally wakes up. Keep her on light, non-critical duty until I let you know otherwise."

"We can accommodate that," Ghent said. He leaned forward to enter duty restrictions on his computer. "Considering how traumatic her acclimation was, I'm surprised you didn't keep her in med section."

"She requested her quarters. I agree, it's, uh," Metchell's pitch dropped. "better to awaken in familiar surroundings."

Now, why would that be funny? "What?"

"Apparently," Metchell said, "her quarters were last occupied by the Sierritame scientist we had with us a couple missions back."

Ghent laughed at the mention of Sierritame.

"Did you ever see those quarters?" Metchell asked.

"Only once," Ghent said, curbing his laugh. "I got out as quickly as I could. What was Kena's reaction?"

"She covered her eyes and moaned." Metchell's voice rose over Ghent's renewed laughter. "Fortunately, she had—several—décor schemes in her computer, so I was able to, uh, stabilize the situation."

"What an appalling shock," Ghent said, "and right after acclimation, too. What instructions did you leave her with?"

"None." Metchell shook his head. "She was asleep before she lay down. I'll return to her when she wakes. Did you have something specific in mind?"

"Simply that I want to talk with her about our Grfdn crew

members before she meets them." Ghent rolled his shoulders and stretched his long arms along the curved backrest of his chair. The charcoal gray fur, which covered his shoulders and upper arms, shifted as his muscles flexed.

"As well you should! Do they know she's here?"

"They do," Ghent said. "I've taken what precautions I can to avert—shall we say, unpleasantness. If she can avoid stirring up trouble, we should be able to maintain a tolerable situation."

"She has more cultural studies in her profile than I'd expect for a navigator," Metchell said. "She responded to my tonal changes like she grew up on Dantokrell. She may be fairly well prepared."

Ghent snorted. "Grfdn describe themselves only from their own point of view. Nor do they permit other races' descriptions to be entered into public information centers. So, I'll be very surprised if she's found study material that will prepare her for them."

"I know, but she's bound to have met Grfdn before," Metchell said. "She's been acclimated to them."

"True, but meeting them is far different than working with them. Her previous assignments were on ships with few Grfdn. Not one of them had any Grfdn navigators."

"You make no sense." Metchell twisted his head to one side. "Why did you want her here if you expect trouble? Is she really that good?"

Ghent spread his hands. "Even among her own race, she is exceptional! Human competitiveness makes them a nuisance as crewmembers, but it does develop outstanding performance levels. This mission has a high level of risk, both at our destination and en route. Kena is a definite asset, even if she does come with the typical Human bad habits."

Metchell's nostrils contracted.

Ah. What was this? "Did she even find a way to annoy you?"

"She presumed to know how I should conduct her acclimation," Metchell said. "She told me I could skip the first step." He shook his head. "No one likes the repetitive description or rehashing their decision, but I will not perform a high trauma acclimation if the subject isn't willing to listen to me."

"I hope you set her straight with utmost clarity."

"Now, how would I have gotten her relaxed if I used your approach?" Metchell said. "I can get my point across without stressing my patient. To her credit, she complied after that. Later on, she also managed to control intense anger very quickly."

Ghent lifted his brow. "So, she has a quick temper, too?"

"There was no indication of that," Metchell said, dropping his pitch. "I won't let you criticize her for anger during acclimation to the likes of you. After what she'd just been through, I'd be more inclined to say she's highly tolerant."

Ghent grinned. "I acquit her of the charge. What else can you tell me about her?"

"Normal, healthy Human. Moderate strength, good flexibility, and quick reflexes. She's the light-skinned variety, brown hair..." Metchell pointed at one of the lighter patches of his hair. "About this color. Fine bone structure, a little taller than average for a female. Her chest looks odd, but that's to be expected. She wore a loose tunic over her navigation suit, so it wasn't too shocking."

"I was hoping for something less physical," Ghent said. "Did you notice her *personality*?"

"We only talked for a few minutes before starting acclimation. When I asked her to reconsider, she was respectful but firm." His lips twitched. "She uses humor in difficult moments, including that one. I'd even guess she adapted her humor for me."

"May I infer that she managed to make a friend?" Ghent asked.

"Of course you may." Metchell turned his hand in the helix gesture common to his race. "Dantokrellie are so accommodating."

"Vya!" Ghent said in his own language, giving the expletive an affectionate twist.

CHAPTER FOUR

Kena woke to gnawing hunger pains. Lingering exhaustion fogged her mind. Where was she? Oh, yeah. She struggled upright and found a protein drink to quiet her stomach's demand. Then, she sat on the side of her bed, grappling with the difficult question of whether to get some coffee or go back to sleep.

Lights flashed, and a shrill tone sounded. Kena startled so badly, she almost fell off the bed.

A command blared over the audio system. "Navigators to stations! Navigators to stations!"

Kena was on her feet and almost out of her quarters before remembering she didn't know the way to navigation command. She snatched up her computer and hurried as best she could, following the path it displayed.

The last to arrive in nav command, Kena hesitated just inside the door as the final words of an order came over the speakers. The man standing at the central directive console couldn't be Frethan. Tall and lean, with short hair clinging to his head—a Grfdn. He swung around and glared at her, his small, thin-lipped mouth pressing into an even tighter line.

"I'm Kena. What do you assign me?"

He pointed to a console in the forward section of the circular room. "That station. Monitor extended area."

Kena hurried past him, slid into her seat, and activated the configuration controls. The station re-formed to accommodate both her physique and task. She exhaled a long breath. He'd assigned her the least demanding duty, which gave her a moment to figure out what had happened.

Her display showed the *Ontrevay's* course and surrounding space. Excellent. They were already through the spatial rift, which saved weeks of travel time. Though they'd only been underway for twelve hours, they were approaching the nebula that formed one border of PitKreelaundun space.

A puzzling designation, that. Kena and the member races of the Interstellar Collaborative found the practice of laying claim to a spatial void inconceivable, but their neighbors were extremely sensitive about the vast area they'd declared to be PitKreelaundun space. They might challenge a ship for even skirting the nebula's edge, as the *Ontrevay's* current course required. The nebula's sporadic debris ejections would both increase navigational risk and afford some protection. The PitKreelaundun might not like the *Ontrevay's* presence, but they would think twice about coming in for a fight.

Kena ran a rapid playback of the past few minutes. An uncharted rock had curved into their path. Collision had been unavoidable. The *Ontrevay's* extended shield had absorbed the impact, but it bowed inward and crushed a sensor array against the rigid hull shielding. So this was what they were dealing with.

Kena studied several types of scans, deciding which debris warranted trajectory analysis. Alternate courses played through the back of her mind, as always.

She glanced at the navigator to her left, a Grfdn female. No need to worry about the short-range area, since the woman had it up on her screen. "You must be Hrndl," Kena murmured. "And I assume Krdn is directing?"

"Yes," Hrndl said in her throaty, Grfdn version of the Prednian language. Her tiny mouth barely moved. "I hope you're also aware that his rank is second navigator."

"Yes. What did I miss on the general order?"

Hrndl's eyes remained locked on her display, and her hands moved over the controls. "Command designation. Frethan is in ex op, assessing damage. Krdn has nav command. We'll hold fifth-dimensional slip."

Kena plotted a trajectory as she waited for more from Hrndl. It didn't come. "Doesn't the captain get involved?"

"Ghent splits his time between shifts, so he may be asleep. He trusts his officers."

Kena let the conversation drop. The other navigators in the command room exchanged occasional, brief statements. Kena absorbed them, but stayed focused on her own console. Several groups of small, uncharted objects were approaching their path. Strange. At least they had time to get out of the way.

She laid out a new course, then said, "Recommend course change. Implement within four minutes."

Krdn ordered, "Continue extended scanning. Netlyn, verify her scan and projections. Delf, check the course parameters."

Kena continued to monitor, while her course recommendation was accepted and Delf prepared to initiate the change.

A moment before implementation, Ghent strode into nav command. His emfrel hit Kena like a shock wave. She swung around to stare at him, her lips parted and eyes wide.

Ghent glanced at her as he joined Krdn at the directive console. "Focus," was all he said.

Krdn sneered in classic Grfdn fashion: eyes narrowed, nostrils lifted, and mouth oddly straight. "Netlyn, check the Human's scans," he ordered.

Kena turned back to her console and pressed cool fingers against her burning cheeks. The distraction of Ghent's emfrel overwhelmed her senses, and it took her several seconds to realize Delf had implemented the course change. She was not only slow to adjust her settings, she even missed some objects on the long-range scans, forcing her to make constant rechecks. Never out of conscious thought was the Plynteth sitting behind her.

A few moments later, Ghent allowed his shoulders to relax. "Emergency status ended," he said. "Resume normal procedures."

Krdn turned to Kena and ordered, "Non-essential crew, get out."

When Kena started to rise, Ghent said, "Kena, stay where you are until Metchell arrives."

The growling inflections of Krdn's speech intensified. "She is disrupting the—"

"Krdn!" Ghent held his gaze, letting the silence stretch. "When you are in command here, I expect you to be aware of the crew, not just the space surrounding us. It's obvious Kena requires medical attention. Why don't you recognize that?" Touching his comm control, he said, "Frethan, come to nav command."

Metchell entered and stopped short. "Ghent! Your first contact with her is *here*?" He strode to Kena.

Ghent softened his voice. "Emergencies do occur. She performed well, given the circumstances, but take care of her now."

Frethan arrived as Metchell escorted Kena out.

The instant the door slid shut behind them, Krdn exclaimed, "Performed well? How can you say that? She became worse than useless in a matter of minutes."

Ghent ground his voice to the low pitch a Grfdn could understand. "I can say it because I considered her state before I judged. Her condition is explained in her duty restrictions, yet you seem ignorant of it. In spite of exhaustion, she scanned thoroughly and laid out a flawless course. Her acclimation to my race is incomplete and more than accounts for her difficulties after I

32

arrived. Do you have any other comment to make on her performance?"

"I stand corrected."

Ghent held his rigid posture. "So you say, but I doubt you believe it. Report to my consult room. Frethan, take charge here while I educate Krdn on the duties of second navigator."

H rndl made quick eye contact with Krdn as he entered the dining hall for third meal. Had he been with Ghent all this time? Just how bad had it been? Ghent was a reasonable captain, but he could make his displeasure felt.

Krdn served himself from the buffet and joined the three Grfdn at their reserved table. As usual, his expression revealed nothing. His upper face lacked the creases of most Grfdn, giving him a passionless demeanor. She knew better.

Hrndl didn't bother to hide her scowl. Rumors had spread of the happenings in nav command. Yet another irritant—as though yesterday's were not enough.

A Prednian crewmember dropped a stool at the end of the table, ignoring due courtesy. He sat down, propped his elbows on the table, and rested his chin on his interlocked fingers. Hrndl exchanged a look with Krdn, but the Prednian only grinned and said, "Do tell. What really happened with our new senior navigator?"

"Nothing of interest," Krdn said.

Their uninvited guest laughed and turned his round eyes to her. "You were there, Hrndl. What happened?"

She glared at the awkward cylinder she'd been drinking from— a reminder of every unpalatable word Ghent had uttered when he summoned the Grfdn yesterday. Now she had to listen to fools mocking her intended mate. She would need to work closely with that pathetic Human, while idiots extolled her fabulous skills. Hrndl's throat tightened, almost causing her breath to rumble.

Those skills were useful only if Kena worked alone. Coordination with Humans was impossible. So obvious, but these imbeciles couldn't see it. She longed to explain this with the precision of a laser knife, but Ghent's warning was fresh in her mind. She must watch every word.

Hrndl kept her voice level as Krdn had. "She came to nav command unfit for duty. Why, I don't know. I can only assume she didn't realize her own state. After working for a while, her condition deteriorated. Krdn ordered her out as soon as he could. It's as simple as that." She brought her eyes up to meet his. "Now that you know, we would like to eat without you reclining on our table."

At least that got rid of the nosy Prednian, but there was no telling when she'd have to deal with more. As if on cue, Rnl launched a complaint about the gossip. Hrndl let the rumble in her throat reach audible level.

"Again?" Krdn said to Rnl. "Is it really that difficult for you to know when to hold silence?"

Rnl glared at Krdn, but to Hrndl's relief, didn't respond. It never ended well for him, and Krdn had been ruthless the past few weeks.

She glanced at Frdn. He made eye contact with no one and didn't open his lips for anything but food. Not surprising, all things considered. This meal couldn't end fast enough. As soon as she swallowed her last bite, she stood to leave.

K rdn watched Hrndl rush through her generous meal, ensuring that he finished at the same moment. He followed her from the dining hall and matched her pace. She hadn't quite reached the stage of needing a mate, but the time neared. She would choose him—he would make that a certainty.

At least the hurried meal spared him the company of Dhgnr. He had entered on the far side of the dining hall, but lingered to

talk with some engineers. His one piercing glance at Krdn boded
nothing good. Dhgnr's rank in the Collaborative equaled Krdn's,
but within their own race he bore the title of khn. If he tried to
attract Hrndl, he could prove a significant rival. The other two
men weren't a concern. Rnl was a fool, and Frdn a child. They
could not compete with him, and he made sure they knew it, lest
they intrude during these moments he contrived to be alone
with Hrndl.

This evening should have been like any other, but he could
think of nothing to say. His lengthy session with Ghent would not
be a topic—that much was beyond doubt.

Hrndl held silence only until they turned down an empty
hallway. The low growl of a Grfdn obscenity merged into words.
"Is it too much to ask? To drink with my meal? I could strangle
Rnl for objecting when Ghent said not to use drinking pouches in
Kena's presence. What good of that?"

"We can always count on Rnl to say the wrong thing."

"Now, Ghent insists we drink from those awful cylinders even
when she's not there. And do not dare say it's for practice. It's
totally unreasonable. Water dribbles out the sides every time I try.
Humiliating! I look no better than those other slobs in the dining
hall."

Krdn drew her into an empty common room. "I know. It's hard
for me, too." He moved nearer and caressed the fine line of her
narrow lips with a fingertip. "With your charming, tiny mouth, it
must be even worse for you. Be patient. I'll convince Ghent that
we be allowed to drink from pouches again."

She sighed and flopped down onto a lounge. "I'm too heated,
beyond doubt. What an awful way to start a mission."

Just as well that she retracted, for he had no intention of
talking to Ghent about it. His single goal was to be chosen as her
mate; he would say whatever pleased her.

Hrndl rolled her shoulders, as though she couldn't get the
muscles to release.

He moved behind her and massaged, feeling for the hard cords

35

within her back and working them loose. Excellent. No need to talk or guard his expression. A perfect way to get her comfortable with his touch.

Hrndl let a sigh drift out with no trace of a rumble. She stretched her slender legs and turned her delicately formed feet. As pretty as the rest of her, right up to the glossy chestnut hair that stirred at his breath. Better yet, she was as intelligent as she was beautiful. Her skill demanded the respect of other navigators, and her Grfdn social position exceeded his own. Becoming her mate could only add to his consequence. He would let nothing come between them.

CHAPTER FIVE

G hent contacted Metchell over the communication system the next morning. "Is Kena adequately rested?" he asked as he secured the strap of his shirt.

"I believe so," Metchell's voice answered from overhead. "I've told her to spend most of the day in her quarters, but I'm really just trying to keep things low key for her." His voice softened. "Let's try this. You avoid navigational emergencies today, and I'll avoid publicly criticizing you for having contact with her."

Ghent smiled. "That almost sounds contrite, but don't worry about it. What you blurted out was actually useful to me. I'll notify all debris to stay out of our path today."

"Excellent. I take it, you're about to go see her?"

"Yes," Ghent said, pulling his stretchy, grip-soled footwear on.

"A few short visits would be better than a single long one. Let me know if she seems unduly stressed."

Ghent reached for the palm-sized computer, which he always carried, but rarely used. "I will."

K ena leaned her folded arms on the round table in her sitting room. A real, paper book lay open before her. The only one she brought on her travels. Smooth hair hung forward as she read; the ends curved inward, almost touching beneath her chin. Plynteth emfrel sifted into her awareness. Her eyes lifted to the door.

Seconds later, Ghent requested entry. She slid her hand lovingly across the page before pushing the book aside. Steeling herself for the encounter, she accessed room controls from her computer and opened the door.

Ghent paused to look around, the corners of his mouth lifting. "You've improved these quarters immeasurably."

She managed a tight smile in spite of his intense emfrel. "Thank you."

Ghent turned in a circle, examining the décor. It gave her opportunity to study him. His shirt, designed in the Plynteth fashion, wrapped only his chest and lower back with a thin strap around his neck. Nothing more was needed—fur covered his back and broad shoulders, ending near his elbows. His powerful build made up for what he lacked in height.

"This mixture of colors," he said, "what do they convey to a Human?"

"An ocean beach." Kena leaned back in her chair. "The carpet is the color of sand, and the couch and chairs match the rocks on my favorite shoreline. The tables are re-formed to the texture of driftwood."

The fur of his brow puckered.

Oh yeah—Plynteth's water was almost entirely underground. "That's wood that has floated in the ocean and been driven ashore by waves." She pointed at ceiling and walls as she described hues. "This blue is one of the lighter shades of the Terran sky. The aqua is shallow waters, the richer blue, deep water. Accent colors are from shellfish. The audio is waves on sand and bird calls."

"Who designed this?" Ghent asked.

"I did."

"So, you are an artist as well as a navigator."

Kena tilted her head. "Why do you say that?"

"If you wanted to see the ocean, you could have simply displayed recorded images. You could have seen the waves as well as heard them. But you designed this instead."

She smiled. "So I did. What do your walls display?"

"Plynteth canyons. You may see them this evening." Still he waited near the door. "You've endured me for a few minutes now. How bad is it today?"

"Better than yesterday."

"May I sit down?"

An odd request, coming from anyone not born on Earth. She gestured to a chair across the table. "Please do."

He took the chair, but said nothing else.

Silence—more uncomfortable than his emfrel. All she could come up with was, "What did you want to see me about?"

"Nothing. We'll call it a social visit, even though it has another obvious purpose."

She tilted her head.

His brow puckered again, as though he was trying to figure her out. "Perhaps I should mention that I never intended to place you in a stressful situation and then distract you with my emfrel. I was planning something more like this, where we could just talk."

"Oh." What was she supposed to talk about?

He filled the gap. "You're interested in racial differences, I gather?"

"Quite so."

"By now, you know it isn't just my emfrel that's unusual. Plynteth have the dubious distinction of being the furriest intelligent race."

Well, at least he had a sense of humor. She relaxed. "Human males hold second place. They have thick facial hair."

"I've seen pictures of that, but the males I've met had shaved their"—he paused then spoke her native word, for which the

Prednian language had no counterpart—"beards. Did I say that correctly?"

She nodded. "I'm told that shaving reduces shocked stares. As a matter of fact, I'm pretty accustomed to being stared at, too."

"I doubt you're accustomed to this," he said, extending one arm and resting it, palm upward, on the table.

"Indeed not," she said, examining his wrist.

Among the biped races, hand structure varied, most often in the number of fingers. A few races even had two thumbs, but none were as unique as a Plynteth hand. Four fingers, with a gap between the middle two. No thumb. Instead, the center of Ghent's thick wrist displayed a patch of loose skin pulled inward, no doubt concealing his shurg—a retractable digit directly opposite the fingers.

"There are so many stories," Ghent said, "so we prefer to simply show it. That way, people don't have to bother trying to hide their curiosity."

He gave his hand a quick jerk. The shurg shot out of the indentation and met the fingertips. A thick muscle rose up along the length of his forearm as he tightened his fist, lending credibility to the Plynteth's reputed strength.

Kena blinked. "It doesn't..."

"Doesn't what?"

"Appear to be jointed," she finished, hoping her observation didn't offend.

"No, it has no bones. Only muscle with specialized tendons." He moved it as he spoke, showing its flexibility. "Our hands cause more consternation than any other feature. That's partly because of how quickly our shurgs extend. Most races interpret a swift, grabbing motion as aggression. Innate interpretations of body language are hard to overcome, even with education." His voice quieted a bit. "Then, there are the reports of Plynteth accidentally breaking bones when grasping a non-Plynteth."

"Has that ever happened to you?" Kena asked.

A corner of his mouth twisted downward. "You had to ask me

that. Long ago, during adolescence. I grabbed the arm of a Meklehon child as she slipped and fell. Her parents forgave me because the fall would have killed her. But feeling her bones snap —and her scream—not a pleasant memory. I assure you, I've been very careful ever since. In fact, when I am going to spend extensive time with someone, I usually take the precaution of learning how much pressure they can comfortably tolerate. We do have very precise control, once we know how much force is appropriate."

"I've heard of the Plynteth doing this." It seemed unnecessary, but if it was significant to him, fine. She extended her arm, laying it between his hands.

He used the hand with the retracted shurg to grasp her wrist.

Despite his previous demonstration, the sudden clench startled her. She uttered a wry laugh and said, "Obviously, Humans are one of those races who interpret that as aggression."

"That's not my intent. Please tell me when it begins to get uncomfortable. And I do mean *begins*."

Her fingers curled to her palm as his grip slowly tightened. His shurg fit neatly into the gap between his fingers. "You're cutting off my circulation," she said.

He released her at once, and she extended her fingers. Blood rushed back into them, and the tingling subsided.

"It's not hard to imagine how you could break a wrist."

"I will not do so." The fur on his brow puckered.

She softened her words. "I didn't think you would. I was merely commenting on your strength."

He gave her a quick nod then gestured to her book. "What is this?"

How abrupt! Kena drew a breath and adjusted. "To give you the English word, it is a *book*."

"The ancient Human method of storing writings?"

Kena relaxed against the chair back. "Ah, you've studied my culture beyond the standard information. It's not so ancient, really. Some paper books are still made, though most writings are stored in electronic format."

"How did you learn to read? From a book or a display?"

"In formal education," she said, "we use displays."

"Then, don't you find it awkward to read from this?"

"Not in the least. I've been surrounded by books my entire life."

"I've never heard a Human language spoken," Ghent said, "other than a few individual words. Will you read some of this to me?"

How different he was from any other captain she'd had. She pulled the book toward her. "This is poetry written, oh, about 3,000 years ago. It's translated to a language called English.

> 'Oh Lord, you search me out and know me.
> You know when I sit and when I stand.
> You understand my thoughts, even from a distance.
> You surround my journeys through the day and my bed
>   through the night,
> And are intimately acquainted with all of my ways.
> Even before a word leaves my tongue, you my Lord, fully
>   comprehend it.
> You encompass me, behind and before, and cover me with
>   your protective hand.
> Such infinite knowledge is too wondrous for me.
> It is lofty.
> I cannot fathom it.

> 'Where could I go to be separated from your Spirit?
> Where could I run to escape your presence?
> If I ascend to the stars, you are there.
> If I descend deep within the earth, you are there.
> If I ride the wings of the dawn's brilliant light,
> Even there your hand guides me and your right hand
>   supports me.
> If I think that darkness will obscure me, or the void will
>   swallow all light,

Even these cannot hide me from you.
Your light shines ever on,
A radiance surpassing both day and night.'"

Kena closed the book and looked up at Ghent. He watched her intently, but did not speak.

"Well," she said after a moment, "what do you think of English?"

He took his time answering. "Its sounds are rich, and its cadence pleasant. Yet I suspect that the meaning of the words is far lovelier than their sound. Your expression is remarkably altered."

Her smile grew deeper. "I am quite fond of this poem. I'm a little surprised, though, that you like English. It's so dissimilar to your native language."

His eyes half closed then widened. She committed the unfamiliar expression to memory while waiting for the first hint of its meaning.

"I admit that is odd. I can't explain it, even to myself." He hesitated again. "I understand it can be difficult with poetry, but could you translate the passage?"

She scanned the page. "The words are figurative, and some concepts are uniquely Human. Perhaps this part—which, by the way, causes it to be called the Navigator's Poem."

If I ascend to the stars, you are there.
If I descend deep within the earth, you are there.
If I ride the wings of the dawn's brilliant light,
Even there your hand guides me and your right hand supports me.

She lifted her gaze to his. "To give you a taste of the figurative; at Earth's dawn, sunlight traces its signature in the atmosphere. Perfectly straight rays are visible, spreading in all directions. We perceive that as a hint of light's nature. In the past few decades, we've come to use the phrase 'riding the wings of the dawn' as a figurative reference to traveling in dimensional slip."

"Ah. Yet you said the poem was old?"

"Indeed. Among other reasons, we preserve this set of poems because we perceive them as timeless—that is, they maintain meaning even as the ages pass."

A slow smile stretched his lips. "Cultures are so fascinating. Who does the poem refer to with the words *I* and *you*?"

That question could open the preverbial can of worms. "Either the author or the reader can assume the role of *I*. The word *you* refers to the creator. Does the Plynteth race embrace the concept of an ancient creator?"

"In a general sense, yes." He angled his head toward the book. "Though, I could not show you milenia-old references to such an entity. I have read that Human's place considerable value on comprehending historical information. It's an unusual trait and not one I grasp easily, but you've given me an inate portrayal of its value. Thank you."

For an instant, she toyed with digging deeper. "You're welcome."

"I would love to spend hours speaking of culture with you," Ghent said, "but Metchell advises brief contact for now, so I will leave you." He stood as he spoke. "I understand that your memories of the bay and ex op command are vague, at best. Jorlit was on duty when you arrived, so Metchell asked him to escort you through those areas. Frethan will also come to see you later."

Kena leaned back. "Hopefully before boredom sets in."

"Ah. The thirst so common in navigators—to always be active." He paused by the door. "Before I go, please tell me how uncomfortable this has been."

"Not uncomfortable, exactly—just a bit intense. The feeling is diminishing."

He gave her one of his quick nods and left.

Kena stared at the book again. She had let another opportunity slip away. If only she were as good at conveying Human culture as she was at learning other cultures. True, Ghent's emfrel was disconcerting, but that wasn't the real barrier. Mistranslations could sting. She remembered the day when a crew member had warped and twisted the words of a cherished song. More of a burn, that one. Kena sighed. She had hoped to initiate significant understanding of human-kind. Six years she'd spent with multi-racial crews. Had she made any difference? On the surface, maybe, but some days her heart longed to be known. She rose and stowed the book, murmuring, "Help me see the opportunities and find the right words."

Kena was half-way through her stretching routine when Jorlit arrived. He introduced himself, no doubt warned that she wouldn't remember him.

"Jorlit," she said, following the Tenelli courtesy of repeating the name when introduced. "You lead second shift, do you not?"

He grinned. "Yes. You've been doing your homework. Frethan will like that."

Kena returned his smile. It would've been hard not to, for the Tenelli smile stirred a homey feeling. His eyes, too. Coal black, but the whites showed at the corners—a trait found in few races. Only his wispy, buff-colored hair would make him stand out in a crowd of Humans. He wore it short, much like the down on some ducklings she'd adopted as a child.

"How are you doing?" he asked.

"Fine, except for feeling cooped up. Let's get on with it." Stepping into the hallway, she said, "Tell me, what's been going on while I've been doing all this sleeping and resting?"

"Our course is still clear, so not much actual navigating. Just standard routine—for being in slip, anyway. Simulations. Training for the junior navigators and anyone who's upping their skill set. Oh, and Frethan told everyone to read up on Human culture. That's one task you'll get out of."

"Ha. Resident teacher."

Jorlit chuckled and turned down another hall. "If you want to do some teaching, let's talk about course design."

"I do it much like everyone else—enter basic parameters,

review the computer's options, tweak them, and let the computer recalculate until I've got a good one."

"Like everyone else? Netlyn saw the same hazard you did and was working on a course revision, too. And she's no rookie. How'd you pull it together that quick?"

"I'd use the word *intuition*. There's no Prednian translation. It means an innate knowing. I can simply tell which option will be best and which parts of it to alter, so there's less time wasted on calculating alternatives. I've tried showing it to others, but it seems to be the one thing I can't teach."

"Can all Humans do it that fast?"

"Some. I can only assume it has to do with how we visualize non-standard dimensions."

"But—S4? Are you telling me, you can *visualize* the fourth spatial dimension?"

"Well, conceptualize it."

Jorlit raised his eyebrows at her as they entered a lift. "If you say so," he said, selecting a lower level. "We'll start in the bay."

A moment later, they stepped across the blue marker of the bay's primary shield. More blue lines intersected across the floor, showing where energy fields could be raised for sectional shielding.

She climbed a flight of stairs to the walkway at level two, hoping a higher view might prompt her memory. The bay doors to her left locked out the vacuum. To her right, the high window of the external operations command room bulged out into the bay, providing a view of the entire floor. Two large craft occupied the center of the bay—they wouldn't have been there when she arrived. Probably several others would have been at the space station as well. Nor would there have been so much activity. Technicians removed crew harnesses from the payload modules of the large craft. The gold-tinted hull of one of the navigation modules stood open for maintenance.

Jorlit waited beside her, while she rested her hands on the railing and looked over the bay. Hope of recollection faded. Not a single thing struck a chord of memory. Oh, well. She took her time identifying craft and memorizing the positions of shields, anchors, and mounts. After a moment, she asked, "Which one did I come in?"

He pointed to a single-pilot craft attached to the struts on the opposite wall. "That one—third level, second position." He lowered his hand to point out a location on the bay floor. "I had you anchor down there when you arrived. You looked around the bay after you disembarked and then came up to ex op command."

Kena looked up to the broad window on the third level. Two navigators surveyed their domain from above, much as Jorlit would have during her arrival. "Let's go up."

They rode another lift up a level. It opened directly into ex op command. Three low-profile consoles lined the window, positioned so they wouldn't block the support navigators' view. Hrndl and a junior navigator were on duty. Hrndl acknowledged Kena but continued to observe the other navigator as he fulfilled a request to lower one of the craft from its wall mount.

The rear of the command room boasted its own 3-D display area. Not huge, but certainly large enough to cover the immediate vicinity. Nice. She was going to have a hard time returning to less well-equipped ships.

"How do you like what you've seen so far?" Jorlit asked.

Kena tilted her head as déjà vu nudged her. "I like it very much, indeed."

Jorlit's grin returned.

"Is that something we said when I arrived?"

"Word for word. Do you remember the rest?"

"Mm, no."

"None of it was really important," Jorlit said. "Besides, I think I managed to annoy you, so I don't mind you forgetting, at all."

"That seems unlikely. Are you sure?"

"I wasn't trying to," he said. "I used the translation of a phrase from your language. I thought it was a compliment."

"What phrase?"

The corners of his smile turned down. "I should have kept my mouth shut. I said, 'Your fame precedes you.' And you said, 'How unfortunate.' Is there something offensive about it?"

Kena laughed. "Not really, but you can't expect me to like that. Preconceptions are always misleading. I'd rather you know me, not just what you've heard about me. Or, least of all, what you've heard about Humans."

Behind Jorlit, Hrndl glanced sideways at Kena.

"Well," Jorlit said, "that's all I can really give you for a memory tour. Do you want to see our simulation room?"

"Of course."

When she entered the room, Frethan turned to the door and smiled. He even stood for their exchange of names—a nice mixture of Human and Tenelli courtesy. Small wonder he had a reputation of being well liked. He wouldn't let her stay, though. Clearly, Metchell's orders had weight.

<hr />

W hen Frethan visited Kena that afternoon, he relieved her boredom by taking her to the astro section, which contained the largest 3-D display in the *Ontrevay*. They were reviewing details of their course around the far side of the nebula, when Frethan paused to check a message. "Ghent will be here soon," he said. "Are you all right with that?"

"Quite."

Despite her assertion, Kena couldn't avoid turning to look when Ghent entered. He acknowledged her from across the room but kept his distance. He conversed with a few scientists for about a quarter hour then left. Was his purpose to let her practice focusing on a task while he was present? A challenge indeed! She concentrated on Frethan's words and the rich warmth of his voice, but even that couldn't drive Ghent's presence from her awareness.

F rethan returned to Kena's quarters again that evening. Somehow, they got off on a tangent, and Kena found herself answering dozens of questions about her past encounters with the PitKreelaundun.

Ghent's voice on the comm system interrupted, and Frethan's eyes darted to the time display. He traced two quick circles in the air.

Kena smiled. That would be the Tenelli gesture for time moving at double speed.

"Better let me answer that." He pressed the comm control and said, "Frethan here."

"Still?" Ghent said. "Just how much time do you need with her?"

Frethan grinned. "Oh, she's just such pleasant company, I can't tear myself away. I suppose you want me to share her with you."

"I would appreciate it," Ghent said.

"I'll walk with you," Frethan said as they left her quarters. "There's one other thing I wanted to mention." He seemed to consider his words. "Many of us are delighted to have a Human navigator with us, particularly one with your reputation. But not everyone perceives the benefits so clearly."

Kena chuckled. "Frethan, how very diplomatic you are."

He grinned and, in typical Tenelli fashion, rested a hand against her back as they walked. "I fear you've encountered this before."

"Ah, yes. Once or twice."

"If it causes undue difficulties," he said, "let me know."

They reached the door of Ghent's consult room. Frethan parted from her with a warm smile as the door slid open. She stepped across the threshold.

CHAPTER SIX

T he room was empty, but Ghent's emfrel pressed against
Kena. Another door stood open on the opposite side,
through which she glimpsed a slice of his private sitting
room.

While waiting for him, she studied the Plynteth images
surrounding her. Three walls and the ceiling blended into a 3-D
panorama. So strange that a room could feel this immense. She
rested her hands on the railing, which heightened the illusion of
standing on a balcony, overlooking a deep canyon. Even the
absence of wind seemed odd. She'd seen pictures of Plynteth
canyon walls, lined with dwellings, but they could never convey
this vastness.

Turning in a complete circle, Kena admired the towering
palisades and openings of distant chasms. How would it feel to fly
through this canyon? Swerving between rock formations that
thrust their jagged peaks high above its fertile floor.

Ghent's emfrel filled the room, interrupting the daydream. She
turned to face him.

"What do you think of Plynteth?" he asked.

"A stark, but majestic beauty."

He paused, resting a hand on the back of his chair. "I wonder how you would render it."

"Hmm." She considered the walls again, pointing as she answered. "Perhaps with the color variations and rippling patterns in these areas. I have no idea how to portray the vastness, though. I'm really a much better navigator than artist."

"That is why you're here, after all," Ghent said. "If you intended to convey anything by that humming sound you made, you failed. Only Humans speak without opening their mouths."

She crimped the corners of her mouth. "Yes, I know. It's innate and occasionally slips out. That particular *hum* merely indicated thoughtfulness and wasn't necessary to my meaning."

Ghent nodded and asked, "Are you reasonably comfortable?"

"I am."

"Good. The rest of this isn't a social visit."

He sat in his big chair, and Kena approached the curved table, stopping directly across from him. Clasping her hands behind her back, she waited for him to speak.

"Kena, there are twelve races on this ship. This creates significant challenges. Every member of the crew is expected to accommodate the customs of other races as much as possible. Sometimes that means foregoing natural behaviors. I assume you are aware of this."

"I am."

Ghent stared up at her. "One challenge is knowing what accommodations need to be made. That's typically dealt with through education. You've studied other races extensively. How helpful do you find your studies when it comes to actual interaction?"

"That depends a great deal on which race we're talking about and who designed the educational material."

"Yes, it does," Ghent said, drawing out the first and last words. "There are significant gaps in the material on some races, particularly on the Grfdn. How do you deal with such gaps?"

"Usually through observation. Or simply by asking for

clarification—if, that is, I'm fairly sure the question itself won't cause offense."

"A reasonable approach," he said. "Apparently, we must interrupt this subject. Why are you still standing?"

Strange remark. Even stranger, his speech slowed and quickened, creating an odd cadence. "Because you haven't asked me to sit," she said.

"I see." His cadence grew more emphatic with every sentence. "I'm aware from my own studies that Humans have an intricate structure of customary courtesy. These customs vary depending on location, social status, age, and gender. If you are expecting anyone on this ship to memorize all these rules and determine which ones must be implemented for you, you will be very disappointed. Do you think you could deign to sit without waiting for the invitation you feel entitled to?"

Kena's eyes widened, and she slid into the nearest chair. "Certainly, sir, but you mistake my reason for standing. It's merely a sign of respect for a superior officer."

"Really? Have you studied Plynteth customs at all?"

"Yes."

Ghent rested his arms on the table. "What did you learn about our customs for standing and sitting?"

"They weren't mentioned."

"Precisely. We have no such custom, nor do we interpret standing as a sign of respect. I'll be convinced of your respect by your responses to me, not by your body language."

"I see." Not a good start! How to reverse the negative impression? "I am puzzled by a couple things. May I ask for clarification?"

"You may."

"When you visited me this morning, why did you ask if you could sit down?"

Ghent paused, leaning back in his chair. The odd cadence faded as he spoke. "Because I was concerned about being too close while you were still acclimating to my race. What was your interpretation?"

"It seemed as though you felt an invitation was necessary. Which surprised me, since I'd found no reference to such a custom."

"Did you fill an apparent gap with observation?"

Kena shook her head. "I don't usually draw conclusions based on only one event, but it never occurred to me that you'd interpret my standing as a—a demand for courtesy."

He nodded. "What else puzzles you?"

How much could she ask? "What does it indicate when you vary the rate of your speech?"

A corner of Ghent's mouth twisted down, and he let out a breath of a laugh. "It means I'm annoyed. From what racial perspectives did you study Plynteth?"

"Plynteth and Dantokrellie."

"Neither will cover verbal emphasis. It's as innate to a Plynteth as your hums are to you. Compared to Dantokrellie vocal changes, it's too insignificant to be worthy of comment." He looked aside at the canyon wall for an instant. "Try asking Frethan. He sometimes mentions my speech patterns and should be able to explain them. By the way, not all of my speech is common to Plynteth. I adopt other races' verbal cues when I need to ensure my meaning is clear. Is anything else puzzling you?"

Kena settled back in her chair. "Not right now."

"Then, we'll return to the subject of Grfdn." Ghent spread his hands wide on the table. "Have you interacted with any of them before?"

"Several times, but never closely. They don't seek Human friends."

"That's an understatement! Fights commonly occur when Humans and Grfdn are on the same ship. Some captains tolerate such behavior. I do not. Is that clear?"

Kena stared. "Are you suggesting that *I* might start a fight with a Grfdn?"

"I wouldn't have mentioned it unless it was a possibility," Ghent said, his lips tight. "It's well known that Humans are extremely competitive. One of your more common methods of developing teamwork is to engage in structured group fighting. Under certain circumstances, Grfdn fight amongst themselves, but they rarely fight with any race other than Humans. This strongly suggests Human instigation, so spare me the evasive incredulity and answer my last question."

Heat surged up the sides of Kena's face. Muscles tensed from her neck down her spine. Derogatory descriptions of Human sports irritated her, but nowhere near as bad as his assumption that she would be the instigator of a fight. She answered through clenched teeth. "I understand you quite clearly. Be assured, I will start no fight with a Grfdn."

G hent returned Kena's fixed gaze. Every aspect of her posture, expression, and voice fit the descriptions of Human anger. He opened his mouth to state the consequences of unrestrained emotion, then closed it as one of Metchell's comments surfaced from memory. Instead, he asked, "How much of your anger is attributable to my emfrel?"

Kena's brows twitched together. Then, her gaze fell, and her hands rose to cover trembling lips. She took a couple deep breaths before she answered. "I—I don't know. I suppose it might be due to emfrel, but...you were making such offensive assumptions that... I can't tell."

Ghent exhaled a quiet breath. She seemed appalled by her reaction, yet she hadn't tried to hide behind a convenient excuse. "Try to relax," he said. "I'll send for Metchell."

"Please don't."

At her sharp words, Ghent paused, his long finger hovering above the comm button.

"I need to learn to control this," she said. "If I always rely on

Metchell's sedatives, neither you nor I will know how I might react in a dangerous situation."

A valid point, but was it too soon for her? How did one go about calming a Human? Ghent shifted back in his chair. "You're trembling. Metchell spoke of—I think he called it adrenlin. He said it prevents relaxation."

"Adrenaline. It enhances strength and speed." She rose and turned away. "So, I hope you don't mind some pacing until it wears off."

"Not at all," he said.

Her pacing only took her to the far side of the room. She clung to the stone railing. Her face was hidden, but the rise and fall of her chest told the same story as the snap in her voice.

He waited until her breathing appeared normal, then he asked, "Are you still angry?"

"No."

She released the railing and brought her fingertips up to her face. Eye level, perhaps. Hard to learn much about expression when her back was turned. Unfortunate.

Ghent's study had led him to believe that firmness was required with Humans. Was that false? "Can you judge how much my emfrel is affecting you right now?"

"I'm very aware of you, but it isn't unsettling." She returned to her chair but kept her gaze low. "I wasn't overly conscious of its impact before the anger surfaced. I really can't explain why it happened. I apologize. It is not my normal behavior."

"Perhaps because I made offensive assumptions," he said.

Kena pressed her lips together.

Ghent studied every nuance of her changing expressions and body language. Her face stiffened, but she kept her eyes averted. Her posture remained passive. "Kena, I don't consider myself infallible. I'd like to know what I said that was offensive."

K ena guarded her breath, lest it reveal her tension. His changes from stern to gentle—so hard to follow. But he did seem to want an honest answer. Where to start? She quoted him, her brows rising. "'Spare me the evasive incredulity.'" She licked her lips. "I wasn't trying to evade you. I really was shocked. Grfdn are physically much stronger than Humans. Speed is our only advantage. A few of our males can match them, but I would almost certainly lose a fight with a Grfdn. I cannot imagine any circumstance that would induce me to start one."

Ghent's fingertips moved in a slow arc across the table.

Kena suppressed a desire to steal a look at him. "I certainly won't start a fight, but it's possible they will. Your—predisposition to blame me places me in a vulnerable position, which I have done nothing to deserve."

She wanted to say more, but she'd already said so much without reaction from Ghent. She forced her eyes to meet his and waited.

"I admit," he said, "I misinterpreted your response. Grfdn do not always win their fights with Humans. It didn't occur to me that you'd be physically incapable of fighting them. My own point of view doesn't suggest it either." He pointed at one section of the wall display, where a cliff face protruded toward the railing. "Do you see the alternating grooves in the rock there?"

Kena could just make them out, running vertically up the face of a cliff. "Yes."

"They're handholds. There's no difference in male or female strength among Plynteth. We all scale walls as easily as you walk a corridor. In fact, mothers often climb with their children on their backs, so if anything, they're stronger. I know Human females are typically smaller than males, but I don't recall reading that they're weaker. Is that a trait of your race?"

"Often, but not always. To some, it's a sensitive issue, so you won't find it in the official Human description."

"You share this trait with the Grfdn, which may protect you to some extent. Male aggression against females has severe consequences. In any case, I've already informed the Grfdn of my orders regarding fighting, and, uh, their other practice that is known to offend Humans. They understand authority very well. I don't expect you'll be attacked or threatened."

Kena nodded, though his reference to the *other practice* puzzled her.

"I haven't perceived any anger during this discussion," Ghent said. "I keep wondering what you've left out."

Kena's eyes widened. The man certainly paid attention. "It is a common irritation to hear Humans criticized for competitiveness. The more I hear it, the more I think it's grossly misunderstood. But I've yet to find a way to convince anyone of this, so I'll let it pass."

"I'll expect you to convince me later, then." The hint of a smile touched his lips. "It appears that you've regained control without Metchell's help. Pleased?"

She shrugged. "I'd be better pleased if it hadn't happened at all."

"You demand a great deal of yourself under difficult circumstances."

"Of course."

"Why *of course?*" he asked, relaxing against one side of his chair. "It is not always wise to do so."

"I wouldn't be the navigator I am if I didn't demand a great deal of myself."

Ghent's smile broadened. "Finally, you begin to sound like yourself."

Kena tilted her head. Did he know her so soon?

"There is one other practice," Ghent said, leaning forward again, "common to navigators of almost every race, I would like to discuss."

"What is that?"

"Most navigators," he said, "delight in the freedom and risks of piloting small craft. Some even enjoy convoluted spinning when their passengers are unaccustomed to zero G. I find no humor in the idea of making passengers sick. Nor will I tolerate unnecessary risks to our craft. Frethan was raised in space and has been navigating since adolescence. He may overlook the milder forms of such antics, but I do not. No matter how excellent your skills, if I discover that you're playing games with our short-range craft, you will find yourself permanently assigned to nav command."

Kena only grinned at the stern words. "Don't worry about me. I do all my *playing* in simulation. The craft will be safe under my control—and my passengers, both safe and comfortable."

Ghent looked sideways at her. "What amuses you? Are you expecting me to believe Humans are shy of risk?"

"Not at all. Some even enjoy it. So much so, we have slang for the flying you described. *Hot-dogging*, for instance. When Human officers catch anyone hot-dogging, they do much worse than simply restricting the offender to a boring duty."

"Really? What are the Human penalties?"

She shook her head. "Varied and creative. I doubt any would be appropriate in your culture."

Ghent's smile returned. "How unfortunate." He lifted himself from his chair, seeming to use his arms more than torso or legs. "It's time for fourth meal. If my emfrel isn't bothering you too much, I'd like you to stay with me a while longer."

"It's all right," she said, rising.

"Do you eat fourth meal?" he asked, walking to the door.

"Sometimes. For a Human, it's more of a snack than a meal."

In the hallway, they passed several second-shift crewmembers. Kena exchanged a quick greeting with Jorlit. What balm a friendly face could be.

The décor of the broad dining hall emphasized the *Ontrevay's* design to accommodate a diverse crew. Kena stopped to look around, and Ghent watched her. Tables in a variety of shapes and sizes filled the space, with several forms of seating. Water flasks, drinking cylinders, and hand cleaners occupied the center of each table. Buffets of freshly prepared food separated the kitchen from the dining area. Though there were no physical barriers, color and decor style divided the room visually.

"Who designed this?" she asked.

Ghent shrugged. "That was before my arrival. What do you think of it?"

"Quite well done. The decor schemes accommodate diverse tastes, while avoiding the blandness that's supposedly acceptable to all races. The schemes have been brought together without clashing, and that is *not* easy."

"I gather your interracial studies included the impact of color. Do you prefer to choose from the buffet or use the synthesizer?"

"The buffet." Kena moved toward the section designated *sweet/sour*. Ghent chose his meal from the other, which bore the *freth/prin* symbol and exuded a faint, indescribable scent. The Prednian influence made an appearance at the buffet. Every dish, whether plate, bowl, or even beverage container, was shaped as a squat cylinder. If ever a race valued sameness, it was the Prednians.

Kena and Ghent joined a small group of diners that increased as others came to the hall. Kena said little, preferring to listen and watch as the varied crew mingled. No separation by either rank or race. The sign of a comfortable crew. Perfect. The only exception was the table occupied solely by the five Grfdn crewmembers. Not that she blamed them. Grfdn were known for their fastidious table manners, and eating with Prednians could strain the most tolerant.

Metchell joined her table, and Ghent exchanged a look with him. As soon as both men had eaten, they left together. Their places were soon taken, and Kena spent the rest of the mealtime between jovial Prednians, who made it their business to introduce her to as many crew members as possible.

CHAPTER SEVEN

K ena leaned back from her console in the astro section and rolled her shoulders, as the computer recalculated a course for her. She'd enjoyed a restful night's sleep and persuaded Metchell to remove her duty restrictions. So good to be fully engaged with a crew again.

About a dozen navigators, as well as Frethan and Krdn, gathered around the huge 3-D display, either working at consoles or lounging against the railing that encircled the main viewing area. One of them fed a proposed course to the display, along with a location for repairing the *Ontrevay's* damaged sensor array.

Kena reviewed the final rendering of her course, then touched the control to display it alongside the first proposal.

Discussion began even before completion of a third option. It proceeded exactly as Kena expected. Her proposal received little consideration. Understandable. It plotted the least direct route.

One of the navigators pointed at the first option. "This is obviously the clearest area for repairs and the best course to get there. Why do we have to keep debating this?"

"You're right," Kena said. "It's extremely obvious. That's why it's the worst choice. Don't forget, we're near PitKreelaundun space. Flying that is much like sending them a course plan."

Frethan's easy grin spread across his face, but he said nothing.

The navigator waved a dark hand, brushing her objection aside. "They've no reason to guess any course for us. They don't know we're here."

Kena leaned forward and emphasized each word. "Never assume that."

"We can avoid the obvious," Krdn said, "without going to extremes. Option three is less predictable, because it takes us closer to the nebula, yet it adds very little time to our trip."

"The timing is good," Kena said, "but the safety margin isn't. Too much rock spews out of that nebula and shows up in places that don't align with our projections. Some of it is remarkably hard to catch on a scan."

One of the junior navigators gave her a sideways look. "You sound awfully cautious, considering your reputation. Where's your Human fearlessness?"

Kena's lip curled. "Fearless navigators are fools. Humans aren't good at this job because we ignore risk. We're good because we understand the risks and how to mitigate them. You may be quite certain that I will remain *cautious* in protecting this ship and every person within it."

His only response was a smirk.

"As will all of the navigators on this ship," Frethan said, pinning the young man with an implacable stare.

"Yes, sir."

Uncomfortable silence lengthened as Frethan continued to hold his gaze. "A senior navigator has addressed you. I'm still waiting for your response to her."

The junior navigator turned back to Kena. "Yes, ma'am. I mean, I beg your pardon, er..."

Kena nodded and turned back to Frethan before he could stumble any worse.

"We're discussing course options," Frethan said.

Krdn spoke as if no interruption had occurred. "It is true, there's an element of risk, but it's manageable. We've traveled through greater densities than this; we can do it again. Our mission is time critical. We cannot afford to go far enough out of the way to avoid all debris."

Ghent entered the room while Krdn spoke, and Kena twisted around to look at him.

Krdn demanded, "Kena, did you hear what I said?"

She quoted Krdn's last sentence.

Krdn turned his back on her while Frethan and Ghent engaged in a telepathic link. A few minutes later Frethan decided on option three, and most navigators left for second meal.

A group hung back, conferring in hushed tones. As Kena neared the door, one of the junior navigators rushed into speech. "Kena, if you could spare us a little time with sim, we're hoping you'd show us how you flew that maneuver with the PitKreelaundun fighter and the hammer-shaped asteroid."

Kena stopped and looked back at them. Ghent was conversing with Frethan, but her silence drew his gaze. She strolled back to the group.

"Whyever would you want to know how to fly that maneuver?" She gestured to the display of their intended course. "Have you found such an object in these scans?"

"Well, no, but if we can dance around a twisted, tumbling asteroid and use it to smash a PitKreelaundun fighter like you did, we'll be good enough to do pretty much anything."

"You'll be good enough to get killed." She paused to let her words sink in. "I've never before seen an object so bizarre. Neither you nor I will likely encounter another, even if we could fly every debris field in the galaxy. Do you honestly expect me to help you waste your simulation time preparing for one specific thing that isn't going to happen?"

A stunned silence met her question.

"You mean—you took a risk like that without practicing it?" one of them demanded.

Kena shrugged. "Oh, I'd flown dozens of sims around that rock, but that's because I was going to sample it. Objects that strange tend to attract the attention of scientists. As for the risk, I'd been hit several times. By PitKreelaundun, I might add, who supposedly didn't know we were there." She made eye contact with each of them before continuing. "My shield was all but worthless. Another hit would have been the last, so it was really only a matter of choosing how to die. If my attacker was fool enough to follow me, then I had a slim chance of getting myself out of trouble. It worked brilliantly, but that does not mean I want anyone to copy that particular maneuver."

She softened her expression and said, "Now, if you're interested in knowing how I train for the unexpected—that is an entirely different matter."

"Well—sure—guess so," a junior navigator said.

"It starts out very boring," Kena said with an impish grin. She pointed at the display again. "The first thing you have to do is get some really thorough scans of that course. Forget all those canned sims you've flown a thousand times. Get as close to reality as possible. When our path is programmed in, I'll show you how to add some spice." With a mischievous grin, she turned and sauntered out.

G hent soaked up every nuance of Kena's intonations and body language.

"Great!" muttered another junior navigator. "Now you've got her expecting us to do hours of scanning."

Frethan's mouth twitched, and his shoulders shook, but he stilled his reaction. "You can all work on it together. Get started soon. Otherwise, you won't have much time for sims before we arrive at the drop-out point. I'm very interested in seeing her training techniques with plenty of time for practice."

Frethan turned back to Ghent and continued their

conversation. When the others had moved out of earshot, though, he paused and threw a glance in their direction. He ran his hands over his dark, wispy hair, then linked them behind his head. "Satisfied?"

"Thus far, I am," Ghent said. "I'd like a report on this training. In particular, I'd like to know what 'spice' consists of."

"You will have it."

CHAPTER EIGHT

couple days later, Ghent strode out of the engineering
section. The faint whish of the closing door stopped
too soon.

"Sir."

Ghent halted at Dhgnr's voice. Odd. They had just spoken.
What could the second engineer want that couldn't have been said
earlier?

Dhgnr moved farther from the door, allowing it to close. "I
request to speak with you in private."

"This is not about maintenance, I gather," Ghent said.

"No. I must speak with you as Grfdn khn."

"My consult room, then," Ghent said, resuming his stride.
Dhgnr had never requested privacy. Not even when Rnl had been
involved in a cultural issue. True to Grfdn nature, Dhgnr had only
told Ghent the problem was resolved, not how. What could he
possibly want to discuss? They turned down an empty hallway. "Is
this about Kena?"

"No," Dhgnr said, "though I'd be interested in your impression
of her."

"She leaves one with so many impressions." Ghent shook his

head. "It's hard to know where to start. She has boundless energy, is highly aware of other's perceptions, and manages to convey her enthusiasm to nearly every race. I've never seen anyone weave into an existing team so quickly. It seems as though she's been here weeks, rather than days." A shame it wasn't universal. He dropped his pitch. "There is only one race that's impervious to her charm. Krdn and Hrndl stay as far away from her as possible."

Dhgnr took several seconds to produce a carefully worded reply. "The training material she is working on is of no interest to Grfdn. Our navigators train according to a very different method."

"I am aware, but the preparation for this training includes highly detailed scanning. Frethan is very pleased." Ghent grinned and added, "Netlyn is ecstatic. She's never had so much voluntary help with her scanning duties, nor so many attentive students."

"That's bound to please her. It's her specialty, is it not?"

"True, but I don't see why any navigator would prefer not to know what they're flying into. Yet Krdn is contemptuous. What Hrndl may think, I cannot tell. She's unusually silent. Has she commented on it?"

"Not on the scans," Dhgnr said, answering slowly again. "She only mentioned that the training is not repeatable. I do not understand how non-repeatable actions can be considered training."

Ghent stopped by the door to his consult room and touched the control panel. The door slid open. "No, I don't suppose you would."

An awkward silence followed as Ghent lowered himself into his wide chair.

Dhgnr also sat, his spine stiffer than the chair's back rest. "It is Hrndl that I must speak of. There is a reason why she may show less interest than usual." Dhgnr swallowed.

"Is there some problem between her and Kena?" Ghent asked.

"No, nothing of that nature." Dhgnr drew a breath. "Forgive my hesitancy, please. This is awkward. A female should give you this information, but since there are no other Grfdn females with us, I must do it." He rushed the unpalatable words, his gaze low. "Hrndl is approaching her first ovulation. She will need to mate, and will then need at least three days of seclusion while she delivers her ovum."

"Ah." Ghent paused, sliding his fingers across the granite table. "I realize this subject is taboo to a Grfdn, which means there is almost no information published on it. I'm reluctant to question you. Perhaps you could just tell me what you think I need to know."

Dhgnr hurried through the critical points. "It is hard to predict how long it will be before Hrndl mates—perhaps about a month. She may become easily distractible, but she should be able to control it when necessary." His nostrils pinched. "The Grfdn males are likely to fight. I know you would not normally allow this. I suggest you ignore it until Hrndl has mated. If a fight concerns you, tell me. I will address the issue."

"I've always been able to rely on you to handle Grfdn affairs," Ghent said, "but—after all, you are also male."

Dhgnr's voice slipped to a guttural rumble as he said, "Yes." He checked it, his next words low but smooth. "I do not intend to court Hrndl. She is in a difficult situation, since there is no female to support her. I cannot provide the majority of that support, but at least I can keep the other males from overstepping boundaries. As khn, I am in the best position to perform that duty for her."

Could this work? Doubtful, considering what he'd heard of Grfdn courtship—all unpublished, of course. Still, Dhgnr was as reliable as the annual floods that had soaked the canyons of Plynteth since time immemorial.

"All right." Ghent said. "I know you don't want this publicly discussed, but at least the section chiefs with Grfdn staff should know. And Metchell, also."

"Why Metchell?"

Ghent raised his brow. "Do you think your men will fight for show only?"

"No, but they will not seek medical attention if they are injured."

"Perhaps not, yet I expect my entire crew to keep themselves fit for duty. Is that understood?"

"Yes." Dhgnr clipped the word short.

Ghent envisioned Dhgnr having to repeat this torturous conversation four more times. Careful to hide what could be viewed as pity, Ghent said, "I can probably communicate this much faster than you, but I don't want to violate your taboo. Would it be acceptable for me to tell the others?"

"You may."

Dhgnr left without further ado, and Ghent strolled to the edge of his balcony. Wrapping fingers and shurgs around the railing, he frowned at the majestic expanse. This could be a problem.

K rdn escorted Hrndl to the dining hall that evening. Several navigators walked with them and kept Hrndl involved in their conversation when they paused beside a table. Annoying, but he hid his impatience. His eyes traveled to the Grfdn table, checking who was present—all three of them.

Dhgnr was watching him. He lifted his clenched fist and pulled it down to his chest.

Krdn's nostrils pinched. How dare Dhgnr summon him away from Hrndl with a khn's command gesture? Dhgnr's dominating eyes never wavered from Krdn's for an instant, leaving no doubt of his meaning. He would enforce obedience.

Krdn held his head erect in defiance, but strode to the table. "Can you defend your right to command me away from Hrndl?" he demanded.

"Sit." Dhgnr pointed at the chair directly across from him.

That would place Krdn at one end of the table next to Rnl. Separate from Hrndl. He opened his mouth to object, but Dhgnr said, "Shut up! Sit."

Krdn threw himself into the chair with enough force to grind the pivot joints.

Dhgnr turned his head; a glint sliding across his dark, glossy hair. He locked eyes with the men one at a time, Krdn to Rnl to Frdn, and back again. "I have spoken with Ghent regarding Hrndl. He has relayed the information to your section chiefs and to Metchell. They will know that aggressive behavior may occur between you. They cannot know what bounds are proper in relation to Hrndl, but I know." Dhgnr let those words hang for a moment. "Do not think that the absence of female support releases you from restraint. Hrndl will have the right to choose whomever she pleases. If any of you overstep proper courtship, you will feel my nerve wand."

Rnl uttered an obscene growl. "You have no right to use any weapon, or even to state a single command, when a mating female is involved!"

"What a fool you are, Rnl," Krdn said. He let the outer corners of his eyebrows lift as he relaxed against the back of his chair. "He retains all his rights as khn if he's not courting the female."

"Beyond doubt, but—oh!"

Dhgnr's voice rumbled. "So glad you comprehend this with such clarity, Krdn. I will not hesitate to exercise those rights."

The threat grated. Hrndl joined them, preventing his response. Just as well. Her gaze swept the array of dishes provided on the table so she wouldn't need to go to the buffet. Her brows tilted upward as she took her seat. "Who has served me so lavishly?"

"Rnl and Frdn, beyond doubt," Krdn said before the others could answer. "Quaint, is it not?"

"What's the matter, Krdn?" Dhgnr asked. "Are you embarrassed that you failed to provide her with such a common courtesy?"

Krdn glared at Dhgnr. What was he doing?

"My thanks to both of you," Hrndl said, spooning food from the nearest dish onto her plate.

Dhgnr kept his eyes locked on Krdn's. An unmistakable challenge.

Krdn finally lowered his gaze and inclined his head a few millimeters. So, Dhgnr was going to be difficult. Why? If he didn't want Hrndl for himself, why should he care? What good to encourage inferior suitors when, beyond doubt, she would choose Krdn?

Had Hrndl noticed Dhgnr's challenge? She gave no sign of it. The high tilt to the corners of her eyebrows revealed her delight as Rnl and Frdn showered her with attention. They vied to engage her in conversation. Hrndl laughed at some remark of Frdn's. Krdn would have less trouble if they had stayed properly cowed; but, in the end, it wouldn't matter. He could afford to let Hrndl enjoy a little fun. In a moment, he'd give her some conversation that actually interested her.

Several times, Krdn changed the subject to navigation, discussing concepts Frdn and Rnl would find difficult to relate to. Hrndl responded just as he hoped, following his lead every time.

He laughed within, let Frdn turn the conversation, and then brought it back again.

"What do you think about the course recommendations, Hrndl? Do you think another correction is necessary before we drop from slip?"

Dhgnr sneered. "Is navigation the only subject you know?"

Krdn's throat vibrated, but he gave no air to the growl. "No, but it is the most interesting one to Hrndl and me."

"You are second navigator, Krdn," Dhgnr said. "Beyond doubt, you're hoping to become a chief navigator at some point. Every captain expects his chief officers to understand broader concerns than their own interests. I wonder when I will see that quality in you."

Krdn held his tongue. Insults from a suitor, he could deal with. But from a khn? No, that would not end to his credit.

Dhgnr drew Frdn and Hrndl into conversation. Several minutes later, he introduced the subject of their newest navigator. Krdn rejoined the conversation, certain Hrndl would agree with his disparaging remarks about Kena.

She seemed more interested in the berries she was passing, one at a time, from her tongs to her small mouth.

Dhgnr interrupted his lengthy criticism. "Tell me something, Krdn. Who on this ship would you judge to be the most skilled at racial interaction?"

What now? "Ghent, I suppose."

"And who would be the best judge of another's abilities in that area?"

Krdn held his posture rigid. "Ghent, of course. What is your point?"

"Ghent is impressed by Kena's interracial skills," Dhgnr said. "He is not impressed by yours. Nor am I." He sipped his water, holding Krdn's gaze over the drinking cylinder. "It's not so many months since you were promoted. If Frethan wasn't so leery of favoring a member of his own race, I doubt you would have that title you think so much of. Kena's piloting skills exceed yours. Consider your position well."

Krdn growled deep in his throat and crushed the fruit he held in his tongs. "Do not dare compare me to that arrogant little Human. You know nothing of the skills required of a navigator."

"Your complaints of Kena's arrogance are like an ocean complaining that raindrops are wet."

CHAPTER NINE

Kena paced, counting the minutes until she could escape from boredom. She'd been stuck in nav command all morning, taking her turn to monitor as the *Ontrevay* traveled along its programmed course. She shared the duty with Elna, a skillful navigator who seemed incapable of any conversation longer than three sentences. Not the sort to enliven a tedious shift.

Kena's relief arrived ten minutes before she was due.

"Netlyn!" Kena exclaimed. "You darling! You're early."

Netlyn laughed. "A little short on excitement? I figured this was the least I could do. You've made my life so much easier these past few days. Anything to report?"

Kena gestured to the displays that ringed the room, turning in a complete circle to encompass them all. "Do but look. Are they not fascinating?"

Netlyn's gaze swept the screens, taking in the symbolic detail at a glance. "Uh...no."

Kena adopted a despairing tone "You are so hard to please."

Netlyn shook her head and gave Kena a playful push toward the door. "Oh, get to your meal before the crowd arrives."

F ew crew members were in the dining hall when Kena entered. She took bread from the buffet, covered it with a Prednian spread, and selected a few varieties of alien produce.

One bowl held a welcome surprise; deep red, juicy strawberries. The label included a description and the information that they were a new addition to the horticulture section. Fresh Terran food on an interracial ship? She must meet this chef who'd ordered a Terran fruit.

A dish that looked much like rice, but smelled like lemon and mint, piqued her interest. Its label contained a Grfdn name, which she couldn't pronounce, but no warning against Human consumption. She added a spoonful of it to her plate.

Kena glanced around the hall. Only Hrndl was seated at the Grfdn table. Just the sort of opportunity she'd been waiting for. She made her way to the table and asked with Grfdn formality, "Pardon the intrusion, but may I join you at meal?"

H rndl had no desire to eat with the Human, but Kena had stated the request with perfect courtesy, even phrasing the Prednian words in Grfdn structure. To refuse when she sat alone would be a boorish insult. There was nothing to do but consent. "You may share my table," she said with equal courtesy.

Kena thanked her and slid into a chair. "I've been hoping to find some time outside of duty to spend with you."

Oh, no. What did *some time* mean? "Why?"

"To get to know you a little." Kena sliced off a piece of strawberry—small enough for Grfdn etiquette—and put it in her mouth.

"Why?"

Unhurried, Kena chewed and swallowed. "Establishing rapport with crewmembers is part of the way Humans coordinate."

"Humans know nothing of coordination."

"Really?" Kena said. "Do you know many Humans?"

Hrndl clasped a morsel in her tongs. "You don't even have a word for it."

"Actually, we do; although many races misunderstand that word, so we don't use it often."

"You must be referring to *teamwork*." Hrndl said, pushing the awkward syllables between her lips. "The organizational structure through which you fight—excuse me, I mean compete—with one another."

Kena only smiled. "What a perfect example of a common misconception."

"Spare me the explanation that teamwork is, in fact, coordination. I already read it in my assigned study of your race, and I am unconvinced. I repeat, Humans know nothing of coordination." Hrndl picked up the wide drinking cylinder with both hands. So clumsy. Prickles moved down her arms. She took a careful sip of water. Kena's eyes were fixed on her. Couldn't she find somewhere else to look?

"Then I'll rely on you to teach me," Kena said.

Teach her! Hrndl quivered in mid-sip. Water spilled from the cylinder and dribbled down the side of her chin. She couldn't even wipe it away with this monstrous cylinder in her hands. She must look like a child. Beyond doubt, this arrogant Human would enjoy hearing her apologize, but there was no way to avoid it.

Kena spoke before Hrndl could utter a word. "Aren't these cylinders the most awkward things imaginable? I grew so tired of them on the Prednian ship *Baktel*. Perhaps they were understandable there, but I see no reason why we must put up with them in a crew as diverse as this one."

Kena rose and went to the re-forming station. She returned with two containers of water: a tall, slender glass, which Humans preferred, and a Grfdn drinking pouch.

Hrndl stared at the pouch Kena placed before her. Just like the pouches she'd grown up with. A broad cone with the pale color and soft texture of animal skin. Its darker tip hid a valve, which opened when squeezed between the front teeth. What else would anyone expect for a race with a deep cultural dislike of exposing any portion of one's little mouth? So much easier to suck water from a pouch than to form thin lips against a cylinder's edge. Hrndl longed for the pouch—almost reached for it. Then, she remembered.

Her eyes darted from the pouch to Kena's chest, where her loose-fitting shirt partially hid twin bulges. If a drinking pouch resembled that unmentionable anatomy as closely as was said— How could Kena have the audacity to even fill a pouch, much less bring it to their table? Oh, and worse! Now Hrndl was staring in the most offensive manner possible. She jerked her eyes back to Kena's face. "You must know I cannot possibly drink from that in your presence. Why do you taunt me? This is a fine example of *establishing rapport*."

Kena's eyes widened. "Why can't you drink from a pouch when I'm present?"

Hrndl hesitated. Kena's surprise seemed genuine. Could a Human really not know? How could she answer without saying the actual word? "Because...because of..."

K rdn entered the dining hall, his eyes going straight to the Grfdn table. A drinking pouch sat in plain view. Beyond belief! How could Hrndl be foolish enough to use such a thing? No one else seemed to have noticed it yet. He still had time to get rid of it. He strode to the table.

"What are you doing with this?" he demanded in an under-voice.

Hrndl straightened. "I didn't get it. Kena did."

Krdn's voice rumbled through a clenched throat. "How dare you?"

"How dare I what?" Kena asked. "It's a common Grfdn article."

She swept a hand toward her glass and the pouch. "Why should it
be so terrible that I brought water in the containers we both
prefer?"

"Everyone knows that drinking from a pouch in the presence
of a Human is the worst possible insult. If Ghent hears that Hrndl
drank from this, she could be demoted. Even forbidden from interracial ships."

"Oh, relax," Kena said. "There may be a few Earth-bound
Humans who would be offended, but the space-faring Humans
wouldn't give it a passing thought. I am certainly not bothered.
And I'll make sure Ghent knows." She turned back to Hrndl and
picked up her glass. "Now, please, enjoy a comfortable drink
with me."

Hrndl stared as though some inconceivable boon was being
granted. "You really don't care?"

"Not in the least."

Hrndl heaved an audible sigh and reached for the pouch.

Krdn closed a hand over it as he brought his sneering face near
Kena's. "If we wish to drink from pouches, we will do so without
your—help." He hurled the pouch against the wall.

A stunned silence followed Krdn's dramatic gesture. Too
vehement for this passive lot—they'd get over it. But the hush
remained. Too late, he saw the reason.

Ghent stood in the doorway of the dining hall, his stern gaze
moving from the water splattered on the wall, to the split pouch
on the floor, and finally to Krdn's face. "Explain your action," he
said, with heavily emphasized cadence.

Krdn drew his head back. "Kena tried to coerce Hrndl into
defying your orders. I was simply making it clear to her that we
will not tolerate such behavior."

Ghent's eyes turned to Kena. "Do you have a response?"

She leaned back in her chair, dangling a hand over the
armrest. "This is nothing more than a misunderstanding. Hrndl
and I both find it awkward to drink from cylinders, so I brought
water for each of us in the container customary for our race. I

had no idea you'd issued orders pertaining to what we drink from. Then, Krdn arrived and drew conclusions that I do not begin to understand. I cannot see how my actions could be considered coercive, nor do I have any desire to cause Hrndl to defy you."

Krdn's breath stopped as Ghent looked at Hrndl. She sat rigid, her thin lips pressed tight. If Ghent said one word of reprimand to her, Kena was going to regret it every moment until he could be rid of her.

Ghent's words flowed without cadence. "Hrndl, I suspect you're in a difficult situation. I will not require any comment from you."

Without the faintest quiver of emotion, Hrndl said, "In fairness, I do not believe Kena intended to cause trouble."

"Then, apparently, nothing at all has happened," Ghent said. Walking past Krdn, he murmured with Grfdn acidity, "You appear to have a mess to clean up."

Mess? Was this an oblique suggestion that he apologize? His stomach seized. No! The split pouch. It had to be that. Krdn picked it up, tossed it into a receptacle, and left the hall without a backward glance.

P ride demanded that Hrndl finish the meal with Kena. She didn't even have support from her own race, for Dhgnr took Frdn and Rnl to another table. Kena's tact minimized the ordeal. She guided the conversation into neutral channels—Grfdn cuisine, of all things. So much easier to accept than the meaningless apologies most races offered in the midst of conflict. And how strange it was to watch a Human savoring a Grfdn food.

As soon as she could reasonably do so, Hrndl made a polite and dignified departure. Once outside the dining hall, she quickened her steps. Reaching Krdn's quarters, she slapped the comm unit and stated her name. The door slid open.

Hrndl eyed the half-finished food on his table. "Enjoying your meal in solitude, Krdn?"

"Not at all. I was hoping you'd join me sooner. What would you like to eat?" he asked reaching for his computer.

Did he think she'd fall for that soothing tone, or the way he pretended not to hear her insult? "Nothing. I'm civil enough to eat in public. I dined with Kena."

"What? An entire meal? Oh, Hrndl, you really didn't need to make such a sacrifice. No wonder you're in a temper."

Hrndl panted, barely able to get enough air. "After the way you acted, I most certainly did have to stay with her. Everyone on the ship would have been talking about Grfdn manners. Your behavior was inexcusable!"

"My behavior?"

"Yes, yours!" Hrndl took an unsteady breath then tried to smooth her exhale. "Fortunately, Kena can maintain calm far better than you can. I believe she and I managed to convey a pleasant interaction."

Krdn shook his head as though he couldn't believe her words. "Think for a moment, Hrndl. What would have happened if I hadn't stopped you drinking from that pouch? Ghent would have walked in and seen it in your mouth. What do you suppose he would've said?"

"Since he takes more time to listen than you do, I doubt he would've said much at all. He might even have realized that Kena doesn't care about pouches in the least, and we'd be free to drink from them again. Instead, you've made a trivial event into a grand scene, and we'll be stuck with cylinders for the rest of the trip."

Krdn mimicked a very non-Grfdn tone of exaggerated concern. "Oh, Hrndl, I had no idea you wanted to be beholden to the Human. If only I'd known, I would have begged her to help you as soon as she arrived."

"Oh, shut up!"

"Sounds repulsive, doesn't it? So why were you accepting help from a Human? You should be glad I stopped you from doing that, too. Do you think she would let you forget it?"

"Yes, I do. If you hadn't created a scene, she would never have thought of it again. She was just getting two containers of water." Hrndl jerked her head back. "Stop pretending you know what you're talking about. You look a fool! And spare me any more of *your* help. I don't want it."

Krdn took a moment to answer. The muscles in his neck relaxed. "I know you do not need it. I've always admired that about you." He stood and took a step toward her. "Hrndl, you must forgive me if I'm too solicitous. My instinct to protect you is nearly overwhelming."

His words pulled her thoughts to a sudden stop. Mating instinct? Was that really the issue? Possible. She could only guess. A strange foreboding tingled through her. The indistinct desire to talk with females—experienced Grfdn females—was morphing into necessity.

"Come," Krdn said. "We had best put this aside. We should return to work before those gossiping Prednians notice our absence."

The threat of enduring gossip was enough to convince Hrndl to walk to the simulation room with him.

CHAPTER TEN

Kena hoped the incident would blow over without further comment. No such luck. Ghent sent for her after fourth meal.

"I assume you know what I want to talk about," Ghent said as Kena sat down opposite him at his curved, granite table.

She leaned back in the chair, allowing her hands to dangle from the armrests. "Oh, I don't think we should guess at it. Assumptions haven't worked out very well for me today. Before we get into whatever you do want to talk about, would you mind telling me what you meant a few days ago when you mentioned the *other* Grfdn habit which is known to offend Humans?"

"I was referring to drinking pouches."

"Oh, good." Kena sighed the words out. "I was afraid there might be another surprise in store for me. Why didn't you tell me?"

"You are Human—I thought you would know. And at that moment, the last thing I wanted to bring up was an embarrassing subject." His fingertips slid back and forth across the granite. "There are likely to be many more surprises. Why were you sitting with Hrndl in the first place? Don't you know Grfdn prefer to eat only with their own race?"

"Yes, of course." Kena shrugged. "But that's because so few races use table manners acceptable to them. Human manners are not so very different from Grfdn's, and I don't mind taking tiny bites, as their etiquette demands. Also, she was the only one there. I understand that Grfdn hate to eat alone. It seemed like a good time to get to know her. I need to work closely with her, and it would be easier if we had at least some basic relationship."

Ghent glanced at a message on his computer before answering her. "It might be easier for you, but it makes no difference to her. What she wants most from you is predictability. Failing that, she wants clear, concise communication. Do you think you're likely to succeed with a friendship she doesn't want?"

"I doubt we'll ever be close friends," Kena said, "but things were civil when Krdn wasn't involved."

"Are you familiar with Grfdn mating customs?"

Kena blinked. "I, uh, believe I understand the basics."

"You have the most interesting expressions," Ghent said, with a hint of a smile. "What does this one mean?"

"I'm rather surprised at the change in subject."

Ghent shook his head. "I haven't changed the subject. Hrndl is approaching first ovulation. I'd like to know what you understand about that."

"Oh!" Kena shifted her position. "Uh, the Grfdn reproductive system becomes active comparatively late. Females don't choose a mate until the first ovum is maturing. The instinct is quite strong, because an ovum can't be delivered without assistance from a mate. Their race has unequal proportions in gender. Only forty percent are female—which makes for very competitive males. And perhaps most important of all, the subject is taboo. I won't be chattering about it."

"That would be disastrous." He leaned forward, resting his folded arms on the table. "I wouldn't normally discuss this, but you haven't been here long enough to recognize the changes that are obvious to me. Krdn is determined to be Hrndl's mate. He is already possessive and protective. I suggest you avoid situations where you could be a hindrance to their relationship."

"I see," Kena said slowly.

Ghent frowned at her. "What annoys you about that?"

Her eyebrows drew together for an instant, then she burst into laughter, tilting her chair back as far as it would give. "Nothing, at all. When Humans draw out words, it shows thoughtfulness, not annoyance."

"Ah." Ghent settled back in his rigid chair.

Kena stilled her mirth and asked, "Do you think Krdn over-reacted because he thought I was trying to cause trouble for Hrndl?"

"Beyond doubt, to borrow their phrase. Believe me, I do not normally overlook such unrestrained temper."

One of his shurgs extended as he enunciated the last two words. Apparently, that scene had bothered him far more than he revealed in the dining hall.

Kena licked her lips. "Have I convinced you that drinking pouches don't offend me? Will you permit Grfdn to drink from them?"

"It's a moot point, Kena. They won't drink from them while you're on this ship."

"Why not?"

"Because," he said, "you obtained that privilege for them."

She tilted her head. "I don't understand. Wouldn't this fit in with their all-important coordination thing?"

"Not at all." Ghent shook his head. "They do not coordinate because they need or want help. Implying that someone needs help is an insult to a Grfdn. The purpose of coordination is to increase efficiency. If employing two people more than doubles the output for a given task, then they coordinate. Both of them expect to gain equal benefits from the synergy. Otherwise, they work alone." He paused and emphasized his next sentence. "The purpose of coordination is never to help someone."

"From a navigator's perspective, this is not good."

"Why do you say that?" he asked as his shurg retracted, an apparent unconscious movement.

"What if someone's craft is damaged," Kena said, "or for any other reason, they can no longer provide their full contribution? Will Hrndl or Krdn just abandon the other navigator and carry on alone?"

"Never!" Ghent said. "Once agreed upon, the commitment cannot be broken. The entire task must be completed. The greatest possible benefit is still equally shared between both parties, even if that benefit is far less than originally envisioned. Grfdn never leave a partner if there is any chance of bringing them back alive."

Kena considered his words for a moment. "This has been most enlightening. Have we covered what you wanted to see me about?"

Ghent laughed. "Yes, ma'am."

What did that mean? "Why are you laughing and calling me ma'am? Did I say something I shouldn't have?"

"Let us rather say that conversations with you are—unique."

"Oh. Uh, good night, then."

"Good night, Kena."

Ghent replayed the conversation in his mind for a few minutes until Frethan entered.

"What amuses you?" Frethan asked.

"Kena. I called her here to talk about a very unpleasant incident between her and our Grfdn navigators. She led the conversation, and then very graciously asked if we had covered what I wanted to see her about."

Frethan chuckled as he smoothed his wispy hair back. "I can well imagine. And yet you let her get away with it?"

Ghent smiled. "Oh, I'm exaggerating a little. She's not disrespectful, and I'm learning a tremendous amount by letting her talk freely. Still, I find her exquisitely humorous at times. Only you and Metchell talk to me as casually as she does."

"We are Tenelli and Dantokrellie, after all."

"Ah, yes. Two races of most friendly repute. But you know it's not that." Ghent swept the fingers of one hand back and forth on his table. "Who would ever have thought that an arrogant Human would interact with me the same way you do."

Frethan's brow creased. "Humans are often criticized for arrogance, but I do not see it in her. Granted, she has an abundance of confidence. Perhaps in Humans that is misinterpreted."

"It's either that or excessive friendliness to high-ranking officers," Ghent murmured.

Frethan only laughed. "She has indeed made many friends—not just among the navigators, either."

"You've had some time to observe her, now. Are you pleased?"

"Entirely! Her navigation skills are everything her records indicated. She can plot a time slip course faster than anyone on this ship. Her training skills are leadership level. She can even teach others how to train."

Ghent leaned forward. "Elaborate, please."

Frethan's gaze wandered then returned. "Giddech has been training Eperia on advanced robotic techniques. She does fine with most of it, but has some problem areas. The equipment is of Human design, so I paired her with Kena. Giddech made one of his snide remarks about Eperia. Something he now seems to regret —for a change."

Frethan shook his head as though still surprised over what had happened. "Kena responded by ordering him to train Eperia while she observed. She figured out that he had one of the controls configured for his own range of motion, rather than Eperia's. It made her clumsy with certain actions." Frethan mimicked a twisting motion with his hand that could only be completed by tilting his upper body as well. "Kena instructed him in recognizing physical restrictions and the finer points of robotics configuration.

Then, she gave him a lesson in cultural perception. As is common for her race, Eperia is sensitive to the word *must*, particularly *you must*."

"Ah, yes," Ghent said. "It's viewed as manipulative and autocratic."

Frethan nodded. "Giddech gives instruction only with the phrase *you must*, never anything like *you should* or *try this*. Kena insisted that he rephrase every instruction."

"Should I assume he now hates her?" Ghent asked.

"You would think so," Frethan said, "but apparently not. She used her authority a few times to check that nasty tongue of his, but otherwise used a respectful tone while she taught him. She also corrected Eperia for taking offense over a cultural difference of expression. They had a rocky start, but Giddech did listen to her. And believe me, listening is not his strong point. After Kena dismissed him, she trained Eperia, who learned from her without any difficulty."

"Excellent. It'll be a shame," Ghent teased, "to see her go when this mission is over. We're unlikely to need so many navigators for the next."

"I will find a way to keep her here."

Ghent grinned and stretched his long arms. "When was all this?"

"Just this afternoon."

"Were Hrndl or Krdn present?" At Frethan's nod, Ghent asked, "Their reactions?"

Frethan stared over Ghent's shoulder, almost as though watching a recording of his memory on the rock wall. "Nothing verbal. Hrndl looked over at them a few times. I can't recall Krdn ever glancing their way." He shook his head. "I've had to start watching his duty assignments. Everyone else, he pairs up efficiently, but he insists on giving Kena trivial, solo tasks. He's not utilizing her skills."

CHAPTER ELEVEN

K ena sat beside Frethan in the simulation room, monitoring results of the run she'd designed in the Human style of training, a sim peppered with random events. She glanced over at Frethan. He leaned back in his chair, smiling as usual. The cause right now, though, was the navigator response statistics rolling across the screen.

Kena studied the techniques revealed on the main screen, which was sectioned to mirror the displays from each of the simulation compartments that lined two sides of the long room. She sighed and shook her head.

"Your training scenarios are successful," Frethan said. "There's a noticeable improvement in high-stress response rates; but, unless I misread your expression, you're not at all happy about it."

Kena only shrugged.

He waved a hand at the screen. "This simulation is demanding, almost impossibly so, but they're doing remarkably well in spite of the difficulty. They don't have the reflexes of a Human, but the improvement rate is excellent."

She nodded, but spoke in a flat voice. "True."

"I'd expect you to be pleased. And so will they. Keep the

importance of morale in mind when they come out of the simulators."

She turned her chair toward him. "I'm not dissatisfied with anyone's navigational skills, Frethan. It's the way these sims are being used that worries me."

From the corner of her eye, movement caught her attention. Hrndl looked up from the console she was using, stared at Kena a moment, then began to study the segmented screen. About time she noticed her fellow navigators.

"Frethan, no one has flown standard sims in two days," Kena said. "And they don't include partners when flying the randomized ones. I even programmed in partners, but the only attention the navigators give them is to avoid hitting them."

Frethan laughed.

"That wasn't a joke."

"I know, Kena, but you're worried about nothing. They know the purpose of the random events is to improve reflexes. They won't forget they have partners when they really fly."

Kena shook her head, the corners of her mouth pulling down. "I don't know, Frethan. I think you should require partnered sims. And it wouldn't hurt to restrict how many random sims they fly in a day. The one they're working on now is going to demoralize most of them. This is their third time through, and they're still flying it all wrong." She spread her restless hands. "Not a single one has brought the simulated partner out. The ones who've tried got smashed into scrap metal. Not even Delf has pulled it off, and he's a senior navigator with the skills to prove it. What good are high response statistics if people die?"

In direct contradiction to her statement, Delf sauntered out of his simulator, as only a Veet could. His long limbs swayed with fluid grace. Beneath a mass of black hair, his dark eyes flashed, and the lines around his mouth deepened. "I must say, Kena, you know how to set up a simulation. That one really pushes the limits. I can't remember when I've enjoyed a sim more."

Netlyn came out of her simulator as he spoke. She plopped

into a chair at the ring of tables in the center of the room. Her wispy, brown hair fell forward, veiling her downcast eyes.

Hrndl sneered at Delf. "I don't know what you're looking so pleased about. You left your partner to be pulverized."

"I don't like leaving a partner behind any more than you do, Hrndl, but sometimes that tough decision has to be made. That's the point of having one in this sim. If you spend time trying to rescue your partner, you get trapped and can't get yourself out. It's a question of whether two people will die, or just one."

"That is not the point of the sim," Kena said. "You can both get out safely."

The rest of the navigators were coming out of their simulators, complaints firing.

"Well, why don't you just show us how?" one of them said.

"What good will that do us? We don't have Human nervous systems and never will."

"It's not a fair comparison. Kena designed the sim; so, of course, she knows the way out."

Kena waited for their griping to subside. "This isn't a competition. It isn't about the capabilities of our nervous systems. It's about making the right decisions under pressure. I'll bet Hrndl could finish it successfully on the first try."

Frethan's brows snapped together. "The Grfdn train differently than the rest of us and are not required to use randomized simulations. Nor do I want to hear any suggestions that could be interpreted as manipulation."

"That is not my intent," Kena said. "I simply think training would be improved if it were a joint effort, incorporating both Grfdn and Human strengths."

Every trace of Frethan's persistent smile vanished. "Enough."

Hrndl strode to a simulator. "She has a valid point, Frethan. The training you've been doing for the last two days worries me. I'm willing to try her simulation for the sake of improving the training program."

As Hrndl slid into the simulator's couch, Netlyn darted

glances between Frethan and Kena, her brow tight. "We should give her at least three runs through before commenting on her results."

H rndl paused, her hand hovering above the door control. "Perhaps you didn't hear Kena. This is not a competition." She closed the door and fed her controls, audio, and view screen to the room's main display.

The simulation placed Hrndl in the role of support navigator. Her partner, in a separate craft, was collecting samples from an area of concentrated debris along the nebula's fringe. The simulation computer controlled both the debris motion and the virtual pilot in the collection craft. Hrndl monitored just outside the danger zone. Some of that debris was going to collide soon. Which rocks, though? The sooner she figured that out, the better her chance of success.

The collection craft dropped its extended shield and began the delicate job of hooking a spinning object.

Hrndl's scan and analysis revealed the threat only seconds before one spinning rock bashed into another. The scattering pieces set up a chain reaction of collisions, spraying debris across both craft. Hrndl's double-shielded craft remained undamaged. The collector was not so fortunate. The impacts sent it farther into danger.

Hrndl made contact with the collector's virtual pilot. "Status?"

"I've lost all nav jets except 14 and 16. I'm down to only one shield generator. Power level is eight percent."

"Stabilize your course," Hrndl said. "What's your weapon status?"

"Undamaged, but I don't have the power to use them."

"I have plenty," she said. "Minimize your shield and keep weapons online."

Hrndl blasted a rock heading for the disabled craft, and it

changed course, heading harmlessly away. Another soon followed it.

D elf shook his head. "She'll never make it now. She's waited too long to protect herself."

Kena turned a smirk his way but said nothing.

Netlyn asked, "Why do you grin? Most of us tried to protect our partner that way, and we never got out to the debris cloud. Hrndl still hasn't even moved. She doesn't stand a chance. What's the point of a sim that kills everyone?"

"I don't recall anyone asking their partner to keep weapons online," Kena said. "She's on the right track."

As if on cue, Hrndl's voice addressed her virtual partner. "I'm sending you a sequence of targets. Do you have them?"

"Yes."

"Begin firing, at once, and don't change the order. My course to you is planned around the sequence."

"Acknowledged."

H rndl held her position until her partner had blasted two oncoming objects. She continued her own firing as she swept a complex course toward the damaged collector. "Prepare for contact. Shut down your nav jets as soon as I've got you."

"I missed the last target."

"I'll get it," she said. "Cease fire and hold steady. I'm coming in on your tail."

"Acknowledged."

Hrndl's maneuver to hit the final target failed. The rock spun close enough to reveal its jagged, fractured edges. A giant spearhead, hurtling through the void. She fed maximum energy to shields and fired thrusters. Her course angled in on the rock's trajectory, closing the distance. The projectile struck her extended shield. Ice burst from its surface as she shoved it away.

Hrndl reversed thrust. The disabled craft was too close. She couldn't avoid dealing it a nasty jerk as she snared it. Her shield wrapped around the linked craft. "Status?" she asked.

She received no response. The nav jets did not shut down. Their thrust skewed her course and pushed the pair toward a spin.

"Navigator, report your status."

Silence.

The virtual pilot must be incapacitated. She compensated for the extra thrust. There'd better not be a delayed shutdown. Worst of all, her plan had included a partner capable of firing weapons. How would she get through all this debris alone?

K ena watched in rapt attention. Like the navigators beside her, she shifted with every movement on the screen. They all had access to the collector craft's data, which Hrndl couldn't see. Its communication transmitter was damaged by the impact. Only the receiver still functioned. The computer interpreted the force of impact as mildly damaging to the pilot. It simulated ten seconds of disorientation, then waited for instructions from Hrndl.

Kena scowled, jumped up from her seat, and ran to a simulator. "What are you doing?" Delf demanded.

Kena slid into the simulator couch. "This was designed to be a partnered sim," she said, jabbing at buttons to take over for the virtual pilot.

Delf swung around to Frethan. "This isn't a fair comparison. She's changing—"

"Pay attention!" Frethan snapped. "See if you're capable of learning something."

I nside her simulator, Hrndl adjusted her course, increased thrust, and blasted two objects out of her path. She considered the few options still available. Her simulated craft jerked sideways then corrected. What was that? Two seconds later, the movement repeated, then again in another two seconds. The other navigator was alive and signaling her. A tingle coursed through her, and the corners of her eyes lifted. Better yet, he hadn't shut down nav jets. He must know she had compensated.

Hrndl almost repeated his signal back to him before realizing communication could be simpler. She broadcast, "I'm not receiving communication from you. If you can hear me, repeat that sequence."

She released a breath as identical jerks rocked her seat.

"Excellent! I'm transmitting a four-second count. Shut down thrust on the fourth mark." As she spoke, Hrndl prepared to deactivate her counter-thrust. At the appointed instant, both navigators simultaneously performed their parts of the correction. The coupled ships continued on course, sailing between two approaching rocks.

Hrndl tested maneuverability. Her craft responded exactly as it should. A tingle surged all the way to her fingertips. Success was within reach. "Let's establish a yes/no signal. I can see the lights in your aft section. Turn them off and on—once for yes, and twice for no."

After her partner repeated the signal, she sent him a series of targets.

The lights flickered once.

They spent the next ten minutes flying through a dense field of debris, both of them firing to clear a path according to Hrndl's precisely coordinated plan. The simulation ended as they came out of the debris field.

Hrndl emerged from her simulator, her steps quick and her eyes tilted high. "You were right, Delf. That was an excellent sim!" She searched the group as she approached. "Where is Kena?"

CHAPTER TWELVE

"I'm here," Kena said, stepping out of another simulator. Hrndl's pleasure froze. "Were you flying the disabled craft in sim?"

"After you caught it, yes."

"So, you think I needed your help," Hrndl said, her voice dropping almost to a rumble.

"Not you, but the computer was in dire need." Kena strolled to the central tables. "I hadn't programmed for that hard of a jolt. It simulated disorientation then waited for your instructions. No navigator would simply wait inactive, so I joined you. Once you knew your partner could function, I only followed your directions." Kena glanced around the circle of navigators. "This sim was designed to show how two navigators working together could get out of an otherwise impossible situation." She turned back to Hrndl. "That's pretty hard to illustrate if one of them stops navigating."

Hrndl stared. Hard to believe from a Human, yet the whole design of the sim supported her explanation. In fact, it was similar to Grfdn training in some ways. Shocking. It called into question everything Hrndl knew about Humans. It wouldn't be wise to jump to conclusions, but—perhaps getting to know Kena wasn't such a bad idea, after all.

Delf broke in on her thoughts. "Kena should never have joined the sim! It created a distorted comparison."

Kena turned to him. "If you really need to have your skills acknowledged, I concede that you won this imagined competition in terms of maneuvering and firing accuracy. But I would still rather fly with Hrndl than with you."

"Why? So you can be there to help her out of trouble?" He aimed a scathing glance at Hrndl.

Hrndl drew her head back, but Kena gave her no chance to respond. "No, Delf. It's partly because you and I have similar skills. Putting us together would be a waste. Much greater synergies are gained by pairing us with others. But mostly, it's because you are much too likely to ignore your partner's capabilities. You may as well fly alone."

Delf's large mouth curved into a sneer, promising a response far from polite.

"That will do," Frethan said. Delf turned to him, but Frethan cut him off again. "Do not utter one more word. You are dismissed."

Delf's face contorted into a grimace before he swung around and headed for the door.

Hrndl shook her head. Bad move. Even she knew what that grimace meant. A facial obscenity. Frethan would never let it pass.

Frethan's voice grew cold and hard. "Now would be a good time to show me perfect respect."

Hrndl held her breath and focused all energy on keeping her face still.

Delf halted. He hesitated an instant then spun to face Frethan. In one fluid movement, he lifted a knee to hip level, raised himself onto tip-toe, and closed his eyes. He held the pose for a few seconds, then he snapped his feet together, turned on his heel, and strode out the door.

Kena pulled her lower lip between her teeth, as Delf turned to Frethan. Oh, no! Not the tin soldier routine. According to the Veet racial profile, it was a posture of deep respect. How that culture had ever come up with such an absurdity was beyond comprehension. It seemed to satisfy Frethan. How could he keep a straight face?

Kena hoped no one noticed she was strangling on suppressed laughter. Frethan either didn't notice or didn't care. He dismissed Kena and Hrndl, but kept the other navigators with him.

Kena hurried to her quarters to have her laugh in private. She was forced to hold it back even longer, for the door of her quarters didn't close behind her. Hrndl stood in the entrance.

Hrndl spoke with Grfdn formality, though it sounded like there was gravel in her throat. "Please forgive the intrusion. May I speak with you for a moment?"

Kena swallowed hard and managed to answer. "Certainly. Please come in."

"I am curious about one of your expressions," Hrndl said. She took another breath. "It wasn't mentioned in the training material, and I respectfully request an explanation."

Was she this stiff on purpose or just uncomfortable? And how to get her past it? "What expression?" Kena asked, trying to sound like this was a normal conversation.

"You pulled your lower lip in so far, your mouth looked almost Grfdn."

Kena almost choked, but somehow controlled her voice. "It's referred to as 'biting one's lip.' The lip is held between the teeth as a physical reminder to control the expression of an emotion."
Kena tried to control that same emotion, but her mouth quivered.

The muscles at Hrndl's temples tightened, pulling the corners of her eyes upward in the Grfdn version of a smile. "What were you suppressing?" she asked, even more gravel tumbling within her throat.

SHARON ROSE

"I find the Veet posture of respect—quite humorous."

Hrndl's voice shook. "As—as do I."

Kena struck a melodramatic pose. "I can imagine myself twenty years from now in the role of a firm chief navigator. A Veet makes a face at me and I sternly declare, 'Now would be a good time to show me your perfect sense of balance.'"

Hrndl collapsed against the wall in helpless laughter. She sounded like a Human gargling. It was more than Kena could endure. She fell onto the couch and laughed until she couldn't breathe. By the time Hrndl quit, Kena was holding her sides and forcing herself to take slow, deep breaths.

She might have succeeded if Hrndl hadn't exclaimed, "Kena, you've changed color!"

Kena doubled over, shaking.

Hrndl's voice firmed. "Are you all right?"

Kena could only nod as Hrndl stared.

"Your face is so red, and your breathing is irregular. I think I should call Metchell."

"No!" Kena twitched her head from side to side. "No, I'm fine. Jus—just don't make me laugh again."

Hrndl sat down, her back not touching the chair.

Kena took a few deep breaths. "Thank you for sharing my laughter."

Hrndl's eyelids drooped in a fleeting expression. "It was most enjoyable. So was flying your sim. It was incredibly realistic. Do Humans always put that much detail into sims?"

Kena leaned back and stretched her legs out. "Uh-huh. We hone our reflexes through repeated practice. The more accurate the simulation, the better we perform in reality."

"Was the—double hum—your sub-vocal form of *yes*?"

"Oops. Yes, it was."

"What do you use for *no*?" Hrndl asked, leaning forward.

"Uh-uh."

"Repeat them, please."

"Uh-huh. Uh-uh."

"Interesting," Hrndl murmured. "I thought Human sub-vocalizations where simply hums. But there's a tonal variation, and it sounds like the letter *H* is included. If not for the vowels, they would sound Grfdn."

Ah! She had noticed a similarity. Promising. "You're much quicker than most to pick up the distinction."

"Just as you are able to pronounce our names better than most non-Grfdn. Perhaps it's because these sub-vocalizations come naturally to you." Hrndl was looking at her—really looking—as though experiencing some profound realization in this odd conversation.

"Maybe." Kena tipped her head, unwilling to claim proficiency with their guttural sounds. "It helps if I can remember not to move my lips while pronouncing Grfdn names, but that is a challenge. Then there is the question of vowel placement. I'm sure you know which letter combinations need them, but it's utterly obscure to the rest of us. I've often wished you would place a vowel indicator within your Prednian version of name spellings."

"It doesn't work," Hrndl said. "Our speech organ is so low and different, no other race can approximate our throat vowels. The closest anyone can get is to use their must guttural vowel wherever they require it. Prednians, for instance, need many vowels. They call me Hur-run-dul. But you can manage Hurn-dul, which I prefer. The last thing we want is to add more vowels than necessary."

"I often wonder about Krdn's name. I can say Kru-dun or Kur-dun. Which is closest to correct?"

"He prefers Kur-dun. Most people say Dhgnr wrong. The *h* is a vowel because it's between sharp consonants. If you can't pronounce it as a vowel, replace it with one you can say. Dug-nur is far better than Duh-gun-nur."

Kena experimented with it then asked, "And the other two?"

"Ru-nul and Fru-dun."

Kena repeated them all. "How's my pronunciation?"

"Good enough for us to recognize them."

That bad? "Does it annoy you that I say your name poorly?"

"Not at all. You say it far better than most. Have you practiced it?"

Kena let out a wry laugh. "Beyond doubt! I could never get close to your names without practice."

"I'm not surprised, but what you said a moment ago—about needing practice to hone your reflexes—that is surprising. I thought Humans were born with quick reflexes."

"So it is said. Were you born with coordination skills?"

"No, but we do learn them at a very young age. Even the simplest chores are coordinated."

Kena shrugged. "My sister and I also learned coordination quite young." Hrndl drew her head back, but Kena didn't wait for her remark. "For instance, we knew we could finish the simple chore of making our beds much quicker if we helped one another."

"To a Grfdn, there is a distinct difference between helping and coordinating. You use the words interchangeably. Am I correct in guessing that the Prednian words *help* and *coordinate* translate to the same word in your language?"

"No, but you probably perceive a greater difference between them than we do," Kena said. "I didn't help my sister because I thought her less capable, and she didn't find my help insulting. It's a simple fact that two people can make a bed much faster than one. We coordinated our movements without any communication. In fact, we were usually talking of something quite different. I still use the word *helping* to describe what we did for each other. But, since there is no shame or insult associated with that, the end result is the same."

"What you described sounds like a matter of mutual benefit. I'm not sure why you call it helping."

"Perhaps because Humans perceive the value of help."

Hrndl's nostrils lifted. "It creates dependence. How can that be valuable?"

"Only if it's taken to extremes—or if the person wants to be dependent. We stop helping in that case."

"Helpful races are poor at recognizing dependence."

"A valid observation, but unhelpful races are poor at recognizing when someone could learn to succeed independently if they were given help."

"We do realize that society as a whole benefits from every member's productivity," Hrndl said, shifting to a different position in the chair. "In some types of coordination, the benefits are shared indirectly. It's not as though we would leave an injured person to starve in the street."

"No doubt, but you give an extreme example. When great shame is attached to requesting or receiving help, opportunities will be missed. Somewhere between the two extremes lies the help that can improve society, without causing either shame or dependence."

"Yes," Hrndl said, "but not help. It's called coordinating, and it involves mutual benefit."

Kena chuckled deep in her throat.

Hrndl's brows rose. "Is that a laugh? It sounds different."

"It's for a different type of amusement. Don't you realize what we're doing?"

"Apparently not."

Kena grinned. "We are agreeing."

"Definitely not!"

"Oh, I know," Kena said. "We have such remote viewpoints that it sounds like complete opposition. But, still, I suspect we are much closer to agreement than either of us would have thought possible."

"Then you clearly do not understand coordination."

"Let's see whether I do or don't."

"How?" Hrndl asked, her eyes narrowing.

"Coordinate with me on the development of training simulations."

Hrndl hesitated. "Your techniques do produce certain benefits, but there appear to be offsetting problems."

"Quite so. Those who lack confidence tend to become rather timid after flying Human sims. Grfdn sims, on the other hand, are very good for standard, repeatable procedures, but they don't teach how to react when standard procedures fail. Did you realize the virtual pilot in my sim was programmed to miss at least one target?"

"I wondered why he missed it. A hit shouldn't have been difficult from his position."

"There's no such thing as a perfect navigator. Your skills are top level, but you didn't look very well-prepared when your partner failed only one instruction."

Hrndl angled her head. "I cannot deny that, after virtually knocking him unconscious. But I still don't see how you can train with randomization. It sounds like you want to teach the crew not to use standard procedures. This will cause chaos. No one will know what to expect from anyone else."

"The environment may be random," Kena said, "but repeatable response patterns can be applied to many situations. The challenge is to pick the best response in the instant danger appears. That's where practice comes in. Perhaps this would be clearer if you review how I fly sims."

"Do the rules not state that randomized sim records cannot be made public?"

Kena picked up her computer and entered the authorization as she replied. "Yes. I suspect it was made after a few fiascoes like the one we just saw. You were the only one to display your full information during training, and look what it did to Delf. Just imagine what he'd do if you published it."

"You need not worry about Delf. He'll get over it. The Veet can be quick tempered, but they recover with equal speed."

Kena looked up from her computer, a faint smile lifting her lips. "I have flown with Veet before."

"Then, I suppose you already knew that," Hrndl said. "Since you also know what dissention it can create, why do you give me your records?"

"Giving them to one navigator is hardly the same as making them public," Kena said. "If you do decide to coordinate with me on training—and I hope you will—you'll need to see Human training. If not, I'd still like you to know what to expect from me when we're flying."

"That would be useful information." A distinctive chime sounded on Hrndl's computer. She stood to leave without bothering to look at the message. "I'll review your records as soon as I can."

CHAPTER THIRTEEN

How could she even do that?

Hrndl took a deep breath, ran her gaze around the screens in nav command, and returned to Kena's data. The simulation records had only whetted her appetite. She'd consumed them in a couple days and now delved into Kena's actual flight records. Fascinating! She'd expected good piloting skills— Human reflexes guaranteed that—but the rest? Some of it didn't even seem possible. Beyond doubt, the woman had earned both her rank and reputation.

Hrndl stretched. She shouldn't have needed to stay up late last night, hunched over Kena's records. Krdn could have studied them with her. One thing they had in common was an endless drive to improve their navigation skills. Here was a promising new avenue, but Krdn's contempt for anything Human prevented that. He'd focused on nothing but her.

Not that she objected to that! The corners of her eyes lifted at the memory of the deserted inner-ring hallway he'd found for their evening walk yesterday. It even provided access to an overlooked common room. How pleasant he had made their time together.

Most of it, anyway. She didn't care for the way he'd ignored her when she talked about Kena's skills.

The junior navigator who shared her duty pointed out a distant object, but said, "Risk is negligible."

Hrndl swiveled to the screen he was using and reviewed the playback and current scans. "Good assessment. Carry on."

All those little rocks from that beautiful nebula, harmless— most of them. Yet, they could not be ignored, for even one could prove devastating. Why did they seem to be a warning about Krdn? Intelligent. A highly skilled navigator. Doing well in his career. Taking pains to show his dedication to her needs. All traits desirable in a mate, yet he disregarded her opinion. Was this like a harmless rock—or something significant? Once she chose, she'd spend her life with her mate. Could his disregard grow from an annoyance to an intolerable irritant?

How could she know? Beyond doubt, it was questions like these that had spawned the ancient imperative, "Never should a female rely wholly on her own judgement while her mating drive is in full force." Older females always coordinated with the younger as that first ovum matured and pumped out chaotic, demanding hormones. Perhaps she should have left with the other Grfdn females who were reassigned to another ship. But leave the *Ontrevay*? No, not something she wanted to do. Besides, Krdn had seemed like such an obvious choice for a mate.

Her pulse quickened. She couldn't deny a certain attraction, at least when he wasn't criticizing Kena. If only Krdn would join her now in studying Human techniques. As second navigator, he really ought to know this information. Where was he, anyway? He'd been starting his split shift early in order to be with her. Would he join her in nav command? Did she want him to?

Hrndl compressed her lips. Simultaneous desire and dissatisfaction were maddening. She needed someone to ask. It wasn't right that there were no Grfdn females to support her! She squelched a growl before it became audible. What good of all this silent ranting?

She captured her unproductive thoughts and focused on Kena's records. They provided the perfect distraction, absorbing her so completely that she didn't look up when Krdn entered.

"What's so interesting, Hrndl?" He leaned over her, resting a hand on her shoulder. "Oh, not Kena's records again. You are wasting your time."

Hrndl dipped her shoulder away from his touch, but turned the motion into a reach for her console to acknowledge their change of command. "I am a navigator. So is she. If I must fly with her, I should understand her techniques."

"A futile attempt. She is unreliable. No matter how well you study her past, her future actions remain unpredictable. Besides, she's likely to be assigned to solo flights. That's what she's best suited for."

Hrndl squirmed as the other navigator's mouth slipped open. How could Krdn stand there and disparage a senior navigator right in front of a junior? "You miss a great deal. Frethan sees that her training contains aspects of coordination."

Krdn snorted. "I doubt that! But if so, Frethan understands coordination as poorly as Humans do. Even if she wanted to learn it, she does not have the control to maintain her focus. She swings around to stare when Ghent enters a room. What more proof do you need?"

"She hasn't done so in days."

"Beyond doubt, she is still doing it internally. Such distractibility is a serious flaw."

Kena had paused in the doorway. She let it slide shut and headed to the forward consoles. "It's not nearly as distracting as you think, Krdn," she said. "But sensitivity to emfrel does give me one sweet advantage. I always know when someone enters a room, even if my back is turned."

Krdn's eyes narrowed. They tightened still further as Hrndl

exhaled a mocking snort. He straightened and glared at Kena. "As unpredictable as usual. What are you doing here?"

Hrndl muttered, "Why shouldn't she be here? She's a navigator."

Kena took the console on Hrndl's right. "Alas! The void's as unpredictable as I am." She touched her console to change the room's central screen and waved a hand at it. "Frethan dislikes the latest scans of our drop-out point and has just changed the location. We drop back to four dimensions at 16:24, which is barely ten minutes away." She touched the re-form control as she spoke, and the console changed its couch, control panel, and display to her specifications. She let the fluid motion soothe her—synthetic matter performing a choreographed dance.

"Is he still planning to use the octopuh repair craft?" Krdn asked.

Kena sat down, ignoring his mispronunciation of the English designation. "No doubt."

"The phrase is *beyond doubt*." Krdn growled his words. "If you must mimic Grfdn, at least get it right."

Kena blinked, her hand pausing over the console. "*No doubt* is a common Human expression."

More navigators entered, and Frethan's voice came over the communication system. "Dimensional transition has been rescheduled to 16:24. Krdn has nav command. I have ex op command. Delf is piloting the robotics craft. I'm sending five navigators out with him to get this done as quickly as possible. Krdn, you and Hrndl perform transition with Kena on oversight. The rest of the navigators are on their way to you. I want the most thorough scans that have ever been done, and I want every one of them double-checked. Watch for PitKreelaundun craft and camouflaged devices. And don't let me hear anyone say they don't know we're here."

Krdn twisted around, looking at the last few navigators who hurried into nav command. "Frethan, most of the first shift is here. Who is handling support with you in ex op?"

"Ghent. I've only got one craft out. I'm not pulling anyone off scanning."

Krdn frowned, but he calmly stated names and assignments. The command room grew quiet as the navigators set up and began their tasks.

Krdn strode to the console on Hrndl's left and raised it to standing height. "Hrndl, I request telepathic coordination."

"Granted."

Kena glanced their way only once, to see how they divided the task. Krdn controlled the dimensional drive, while Hrndl piloted.

Kena monitored the *Ontrevay's* artificial dimensional rift, ready to compensate for any problem before it could have devastating effects. The shields were under her control, along with mitigation strategies for dimensional faults. In the realm that most people called reality, the rift was invisible. On her display, it was depicted as tunnels within tunnels, some moving in opposite directions. No worries when they were stable, but that was about to change. She watched the exit form and verified symmetry. The slip detachment from the S_4 and T_2 dimensions had to be perfect, or Hrndl would be in for some wild piloting.

Krdn and Hrndl executed in perfect synchronization, giving Kena nothing to do.

When the *Ontrevay* had returned to normal space/time, Kena said, "Excellent transition!"

"Of course," said Krdn. "It is the product of Grfdn simulations without a single random event." He glanced across several screens then touched a communication control. "Frethan, we are stable, and the area is clear."

Frethan's voice transmitted to both nav command and the repair craft. "We're opening the bay." A minute later, he said, "Delf, you are clear to launch."

Delf said, "On our way."

Krdn closed the channel and said, "Hrndl, monitor the repair area. Kena, review scans for signs of PitKreelaundun craft or tactical manipulations."

Repairs proceeded smoothly, and nav command grew quiet. The main display screen showed Delf's craft and a section of the *Ontrevay's* hull. Robotic arms, operated by four of Delf's crewmembers, attached the newly fabricated sensors.

Most were in place when Netlyn opened a comm channel and announced, "I've found an object on a strike course: 20 centimeters in diameter, high mass, impact in three minutes. Delf, do you have the full scan?"

"Yep."

Kena switched her scan to the object. The rock approached at an oblique angle in relation to the ship.

A few seconds passed in tense silence before Delf said, "Thanks for the notice. I've got plenty of time to net this pebble."

Kena studied it as energy beams extended from the perimeter of Delf's craft and wove a containment field in the rock's path. The danger seemed minimal, but why was a high-mass object mixed in with the other debris heading in their general direction? Stranger yet, its chemical signature was oddly distorted, and the mass reading kept fluctuating. Something must be interfering with the scan.

Kena touched a button on her console. "Delf, I sure would like a look at that thing if you can bring it in for me."

"You'll have it in the hour. Unless, that is, you want it wrapped in some of that fancy Terran gift paper. That will take longer."

Kena grinned. "Hmm. I think I would prefer energy field gift wrap. We'll start a new trend on Earth."

Then, the object hit his containment field, and Kena sucked her breath in. It bounced crazily inside, gaining momentum rather than losing it. It behaved like a tiny craft with damaged controls. The field hadn't been powered to absorb so much energy, and it weakened before Delf could compensate. The object careened through it, plunged toward the array, and nicked a sensor that hadn't yet been fastened down. The long, curved blade spun away from the ship. The rock bounced off the hull shield and continued its aimless journey through space.

Kena's lips pinched as expletives in two languages came over the comm system.

"Shut up, back there," Delf said, his tone unperturbed. "A sensor is loose, Frethan, but there shouldn't be a problem. It's not moving that fast. I'll just run over and fetch it."

"Stay where you are, Delf," Frethan said. "I want that array completed now! I'll take a craft out myself to retrieve the sensor. Krdn, send a navigator down here for support."

"Quon, ex op," Krdn ordered.

Quon sprinted to the exit. His feet pounded down the hall as the door slid shut behind him.

In a couple minutes, Ghent's voice came over the comm channel. "Support has arrived. Frethan, you're clear to launch."

A small craft entered Kena's scans. Frethan's years of experience were obvious. He made it look easy to intercept the sensor, capture it in an energy field, stop its spin, and transfer it to a robotic arm.

As Frethan turned his course back toward the *Ontrevay*, Delf reported his status. "Repairs complete except for that last piece."

"Get back inside, Delf," Frethan said. "I can set this one myself."

The minutes ticked by. Kena heard the external communications but paid little heed. Awareness of critical points was enough. Delf had brought his craft in. Ghent had sent the crew to astro for additional scanning support. Frethan was almost finished. Kena rolled her shoulders, but kept her eyes on her display.

She and Netlyn focused entirely on scanning for near, high-mass objects. No more had appeared. Impossible to relax, though. Explosives encountered near the PitKreelaundun border usually occurred in clusters. Kena stretched her neck from side to side. Only one today, it seemed. Frethan was heading back to the bay, passing between the *Ontrevay* and a large rock on a stable trajectory. She'd already analyzed it and found no risk. Wait —what now?

"Mass variations." Kena said, highlighting the rock on the display. "It's close, but not on strike—"

The rock exploded. Debris hammered Frethan's craft. It slammed sideways against the *Ontrevay's* hull shield with a neck-snapping jerk.

CHAPTER FOURTEEN

Kena gasped. The shock of the explosion was nothing compared to Frethan's silent cry. His emfrel surged into her mind then faded with equal speed. She pursued his failing essence and surrounded the last feeble spark of his life energy.

Ghent's voice demanded Frethan's status. No reply came over the comm system.

Kena tracked Frethan's craft on her display as she steadied herself and extended telepathic energy. She felt him—barely. No thought, no sensation. Nothing beyond existence. His craft spun, sidewinding away from the *Ontrevay*.

"Frethan, report your status," Ghent said again.

The words should be as clear in Frethan's craft as they were in nav command. Kena strained to hear them through his ears. Still nothing.

Ghent kept trying. "Frethan, I'm not receiving your answer. Ensure your comm channel is open."

There. A fragment of the sentence reached Kena through Frethan's awareness. Confusion swirled within him, and she lost the sliver of telepathic contact.

"Kena, what's going on," Hrndl said, her voice hushed.

Ah, Hrndl was aware. Kena's shoulders relaxed a tad. "Get me a remote nav communication beam," she whispered, not wanting even her own voice to interfere while she struggled to sense anything Frethan might hear.

Hrndl's hands flew over her console, while Kena tracked Frethan's craft. Its tumble rate increased, with most nav jets still operational—under no one's control.

Ghent's tone changed with each statement. No longer a rapid demand, it now directed with slow, firm patience. "Frethan, I'm not receiving communication. Shut down all of your navigation jets."

An echo of the words reached Kena through Frethan. Confusion overwhelmed their meaning. And pain. He slipped away from her again.

The craft's spin grew ever more unstable, impossible to catch through robotics. Kena fidgeted in her seat, aware of Hrndl's scrutiny.

"Frethan, shut down all of your nav jets," Ghent said.

Kena detected Ghent's words through Frethan's awareness, along with his hammering pulse. She pushed her own perception of those words through his confusion and spoke telepathically to him. *Frethan, I am Kena. Link with me. Link with me!*

Frethan finally turned his attention to her, puzzled but willing. She embraced him, feather-soft, establishing and sustaining the link with her own energy. She exhaled with a faint whisper. "I have him."

Kena jabbed the configuration controls. Her console re-formed to the specifications of Frethan's craft.

Hrndl's fingers still moved over her console, as confident as her low, calm voice. "The comm beam is ready. I'll coordinate for you. I saw the record from when you did this before."

One less thing to worry about. Kena held her focus against the confusion, pain, nausea, and fear muddling Frethan's mind. She channeled comfort to him. *You will only rest and watch. Nothing else. I will navigate and bring you in.*

Kena's remote controls activated. She urged Frethan to look at his displays so she could confirm her ability to pilot his craft.

His gaze settled first on his hands floating before his chest, the fingers curled and relaxed as though he slept. She sensed his knowledge of paralysis, his belief that it was temporary, and a transient thought about his spinal sheathe—whatever that was.

She needed focus. *Look at the console, Frethan.*

He lifted his eyes, the tiny movement sending pain through Kena's senses. His temples throbbed with his pulse, making her head twitch. At least he knew what she was doing and forced his eyes to follow her suggestion.

She chose an insignificant control and operated it, watching Frethan's view to validate the result. Hrndl's communication beam was spot on.

A smile reached her lips. She whispered, "Control confirmed."

Hrndl opened a comm channel to ex op command. "Frethan is alive. Kena has control of his craft. I am coordinating."

Kena shut down his thrusters and slowed the roll with others. She turned the craft's trajectory back toward the *Ontrevay.*

Hrndl adjusted the communication beam to match. She lost it once, but recovered in seconds.

This was tricky work. All operations must be smooth and balanced so loss of control wouldn't mean disaster. Kena selected a consistent arc for the course. Most would have chosen a straight path, but that would require a course correction, increasing the risk of communication failure.

Kena relaxed despite her intense concentration. She had the course exactly the way she wanted it. Through her link with him, she framed peaceful words. *Not long now. You're almost in.*

His emotion brushed her mind—relief, trust, fondness? Warmth flooded her.

K rdn frowned at his displays, his shoulders tightening. Kena was down to the easy part. Why did she maintain this curve instead of straightening it out? Beyond doubt, she wanted to impress them all with how well she handled complexity.

His fingers extended with his longing for access to Frethan's controls. He dared not interrupt, but—there must be something else he could do. An energy field with a tenuous surface deployed on the outside edge of the curve? The craft would drag and straighten its course. He'd have to hurry with the calculations. That craft was too close for safety with this curved course.

His haste introduced a flaw. The field's surface was too dense, and Frethan's craft didn't drag. It bounced. It struck the edge of the open bay doors, and the weakened hull split.

P eace turned to horror, giving Kena only an instant to grasp that something was terribly wrong. She had no time to respond. A strangled cry escaped her as Frethan's hull crumpled. He would die! Frethan's awareness mirrored hers, and he severed the link to spare her his death throes. But the vacuum was faster than he. She felt the air savagely rip from his lungs as he jerked himself from her mind. Kena went rigid, certain she would never inhale again.

Hrndl swung around to Krdn. "What...have...you...done?"

"You could see how curved her course was. I had to put up a field to straighten it."

Hrndl rose from her seat like a cat stalking prey. "Had to? You had to? I was coordinating. Her course was balanced and stable. Your field threw it off. You killed Frethan!"

Their words intertwined with the shock and grief paralyzing Kena's mind.

Krdn's grating voice ended a tense pause. "How could I kill

someone who was already dead? He never responded to us in any way. Kena's heroics were a showy waste of time."

Hrndl gasped. "Kena felt him alive."

"She couldn't have. Not at that distance."

Hrndl drew back from him as though he carried a contagious disease. "You fool! She was linked with him, and you didn't even know it."

"Impossible. Humans aren't telepathic. Frethan was dead. Get back to your console."

Dead? Krdn's words drove a spike into Kena's anguish. The last moments of Frethan's life remained precious within her. Krdn discarded them. Dishonored them. As though Frethan's life were of no value at all. She ground two words through her constricted throat. "He lived."

"You have no proof," Krdn said.

Heat surged through Kena. She jerked herself up, barely getting her feet beneath her. She braced herself against the couch with a white-knuckled grip and took her first full breath. "He lived!" she shouted.

Ghent burst into nav command with Metchell close behind, just as Krdn demanded, "Prove to us that he lived."

"Silence!" Ghent ordered.

Kena's pulse hammered, drowning out Ghent's voice. She staggered toward Krdn, determined to make him acknowledge Frethan's life. Something was in her way. She sidestepped—struggled to get past. She couldn't see what blocked her. It was lost in the nothingness beyond the shifting tunnel to Krdn. She wouldn't lose sight of him, though. She would make him admit Frethan had lived. Her entire body shuddered.

She tried to shout. "He lived!" It came out strangled. "I was with him. I felt the vacuum—rip the air from his lungs."

H rndl and Metchell strove to support and restrain Kena. She drew loud, rasping breaths. Her knees wobbled, but still she struggled forward.

Hrndl kicked an empty couch around and tried to guide Kena toward it. "Sit down, Kena. Just bend your legs, and we'll get you onto the couch."

"I doubt she can hear you," Metchell said, clutching Kena's arm as she swayed. "She's in sairital shock."

Kena's legs collapsed, and she lurched hard against Hrndl's chest. Hrndl dropped to her knees and prevented Kena from hitting the floor. She grabbed Kena in a bear hug, pinning her arms to her sides. Kena struggled, but Hrndl held fast.

Metchell inserted a drug tube into a mask and placed it over Kena's nose and mouth. She drew another rasping breath then grew still. Her eyes stared blankly. She let out a gentle breath, and her body relaxed in Hrndl's arms. Together, they laid her on the floor. Metchell removed the mask and reached for another instrument.

Hrndl gazed at Kena's inanimate face, only vaguely aware of Metchell's actions. Frethan dead. Kena injured from the link. It was dreadful—unbearable. She narrowed her eyes then flashed them to Krdn's rigid face. In an instant, she was on her feet, advancing on him. "I'll kill you!"

"You will not. You will return to your console and follow Ghent's orders."

Hrndl turned and stared at Dhgnr. When had he come to nav command? He stood beside the directive console, his expression unyielding, a nerve wand in his hand. Her chest tightened. The Grfdn khn actually had to come to nav command—with a weapon —to get the situation under control. She'd been so enmeshed in the drama, she'd lost touch. Had Ghent issued orders? Or spoken to her? Hiding her shame, she pulled her couch around and plopped into it.

How could this have happened? Krdn! She'd wanted him for

her mate. Now he had violated coordination, injured a senior navigator, and killed their chief navigator. Her stomach roiled, forcing bile to the back of her throat. His execution could not happen quickly enough. Oh, in one dreadful second, they'd lost three navigators. The three best. And her mate—she had lost her mate!

Dhgnr growled one word in his own language. Hrndl suppressed a cringe as he took Krdn out. The vacant consoles on either side of her shouted a silent emptiness. Ghent helped to lift Kena and settle her in Metchell's arms—her body so limp. The door slid open, then closed, as Metchell carried Kena out. Hrndl shuddered.

Ghent rested a hand on her shoulder. He leaned over and spoke into her ear. "Your coordination with Kena was admirable. We need you now—even more than she did. Can you continue?"

Hrndl inhaled, straightened her back, and answered with tight control. "Yes."

CHAPTER FIFTEEN

Every muscle in Kena's body shook in violent spasms as her mind plummeted into the past. Searing pain tore through her throat. Air ripped from her lungs as Frethan's life ripped from her mind. Limbo swallowed up place, movement, and air. She couldn't react—only exist in agonized grief.

Distant words intruded, bringing her back into herself. Challenging words. Denying the existence of Frethan's precious life. Rage consumed her. She would make him unsay those vile words!

But she couldn't reach him. They held her from him. Confusion swirled. Why was she on her back? She thrust again. No hands held her. An energy restraint pinned her. Time and location disassociated, then reassembled into now. Her eyes batted open. She wasn't in nav command.

Metchell's voice grounded her. "Kena, you are in medical section. Relax." He touched her arm, and it spasmed. His fingers wrapped her wrist. "I'm inserting an IV. Relax."

Her pulse throbbed, and her breath panted. She fought the restraints. "He will not say Frethan didn't live. His life was precious. I won't let him diminish it. Not even one second. I won't let him!"

Metchell massaged the center of her forehead. "Frethan lived. We valued him greatly. You are in shock. You need to rest."

The drug he'd administered took effect. Her muscles refused the struggle she demanded of them. Metchell's hands moved, touching pressure points at the sides of her head and neck, then down to knead her shoulders. His gaze was fixed on a medical monitor. She didn't care what he saw there. Her condition meant nothing, for Frethan was...was...

"Frethan!" she whispered. Her breathing grew labored; she squeezed her eyes closed. She uttered an anguished cry. Her breath rushed out, but she could not inhale. The anguish ended abruptly, and her rigid body went limp on the couch. Sobs shook her chest.

A soft cloth wiped away her tears. "Look at me, Kena," Metchell said.

She gasped the sobs down and tried to still her trembling chin, as she turned unwilling eyes to his face. Gentle concern creased his brow.

He pressed the cloth to the outside corner of her eye, capturing another tear before it reached her hairline. "I know this is difficult, but don't despair." He firmed his changeable tone. "You will recover." His voice gentled again. "Rest, now."

Hrndl tossed and turned through an endless night then woke exhausted. She dragged herself out of bed, dressed by rote, and ran a brush through her chestnut hair. The mirror, she avoided. Her stomach rumbled. Would she be able to stand the dining hall? All those people asking questions—or avoiding asking questions. Probably not.

Her computer beeped its command signal. She picked it up and read the message. A summons to Ghent's consult room.

Hrndl kept her gaze on the floor as she hurried past crew

members in the hallway. She reached Ghent's door at the same moment as Metchell. His eyelids drooped—a long night for him, too? The door slid open before she could ask about Kena. She entered then halted so quick that Metchell brushed against her back. Krdn!

He sat rigid at one end of Ghent's curved table, his eyes on the granite surface. Ghent watched her from his large chair. To his left, Dhgnr leaned against the wall near Krdn.

Dhgnr held Hrndl's gaze for a moment. Then, his eyes moved to the chair at the far end of the table and back to her face. She suppressed her loathing and took the chair Dhgnr had indicated. At least it was the farthest from Krdn.

Ghent waited until Metchell sat between the two Grfdn before asking, "What is Kena's condition?"

"She experienced a portion of Frethan's death throes," Metchell said. "Fortunately, the link was broken before the instant of his death. She'll recover, but she needs rest. I have her sedated. She'll be awake tomorrow, but I'll be keeping her deeply relaxed. If her recovery proceeds well, she may be able to take light duty by the next day."

Ghent let out a sigh. "That's a relief. What are the chances of a relapse?"

"Always a possibility with this type of injury," Metchell said, turning his head. "It'll take some time to determine just how much of a problem that will be. Often, a point of fixation can trigger re-experience of the trauma. I already know what that point is, so it should be easy to avoid."

"How can you know so soon?" Ghent asked.

"She's had several nightmares. She woke from each with one thing in mind: Krdn challenging the time of Frethan's death. It triggered re-experience every time. I've been able to stop the nightmare recurrence, but..." Metchell turned to Krdn. His tone altered, implacable and harsh. "I do not ever want to hear anyone question whether Frethan was still alive when his craft ruptured."

"How convenient for her," Krdn said.

Hrndl quivered, her fists clenching. How dare he! She tensed to attack, but subsided when Dhgnr pulled his nerve wand from his belt.

With an almost hopeful sneer, he thumbed the release, and the flexible rod extended a half-meter from the grip, humming with its charge—a charged that sensitized nerve endings with every stroke.

Krdn's gaze followed Dhgnr warily. How stiff he sat, his torso well away from the back rest. Ah! Dhgnr had already beaten him. Hrndl gloated. She could wait.

"Respectfully, sir," Krdn said, "I am within my rights. If I am to be charged with the crime of causing Frethan's death, it is necessary to prove he was alive. The only person who claims to have had contact with him cannot be questioned. It can be argued that this particular fixation is assumed. Her distress could simply be an example of the intense emotional responses Humans are known to experience."

Hrndl lunged at Krdn.

Metchell grabbed her shoulders, bracing her a few inches from Krdn.

"Sit down, Hrndl," Ghent ordered. "I sympathize with your fury, but I insist that you control it."

Hrndl's exhalation rumbled as she allowed Metchell to push her back into her chair.

Ghent turned back to Krdn, his voice dangerously quiet. "You mistake, Krdn. No one is charging you with a crime."

Hrndl's quick intake of breath drew Ghent's attention back to her.

"Here, that is." His eyes locked on hers. "When this mission is complete, I will ask your Judgement Council to take custody of him."

"His behavior was inexcusable!" she said. "How can you possibly ignore it?"

"Be...very...certain...that I am not ignoring it." Ghent paused and calmed his harsh cadence. "Consider for a moment. When we reach our destination, we'll be pulling samples from a huge area of debris—all of it in unstable orbit. This will be dangerous, grueling work. It's never acceptable to lose any navigator, but losing the top level is disastrous."

Ghent tightened his lips. "Frethan is gone, and nothing can change that." He drew a deep breath and let it out. "Under normal circumstances, the second navigator would be promoted to chief. I will not do so, of course, since Krdn is implicated in his superior's death."

Ghent's shurgs massaged his knuckles. "That means, one of the senior navigators should be promoted. There are only three of you. I'm sure you realize, that is not enough. Jorlit's and Netlyn's informal command relationship with Frethan is now in limbo. You and Kena are in—I think I will say *sensitive* condition. That leaves Delf. He has excellent piloting skills and leads missions effectively, but I have yet to witness the patience or tact that seems to come later in life for the Veet."

Everything he said was true, and his depth of understanding afforded Hrndl a measure of relief. She inclined her head, for she didn't trust her voice to convey respect.

"While Krdn," Ghent said, "has shown himself undeserving of a leadership position, he is skilled at organizing complex activities. I intend to use him in that role."

Hrndl tried to keep her opinion from her face. She failed, but at least kept her lips sealed.

Ghent turned back to Krdn, and his voice grew harsh. "Understand this. I will be acting as chief navigator, not you. Your authority is limited to crew assignments only. While I doubt your ability to coordinate in a Grfdn manner, you will continue to organize navigational activities as Frethan taught you. I will monitor your work closely. If you interfere with—or even mildly annoy—either Hrndl or Kena, you will be subject to discipline. Make absolutely certain that they come to no harm, whatsoever, from your activities. Is all of this clear?"

"It is clear."

"Do you intend to obey my orders?"

Krdn drew his head back. "Beyond doubt!"

Dhgnr seized Krdn's neck beneath the jaw and forced his head backward at a sharp angle. His muscles jerked. The nerve wand hummed centimeters away. "Beyond doubt? What could ever be beyond doubt with you? Do not dare flaunt your arrogance again. You have disgraced both yourself and Grfdn. I allow you to continue serving only because it is necessary." Dhgnr's voice grated ever lower as he drove the words home. "Whatever discipline you require, in either Ghent's opinion or mine, will be administered by me. It will be long and painful. If you hope to avoid it, you will obey Ghent's orders scrupulously."

Dhgnr paused, staring down at his victim. Krdn's only sound was his constricted breathing.

"Since your powers of self-deception are so astounding," Dhgnr said, "I will be explicit. You will not court Hrndl, nor interfere with anyone who does. You will speak to her only as your duty requires. You will eat only in your quarters. Regarding Kena, you will speak to her, and of her, with full respect. You will never state, nor even vaguely imply, that Frethan was dead before his craft ruptured. If asked, you will state that he was unquestionably alive until that time. Do you submit to my will?"

Krdn rasped out the words, "Yes, Khn Dhgnr."

"I am unconvinced. Your neck muscles still resist my grip."

Hrndl gloated. He was using a surrender grip—so named for good reason.

Krdn closed his eyes and relaxed his neck. Dhgnr's fingers closed cruelly around his throat. The only sign Krdn gave of the pain was a tightening around his eyes. For a full minute, he remained unresisting under the strangling grip. Dhgnr finally released him with a jerk that forced his back against the chair.

Dhgnr swiveled his gaze to meet Hrndl's.

She lowered her head in a tiny nod, answering his unspoken question. It would be enough, for now.

He flicked the control of his nerve wand and clipped it to his belt while addressing Metchell. "I hate to trouble you with the pitiful thing, but that particular hold sometimes prevents speech for several days. Much as I detest the sound of his voice, he must speak in order to perform. Please repair his vocal organ, if the damage is that severe."

Metchell stood, grabbed Krdn's arm, and pulled him to his feet. Krdn stiffened, revealing the pain that spiked through his back. Metchell paused and glanced at Dhgnr.

"I hope your medical ethics don't compel you to treat his back," Dhgnr said in a low purr. "That would make it necessary for me to beat him again."

"I don't have time to bother with his superficial nerves," Metchell said then pushed Krdn toward the door.

When the door closed behind them, Ghent turned to Hrndl, and his voice softened. "I hate putting you in this position, Hrndl. Can you tolerate it?"

"I understand the need," she said. "I will do what is necessary for the benefit of the crew and the mission."

"Your cooperation is appreciated." Ghent stood as he spoke. "Let's get something to eat."

Hrndl also rose and took a firm stance. "There is one other thing I will do."

Ghent turned back to her. "What is that?"

"I will bring the charge against Krdn to the Grfdn Judgment Council. Kena need not provide witness, nor be troubled by him ever again."

Dhgnr sucked a breath in.

Ghent looked between the two Grfdn. When neither spoke, he asked, "Do you need privacy?"

"No," Hrndl said.

Dhgnr looked like he would have said *yes*, but she had no choice.

His low voice hovered at the edge of rumbling. "That decision has additional consequences at this time."

Hrndl kept her back straight. "Regardless, we were coordinating when she was injured and Frethan was killed. I will complete my commitment."

CHAPTER SIXTEEN

Kena approached the open doorway of the common room Netlyn had reserved. Faint blue light spilled into the hallway—the Tenelli color of mourning. She focused on the emfrel. Only Tenelli—just as she'd hoped.

Voices reached her as she neared: Netlyn's soft tones, then Jorlit's, edged with frustration.

"There's just so many questions that can't be answered, so they go `round and—"

"Kena!" Netlyn exclaimed.

Jorlit jumped to his feet and spun to the door. His wide eyes met Kena's as she paused in the doorway, but he couldn't seem to speak. Was that because she hadn't seen him these three days since Frethan's death? Or because of what she overheard?

"My dear," Netlyn said, "why are you up at this hour? I'm sure you should be resting."

She nestled in her husband's arm on the blue sofa facing the door. Inewin swept his free hand inward, their gesture of welcome.

"Do you have any idea," Kena said, "how much I've rested in the last few days? I assure you, I am not one tiny bit tired."

Jorlit came to her as she crossed the room. He put his hands on her shoulders and looked into her eyes, his brow creased. "Are you all right?"

A small sigh escaped her. "Am I happy right at this moment? No. Will I recover? Yes." She swept a glance across all of them. "Everyone has been very kind and concerned about me, and I do appreciate that. But I was hoping, maybe if I was with Tenelli... well, that maybe you'd be more aware of Frethan, and less focused on me."

Jorlit's mouth gaped, then he swallowed. "A–aware? Of Frethan?"

"Doesn't that make sense to you?" Kena asked.

"Uh, I, uh..."

Inewin filled the gap. "Netlyn and I spent the day studying whatever we could find about Human grieving, and I have to—"

"The whole day?" Kena tilted her head, a tease in her voice. "How depressing!"

Inewin let out a startled laugh, quickly suppressed. "Oh, that's right. There was mention of humor intermixed with grieving. And no, not every moment. I meant when we were off duty. But what I was going to say was that—well, frankly, we don't fully understand it. However, there's one thing all the Tenelli have been talking about—wanting to tell you." His brow lifted. "We just haven't been sure about when, or how, or even if we should."

Jorlit found his voice again. "It sounds like maybe now is the right time?"

Kena nodded and waited.

"We want you to know, we're very appreciative and grateful for what you did to save Frethan's life." Jorlit's eyes moved over her face as he spoke in a practiced cadence. "We know you took an incredible risk to even try it. The strain must have been intense. We're amazed that you would do such a thing for someone who isn't even of your own race, and we want you to know we hold you in the highest regard for it."

Tears dampened Kena's eyes.

Jorlit hesitated then took a breath and forged ahead. "Tenelli have a custom when we leave our planet. We take a stone with us, often a gemstone, that came from Tenel. We know Humans have a custom of giving, and we would like to give you the one Frethan carried." He reached into his pocket as he spoke, then took her hand and laid a cool stone in her palm. "It's called a purnel. They're only found on Tenel."

Kena rubbed a fingertip across its polished surface. It was a few centimeters long, the color of jade, swirled through with lighter shades. Its teardrop shape complemented the delicate pattern of swirls. Her throat tightened.

Jorlit waited a moment. "Uh, we weren't at all sure if this would be appropriate, so please don't feel obligated to—"

Kena stopped him with a quick shake of her head. "It's perfect," she whispered. "I treasure it." A tear slipped from the corner of one eye.

"Oh, Kena! I didn't want to bring you more grief."

A wavering smile was the best she could manage. She wiped the tear away. "You haven't. You've brought me joy."

"I have?"

Kena giggled and took his arm, turning him toward the other sofa, which was as blue as the rest of the room. "Yes, you have. Now, let me sit and talk with you. I interrupted you when I came in. What are all these questions that supposedly cannot be answered?"

Jorlit stiffened as he sat next to her, not quite meeting her eyes. "Oh, nothing you need to be concerned about."

"Do you know what happened when I walked into the dining hall earlier today?" Kena asked.

His lips parted, and he stared.

Of course, he hadn't been there. Kena looked to Netlyn and Inewin, raising her brow.

The corners of Netlyn's mouth turned downward. "Every conversation stopped."

"Yes, they did," Kena said. "But sooner or later, I will overhear bits and pieces of whatever is being hidden from me."

"Why assume something is being hidden?" Inewin asked. "Maybe they just didn't want to remind you. We all know it must have been a horrible experience."

"Perhaps." Kena shrugged. "Yet, Jorlit did use the word *questions* a moment ago. Wouldn't it be better if I heard them first among friends?"

They offered no answer beyond uncertain looks.

She turned to Jorlit, shifting sideways and tucking one foot beneath her. "What questions?"

He frowned and laid an arm along the back of the couch, taking a moment to answer. "Oh, they tend to be circular, with a lot of speculation. Things like, how could you have reached so far? Which prompts the question of exactly when and at what distance you established the link." He gestured in a side-to-side hand motion as he stated each new question. "Some assume you must have done it within seconds of when he was hit. But then, why didn't a Tenelli link with him? It should have been easier for us than for any other race. Some have heard that Humans have unusually long range, but no one can find any confirmation of it. In fact, for a race that's very free with information, Humans say precious little about their sairital traits—telepathic or otherwise."

"There's a reason." Kena tilted her head. "Have you heard of the technique of comparing native languages when studying the differences and similarities between cultures?"

"Sure."

"We have no word that translates to sairit," Kena said, "so how can we document our sairital traits? Some of these questions don't apply, because they're based on assumptions that are true for you, but not for Humans."

"I know Humans aren't natural telepaths," Jorlit said, "so there are bound to be some challenges in discussing telepathy, but..." He faltered as she closed her eyes and shook her head. "What?"

"You completely missed the point." She took a breath and slowed her words. "I didn't say we don't have a native word for telepathy. We do. It's *sairit* that cannot be translated."

Jorlit's eyes widened. Was he even breathing? He swallowed. "You're telling me, a non-telepathic race has a native word for telepathy?"

Kena quirked a half-smile at him. "Yeah, that one is a little hard to explain. Remember, we're talking about sairit. A *sairit* is the thing we don't have."

"But...but...telepathy is a sairital function."

"It is for you." Kena raised an eyebrow. "Does that mean it is for me?"

"What else could it be?"

"Two English words: *mind* and *spirit*." She paused to emphasize them. "In the early attempts to translate our languages, the Tenelli assumed the words were synonymous and translated to your word for sairit. But that isn't so." Kena glanced at Netlyn and Inewin. "By the way, that's probably why you don't understand the Human information about grieving. The most significant aspects can't even be addressed." She turned back to Jorlit. "No wonder you looked at me like I was out of my mind when I said, 'aware of Frethan.'"

Jorlit's hand moved forward and back in his gesture for retraction. "For an instant—it seemed as though you thought he still existed. I realized at once I'd misunderstood."

Kena's lips tightened despite her effort to keep a neutral expression. She didn't dare answer, for her voice would surely break. So strange that a concept dear to her meant nothing at all to a Tenelli.

Jorlit's brow creased again, and he took her hands in his. "This must be hard for you—with no Humans here."

She shook her head. "Jorlit, you look so tired."

"I am." He let out a long sigh. "And still as puzzled as when I walked in here. Can you at least tell me when you linked with Frethan?"

"Do you mean when did Frethan link with me?"

"Oh, Kena!" Jorlit closed his eyes. "It's the same question."

"Fine." She shrugged. "I don't know the exact time, but I'm

sure I said it right afterwards. Hrndl heard me and said she'd coordinate. Isn't that in the record?"

"That part is but..." He ducked his head. "Well, everyone thinks it must have been earlier and it just took you a while to say so. After all, it was only a whisper. No one heard you except Hrndl. How could you possibly have reached him so far out? And why wait so long if you were going to do it at all?"

"I didn't wait that long," Kena said, shaking her head. "I tried from the very beginning. I used Ghent's voice for a cue, because we could both hear it. But Frethan was unconscious at first, and then he was so confused, he couldn't even tell I was there."

Jorlit stared, his brow contracting. "There? What does that mean?"

"Um—he couldn't sense me. Does that work for you?"

Jorlit closed his eyes for a moment. "Sorry. I thought you meant *there*—as though you were present." His hand slid forward and back again while he spoke.

Kena stared into his troubled eyes. Yes, *present* would be a good interpretation, but not one he was capable of comprehending. It would only confuse him further.

He took another breath. "All right. So you tried to link earlier, but couldn't. In spite of his increasing speed, you kept trying. I can't imagine why, but you did. When you finally succeeded— Kena, do you realize how far away he was by then?"

She gave him a long, solemn look before answering. "What does distance have to do with it? I knew exactly where he was."

Jorlit made a couple unsuccessful attempts to speak.

Inewin leaned forward. "The foundation is missing, Kena." He waited for her to meet his gaze. "I'm old enough to remember that Humans published an explanation of mind and spirit, then later withdrew it because of misunderstandings. Everything from 'Humans think they're better than us because they have a spirit,' to 'Humans have pathetically weak minds, but we can fix them.' I do understand why your race pulled the explanation, but it leaves a void."

Could she succeed where others had failed? The last thing she wanted was to stir up another vortex of misunderstanding. On the other hand, she would never get a better opportunity. "Let me try it this way. You have everything you need in one package, called a sairit. We have everything we need in two, tightly-integrated packages, called mind and spirit. Neither arrangement is better nor worse, but they are different."

She turned back to Jorlit. "Distance is not relevant to my spirit, but my mind is limited in that regard, much like your sairit. So, my spirit did the searching, but my mind managed the telepathic contact. If a Tenelli could have reached him, they could have initiated contact even while he was unconscious, but my mind cannot do that. My telepathic voice is so much softer than yours that I—well, I almost have to wait to be noticed."

His frown lessened. "At least that puts it in a reasonable context. I'm not going to pretend any understanding of how I could function with my sairit split into two parts."

She shrugged. "We rarely think of them as separate, but it becomes quite necessary when we use telepathy."

"Ah." Inewin narrowed his eyes. "That incompatibility issue. We try to think of our sairit as only partially compatible with a Human sairit, but that is counter-intuitive. It makes more sense to think of a sairit as compatible with a mind, but not with a spirit."

"It still seems strange, though," Jorlit said. "Human is the only race with a two-part sairit."

He still couldn't stop using the word sairit. Oh, well. Maybe she'd made some progress. "The only race we've discovered, anyway," Kena said. "There's parallels in anatomy. It seems every race has something totally unique." She flexed fingers and wrist as she spoke. "Hands, for instance. They're a little different in every race, but the digits are always on the hand. Except for Plynteth, who have a digit extending from the wrist." She studied her own motions. "It seems terribly awkward to me, but when I watch the way Ghent moves, I see a distinctive grace that is really quite beautiful."

Netlyn grinned. "I'm sure any Plynteth would think theirs is the best hand configuration, but no one else would. The concept of *better-than* has little meaning physically. I suppose the same holds true for your unique sairital configuration."

"You're all unique, too," Kena said. "Otherwise, none of us would need emfrel acclimation. I often wonder how sairital differences fit with the unique capabilities of races."

Netlyn's brow lifted. "What do you mean, my dear?"

"Oh, for example, the Prednians and Tenelli are fabulous at bringing other races into community. The Interstellar Collaborative wouldn't exist without you. Can you imagine the Grfdn and Plynteth creating such an organization?"

That drew chuckles from all three of them.

"But for any complex and technical endeavor," she said, "no one could manage it better than a Grfdn."

Inewin cocked an eyebrow. "I sometimes wonder if they could build an entire planet from scratch."

Kena huffed a laugh. "And you're only half kidding."

He acknowledged with a grin.

She tilted her head and drew a deep breath. "Speaking of Grfdn, there is something I've been wondering about. I'm hoping you could shed a little light on it."

"What, my dear?" Netlyn asked.

"Hrndl! Don't get me wrong"—Kena spread her hands as her voice rose—"I would never expect her to be happy with Krdn after what he did. But the things she says! Not least of which is her longing for his execution. Is this normal Grfdn behavior, or something to do with her mating instincts, or what?"

Netlyn's hands arched in a spontaneous gesture Kena had never seen.

Inewin laughed and said, "Hrndl is tense, is she?"

Netlyn's speech quickened. "Venom is hidden under her tongue!"

"Not hidden very well," Kena said.

Netlyn huffed. "Oh, I'm sure she gets plenty of poisonous stabs in that we don't realize."

"No doubt, but—execution?" Kena tilted her head again. "Is that really what Grfdn do to someone who makes an error of judgment?"

"I think it depends on the circumstances," Inewin said. "I'm sure they consider him guilty of multiple crimes."

"Multiple?"

Inewin directed an odd look at Kena, raising his brows and tilting his head. "Well, there are the two obvious ones: killing Frethan and injuring you." He paused, but continued when she said nothing. "Then, there's the matter of interfering with coordination. That might seem like an irritant to you, but it's a very serious matter to a Grfdn. And last, there are strict rules on what a male can and cannot do with a female when she's ready to mate. The subject is not discussed, so I'm not sure what all those rules are. But interfering when a mating female is coordinating— well, I saw it happen once. Let's just say it's unpardonable."

"When was this?" Jorlit asked.

"Oh, decades ago. It was before I knew Netlyn." He smoothed a hand over her hair. "There were quite a few Grfdn on that ship, and three of them worked in communications with me. One of them was too young to even be a suitor. The female was mentoring him, and this particular day she linked with him while they calibrated some new interchange relays. An older male walked in halfway through it. He broke their link and shoved her apprentice on the floor."

Inewin shook his head. "Everything happened really fast after that. She went for him in an instant, but he controlled her easily. He didn't let her go until three older females showed up." He squirmed at the memory. "They slammed him down on a table so hard, the legs went flying out from under it. Then all four of them started beating him. Punching, kicking, thrashing him with broken table legs. I thought they were going to kill him. The khn showed up, linked with the apprentice for a moment, and then just watched."

Inewin uttered a mirthless laugh. "Somebody asked if he wasn't going to stop them. All he said was,"—he mimicked a Grfdn rumble—"'They are not finished yet.'" He shook his head again, as though he still couldn't quite believe it. "The khn didn't interfere until the guy spewed vomit and blood all over the floor. In the end, the older ones had to drag the mating female from the room. And that was no easy task, even for the three of them."

"You've never even told me about this," Netlyn said.

"No, I never talk about it," Inewin said. "For one thing, the khn asked us not to. For another, it makes the Grfdn seem like crazed animals, and you know that's not true. They're normally rational and extremely dependable. It would be unfair to emphasize something that occurs only once in their lifetime." He shook his head. "Besides, when I remember how easily that suitor overpowered a single female, I think it is quite reasonable that a group of them would be allowed to gang up on him. Otherwise, I don't suppose the women would ever get to choose their own mates."

Inewin rested his elbows on his knees and looked straight across at Kena. "We don't know each other very well yet, Kena, so I need to make sure you understand. I only told you this because of what you just asked, and because of what Hrndl is going through. This story is not to be repeated."

"It will not be heard from my lips. I have a couple questions though, if you don't mind my asking."

His brows rose, but he leaned back and asked, "What are they?"

"Her apprentice," Kena said, "did they continue that relationship?"

"Yes, they did. Some non-Grfdn suggested getting him a different mentor until after she'd mated. Neither of them would consider it."

"And the other women that came to help her—"

"No, Kena," Inewin said. "Came to support her. Make sure you say that correctly."

"My mistake. Did they provide her...oh, any ongoing support?"

Inewin gazed at nothing for a few seconds. "There were always a couple women with her when she was off duty. Toward the end, her suitors would sometimes come to the communication section. Within minutes, a supporting female would arrive."

"Were they just there to make sure she wasn't physically attacked," Kena asked, "or was there more to it?"

Inewin's eyes narrowed. "I'm pretty sure there was more to it, but I can't tell you what. Their conversation was in Grfdn. The crew didn't emphasize speaking a common language as we do on the *Ontrevay*." He paused. "Anything else?"

Kena shrugged. "I'm still unsure why Hrndl is so determined Krdn be executed, but I probably won't ever understand that. I just hope it doesn't get her into trouble with the other Grfdn or with Ghent."

Inewin laughed. "Don't worry about the Grfdn. They're in complete agreement with her."

Netlyn's lips twitched. "I don't think you need to be concerned about Ghent either. He understands racial viewpoints better than most. Besides, he has never been completely satisfied with Krdn. He was furious with him after your first time in nav command." She rose as she spoke. "You may not be tired, Kena, but I am. Come walk with me. Our quarters aren't so far apart."

CHAPTER SEVENTEEN

Kena frowned at the nebula sector in the 3-D display as she overlaid various scans on the visible light image. "I just don't see it." She stood and stretched her back.

Netlyn swept the wispy hair from her creased brow and rotated the image. "No, neither do I." She pulled up some older data and reran the time-lapse.

The astro section hummed with conversations. As many scientists gathered there as navigators. Not to mention crew members who were simply taking a break. After all, the room had the best view in the ship.

Piert, the Veet chief scientist, hovered nearby, while Kena and Netlyn searched for the source of a mysterious spectral signature that had made a fleeting appearance. He broke off his conversation with Ghent to exclaim, "That's a relief!"

Kena glanced in the direction he pointed—the portion of the display showing their course and current location.

A few others murmured agreement, and one of the Prednian scientists said, "This calls for a celebration."

Delf grinned in his lopsided way. "Opyera is already planning a gala."

"What is this great event," Kena asked, "which causes such relief and celebration?"

"We just passed the farthest edge of the PitKreelaundun border," Ghent said. "Didn't you know?"

She glanced at the 3-D display then back at Ghent. "The void looks pretty much the same on both sides of the border."

Those nearby laughed. Kena raised an eyebrow and watched them with a half-smile.

Piert cocked his head. "Uh-oh, I don't think she was joking that time."

Netlyn looked stricken. "Was it impolite of us to laugh?"

"Netlyn!" Kena exclaimed. "When have you ever known me to object to laughter?"

"Oh, Kena, how like you," Netlyn said, wrapping her in an impulsive Tenelli hug. "Admit it, now. You know exactly where we are."

"True. It's just that their border is so—boring! You'd think they could at least put up a clever sign or something."

"A sign?" Netlyn stretched the word out, her pitch rising to a squeak.

Kena's grin deepened with the joy of leading Netlyn on. "Yeah. Something like..." She assumed a cheerful, plastic tone. "Thank you for visiting the PitKreelaundun void. Please come again soon."

Netlyn's mouth hung open. Across the room, Hrndl pressed a hand to her mouth but failed to suppress her gargling laugh.

When Ghent stopped laughing, Piert said to him, "I can't even imagine what she's talking about. How was that funny?"

Ghent shook his head. "You know how hard it is to explain a joke across cultures. This one has the incongruity of mixing Human hospitality with the ludicrous idea of borders in space."

"I see," Piert said, but he watched Kena. "She's got her mischievous look again. We'll never find the source that way."

Kena gave him a sympathetic smile. "What do you think, Netlyn? Is it even possible to get more data for him?"

Netlyn shook her head. "Pretty hard to get improved scans when we're moving away, Piert."

He sighed. "All right. On the list for the journey back, then."

"Will do." Netlyn tapped reference points on her console to record his request.

Piert's gaze lingered on Kena. She tilted her head and waited.

He took a deep breath. "Kena, I've been wondering about something for the past week."

A week? The time since Frethan's death. Everyone still tiptoed around that subject. The entire event, in fact. She wished they wouldn't. Life went on. She hadn't had a nightmare in—was it three or four days?

"Then, I think you should ask." Kena said.

"That small rock—the one that got through Delf's containment field. You wanted it brought in." Piert frowned. "What did you suspect?"

She shrugged. "That was one strange little object. Not that we had much time to look at it, but it's the sort of thing I'd expect your team to want."

"Agreed, but...it must have been a PitKreelaundun device."

Her eyebrows twitched together. "I know it changed course and headed for the *Ontrevay*, much like their devices do. But it was this big." She held up her hands as though grasping an invisible soccer ball. "What could they possibly hide in such a little package that would matter to a shielded vessel?"

Kena sensed Grfdn emfrel near the door, and she turned to see who entered. Rnl. She disliked him more every day. "Apparently, he thinks she can't find the dining hall," Kena said under her breath.

Rnl made his way to Hrndl, who looked toward Kena. Predictable. For the past week, she had done exactly that every time either Rnl or Frdn approached her.

"And earlier every day," Ghent said. "Hrndl and Kena, join me for a moment before your meal." He led them aside.

Rnl followed until Ghent's cold stare drove him back.

"A question first," Ghent said once they'd entered a private room. "Have either of you had any difficulties at all from Krdn?"

Hrndl ground the words out. "Not since that first day."

Kena crimped her lips, remembering Hrndl's reaction when Krdn tried to assign them to separate shifts.

Ghent looked to Kena.

"No problems," she said. "Since he's with third shift, we don't see him more than an hour a day. For which, I thank you."

Ghent nodded. "It's time we get enough senior navigators—formally, that is. I'm considering promoting Jorlit and Netlyn, so this is your chance to tell me any concerns or comments. Hrndl?"

"I concur. To a certain degree, they've been in that role for a while. Jorlit already leads second shift, and Netlyn directs the teams on scanning duty. Transition will be smooth."

"Kena?" Ghent asked.

She shifted a bit. "I've known them all of three weeks. You and Hrndl have so much more experience with them."

"I still want your opinion."

"I've seen Jorlit's skills in simulation," Kena said. "They're excellent. Netlyn's not quite as impressive as a pilot, but she can tease more information out of a scan than anyone—and faster. She's also good at teaching that skill. I've seen them both lead successfully in low-stress situations, but I haven't observed them in high-stress. There's no one else I'd prefer."

Ghent ended the discussion with his quick nod. "Thank you. You're dismissed."

As they walked away together, Kena murmured, "I don't know anyone who can get through a conversation faster."

"No one could doubt he is Plynteth." Hrndl looked around the astro section. Rnl was gone. She let out a sigh, and her shoulders relaxed.

In the hallway, Hrndl darted a look to meet Kena's sideways glance. "Uh, I hope you don't mind joining me, even though it's hard to converse during meals now. I do appreciate your company."

"Then you are welcome to it. I often wonder if there is something I should know—something that I dare not ask."

"If you don't dare ask," Hrndl said, "then you must already know."

Hmm. How much could be said without violating taboo? "I gather that you will choose a mate soon, but that's not what I meant. At times, it seems as though—additional knowledge would enable me to be more useful."

Their footsteps echoed unnaturally loud in the silence. Hrndl finally ended it. "Your presence alone is useful. It would be unreasonable to expect you to provide the full role of a Grfdn female. Dhgnr is aware and provides what is critical."

Kena mulled over her answer. It should have relieved her. Dhgnr was khn, after all, so maybe that made sense. Why then did she feel the answer skipped over a gaping pit?

Ghent made his way through the crowded common rooms, which had been joined for the gala. Not relaxing entertainment for a Plynteth, but he had learned how useful these events were. They showed him the state of morale and improved it at the same time. Even the timing was opportune, for Gordahl had inquired about Kena in his last message.

Ghent reached Kena's side as the Grfdn percussion music started. Her chest still heaved from her last dance with Delf, and her eyes sparkled greener than usual. Strange that expending energy seemed to invigorate rather than deplete her.

Kena greeted him with her welcoming smile.

"I'm beginning to wonder if you know the dances of every race," Ghent said.

"I'm working on it. Jorlit taught me the Tenelli kyinatti tonight."

"So I saw. Much slower than the jig you just danced."

"True, but charmingly graceful." She shifted her torso in one of the kyinatti's side-to-side rolls. The full skirt of her dress swayed. A traditional garment, apparently. Dark emerald with a smooth sheen. It left her arms and legs bare, although it hung below her knees—at least when she wasn't twirling. Gems hung from her earlobes and around her neck, and her hair swept back from her face in intricate twists. Unique styles were common at a gala— what surprised him was her figure. The garment's neckline cascaded down in loose folds, but somehow the fabric clung to the curves of her torso, revealing her shape more than usual. He'd been a little worried that he might need to deal with a cultural incident, but Kena seemed oblivious to shocked stares that darted away.

Kena's gaze strayed to the dance floor where Hrndl stepped through a complex pattern with Dhgnr.

"Are you going to learn a Grfdn dance, too?" Ghent asked.

"Not just yet." She studied their movement. "They seem to anticipate the tempo changes, but I have no idea how. Then, there are all those right-angled turns. Perfectly choreographed, but the form is a mystery to me."

"It's a shame there's no Human to dance with you to your own music, Kena. I suspect Quon's version of the waltz would not be seen on Earth."

Kena smiled. "He didn't do so bad for a first try."

Generous, perhaps. "Did you choose the Human music for the gala?"

"Yes. Opyera asked me to."

"Amazingly diverse," Ghent said, "but I didn't hear any vocal music."

"No."

Her reply didn't surprise him, except in its brevity. He'd overheard Kena decline a request to sing. Since Humans were the only race that could produce music from within their bodies, novelty placed it in high demand. It was said to be very beautiful. But she hadn't even included vocal recordings.

"Don't you miss it?" Ghent asked.

Kena shook her head. "I often play it in my quarters."

"Why not here?"

"The words are all in my own language."

The spark had left her eyes. She wasn't telling him something. "Our directive to speak a common language is not that rigid. Could we enjoy musical voice without understanding the words?"

"You could," Kena said, "but I assure you, Prednians will want translation. The words are nuanced poetry. They may sound literal, but often contain quite different meanings. Delivery style modifies them even more. Translations can be nothing short of appalling."

"I've watched you with Prednians. It never seems that their— shall we call it *curiosity*—disturbs you."

"I don't usually let it. Even though it can get overwhelming, their interest in others is truly welcoming and inclusive." Her brow lifted. "On the other hand, I've had them translate one of my songs, so I do know what I'm talking about. When will I get to hear Plynteth music?"

That subject change was abrupt—at least for Kena. Just how appalling had that translation been? Enough for her to formally claim cultural interference? Hard to envision her going that far. But apparently, he'd asked too much, so he followed her lead. "I told Opyera to play it near the end, and only a few pieces. Plynteth music is not widely appreciated."

"There won't be any Plynteth to dance with you either," she said.

"We are one of the few races who don't dance."

Kena tilted her head. "Still, no one to enjoy your music with you."

Ghent sensed an unspoken question. "True, but I plan to soon add a Plynteth astro biologist to the crew."

Kena raised her arched brows. "Someone specific, I gather?"

"My wife. She will bring our son, as well." There was her sudden blink. He'd thought that would surprise.

"Ah! I didn't realize. Has he been too young to leave Plynteth?"

"Yes." Ghent smiled at her understanding. "Is there any race you have not studied?"

"No known race," she said, "but I am sure there's a great deal I do not know."

"Does it seem strange to you that we keep our children on Plynteth throughout childhood?"

"Not in the least. The only reason my parents returned to Earth was so their children would be raised there." She tilted her head, the corners of her eyes narrowing. "You see? Even Humans and Plynteth have similarities."

He chuckled and turned to Remlishos, his chief engineering officer and second in command.

Remlishos greeted Kena with his formal Meklehon bow, which she returned before moving away. "May I have a moment to link with you, sir?"

Ghent's need for Remlishos had increased in the wake of Frethan's death. Their telepathic links to exchange information had become so commonplace, they no longer even needed the audible cue they had used in the past. Ghent engaged the link and absorbed the offered knowledge.

CHAPTER EIGHTEEN

Unnatural silence echoed in the crowded astro section. A disquiet so intense, it even permeated the emfrel.

Kena stared at the display, as did every scientist and most of the navigators from all three shifts. Shared eagerness pulled them in to see the first short-range scans of the SMG76428 system—to know what it really looked like now that they were out of dimensional slip and close enough for detail.

Kena leaned close to Hrndl and murmured, "Could have done without this."

Hrndl responded with a silent nod.

Netlyn compiled numerous scans into live-action composites, rich with symbolized detail far beyond what the unaided eye could detect. Brilliant, as usual. Pity that the contents were pure chaos.

The two planets had fragmented into much smaller pieces than expected. Kena wouldn't have cared so much if the debris had followed predictable paths. By now, it should be scattered enough for reasonably safe maneuvering, even at high speeds. Instead, fragments of all shapes and sizes jostled one another within the 3-D display. Speeds and direction appeared completely random.

She glanced around to gauge other reactions. Scientists glanced uneasily from the display to the navigators' somber faces.

"This can't possibly be correct," an astro physicist said. "How can the debris be traveling in so many different directions? It's even heading inward and counter-orbit."

"Subsequent collisions, maybe," Jorlit said.

"But the debris would have radiated outward from the original explosions. Collisions should have been rare—not nearly enough to produce a maelstrom like this."

"No, I wouldn't think so," Jorlit said, "but something is causing it. The data is accurate, whether we understand it or not."

Betnorel, a Prednian scientist, spoke up. "The speeds are a significant anomaly, too. Netlyn, are you using standard coloration for velocity indicators?"

"Yes, of course."

Kena offered her a sympathetic smile. As if Netlyn didn't have enough to deal with, now she had to put up with insulting questions.

Piert moved close to Delf. "What do you think of the scanning results?" he asked in an undertone. "Are they being correctly interpreted?"

Kena could only hope his words hadn't reached Netlyn's ears.

Delf didn't keep his voice down. "Netlyn is overseeing the scanning. You can balance your life on the accuracy. Believe me, when she sees velocity variations this extreme, she's checking both the data and the interpretation."

Netlyn turned her head toward Delf and mouthed the words *Thank you.*

He answered her with only his lopsided grin.

Piert raised his voice. "Science team."

The murmured arguments around the room came to an abrupt halt.

He strolled among them, pivoting to address everyone. "We came here to solve a mystery. Now, a bigger mystery than we expected. We have two choices. We can deny that what we're looking at is reality. Comfortable, perhaps." He flicked his hands outward. "But we'll learn nothing. Or we can acknowledge the facts and get to work on solving the riddle. Anyone who wants to stay ignorant is dismissed. Those willing to work on a solution—we'll convene in the science section." He turned on his heel and left.

Once the door slid shut behind the last of the scientists, Ghent addressed the navigators. "I'm sure you all realize our earlier projections are useless. We must find a method to predict trajectories. Start searching for patterns. Krdn and Netlyn, join me. Let's find a meaningful way to divide this mess up for study."

Hours later, they were still at it. A subtle change enveloped the navigators. Perhaps it was the snug nav suits they had all donned that morning—ready for immediate external missions. Or perhaps the result of switching from simulation to reality. Discussions broke out from time to time, all seasoned with the understanding that lives would soon hang in the balance. Kena absorbed them in silence, intent on the scenario she studied.

Hrndl put a hand on her shoulder. "Second meal has already begun."

"I need to finish this," Kena said, glancing up at Hrndl in her beige nav suit. It emphasized her straight, slender figure.

"All of this debris will still be here after meal. You need to eat, though I admit, not as much as I do. Please join me."

Kena stood and arched her back.

Hrndl's gaze moved down Kena's charcoal gray nav suit, much the same as Hrndl's, but designed for Human curves. Her eyes lingered on the belt, which hid the waistband and made the suit look like a single garment from neck to ankles. "I'm not used to seeing you without a tunic."

"I know," Kena said, side-stepping away from her console. "Thank you for not looking shocked."

"No chance of that." Hrndl turned for the door. "I've seen your face when people stare and then look at anything but you. Besides, I already made that mistake the first day we ate together."

Kena hoped everyone in the astro section was listening. "I'd like to find all references to the Human female figure in all the interracial training material and delete them."

"Something must be said about a difference that obvious. What would you replace them with?"

"Don't touch the front of a woman's chest. Period. Nothing more. Making a big deal about not looking is ridiculous! Who goes around avoiding looking at Ghent's hands? People notice the difference, then it's ordinary."

A couple Prednians stared with their customary arrested expression, their rounded eyes almost perfect circles. Her exact words would be repeated all over the ship in a matter of hours.

K ena checked the Grfdn table as soon as they entered the dining hall. The expressions on Rnl's and Frdn's faces changed from disconsolate to eager, much like actors in a farce. Dhgnr sat with his back to the door.

Kena helped herself at the buffet. Hrndl stayed with her even though an array of dishes awaited her on the Grfdn table. Typical. At least Rnl had learned manners a few days ago, when he'd tried taking Hrndl's arm to draw her away from Kena. Hrndl's Grfdn reply drove him backward a full meter. Kena tried to ignore all such interactions, but they grew tiresome.

The seating arrangement was also repeated from the last few days. Dhgnr sat in the center on one side, causing Hrndl and Kena to separate at the table. Hrndl had objected to this at first, but Dhgnr seemed to have a purpose, so Kena complied. Besides, it placed her as far from Rnl as possible. A definite advantage.

Kena had assumed Dhgnr wanted better opportunity to talk
with Hrndl, but he rarely said a word to her. Instead, he conversed
with Kena—while watching the other two men. As always, he had
a topic ready the instant she took her seat.

"You were assigned to the *Baktel*, were you not?" he asked,
passing a water flask to her.

"Yes. Why do you ask?" Kena filled her glass. At least this table
held Human-style drinkware rather than Prednian. The Grfdn still
wouldn't use their native drinking pouches. Talk about stubborn!

"A friend of mine was recently on the *Baktel*," Dhgnr said.
"Nlnr. Did you meet him?"

"Ah, yes," Kena said, cutting her food into tiny pieces. "A
dimensional physicist. He disembarked when I arrived, but I met
him at the space station. We had a rather interesting
conversation."

"About what?"

"The nature of T1 and T2 dimensional linkage," Kena said,
"and a couple of theories for why it disengages at the boundaries of
a dimensional rift."

"Ah!"

Kena tilted her head. "Your friend is really quite brilliant."

Dhgnr turned to her, a smile lifting the skin beside his eyes.
Unusual. "Has he made progress on that particular riddle?" he
asked before taking a bite of reconstituted meat.

"I'm not sure. He described two theories." Kena altered her
voice to a more precise speech pattern. "One of them accounts
well for the observed effects. But, to his apparent chagrin, it does
not answer the question of why—at least, not to his satisfaction.
The other predicts certain effects that are impossible to measure.
Very frustrating, I'm sure, but he seems to like the theory's elegant
explanation of causation."

Dhgnr uttered a soft laugh. "How well you capture Nlnr's style.
Which theory do you favor?"

That worked rather well. She resumed her normal voice.
"The first. I must admit, my practical mind had a hard time

following the second." She slipped a morsel of bread between her lips.

"I think I'm relieved I did not have to take part in this conversation."

She looked sideways at him. "It was actually quite intriguing. Only a little of his discourse was too obscure to follow."

"You seem pleased with Nlnr," Dhgnr said.

She raised an eyebrow. "Why not? As a Human would say, he was good company." A memory warmed her. "He even accessed a language translator when he was about to leave, and parted from me with the English phrase *Good day*."

Dhgnr stared at her. Not in the sneering or cold way of the other Grfdn men. His eyes widened, and his dark hairline pulled back. Intrigued, if her interracial sources were correct.

The expression lasted only a second, for he swung around to interrupt some remark from Rnl. A moment later, he returned his attention to her. "Please forgive me for the interruption and for speaking Grfdn to them."

"I don't mind," Kena said. "By the way, I am curious about something. There were two Grfdn khn on the *Baktel*. Nlnr, who was part of the science staff, and another one named Drnld, who also disembarked. I understand that Drnld had no duties pertaining to the ship or the mission. Yet, there were only eight Grfdn. Even after they left, people speculated over why they needed the extra khn."

Dhgnr laughed in his throat. "Nlnr's rank is high, so it wasn't necessary. His first act before any journey from Grfdn is to select another khn to accompany him and delegate all of his duties."

Kena chuckled. "Did I not say that he was brilliant?"

In that instant, Hrndl snapped back at a remark from Frdn.

"Unfortunate that I could not follow his example on this trip," Dhgnr murmured, clasping his tongs around the last morsel on his plate.

Kena looked at Frdn and Rnl, then back to the glass she held. She dipped her voice an octave. "Most unfortunate!"

Dhgnr's tongs paused in mid-air, and he stared at her again. Something different in this expression. She hoped for a hint of his thoughts, but he looked away and slipped the food between his lips. Ugh! What was going on?

For once, Dhgnr didn't try to occupy her. Rnl's voice caught her attention as he expounded the advantages of a career in resource management.

Kena's brows lowered as she listened to his persuasions. She kept her voice down but made no secret of how appalled she felt. "Dhgnr, is Hrndl required to change her career if her mate insists on it?"

"No," he said.

"Why do they both keep talking about it?"

It took him a moment to answer. "Navigation may be an admirable career among Humans, but Grfdn typically view it as dangerous. Suitors tend to be over-protective, hence their suggestions." He took a quick breath. "A question occurred to me after we discussed cultures yesterday. How many languages can you speak?"

Well! He certainly didn't want her involved in courtship. She felt like rolling out one of those Grfdn growls, but made herself answer. "Three Human and five non-Human."

His hairline pulled back again as he focused on her. "You're a navigator and have not been in space many years. How do you come by so much cultural knowledge?"

"Humans pursue dual studies in their career training. My secondary was cultural studies. Also, my parents pursued their careers in space before I was born. My father—"

Kena's breath caught as Rnl included a mispronunciation of *Human* with some words of his own language.

Dhgnr once again darted a glare at the two Grfdn men and snarled a reprimand.

Frdn lowered his head, but Rnl said, "Hrndl, you deserve better company than a Human. If you want a female companion, choose from a race able to contribute something of value.

Kena clamped her lips. From a Grfdn viewpoint, no insult could be worse. He'd called her—indeed, all of her kind—worthless leeches.

"Idiot!" Hrndl sneered. "Human's produce the finest navigators, and Kena is a prime example."

"Our best robotics," Dhgnr said, "are designed by Humans." Frdn's gaze steadied on Hrndl. "In communication, we use Human encryption algorithms exclusively, and their translation technology is also impressive."

His words were so blatantly intended to please Hrndl rather than compliment Humans, Kena had to suppress a laugh. At least it defused her anger.

"Well, they've made no contributions to resource management," Rnl said. "Besides that, they're dangerous. They war so viciously, they would have destroyed their own planet if the Tenelli hadn't stepped in."

"Oh, now that is just ridiculous." Kena let her hand fall to the table. "You never learned that from any Human or Tenelli. What is your source?"

"Well, you had a world-wide war for seven years, didn't you?"

"You're partially right. Seven years of what you would call natural disasters, punctuated by some very shocking battles. But the Tenelli didn't arrive until almost a decade after it ended.

"Who did end it?" Hrndl asked.

"Humans, of course, led by a very special Human. One capable of establishing a government of lasting peace. It's because of him, and all who cooperate with him, that Earth is once again a lush garden. Our recovery has nothing to do with any other race."

Rnl's nostrils lifted. "Only a race of war-mongers would claim ending a war as an accomplishment. And these other achievements are nothing compared to the value we—"

Dhgnr silenced Rnl with a single Grfdn word, waited for Frdn to engage Hrndl's attention, then turned back to Kena. "Again, I must apologize."

"No more apologies. The cause is quite clear. While I

appreciate your courtesy in talking with me, Dhgnr, it need not be constant."

"It's the least I can do." He picked up his glass, lifting it higher than usual. "You may not realize it, but we much appreciate this change. The drinking cylinders of Earth are so much easier for us to use than those of Prednia. Also, you are very thorough in adopting our table manners."

"For the most part, my table manners are from Human culture."

"Would any of our Grfdn manners be unacceptable on Earth?"

Rnl's voice was rumbling down again. Kena struggled to keep her expression calm. "Hmm. Children who squabble during meals are sent away from the table. Their stomachs soon teach them to control their tongues."

Rnl stopped mid-sentence and demanded, "What?"

"I was speaking to Dhgnr of Human culture," she said, all innocence. "Did you feel that it applied to you?"

Rnl panted a couple breaths before a growl began deep in his throat. It stopped when Dhgnr slammed a fist onto the table.

Rnl changed to words. "Humans are not welcome at the Grfdn table."

Hrndl's voice grated. "I invited her to my table. Accept her or leave."

Kena exhaled through pursed lips when Ghent stood up and said, "Navigators, we're meeting in the astro section in five minutes."

Hrndl linked arms with Kena in the hallway. Kena's memory skipped back to Ghent telling her that Hrndl would never want her friendship. There was a first for everything—and this was definitely a first!

"Oh, my dear," Hrndl said. "That was the most wonderful line."

She made an attempt to reach Kena's pitch and quoted, "Did you feel that it applied to you?"

Kena chuckled along with Hrndl's gargling laughter. Anything to lighten the mood after that unpleasant meal.

A few minutes later, Kena sat at a console next to Hrndl and surveyed the astro section. "What a relief," she whispered. "The whole gang isn't here."

"Three scientists are more than enough for a lengthy argument," Hrndl murmured.

Apparently, Ghent thought so, too. Instead of sitting, he leaned against the railing that encircled the 3-D display. Focusing on the scientists, he said, "We are not here to debate which theory is correct. We know it's far too early to do more than guess. The purpose of this meeting is to give the navigators an idea of the possibilities, and to determine our first steps in understanding the explosions." Ghent slid a hand along the railing. "I'd like each of you to give a *brief* summary of your theory. Focus on why the debris is so much smaller than we expected, and why the trajectories are inconsistent with earlier data." He nodded at Betnorel, the Prednian scientist.

"We think the initial fracturing occurred to a much higher degree than originally estimated. Hence, the pieces started out smaller. Since we don't know what triggered the break-up, it's quite possible that the initial force was underestimated. Therefore, debris from the two planets may have already mixed, rather than just now coming together as we expected. The material that we thought to be the alpha planet may really be a mixture of both the alpha and beta planets, and vice versa. This explains why some material appears to be heading inward. At issue, is the—"

"Thank you," Ghent said. "That will do." He nodded to Thrayl.

"We've always suspected," Thrayl said, "that gravitational anomalies were involved in this phenomenon. We've found indications that significant portions of the material in both planets and in the large moon have unusually high mass. This would have skewed earlier projections of the overall composition. We've also found unrecognizable chemical signatures. We may be looking at an element never before identified. If it's volatile, it could account for variations in velocity. This could result in more collisions than were anticipated. Subsequent collisions would break fragments into smaller and smaller pieces." Thrayl stopped and looked back at Ghent.

Ghent extended his hand, palm up, in the Tenelli gesture of thanks, and nodded to the third scientist, a Dantokrellie.

Salsheen used a tone that Kena identified as strictly-business, but her body language was defensive. "A few of us recognize the possibility that the original estimates of fragment size, speed, and directions were approximately correct. We think the break-up activity may have continued for an unknown period of time. This hypothesis has some definite problems, but we bring it up because it suggests added risk. It's conceivable that additional fragmentation could still occur."

Every navigator stared at Salsheen. Kena's imagination conjured up visions of flying amidst debris that could explode without warning. A few navigators gave vent to their cultural expletives. Sadly, this loosened Betnorel's tongue.

"There is no particular reason to believe this is still happening. Remember, there was an unusual energy reading from the star before the break-up. That has not recurred, so this hypothesis is very unlikely."

Before anyone could respond, Ghent asked, "Did you calculate probabilities for the theories, as I asked?"

"Yes," Betnorel replied. "The theory I described has a probability of 60-65 percent."

Thrayl turned to Ghent and said, "30-35 percent, sir."

Kena grinned and said to Salsheen, "They didn't leave you much, did they?"

She returned the smile. "I agreed to an estimated probability of 5-10 percent to avoid argument."

"How wise," Kena said. "Unfortunately, I think that estimate may be low. The trajectory data I've analyzed fits better with your theory than with the others."

"Yes," Ghent said, "I've seen indication of that, too. Regardless, we must take precautions. All samples brought into the hold must be enclosed in containment fields."

Betnorel's eyes rounded. "But we need to—"

Ghent employed his cold stare. "Do not suggest placing the ship and crew at risk."

Betnorel swallowed.

"What are the sampling needs?" Ghent asked

"We'll need control samples," Thrayl said. "Material that we are absolutely certain is from the alpha planet and from the beta planet."

"We should be able to pick that up this afternoon," Delf said. "We're sure the rocks at the outermost edge of the debris field haven't been knocked around since the original break-up. It's easy enough to know which planet they came from."

Thrayl nodded and said, "As we get closer, we'll try to determine from scans which pieces broke up from collisions and which show signs of other forces. We'll need samples from both sets. And obviously, we want samples of the unidentified substance." He frowned and turned to Ghent. "We really need samples from the two moons if there's any way to get them without excessive risk. We'll leave that decision to you, of course."

Ghent turned to Netlyn. "How are you doing on finding the small moon?"

"I'm not positive yet, but I think I've found it. There's a large object surrounded by several fragments. They're a ways off the moon's orbital path, but within the realm of possibility."

"Let me know when it's confirmed." He looked back to the three scientists. "Thank you for the information. You're dismissed." As they headed out, Ghent said, "Delf, you get samples from alpha. Kena, collect from beta. Take solo craft; we aren't looking for quantity on this run, just representative samples. Krdn, partner them each with a junior navigator. We'll get some training value out of this, as well. The rest of you, continue with your current assignments. I'll be with Piert if you need me."

CHAPTER NINETEEN

Alone in a small collector craft, Kena aligned her course with an irregular chunk of rock that had once been part of the beta planet's crust. She circled it to get a complete scan, and then slowed its tumble with nudges from an energy beam. When it was stable, she anchored it in a containment field with the rest of her samples.

This was her delight: Zero G. A responsive craft under her control. Vistas never before seen, spread out for her discovery.

This trip had an added bonus, since she was in a solo craft. No emfrel. Pleasure simmered deep within Kena's heart. For some reason, all the nuances of her creator's love were so much more tangible when she was alone in space. Beloved protector, guide, comforter, friend, father—the list could go on and on. She didn't need words with him. He was just intensely present while she worked.

She gripped the control stick with her right hand, while skimming her left across the console to configure the containment field for towing. She swung the little craft around to get a visual of her partner. Her movements were instinctive, and the craft responded as smoothly as if it were her own body. Without looking at the console, she slid her hand to the far left and touched a communication control.

"Are your samples stable?" she asked the other navigator.

"Yes, ma'am."

"Right. Let's head back to the *Ontrevay*."

The return trip took a couple hours. Kena filled the time by studying the scans she'd recorded of her samples. Nothing unusual. She paused to admire some crystals that flashed a rainbow of colors as they turned under the craft's lights. They'd probably end up in a museum somewhere. A memorial to a planet that was no more. She hoped they wouldn't be accompanied by artifacts of an intelligent race. At least she'd found no hints of that in her small collection.

As they decelerated for final approach to the *Ontrevay*, only Delf's craft came into Kena's view, aligned belly-to-belly with the ship. His partner must already be inside. He nudged his sample collection into the broad hold beneath the ship's gravity plane. The containment field snared it and drew it into position. Delf angled away from the hold, executed a half-flip reversal, and slipped neatly into the bay on the ship's side.

He opened the comm channel and said, "Your turn, Kena."

She grinned at his jaunty tone. Delf was never so happy as when he was flying.

A support navigator in ex op command said, "Kena, I'm sending target coordinates. Do you want to talk your partner through, or shall I?"

"I'll do it," she said. This took longer than Delf's polished maneuver, but was soon complete. She'd aligned her own load by the time her partner entered the bay.

"It looks like you've already figured out your target coordinates," the support navigator said, "but here they are for confirmation."

She gave them a quick check and replied, "Yes, that will do nicely. Releasing samples." She sent the collection toward the designated point and watched until the containment field engaged it.

"Another perfect shot," the support navigator said. "Come on in."

"If you insist," Kena said. She closed communication, enjoying the last couple moments of her trip as she adjusted her course for a curved entry into the bay.

An alarm sounded. The word *FIRE* flashed on her console. Damage indicators lit. She reached for the communication control, but the panel beside her blew apart. Twisted metal smashed into her left side.

Pain spiked through her ribs, and her diaphragm seized. Only her restraint harness kept her from curling into a ball. The agony overwhelmed her, then fueled a screaming need to reach the comm control.

She forced her head up and tried again, but her hand wouldn't respond. Her left wrist throbbed, and needles prickled through her fingers. Not good! She tried with her trembling right hand, but twisting her torso was unbearable. Debris still ricocheted around the cockpit. Something bounced against her windpipe. She blinked tears from her eyes.

A portion of her brain shouted through the pain. *Think!*

Her gaze flew to the window. She was off course. She would miss the bay doors, but not the *Ontrevay*. No!

Kena tried to correct, but the craft didn't adjust course. She checked her navigation console. The entire left bank of nav jets was down. She had to get control.

Her diaphragm was still locked in a spasm. Her pulse pounded in her head. Blood spread across her shirt. The *Ontrevay's* hull filled the window, closing in. She had very little time. "*Help me, father.*"

She overrode primary control and turned the upper and lower jets as far aside as possible, working them against each other. Her craft shifted sideways, returning to its course. It wasn't quite aligned. She tweaked with the right, rear thrusters. She was risking a spin, but could do nothing more to correct. Krdn was in ex op command; he'd be quick to see the danger and protect the bay.

G hent stood beside the consoles in ex op command, talking with Krdn, as Delf came up from the bay to watch Kena's entry. Ghent only half listened to the routine procedures and the casual conversation between Kena and the support navigator. Neither he nor Krdn paid much attention to Kena's maneuvers.

The support navigator frowned at the course projection and said, "I hate these curved entries. They're so hard to predict."

Delf leaned back in his chair with one foot on the console's edge, his hands linked behind his head and a smile twisting his lips. "Don't worry about it. She knows what she's doing." He shook his head. "Thias! That woman can fly! A perfect arc for approach. She won't even have to adjust it en route—just a little tweak at entry. Watch and learn."

Krdn looked over at the display, a guarded frown on his brow. He dug his fingers into the back of the couch he stood beside.

"What is she doing?" Ghent asked.

"Coming in with only three banks of the nav jets operating," Krdn said. "On a curved course—just like the one she used to bring Frethan in."

Ah—that was the reason for Krdn's tension. "Three banks? Why?"

"Impressing us with her prowess, I suppose." Krdn's voice rumbled. "There's no sign of any damage."

True enough—her craft looked fine. Krdn didn't. His lips compressed, and his knuckles whitened, but he made no move toward the console. The reason dawned on Ghent. Krdn was damned if he did and damned if he didn't. Was Kena taunting him? Would she go so far as to put the ship at risk?

Kena execute a one-sided course correction. It pushed her toward a spin.

Ghent's nostrils flared. He dove for the containment controls. "Protective fields!" They barely had time to get the internal fields energized.

Kena's craft sailed into the bay in an unsteady spin, nav jets still firing. They flared against the energy shields, encircling her in a halo as she spun. It took her a full turn to get them shut down.

Ghent's shurgs wrapped his fists. She would have damaged all the craft on second level if they hadn't gotten the shields up. He swung around to the lift. "Stop that spin and pull her craft down so I can get in there and—educate her."

Krdn took the controls. He snapped orders to the other two navigators. "Anchor the craft. Rapid pressurization. Engage—"

The lift door slid shut, cutting off his words. By the time Ghent reached the bay, the gravitational field had re-engaged. He waited only for minimal pressure before opening the lift door. His eardrums fluttered, and air rushed past him to complete pressurization. The left side of Kena's craft faced the lift. Ghent half expected to find damage. Its flawless condition fanned his anger.

He crossed the bay at a run, flipped open the panel beside the hatch, and pulled the manual release. He swung himself inside without waiting for the hatch to fully open. "Do you think I am impressed?" he demanded.

Two steps took him into the cockpit. He grabbed the top of the high-backed couch to jerk it around.

The stench halted him. His eyes swept over the damaged panel and Kena's right hand, gripping the armrest. Careful to bump nothing, he maneuvered around her in the cramped cockpit to get a better look. The fur on his brow puckered, and a Plynteth exclamation passed his lips.

He reached across the console and jabbed the comm control. "Get Metchell down here." Dropping to a gentler tone, he said, "Kena, tell me what's injured."

Kena tried to point, but her hand wavered. She mouthed soundless words.

"I can't hear you." Ghent leaned close to her face.

"Can't—breathe." Her faint, strangled words slipped between pale lips, and her eyes rolled in a disturbing fashion.

"Tell Metchell there's blood on her chest, and she's barely breathing." He twisted around to open a cabinet.

Delf's voice came over the speaker. "There should be an oxygen mask in the emergency cabinet."

"Yes, I have it," Ghent said, jerking it out and letting other supplies fall to the floor. Careful not to move Kena, he formed the mask over her nose and mouth. "This is oxygen. Try to breathe."

K ena felt the mask press against her face, but Ghent seemed very distant. What good would oxygen do when she couldn't inhale?

"Kena, breathe," he ordered.

She tried to draw air through her swelling throat. Fresh pain shot through her chest. Her eyes clenched.

"Again. A little deeper," he said.

She sat there helpless, her diaphragm wrenched in a spasm, her throat closing, and her head throbbing.

"Kena, breathe," he ordered again.

She could barely hear him over the roaring in her ears. Strange tingling sensations prickled through her. Someone tipped her head back. Garbled sounds. Darkness.

Her head seemed stuffed with cotton. She tried to move it but couldn't. Dizziness swept through her. She was numb and floating. Strange. She'd gotten into the bay. Something had fallen when the gravity field engaged. So why was she floating?

The memory of pain lingered, but she felt nothing. Confused, she opened her eyes. Ghent's and Metchell's faces hovered at odd angles. Her stomach convulsed, and she fainted.

G hent cringed as Kena's eyes rolled back and their white showed. Unnerving.

"Let me get next to her," Metchell said.

Ghent sidestepped out of the cockpit to switch places with him. They tilted the couch as far as possible without allowing her body to shift.

Metchell slit her nav suit open and exposed the wound: a long, jagged gash, sluggishly bleeding. He glanced at the image on his handheld med scanner.

Ghent endured several long seconds before saying, "You could talk, Metchell."

"Three ribs are broken. There's bruising over her diaphragm and on her neck, which explains breathing difficulty."

Metchell secured a gel bandage over the open wound and reached for a chill pack, which he formed around her neck. He frowned at his med scanner as he moved it down her limbs.

"Her left forearm is broken." When he finished checking, he said. "A few more bruises, but no other serious injuries."

She still looked terribly pale, but at least her chest was moving in a steady rhythm.

Metchell eased Kena's left arm into an immobilization cuff, forming it around her wrist and hand. Then, he filled a syringe.

"What's that for?" Ghent asked.

"She'll wake soon. I'd rather keep her unconscious for now." Metchell finished the injection and met his eyes. "She'll be all right, Ghent. They're painful injuries, but I won't let her feel any more of it. There shouldn't be any problem with healing."

Ghent let out a long breath, taking as much comfort from Metchell's unworried face as from his words.

Metchell glanced around the cockpit, lines edging his eyes. "What's that awful smell?"

"Two smells, really," Ghent said. "Charred insulation and fire suppressant."

"I'll never understand how you can differentiate odors. Support

her so I can recline the couch and get a brace behind her back."
Metchell slid the re-formable frame into place, then engaged the
energy field to secure her body. "Help me lift her out. I'll take her
legs. You lift by the frame."

K ena woke in the medical section. She took a quick look at
her surroundings and murmured, "Not again."
Metchell walked over to her. "What's wrong, Kena?"
"I'm spending...far too much of...this trip in med section."
Metchell feigned an offended tone. "I thought you liked me."
"Sure, I do but...can't we just...chat in the dining hall an'...skip
this part?"
"Not this time. Have you ever had bone regenerated?"
"No. And I don't have time...for it now."
"Too true. I've accelerated the process. You probably know
that's excruciating. I've completely numbed several nerves in your
chest and arm. You're going to have to put up with that for at least
a day. You won't be operating anything for a couple days, but
Ghent seems to want your brain back on duty."
"Actually, my brain is...operating way below light speed. Can
you give me something...to pull me out of this fog?"
"No. You're off duty."
"Quite. That's the problem. I need to be on duty."
"Kena, it's third shift. You're supposed to be asleep."
"Oh."
"I only let you wake up so I can get some food into you. I'll
just confirm that pain control is complete first. Take a deep
breath."
She did as he asked, or rather, she thought she did.
"A deep breath," he insisted.
She tried again.
"Come on. You can pull in more than that. Imagine you're
going to yell at me long and hard for being such a pest."

She managed a shaky laugh and a replenishing breath that satisfied him.

"Do you feel any pain with that?"

"No. Breathing feels very one-sided."

"Good. You are breathing with both lungs, though. It probably felt like your left lung was seriously injured, but it wasn't. Sit up now. I'll help you a little, but I want you to use your muscles."

She strained to pull herself up as he raised the couch's back.

"That's enough," he said.

She relaxed. Not that she wanted to, but her weakness left her no choice.

He reviewed internal images of the motion then stared at her face. "The scan looks fine, but that frown doesn't. Did it hurt to move?"

"No, I just don't like feeling so weak and awkward."

"Accelerated regeneration consumes a lot of energy. You'll tire easily. Ghent knows your condition, so if you need a break while you're on duty tomorrow, just say so. It won't cause any problems." He slid an instrument across her left hand and asked, "Can you feel that?"

"No, nothing."

"Good." He turned her nerveless arm over and pushed the sleeve back, revealing a narrow cylinder filled with a milky fluid.

One end of it tapered to a thin tube that disappeared into her bruised skin. The other end held a pressure device that forced the contents slowly into her arm. A clear cast covered the tube and her arm from elbow to palm.

"You have three more of these tubes on your rib cage. I'll wrap your chest when you're up moving around, but I can't immobilize it as firmly as your arm. You'll need to move carefully, since you can't feel."

"All right."

Metchell picked up a glass from the counter. "Here's your midnight snack."

The beverage was thick and filling—more than she really

wanted, but she forced it down without comment. He took the glass from her and handed her another small one of clear liquid.

"I'm full," she muttered.

"Drink it."

Kena met his eyes. He wasn't going to take *no*. She drained it. Metchell began lowering her couch. The movement felt strange. She tried to set the glass down, but the side table seemed to be moving.

Metchell caught her wavering hand and took the glass from her. "Go to sleep."

"Oh." She sighed. Lassitude overwhelmed her. She closed her eyes and let the drug carry her to oblivion.

CHAPTER TWENTY

The next morning, Kena shoveled a heaping spoonful of hash browns into her mouth as Hrndl walked into her room in the med section.

"Feeling better?" Hrndl asked.

"Uh-huh." Kena swallowed, drank some juice, and said, "You picked a terrible time to visit. Metchell's treatment has got my appetite pretty near insatiable. I can't get the food in fast enough, so you're likely to be disgusted."

"I'll survive. I've eaten in the same room as Prednians, after all. It can't be worse than that."

"I certainly hope not. Speaking of eating, why aren't you?"

Hrndl took a step to the side, as though she needed to distance herself from something. "I left early so I could visit you."

Kena consumed a close imitation of scrambled eggs and cheese before responding. "It's not that I don't enjoy your company, but shouldn't you spend what little free time you have with the other Grfdn?"

"Why should I? I already know far more than I want to about the incredibly complex task of converting various types of waste into useful resources."

Fortunately, the next spoonful hadn't yet reached Kena's mouth. She broke into weak laughter, and Hrndl's eyes tilted upward. The tension in her face eased for a moment, but then the tilt of her eyes sagged.

Hrndl gave her head a little shake. "I do have another reason to be here. I'm to brief you on the latest developments."

"Ah, good. Have the scientists come up with anything more yet?"

"Nothing definitive," Hrndl said. "They're all pondering unrecognized chemical signatures that are showing up on the scans. Not that I blame them. The signatures are incredibly strange! It appears the substance morphs into something else and then back. Or maybe it just fades into and out of existence."

"That must be driving Netlyn crazy."

"It's certainly causing her difficulties. Speaking of Netlyn— Giddech was disrespectful to her. Jealous of her promotion, I suppose. He's not likely to make that mistake again. She's so universally pleasant, I wasn't sure she could do firm authority, but she accomplished it quite thoroughly."

Kena said, "Excellent," between mouthfuls.

"Getting back to this peculiar substance—it's estimated to be present in about 15 percent of the objects, but there's none in the crust samples you and Delf retrieved." Hrndl extended the display of her computer and used it while she talked. "Netlyn has confirmed that the objects she has been tracking are, in fact, remnants of the small moon. Unfortunately, it'll be risky to get near them." She showed Kena the image she'd pulled up.

Kena frowned at it as she chewed then waved it away.

Hrndl clipped her computer to her belt. "We now suspect that this system once had a close encounter with another. We're trying to determine which one. There's an unusually broad, elliptical asteroid belt, fifty-six degrees off the planetary orbital plane. Overall, the system is very cluttered. To use Delf's phrase, it's swarming with dirtballs."

Kena finished her juice and said, "That sounds like Delf. Is he all excited to get out in it?"

"Not as much as you'd expect."

"Oh? Why not?"

"Morale in the nav section is about as low as it can get."

Kena frowned. "I suppose. Three accidents already, and we haven't even done anything difficult yet."

"That's the common thought," Hrndl said.

"We'll have to see what we can do about that."

Hrndl shrugged. "I'll leave that to you. The Grfdn aren't known for morale-boosting effervescence."

"Actually, I'm not likely to score high on effervescence today. Metchell says I'll tire easily, but I'll do my best to hide it."

"That won't be hard," Hrndl said. "You, Netlyn, and I are going to be in the astro section today. I expect Ghent will be there as much as possible, too. Everyone else is flying sims through the debris field or taking a turn in nav command."

Metchell walked in, just then, with a thermal mug in his hand. He gave it to Kena and said, "Delatin came out of the kitchen with this and asked me to bring it to you. He said to tell you that it's 'fresh brewed from real beans.' Whatever that means."

Kena made a fumbling attempt to unscrew the lid. "Such fun it is, to have one arm that's as useful as a block of wood!"

Hrndl reached over and opened it. "What is that?" she asked, her nose crinkling as she stared at the dark brown liquid. "It smells horrible!"

Kena raised the cup and inhaled the aroma. "Ahhh!" She exhaled, making a show of ecstasy. She sipped it and said, "Delicious! This is so kind of Delatin."

"What is it?" Hrndl demanded again.

"Coffee. I'd offer you some, but it contains a stimulant. It's a restricted drink to all races but mine."

"Why?"

Metchell answered her. "Drugs don't necessarily work the same for all races, particularly if they affect the brain."

"Too bad, Hrndl. No coffee for you."

"What a shame," Hrndl said, lacing her words with feigned regret.

Kena chuckled and sipped her coffee, while Metchell checked the progress of bone regeneration.

When he finished refilling the tubes, he said, "I'm going to need to do this every few hours, but you needn't come here. I will come to you." He re-secured a stiff chest-wrap. "There are motion sensors in this. The top band will vibrate if you're getting close to injuring yourself. If you feel that, just straighten your torso." He pulled her tunic down, covering the wrap. "You can go now, but remember, move carefully."

"I will," she said, sliding her legs over the edge of the couch and standing. Raising her pitch, she added in his language, "Coo en la!"

Metchell smiled and performed the Dantokrellie gesture of acknowledgment, bringing his fingertips together. "I suppose I shouldn't be surprised that you would thank me in my own language. Get to work, you little charmer."

Hrndl walked out with Kena and said, "You're amazing."

"Am I? How so?"

"You have some very surprising friends. I heard that you stayed at the Prednian gala through the music of every single race."

"Why not?" Kena asked. "What Human isn't interested in music? Besides, Prednian music has complexity and nuances that Humans particularly like."

"Yes. So much so, you and Delf danced one of their jigs in double-time."

Kena grinned. "Well, who else on this ship could keep up with me, except a Veet?"

Hrndl glanced over her shoulder. Making sure the hallway was empty? "The point is, you won't go near the Prednians in the dining hall, but you do attend one of their endless parties."

"But of course. Prednians don't serve food at their parties. There was no chance of having to watch them paw food into their mouths."

"An apt description," Hrndl said. "You find their manners as disgusting as I do. And yet, the Prednian chef prepares a drink especially for you and ensures that it's delivered to med section. If you're going to explain why that is not surprising, spare your breath. Then, there is Metchell. It's hard to decide whether he treats you as a favored niece or merely a friend of many years. You've even learned some of his language."

Kena used an apologetic tone. "All of it, in fact, but that was a few years ago."

"Do you really like him as much as you appear to?"

"Of course, I do. Is there some reason I shouldn't?"

"No particular reason," Hrndl said as they turned down another hall. "But he is so four-dimensional, after all."

Kena chuckled even though this disparaging comment was an old joke. Navigators used it to describe those who couldn't grasp the fifth and sixth dimensions. "Actually, Hrndl, I suspect he is three-dimensional."

"Oh?"

"The first day I met him, he used the terms *twists* and *eddies* in relation to flying a spatial rift."

Hrndl snorted. "My point exactly."

Kena chuckled again but defended Metchell. "I admit, he'd never be able to hold his own in the astro section, but he's as good at his profession as we are at ours. Besides, it's easy to make him laugh, and that's always a plus in my view."

Hrndl fell silent, and Kena stole a sideways look at her. Now what had she said to make Hrndl scowl? Still—she'd scowl too if she had to choose between Rnl and Frdn. They were certainly no more than three-dimensional either. And they had no redeeming qualities that she'd ever noticed. Why didn't Dhgnr pursue her?

"You forgot to mention my most surprising friend," Kena said.

"Who? Me?" Hrndl glanced at Kena's teasing grin and said, "That one is too bizarre for words!"

"Quite!" Kena chuckled. "Thank you, by the way, for bringing me fresh clothes." She ran her good hand around the hem of her tunic.

Hrndl shrugged. "Not much effort. You startled me, though, with the way you have your sitting room configured. I thought for a second I was in the wrong quarters."

A few crewmembers hurried up to them from an intersecting hall. They greeted Kena with far more exuberance than seemed necessary.

Hrndl fended off a Tenelli, who approached from behind with the apparent intention of hugging Kena.

They finally reached the astro section, and Kena murmured, "Safety, at last. I had no idea the hallway would be so fraught with danger."

<hr />

The morning was long and frustrating. Kena struggled to stay alert. Breaks didn't help much, and having only one useful hand made work cumbersome. It was almost time for second meal when she finally admitted she couldn't function without a nap. Kena turned to tell Ghent but paused, for he was staring at Netlyn.

She jabbed at console buttons, activating screen after screen with multiple views of a tumbling object. "Oh, no!" Netlyn exclaimed, stabbing at a few more buttons. The recorded images that she had assembled appeared in the 3-D display area. "You were right, Kena. A probability of 5-10 percent wasn't nearly high enough."

The rock tumbled before them, viewed from all angles. No other debris approached it. Then, without warning, it burst apart, flinging remnants in all directions.

Kena muttered, "I could've done without being right."

Ghent joined Netlyn, helping her target the easiest fragments to collect. Without looking back, he said, "You two get something to eat. We'll wait until you come back."

Kena sighed. "Sorry about the timing, but I think I need to sleep."

"Take as long as you need."

H rndl searched Kena's face. "I'd better walk you to your quarters in case I need to protect you from more of your fans."

When they reached their destination, Hrndl followed Kena inside without waiting for an invitation, then ordered two meals.

Kena barely seemed to notice what Hrndl was doing. She said little while she ate and then went to her sleeping room.

Hrndl took her time finishing her own large meal. She should leave. Instead, she leaned back in her chair, surveying the images that covered the sitting room walls. A hilly, Terran forest surrounded her, complete with audio. Branches swayed in a fitful breeze. To one side, a stream gushed between brilliantly flowered bushes—rhododendrons, Kena had called them. The stream splashed over rocks and cast droplets up to flicker in the patchy sunlight. Hrndl closed her eyes and listened to rustling leaves, birdsong, and a gurgling brook. In spite of the sounds, or perhaps because of them, the room was blissfully quiet. Hrndl relaxed, drawing deep, soothing breaths.

Several minutes later, the door signal and Metchell's voice interrupted her. Hrndl's eyes tilted upward—a forest with a comm system. She reached lazily for the door control and opened it.

Metchell eyed her for a moment before asking in his gentle way, "What are you doing here?"

"So many people are delighted by Kena's recovery; I felt it would be best if I made sure she reached her quarters and had the opportunity to eat and sleep. She went to the other room about ten minutes ago, and I stayed to relax before returning to duty."

Metchell's gaze held. Finally, he said, "While I approve of the support you provide her, the fact that you linger here worries me."

"Do you think she would object?" Hrndl asked in innocent surprise.

"You know perfectly well, that is not what I meant. I have no intension of prying into personal affairs, but I am concerned."

Hrndl gave up trying to avoid his true meaning. She looked aside for a moment, considering her answer. Then, she stood and replied with calm dignity, "I am still capable of conducting my affairs. However, I do not forget your profession and your vital contribution to the crew. If I do find myself in need of your skills, I will inform you. Now, if you'll excuse me, I must relieve Netlyn."

Metchell stepped aside and let her leave.

His gaze seemed to cling to her, even after the door closed.

CHAPTER TWENTY-ONE

A few hours later, Hrndl glanced up as Metchell came into astro section.

He leaned over Kena and said something about movement therapy, then they left together.

Had he timed his arrival, shortly before third meal, for Hrndl's sake, as well as for Kena's? Hrndl straightened and curled her tense fingers. Unnecessary interference. The break from her suitors had been wonderful, but the intensity of her mating instinct could not be ignored. Nor could her stomach's demand.

She made her way to the dining hall, where Rnl and Frdn awaited her. Dhgnr was absent, as she'd expected. Two craft had sustained damage while retrieving samples that afternoon. He would monitor repairs.

Throughout the meal, Hrndl's preoccupation with navigational problems thwarted her suitors' attempts to hold her attention. They made little effort. The proverbial appetite of a mating woman was in full force. She'd consumed nearly everything they brought her before the subdued conversations and whisperings in the dining hall finally penetrated her abstraction.

"What's going on?" she asked the two men.

Rnl jerked his head back. "Haven't you heard the rumors?"

"I've been in the astro section all day. With Ghent, I might add. How could I hear rumors?"

"No one is repeating it directly to the Grfdn, anyway," Frdn said. "We've only overheard bits and pieces, but some believe Kena's craft was sabotaged." His tone ground, and he shifted aside. "Krdn's name is mentioned."

Hrndl stared. Every nerve, every muscle in her body went to high alert.

"It could have been someone else," Rnl said. "Why must they assume—"

"Who else?" Hrndl demanded.

"I once heard that Delf has no great liking for her," Rnl said.

Hrndl shrugged off his stupidity. "He was angry with her once, but that was weeks ago. He respects her skill and treats her as a friend."

"How would you expect him to act," Rnl asked, "if he was planning a subtle revenge?"

She uttered a contemptuous growl. "I know both Delf and Krdn far better than you do." She rose and scanned the room. "Where is Ghent?"

A nearby navigator glanced over her shoulder and said, "He just left a minute ago with some of the section chiefs."

Hrndl turned and ran from the dining hall. She reached the corridor outside the consult room just as Ghent was about to enter it. Ignoring the half dozen section chiefs in the hallway, she called out, "Ghent!"

He stopped and looked toward her, his hand resting on the doorframe.

She forced herself to slow down and tried to sound calm. "Your pardon, sir, but I need a moment with you in private."

Ghent stared at her for a few seconds. So still. Less than pleased, it seemed. He glanced over his shoulder at the section chiefs and said, "Two minutes." To Hrndl, he said, "Come," and walked into his consult room.

The instant the door slid shut behind her, Hrndl asked, "What caused the accident to Kena's craft?"

"I assume you've heard rumors," Ghent said. "I suggest you ignore them. It's not possible to determine the exact cause of the accident. There is no evidence of sabotage, only supposition that it could have happened."

"I see. I would like to inspect the damage."

"I have already ordered it repaired."

"Under these circumstances?" she demanded.

"Yes, Hrndl. I have to think of all the circumstances, and we need every craft. I was the first to enter after Kena's injury, and I stayed to inspect the damage after Metchell took her to med section. I examined it thoroughly, and—I repeat—there is no evidence of sabotage."

Hrndl's words tumbled faster, emphasizing her guttural accent. "But if we don't know the exact cause, we cannot rule it out. Please tell me what you did find."

"I've already spent twenty minutes going over the fine details of this with Dhgnr. I don't have time to do it again. I suggest you discuss your concerns with him—after all repairs are finished."

Ghent's eyes swept over her. She stilled the unconscious movement of her hands sliding up and down her thighs.

"You've done enough for today," he said. "Take some time to refresh yourself." Her face must have betrayed her, for he said, "I don't want you looking at any navigational data for at least two hours. Understood?"

Hrndl hid her emotions. "Yes, sir."

"Good." He ushered her out and looked down the hallway where Rnl and Frdn waited, before motioning the section chiefs into his consult room.

Hrndl let her suitors guide her steps, not caring where they went. They found an empty common room and sat down with her, vying continuously for her attention and favor. Her thoughts wavered between mating and the horrible suspicion that Krdn was trying to kill Kena.

Finally, she demanded, "Why must you go on and on about trivialities in a situation like this?"

Dead silence.

Rnl broke the long pause. "I know the flying is more stressful with all this explosive debris out there, but I've heard you're a good navigator. If you'd like, I'll talk with Ghent about how Krdn assigns your flights and make sure he doesn't send you into danger. In the meantime, let me get you something to eat. You didn't get a chance to finish your meal."

Hrndl stared at him, her breath coming fast. "What are you talking about?"

Rnl stammered, and Frdn seized the opportunity. "What did Ghent tell you about the accident?"

"The cause is unknown. There isn't clear enough evidence to prove it was sabotage."

"I'll do some checking," Frdn said. "I know some of the maintenance crew and might be able to find out something."

"Don't you understand? It's not enough to prove sabotage. I have to stop it from happening again."

"I'll work on finding out who could have done it," Rnl said. "I'll check out who had access to that craft, who assigned it to her, and who knew about it. The only problem is, quite a few people could've had the opportunity. Are you sure it's really worth all this trouble? Kena is recovering, so no long-term harm was done."

Hrndl growled. How could they be so obtuse? "Intentionally injuring a navigator on a solo flight is attempted murder. We must stop this...this *criminal* before he tries again."

"If we aren't sure who he is," Rnl asked, "how are we going to stop him?"

Hrndl jumped up and paced. Her suitors stood, but refrained from following her back and forth across the room. "Oh, I know who he is. It couldn't be more obvious." She paced faster. "First, he gets away with killing Frethan and injuring Kena. I was coordinating, but I'm forbidden from charging him here. How can I possibly fulfill my duty to Kena with such a restriction?"

Frdn tried to soothe her. "Ghent is sending him to Grfdn as soon as this mission is over. He'll be charged and tried there, which is far better than a trial here."

"Are you blind? Kena, herself, is the proof of the charge against him. She suffers a mysterious accident. Doesn't that suggest something to you? If Krdn gets away with this, he will try again."

Rnl grasped Hrndl's hands and stopped her pacing. "I will go to Dhgnr, if you like, and explain your concerns. He's as angry as you are that Krdn has shamed us. He will not let him do it again." Hrndl stared at him, panting, and he hurried on. "If that's not enough, I promise you will have my support in any form you like."

Frdn laid a hand on her arm and said, "We will work out a method to protect Kena. You know Krdn's opportunities better than I do. Just tell me what is necessary, and I will do it for you."

Hrndl looked from one to the other, her lips a hard line. "Krdn used to make promises to me, too, but he never fulfilled one of them." She thrust their hands away.

Rnl clenched his fists. "He was never worthy of you."

"I will fulfill what I have said!" Frdn declared. "Only tell me what you desire."

"I desire that Krdn know, *today,* that he cannot escape punishment for this attack or any other. I desire that he pay, *today,* for both times he has injured Kena. I desire that he suffer, *today,* all the pain that she has suffered and more. I know where he walks in the evening. If your promises mean anything, come with me now."

Hrndl swept out of the room, certain that both men followed, eager to prove themselves.

They found Krdn passing through an empty common room. One look at the three of them, and he pressed his back to the wall.

"I find it very strange," Hrndl said, approaching him with measured steps, "that the one person who can establish the exact time of Frethan's death has suffered a dangerous and mysterious accident."

Krdn held silence. He drew his head back and stared down at her.

"Did you sabotage her craft, Krdn?" Hrndl asked. "Why don't you answer me?"

His face was like a mask—impossible to read. "If I didn't do it, I would say no. If I did do it, I would still say no. Don't ask me stupid questions, Hrndl."

That was more than enough provocation. All three attacked. Krdn brought his arms up to shield his face, but Rnl and Frdn pummeled his head from opposite sides. Hrndl drove her knee into his gut.

Kena paused on the way to her quarters from med section. Was that...? Yes, muffled thuds and grunts came from the hallway to her right. She followed the sounds.

Kena stopped at the entrance on the far side of a common room. Three Grfdn were attacking someone. Rnl kicked the victim's legs out from under him, and Frdn followed up with a kick to his chest. Krdn struggled to keep his head out of their range.

Kena raised her voice. "Forgive the intrusion, but I'm curious. Do you intend to kill him, or merely beat him senseless?"

The three attackers turned to stare at Kena. Krdn took advantage of the lull, slowly pushing himself up to sit against the wall. He drew one knee to his chest, but the other leg settled awkwardly.

Rnl growled at Kena. "This is not your concern. Out!"

Hrndl stopped him with a hand on his arm. Her eyes met Kena's, and their corners lifted. "Kena must think he needs help." Turning to survey her victim, she sweetened her tone. "Perhaps she is right."

Krdn swore deep in his throat, while the other two men laughed.

Frdn caught Hrndl's hand and drew her aside. "Better let her through, so she can care for him."

Kena strolled forward. Would they continue beating him if she left? How to get rid of them?

As Kena passed her, Hrndl murmured, "No closer."

Kena stopped a few meters away from Krdn. Not a pretty sight.

Through clenched teeth, he growled, "Get out. I won't have your help."

"That is such a pity," Kena said, "because I don't intend to change my standards to pander to your supposed honor."

Hrndl laughed and ran from the room, her suitors following. That worked rather well.

"I still have strength enough," Krdn said. "Dare touch me, and you will feel it."

In the hallway, Frdn stepped back into her line of sight. He made not a sound, nor did he let Krdn see him.

"My intention is merely to prevent your premature death. Can you stand?"

"Get out!"

"As you wish." She turned and left, taking one backward glance toward the opposite doorway. Frdn was gone. She headed for her quarters, frowning over what to do. Her insult had gotten rid of Krdn's attackers far better than a reasonable request would have. But it wasn't enough. She suspected internal injuries and doubted he could walk.

That hallway was not the direct route to anything—it could be hours before he was found. She had to tell someone he was hurt, but who? Metchell was the obvious choice, but his questions would bring Hrndl's involvement to light. The last thing Kena wanted.

What about Dhgnr? True, he conversed with her more easily than the other Grfdn males did, but it seemed more like a means of excluding her. Would he be angry or pleased if she sought him out? Impossible to guess, but two things were certain. He would protect Grfdn honor, and he would keep the navigators available to Ghent.

Kena pulled her computer from her belt and used it to find Dhgnr's quarters. A few minutes later, she touched the panel beside his door and stated her name. Several long seconds passed before the door slid open, but still not enough time to figure out what she should say.

Dhgnr stood rigid in the middle of his sitting room. She stepped across the threshold into beige hues, sunny lighting, and right-angles. The door closed with a faint whoosh.

"Why do you come to me?" Dhgnr asked.

"Because I have found a Grfdn—seriously injured—on the floor of a common room. I doubt he can stand or walk."

Dhgnr quivered as she spoke until she said the word *he*. Then his rigid stance deflated, and his breath eased out. Oh, now that was interesting.

"Rival suitors often fight," Dhgnr said. "Why not tell Metchell? I am no doctor."

She blinked. "It's Krdn."

"Ah! Wh—" His eyes narrowed. "Why do you come to me instead of Metchell?"

Kena licked her lips and chose her words with care. "He will likely ask me questions. Since I disapprove of lying, I would need to speak of—various Grfdn who were present when I found Krdn. It occurred to me that you might prefer to find Krdn alone and inform Metchell yourself."

His gaze held hers through a slight nod. "Do you have any suggestions on where I should stroll, this evening?"

"The vicinity of D34 might be a good choice," Kena said.

As she left, Dhgnr's footsteps headed the opposite direction, his emfrel receding from her awareness. It had settled—unlike what she'd sensed that first moment in his quarters, the instant before he'd realized the injured Grfdn couldn't be Hrndl. So, his disinterest was a front. Not surprising, but why? Why didn't he court her? Why hide what he felt? Particularly, considering how irritated Hrndl was with Rnl and Frdn.

CHAPTER TWENTY-TWO

Kena paused in the middle of spooning strawberries over the Tenelli version of a pancake. A Prednian she barely knew chattered at her from across the buffet.

"Did you hear what happened to Krdn?"

"No. Nor do I have any particular interest in Krdn." She resumed serving herself.

"But he was beaten. Bad!"

"I see. Now that I know, I hope I don't have to hear anything else about him."

The poor guy looked taken aback, but his eyes perked up when Hrndl came to the buffet. "Hrndl, did you hear—"

Kena dropped her voice an octave. "She has less interest than I do."

They walked to the empty Grfdn table, where Hrndl insisted that Kena sit in the chair Dhgnr had occupied of late. Did she dread a conversation with him?

Dhgnr joined them and sat directly across from Hrndl. "Rnl and Frdn will not be with us this morning," he said.

Hrndl nodded.

Dhgnr kept his voice quiet. "It would seem that you had an eventful evening, Hrndl. Did it satisfy you?"

She nodded again.

"Good, because Rnl and Frdn will not participate in such an activity again."

Hrndl took a deep breath. "I understand." She picked up her glass and took a slow drink.

After a moment, Dhgnr spoke in a more natural tone. "Do you need the presence of a khn, Hrndl?"

"That will not be necessary."

His face revealed nothing. "Do you know, yet, whom you will work with today?"

"I assume Kena, unless..." she looked sideways to Kena.

"Metchell removed the bone regeneration tubes a half-hour ago. I shouldn't need to leave."

Conversation drifted to them from the nearest tables: speculation about Krdn. Hrndl's nostrils pinched, and her breath thrummed.

The rest of the day followed the same pattern. Rumors abounded on all sides. Rnl and Frdn made things no better over lunch. Brilliant. The details escaped Kena, for much of the conversation was in Grfdn, but Hrndl sounded about ready to beat them as viciously as she had gone after Krdn.

Later, Hrndl stayed close as they left nav section for third meal. More talk of the beating followed them in the hallway. Hrndl scowled.

Kena glanced at her and said under her breath, "I'm not listening to this through another meal. Care to join me in my quarters?"

"Beyond doubt," Hrndl whispered.

They slipped away then shared a leisurely meal, surrounded by a Terran forest. When Hrndl showed no desire to leave, Kena indulged her with conversation far removed from both navigation and mating. Tension faded from Hrndl's face; yet, every now and then, the outer corners of her eyes lowered while she stared at nothing.

All too soon, the door chime interrupted, and Dhgnr asked for admittance.

Kena hesitated. At Hrndl's tightening expression, she used a comm channel to answer him. "I'm resting and do not desire more visitors."

A pause. Maybe he would leave.

His voice came over the comm channel again. "I will not disturb you for long. Hrndl is missing and doesn't answer communications. Do you have information I can use to locate her?"

Kena's mouth crimped at the corners. She said to Hrndl, "Looks like we can't avoid this."

"No," Hrndl said, standing. "It's time I was leaving anyway."

Kena touched the comm control again to answer Dhgnr. "That, I do." She pushed another button, and the door slid open.

Hrndl spoke as he entered. "I was just about to leave. Did you want to talk with me or merely verify my whereabouts?"

Dhgnr regarded her for a moment. "Is it well with you?"

"It is." She skirted around him and left.

He watched her walk out and then turned his gaze on Kena.

She returned the look, sensing his tension. What could she say to him? She'd never know if she didn't at least start a dialog. "Would you like to sit down?" she asked, gesturing to the chair Hrndl had vacated.

I n the hallway, Hrndl glanced from side to side. Neither Frdn nor Rnl waited there. She released her tight shoulders. To evade them, she chose a convoluted route through the least frequented hallways and finally arrived in med section.

Metchell sat at his table. He glanced up from his computer, then locked his gaze on her and straightened.

"I require your assistance," Hrndl blurted out.

"In what way?" His voice was so calm in contrast to hers.

"I want you to remove my active ovary."

Metchell remained silent, his expression grave. He was going to be difficult. As if things weren't bad enough already, now she would have to argue for her rights.

Metchell finally spoke. "Come with me." He stood and led her into a private room.

Metchell strode past a sofa and some chairs, arranged for conversation, and stopped at a console near a synthesizer. At his touch, the décor changed from the bland coloring considered acceptable to all races. Yellow, beige, and green swept over every surface, and the lighting took on a golden glow. The room's low cabinets acquired Grfdn carvings, featuring their traditional, right-angled motif.

"How cozy," Hrndl said. "It makes me feel right at home."

"Sit down, Hrndl," Metchell said as he took a chair, "and remember that sarcasm is wasted on me. Before we go any further, I want to make sure you understand what you're asking me to do. Are you aware that ovaries cannot be regenerated?"

"I am."

"Each of your ovaries has its own four-year cycle. The remaining ovary will not produce more frequently because the other is gone. You will be limited to reproducing once every four years. If that ovary should fail for some reason, you will be sterile. Do you understand this?"

Hrndl fidgeted. "I know my own reproductive system. You do not need to explain it to me. I have a right to request this procedure. It is not your prerogative to make the decision for me."

"It is my job to heal, not to harm. I will not perform an optional, destructive procedure without—"

Hrndl's control evaporated. "It is not optional. I will not be condemned to a lifetime with either Rnl or Frdn. I would rather have my children far apart or not at all, than to be forced into mating with a man I despise."

Metchell held his silence.

Had she done more harm than good? She uncurled her fists and laid her hands in her lap, trying to calm herself.

After a moment, Metchell asked, "How much longer do you think it will be until you complete ovulation?"

"I don't know, but it must be soon."

Metchell opened a cabinet beside his chair and said, "I want to analyze a blood sample to determine how soon."

"Pointless. Nothing will change. I want to get this over with, now."

Metchell continued his preparations, then leaned forward and held out his hand, palm up. "Your wrist, please." Kind, gentle, and immoveable.

Hrndl reluctantly laid her wrist in his hand.

He drew the sample in silence and deposited it in a tube of solution. The simple test would yield results almost immediately. She even knew how to read it. To emphasize her disinterest, she stared at the opposite wall.

After a moment, Metchell said, "You have at least two more days, probably three. How long have you been considering this?"

Hrndl shrugged. "A few days, I suppose."

"Have you talked with anyone else about it?"

"No."

"I realize it's awkward for you, since there are no other Grfdn females with us. Would it be possible for you to talk with Kena about this?"

Hrndl had longed to do so several times. She framed her answer carefully. "Kena has been very supportive, and there are many subjects on which we converse. However, she does not understand either Grfdn mating or female coordination during that time."

"Then, would it be possible to discuss this with Dhgnr?"

Her chest tightened, slowing her breath, but she couldn't

blame Metchell for not realizing how painful his question was. She'd bound and gagged her feelings with the rigid discipline of Grfdn obligation. She was certain even Dhgnr himself didn't know how she felt. Her commitment to Kena would not be broken.

"Dhgnr understands what form of coordination I need from him," she said. "He will not disagree with my decision."

Metchell opened his lips to speak, then closed them when the urgent comm tone sounded from his computer. He read the message and stood. "I'm sorry, Hrndl. I need to go."

She spoke quickly, lest he tell her to leave. "I understand. I'll await your return."

"I'd prefer that you go to your quarters and rest. However, I don't suppose Rnl or Frdn would have the sense to leave you alone."

"I assure you, they have no sense at all!"

"You may use this room as long as you like," he said as he strode to the door. "Make yourself comfortable and relax."

Meanwhile, Kena sat across the table from Dhgnr. His eyes, dark brown and streaked with taupe, stared into hers. His lips parted, but no words made it past them.

"Taboos are a rather interesting concept," Kena said. "They can protect much needed privacy, but they can also conceal much needed information."

"Do you think Hrndl will be pleased with either of us if I break our taboo?"

"Perhaps not, but pleasing her isn't my greatest concern. I fear my ignorance of her needs will harm her. Are you willing to risk her harm in order to maintain a taboo?"

He looked away, his small mouth compressing.

Kena tried again. "Hrndl once mentioned a type of social coordination with indirect benefits. The concept is not unfamiliar to Humans. I'm willing to coordinate in such a way—if only I knew what to do."

"She needs to be encouraged to choose her mate," Dhgnr said. "Soon! Has she given you any indication of whom she prefers?"

Kena sighed and leaned back. "She complains about Frdn slightly less than she complains about Rnl. Hard to call that a preference, unless it's normal for Grfdn females to dislike their mates. Is it?"

Dhgnr's nostrils pinched. "No."

There it was again—that strange surge in his emfrel. She gave him a moment, but he said nothing more.

"Dhgnr, is there something a coordinating female would do other than simply being present?"

"They, uh, may point out flaws or advantages of suitors, particularly if they think the mating female is overlooking something with far-reaching implications." He repositioned himself as though the chair were a foreign thing. "They sometimes arrange for her to have private time with a suitor she favors—or whom they think she ought to favor. I do not see how you can do these things for her, for you do not know what is normal in Grfdn relationships."

Kena stared at her hands. What could she actually do? After a moment, she said, "Well, there are four Grfdn for her to choose from."

"Four?" His eyes opened wide. Good—she had his attention.

"Krdn, of course, she would far rather kill than mate with. Rnl?" Kena shuddered. "Oh, that choice would be hard to endure. There's Frdn. He seems so—unsure of himself."

"He is younger than Hrndl," Dhgnr said, sounding almost breathless in his hurry to speak. "He will likely improve with maturity."

That tone would convince no one. "Of course, there is one other Grfdn. One who—sometimes—seems to have Hrndl's best interests in mind."

"Sometimes?"

Ah, a flash of anger with that. "She has one need that you seem reluctant to meet. If you really are unwilling, this would, of course, exclude you. But I can never quite tell if you actually are as disinterested as you...portray."

He hardly seemed to breathe. "There is...considerably more to this than you are aware of."

"Not surprising." She fixed a pointed gaze on him. "There is a taboo hiding what I need to know."

He shook his head. "It's not the taboo. Hrndl needs my coordination in another matter."

Kena blinked. "You lost me. What other matter?"

"I, uh, I cannot tell you."

Kena placed her fists side by side on the edge of the table and leaned over them. Dhgnr leaned away from her. "I am doing the best I can, groping around in the dark, risking the possibility of saying the wrong thing, while you say nothing. Do you care enough about Hrndl to take a little risk yourself? Such as being forthright?"

The muscles of his forehead worked. "Hrndl still needs to complete her coordination with you."

What? Kena shook her head and raised her brows. "What coordination?"

"From when Frethan was killed."

Kena extended her hands, fingers spread. "What is incomplete?"

"Krdn must be charged before the Grfdn Judgment Council," Dhgnr said. "Hrndl intends to bring that charge. Under the circumstances, she will fail unless she has the support of her khn. If she has recently chosen me as mate, the Council will not consider my contribution."

Kena knit her brow as she thought through this. "Why not?"

The corners of Dhgnr's eyes tilted upward in spite of his tension. "Males have a tendency to do anything a mating female requests. I wouldn't even be permitted to speak before the Council."

"That, I can understand." Kena smirked. "I could name two males who have clearly thrown wisdom to the winds."

Dhgnr's brow shifted. "Thrown wisdom to the winds? A Grfdn would use the phrase *cast their minds to the currents.*"

"Rather surprising how many similar expressions our races have," Kena said, absently tapping her fingers on the table. After a moment, she asked, "Must it be Hrndl who brings the charge against Krdn?"

"In most cases," he said, "only the injured party may bring a charge. In the case of death, the person who was most closely involved in the incident must bring it. Since Hrndl was actively coordinating with you, she has the greatest chance of successfully charging him."

Kena's eyebrows drew together. "Let me be sure I understand this. Hrndl was coordinating with me, but I was the only one in contact with Frethan. Didn't you just say the case would be stronger if I bring the charge instead of Hrndl?"

Dhgnr tensed again. "You are not obligated by Grfdn law."

"But I can bring a charge before your Council if I choose to, can I not?"

"You must not consider such a thing."

"Why not?" she asked.

"The, uh—are you sure you want to talk about this?"

"Quite sure."

"The possibility of a relapse," he said, watching her closely.

"I haven't had relapses—well, not after the first few days, that is."

"Kena, no one speaks of it here. Don't you realize, if you go before the Council, you must give a detailed account of the actual event? Krdn will give his own account."

Kena grew quiet, bringing her hands together and interlacing her fingers. They tightened as her eyebrows bunched together.

Dhgnr grabbed his computer from his belt and tapped out a rapid message.

"He will say there is no proof..." Kena broke off, drew an

audible breath, and swallowed hard. "Is the lack of direct proof why Hrndl will fail if you cannot also speak before the Council?"

"Kena, I've sent for Metchell. Turn your thoughts away from this."

"When you have answered my question, I will do so."

"Yes," he said. "Now turn your thoughts away."

Kena leaned back in her chair, her eyes almost closed. "Turn the audio level up, would you, please?"

Dhgnr reached for the console. The stream and woodland sounds grew louder.

Kena began her relaxation technique, shifting her awareness to the light that dwelled within. The soft whoosh of the door ended it.

Metchell entered. "What's wrong?" he asked, setting his med kit on the table.

"Nothing," Kena said, her voice the essence of peace. "I asked Dhgnr questions pertaining to Krdn and Frethan, which he thought might cause a relapse. But, as you see, it didn't." She sat up straighter and rested her hands on the table. "However, I'm glad you're here. I want to record my memory of being linked with Frethan. Since that could prompt a relapse, I'd like you nearby."

Metchell's mouth dropped open. It took him a moment to respond. "You mean—record the actual memory, not just the recall patterns?"

"The actual memory."

Metchell's mouth still gaped. He swung his gaze around to Dhgnr. "Did you ask her for this?"

"I would never make such a suggestion."

Kena spoke in a firm but calm voice. "I have already told you I was asking the questions. This is my idea."

"Well, it's not a good one," Metchell said. "Do you *want* to have a relapse?"

"No," Kena said. "Nor do I want to have *several* relapses. But that is the risk I face."

Her words made no impact on Metchell's expression.

"What disturbs me—be it ever so irrational—is the question of whether Frethan was still alive when the hull breached. With a permanent record of my memory, that question will be indisputably resolved. I need never again fear that a chance comment will leave me writhing on the floor, gasping for breath. Not a pleasant experience, that. Even if the vacuum stealing my air is only a phantom of memory."

Metchell sighed as understanding registered on his face. "Do you realize this will feel very much like you are actually experiencing it again?"

"Of course." She couldn't avoid the way strain pulled at her lips. "That's why I want you with me. I don't expect to enjoy this, but I really do believe it's worth it."

Metchell drew a breath and let it out. "If you're absolutely certain..."

"I am certain, Metchell."

"I will help you, then. We can do it here, but there are a couple things I must take care of first. Until I'm ready, I don't want you thinking about this. Go lie down and focus entirely on your relaxation technique. I'll join you in a few minutes."

Dhgnr stood to leave, and Kena went to her sleeping room.

As Kena laid her computer on her dresser, Metchell murmured, "What a mission! This is the third time I've been asked to hurt someone in order to help them."

Dhgnr's steps halted, pulling Kena's attention back to the men. He stared at Metchell.

"I left Hrndl in a private consultation room in med section," Metchell said, keeping his voice down. "It's the first door on the right. Will you go tell her I'll be detained for quite a while?"

Dhgnr frowned. "Is she all right?"

"Physically, she's fine, but she's considering a difficult decision."

Kena's eyebrows bunched. Should she go to Hrndl? Dhgnr's words returned to her, and a smile touched her lips. No, she would encourage a little private time for Hrndl and the man she ought to favor.

CHAPTER TWENTY-THREE

Hrndl startled at Dhgnr's voice on the comm system. "Please pardon the intrusion, Hrndl. May I come in?"

She jumped up from the couch and smoothed her hair before pressing the door control. She straightened as it slid open.

Dhgnr took a couple steps into the room, but held silence.

"Did Metchell tell you to come and dissuade me?" she demanded.

"No." How very calm he held his voice. "He asked me to tell you he would be delayed. He did say you were considering a difficult decision, but nothing more than that."

"Not considering, really. I've already decided." Hrndl tried to ease her voice, as though this were something she would normally discuss. "I assume you know what I mean. It's not hard to figure out. You also know that I, alone, have the right to make this decision. Metchell seems to think otherwise. I may need to ask you to support my rights."

He held silence again.

"Well?"

"I'm just trying to envision how I'll get through such a conversation with Metchell."

She understood what he meant. All too well. She swallowed and shifted. "He is direct—not shy of using the actual words or explaining ramifications."

Dhgnr had the courtesy to avert his gaze. "That…must have been unpleasant for you. And frustrating, too, that you have no female for support. I would prefer to—"

"Oh, stop! This only makes it worse. Nothing will change."

Silence stretched. Her body vibrated like a hammered chime. She let a slow breath out to still herself.

"The situation is changing, right now," Dhgnr said, holding to a dispassionate tone. "You need to hear this, so you make your decision with all of the facts. I wish a female were here for you, but I'm the only one available. Will you let me tell you?"

She could no longer be still. Her feet struck the floor as she took a wide stance. "Fine! But I'd like the quick version."

"I'm concerned you will grab at the first conclusion if you don't hear how this came about."

Hrndl uttered a low rumble.

Dhgnr sighed. "As you wish, then. Kena is recording her memory. This will provide clear proof of the exact time and manner of Frethan's death."

Hrndl gasped. "No!" she cried, dashing for the door. "I will not let her."

Dhgnr stepped between her and the door. "You are doing exactly what I feared."

"Get out of my way!"

"You will only cause harm if you interfere now. The decision is Kena's, not yours."

For an instant, she considered thrusting him aside. But he would grasp her and, oh, what then? She couldn't allow physical contact. She spun away to pace the room.

"Was the urgent call to Metchell for Kena?" Hrndl demanded. "How do you know what she is doing?"

"She invited me to stay and talk with her," Dhgnr said. "I sent for Metchell because I felt the conversation was leading her close to a relapse. I was wrong." He inclined his head. "But when Metchell arrived, she asked him to stay with her while she records the memory."

Hrndl stopped pacing and regarded him through narrowed eyes. "So, now there will be proof. Which removes my need for your support before the Council. Oh, yes, I see. That does change things, doesn't it? Now, you can become one of my suitors."

He frowned, slow to answer. "Yes."

"And to accomplish this"—her voice rumbled—"you led Kena right up to a relapse. The very thing I have tried so hard to avoid. In fact, she's probably having a relapse right now. You have intentionally harmed my coordination partner so that you may court me."

"No, Hrndl. You misunderstand."

"How can you possibly think I will ever look at you again? How dare you even come here?"

Dhgnr's voice grated, his calm swept away. "You are lunging at false assumptions. Do you want to know what really happened, or would you rather cling to your imagined version?"

"Must you insult me, too?" Her façade slipped, allowing her voice to crack.

The heat left his brow, and his back relaxed. "Have I said something worse than what you just flung at me?" His voice steadied. "Hrndl, I am only trying to get you to listen. If I cannot speak to you as a friend, then I must speak to you as a khn. You *need* this conversation. Try to calm yourself...please!"

As he did? Far beyond calm, that emotion she heard in his voice. No, she must not mislead herself. Hrndl sank onto the end of the sofa, at the extreme edge of the seat.

Dhgnr took the opposite chair, watching her. She averted her face, but not so far she couldn't see him.

"I didn't lead the conversation with Kena," he said, "and we weren't talking about Frethan or Krdn at first. She wanted to know how Grfdn females coordinate during courtship." He slid his hands back and forth on the armrests of the chair. "The conversation was —surprising. It turned quickly. All of a sudden, she wanted to know why you needed my support in bringing a charge before the Judgment Council. Perhaps you would have realized where she was taking this, but I did not. Then, she conceived the idea of bringing the charge herself."

Hrndl faced him with a gasp and widened eyes. "No! She must not. She'll—"

He nodded. "My reaction, exactly. I intended to convince her that she shouldn't take such a risk. She started to think about what it would entail. That's when I sent for Metchell. She asked if the lack of proof was the reason why your charge was likely to fail. I tried, Hrndl, to get her off this line of thought, but she refused to let it go until I answered her."

"What then?"

"I told her that it was, and then she...well, she just leaned back and relaxed. It cannot be denied, she is extremely proficient at her technique. When Metchell arrived, she told him she wanted to record her memory."

"And he agreed to that?" she asked, incredulous.

"Yes, but..." Dhgnr shifted and propped his weight on his knees. "The reason she gave him had nothing to do with needing proof for charging Krdn. It seemed to be a product of her thoughts about...I suppose, about hearing anyone question when Frethan died. She argued that it would be better to face one relapse than to risk multiple, unexpected relapses." He leaned back. "I don't pretend to know whether that's a valid argument, but Metchell seemed to accept it. He questioned her, making sure she understood the ramifications, and then he agreed to help her. That's when he asked me to come to you."

Hrndl rose and took a few steps, clasping her hands until the knuckles whitened. "Oh, if only you had let me go at once, I might have been able to stop this."

He, too, stood. He took her gently by the arms and turned her to face him. "Hrndl, I strongly doubt the wisdom of that. I wondered, at first, if her reason was to support you. But in the end, I think she was motivated as much by her own needs as by yours."

Hrndl only shook her head, each movement causing it to hang lower. So aware of his touch, yet so awash with memory of what Kena had experienced—was experiencing—she couldn't even respond to him.

Dhgnr waited.

She needed to say something...or do something. She had no idea what. The moment escaped her grasp.

He slid his hands up to her shoulders. His voice changed again...dulled. "In one way, you were right, at the beginning. This does not necessarily change your own decision. If you insist, as khn, I will support your rights to Metchell."

Hrndl's shoulders stopped moving beneath his hands as her breath caught. A stillness like death. Even though he was free to court her, he would tell Metchell to remove her ovary? Air escaped through her constricted throat.

He jerked at the sound, as though he'd been straining against bands that finally snapped. He clamped his freed arms around her, crushing her against his chest. "I dread you asking that of me!"

Hrndl melted into his embrace, her breath fast and panting.

He loosened his grip. "Hrndl, are you all right?"

"I...I don't know. I didn't sleep at all last night. I'm—I'm so exhausted, I just can't—"

He supported her with one arm and used the other hand to tilt her face upward.

She turned tired eyes up to his and gazed without restraint. His eyes tilted. She leaned onto his arm, so completely, she would have fallen if his strength failed. Her weight seemed to tug his eyes into the highest smile she'd ever seen on him.

"Then I had better get you rested tonight. I'm taking you to your quarters. And don't worry, I won't let the fools disturb you."

Hrndl let him lead her there, tucked within the haven of his embrace all the way.

CHAPTER TWENTY-FOUR

Hrndl arrived at Kena's quarters early the next morning. She paused just inside the door, concern in her eyes. Kena answered her unspoken question with a smile. "I'm fine. I slept like a baby all night. Most of the evening, too, now that I think of it. Sorry to have deserted you. How was your evening?"

Hrndl's eyelids dropped, but she couldn't stop their corners from rising. "It started dreadfully and ended delightfully."

"Excellent!"

"Kena—I must ask you something. I'm not sure if you'll like it."

"I suppose that explains why you're still standing over by the door as though you don't know you're welcome. I hope you don't intend to stay there, because I'm not ready." Kena turned back into her sleeping room and went to the mirror.

Hrndl followed her and leaned against the doorframe.

"What is this thing I may not like?" Kena asked as she combed her hair.

"Well, in a way, it's something you've already been doing. But things have changed a little…a lot, in fact. I need to formally ask if you will coordinate with me through the end of my courtship."

Kena laid her comb aside and hid her grin by searching for a pair of earrings in one of the dresser's compartments. "Certainly, my dear. No, I have that wrong. I should have said beyond doubt." She met Hrndl's eyes in the mirror as she put an earring in. "If we're going to coordinate, though, you can't leave me guessing. You'll have to tell me what you need, whether it's taboo or not."

"I realized that last night. First of all, I'm down to the last few days, so I need you to stay with me when I'm not in my quarters. Dhgnr has been doing that lately when you weren't available, but he is not…His perception can no longer be considered… uh…impartial."

Kena laughed. "Hrndl, you look so coy. I had no idea you could even make such an expression."

Hrndl assumed her most dignified posture, but her eyes still smiled. "Second, when I have made my decision, I will need you to tell my other suitors."

"Ooh. Won't they love to hear that from me!"

"No, they won't," Hrndl said. "That's why I thought you wouldn't like this. As soon as we get to the dining hall, I'm going to tell them I've asked you for courtship coordination. They must respect whatever you say. But I don't think anyone has ever asked this of a non-Grfdn."

"I see," Kena said dryly. "Do I have to break the news to them in private?"

"No, but neither I nor my accepted suitor should be present. The others won't appreciate a public statement, but you needn't be completely alone with them."

"That's good. Do you need to be released from duty?"

"Not now. That would be awful! I intend to stay as busy as I possibly can. I've already requested simulation time for us this morning. I'm sure we'll be in astro after that."

"This is so confusing," Kena said as she closed the dresser's cover. "I thought I was supposed to make sure you're with your suitors. Now, you've planned the day so as to avoid them."

"Not exactly. They can still come to me if they want to—if they are off duty." Hrndl repositioned her computer on her belt. "It so happens, Dhgnr is off duty today."

Kena leaned against her dresser with her arms folded. "What a coincidence that he has an extra day off at this particular time."

Hrndl uttered her gargling laugh and walked back into the sitting room. Kena followed.

"Once I tell them you're providing courtship coordination," Hrndl said, "you have a certain degree of authority over them. If you object to their courtship behavior, you are to demand that they stop immediately."

Kena raised her brows. "And if they don't?"

Hrndl's eyes narrowed, and her low voice rumbled. "They wouldn't dare!"

As soon as Kena and Hrndl sat down at the Grfdn table for first meal, Hrndl made her statement.

Kena watched Rnl's reaction. What would or wouldn't he dare?

He threw her a contemptuous glance. "There is no reason to bring a non-Grfdn into matters of courtship."

"It is Hrndl's prerogative, not yours," Dhgnr said. "If you want to dispute it, you will need to state your complaint to a female khn. Since Hrndl now has a companion, I have decided to court her."

Second meal increased Kena's concerns. Hrndl went immediately to the lavish feast spread across her table—plenty to sate the appetite of a troop, or of one mating female. Dhgnr and Rnl sat on either side of her. Kena selected her own meal from the buffet and turned around in time to see Rnl's hand slide up Hrndl's back. She jerked and arched her spine. Dhgnr twisted around to see, his sneer transforming his face.

Kena strode to the table as the two men came to their feet,

fists clenched. "Gentlemen, do not crowd Hrndl. Move to the other side."

Dhgnr redirected his motion to step around the table, but Rnl drew himself up to full height, shoulders wide and chest thrust forward.

He was a big man. Formidable. Kena let none of these thoughts show in her eyes, which never flinched from his.

"You are ignorant," Rnl snapped. "You have no idea what she needs. Do not interfere!"

"My concern is for Hrndl, and that she has time to eat in peace. What are you concerned about? Or perhaps I should ask, who?" Kena took the chair Dhgnr had vacated.

Rnl's voice ground. "Hrndl, beyond doubt." He handed her a serving dish, which she had yet to sample, and took the chair on the other side of the table.

While Rnl seethed and Dhgnr conversed with Hrndl, Frdn stared at Kena as though he was suddenly realizing she was significant.

In the hallway several minutes later, Hrndl linked her arm through Kena's. "You were perfect, my dear!"

Kena turned her head to stare at her as they walked. "But I hardly said anything."

"Asking Rnl what or who he cared about: you revealed a character flaw—that he was more interested in his own desire than my right to choose. That's exactly the sort of thing a Grfdn female would say. How did you figure out what fits in my culture?"

"I didn't figure anything out." Warmth rose in Kena's chest. "It's just what I would say."

G hent strode through the astro section, searching for key navigators to make sure they were all present. His gaze rested on Kena for a moment, judging her condition. Hrndl murmured something to her, and Kena's musical laughter reached

Ghent's ears. He breathed a sigh and turned his attention to Hrndl. She was looking up at Dhgnr now, her eyes tilted.

His presence was a minor infraction, since Ghent had withdrawn approval for lounging in astro section. Too much work to be done—too many people who really needed to be there. Dhgnr didn't fit that description, but if he could keep Hrndl calm, he was welcome. So long as the other two didn't show up and create a disturbance.

Ghent continued toward the central 3-D display area. The remnants of the two moons drifted in their erratic orbits as other objects sped by. This wasn't a live image, but a projection of debris locations ten hours from now. Gray shading was superimposed over the blackness of space, showing density of fragments too small to see on the image. The lightest gray indicated thickest density. Two course plans ran together through a dark tunnel then forked, one path leading to the large moon and the other to the small one.

Delf glanced up as Ghent approached. "Looks more like a foggy morning than a starry night, doesn't it?"

Ghent studied the image. "Yes, unfortunately, it does."

"The good news," Delf said, "is that our projections are good for 36 hours out. Don't talk to Netlyn about it, though. She'll tell you we're only 19 percent accurate that far ahead. She's such a pessimist."

Ghent smiled, but said, "Display the sampling needs for me."

"As you order, sir." Delf strung the words out, reaching for his console, "But I'm only displaying an image. I had nothing to do with the sample request."

Ghent shot him a quizzical look before turning back to the display. "What is—" He swung around to find a scientist. Betnorel had the misfortune of being nearby. "Betnorel, what is that?" Ghent demanded, pointing at the display.

The startled scientist looked up at the yellow areas spreading across large sections of the display. "Oh...well...it's our sampling needs, sir."

"How can you possibly need this much material? What are you trying to do? Reconstruct a moon?"

"No, no. Of course not. We just want that material dragged clear of the debris field and anchored in a safe area. Then, we'll be able to inspect it and get the specific samples we need."

"Oh, is that all?"

Betnorel squirmed at the choppy sarcasm. One of his colleagues tried to support him. "We understand that..."

"You understand nothing!" The room grew silent as Ghent strode to a console and swept his hands across the controls. "What I said was, we had a window of opportunity to reach the moon debris and collect samples." Objects in the display began to move, and Ghent addressed all of the scientists. "I know this looks safe in the timeframe displayed, but look at the progression. Within 28 hours, the routes will be inundated with debris. What you have asked for will take more than a week to pull out. We have a day. Apparently, you're used to working without time constraints. You do not have that luxury here."

Piert, the Veet chief scientist, crossed the room while Ghent spoke. "Sorry I wasn't here when you saw this, sir. We don't really want this much matter, but let me explain. The problem is, we can't get accurate enough scans to know which specific objects we need. We can only identify the areas of highest concentrations."

"Do you think, perhaps, you could exclude a few areas? Say, about 90 percent of them."

"Yes, we can. But then, we risk sending the navigators into that mess for twenty-eight hours, only to have them come back with inadequate material."

Ghent kept his lips closed, yielding nothing.

Betnorel hurried into speech, apparently trying to make at least a small sacrifice. "Well, I'm not sure who added this," he said, pointing to one area. "It's kind of out of the way. We can do without it and save some time."

"Netlyn added that one," Thrayl said.

Ghent looked at her. "Reason?"

Leaning against a table with her arms folded, she said, "It has a high concentration of benzlium."

"Ah. I'm glad someone considers energy sources. The benzlium will be brought back in the first collection run. As for the rest, the sample size must be reduced. Netlyn, can you help them with their scans?"

"I already have. I've also trained several of them in refined techniques, and I've checked their work. Even I can't get better isolation in all that chaos. There's only one way to do it."

"Well?" Ghent prompted.

Netlyn walked slowly forward, perhaps thinking her idea would gain little favor. "We go in close to the clusters, scan at short range, choose our samples based on the new data, and then drag them out."

Delf shook his head. "We'd have to devote too many navigators to scanning. With all the time that'll consume, and with so few of us piloting, we won't get nearly as much as they actually need. You must know that, Netlyn."

"I can calculate the numbers as well as you can, but I'm not leaving out a significant portion of the crew. Think beyond the navigators. They aren't the only people on the *Ontrevay* capable of scanning."

"Are you suggesting we bring scientists with us to scan?" Kena asked.

Netlyn nodded, though several navigators made sounds of scorn or disbelief.

Piert scowled and declared, "We are no more afraid to fly the debris field than you are. We are willing to do our part."

"It's not a question of daring or willingness," Delf said. "I know a lot of you can scan for composition, but there is a huge difference between that and scanning for trajectory. And once we're flying, it's trajectory that matters most."

"All true," Netlyn said, "but the scientists needn't do both. We'll assign two navigators to each craft. We'd do that anyway, so one can monitor the extended range while the other pilots. The scientists can focus entirely on identifying samples."

"It will still take too long," Giddech said, "for them to get the composition data they need."

Netlyn shook her head. "Not as long as you think. I've taught a lot of them enough about projection so they can keep their scans focused, even for unstable movement. They already knew the basics, and they do fairly well. We can fit eight extra scanning consoles into each of our two transport craft and use them as command ships. The mid-sized craft will each hold two to four extra consoles. They can do additional scanning while the navigators work on collection. The hardest part is, we will all need to fly during the entire period and take turns sleeping en route. Considering capacity and timing, we should be able to make three runs, there and back. I've worked the numbers. It's tight, but doable. I estimate we'll be able to get about 90 percent of the material they really want."

Dhgnr leaned close to Hrndl and whispered, "Will this work?"

Hrndl said, "Netlyn knows scanning better than anyone on the *Ontrevay*. She also knows how to assess skills and train. This is the best proposal I've heard yet."

Ghent looked around the room, his eyes sweeping across each face. "Other suggestions?"

No one looked happy, but no one spoke. He focused on Kena. She nodded. "I concur."

He turned to Delf, who exhaled and said, "I can go with it."

"All right; we'll do it," Ghent said, at last, moving his hands over the console as he spoke. "We're only nine hours from final launch preparation. Krdn, pick minimum staff to stay on duty. All other navigators are now off duty. You'll have time for third meal, then sleep. The same goes for any of the scientists who're going out. You'll be flying until the window closes, so get rested now. If any of you have inflexible sleep cycles, talk to Metchell. I'm sure he can artificially alter them.

Ghent looked around at specific individuals. "Krdn, Netlyn,

and Piert, I want you in my consult room in ten minutes for crew assignments. Dhgnr, you may as well come with me, now. Remlishos is on his way to meet with me already. The maintenance crews don't sleep until the craft have been outfitted with the extra consoles."

Ghent headed for the door. In his peripheral vision, he saw Hrndl lean close to Kena's ear, then hurry to her feet. He was hoping to talk with Dhgnr alone, but Hrndl came with him, rendering the discreet inquiry he'd wanted to make impossible. He waited until the three of them were alone in the hallway before saying, "Hrndl, forgive me for prying into your personal affairs, but I need to know how long you'll be able to fly."

"Metchell checked my hormone levels yesterday evening. I should be able to make it to the end of this expedition."

"I'd like Metchell to check on you each time you bring in a collection. Do you want to fly with Kena?"

"Beyond doubt, but I'd so much rather have Dhgnr check on me than Metchell."

Ghent glanced over at her. Not only were her eyes tilted upward, but her thin eyebrows also slanted toward her temples. Dhgnr appeared to be massaging her lower back as they walked, much to her pleasure. "You can have both of them," Ghent said. "Is there anything else you need?"

"No, not unless you'd like to confine Rnl and Frdn to their quarters for the next few days. I could probably get them to fight, if you need an infraction."

Ghent laughed and led the way into his consult room. "I'd rather just keep them busy, if you don't mind too much."

CHAPTER TWENTY-FIVE

Kena took her time, while everyone else converged on the dining hall. It would be best if the others were settled before she arrived. She didn't intend to eat there anyway. She felt an urge to spend the evening before this particular mission alone. How convenient—and how predictable—that Hrndl had already chosen her mate. That whispered information left Kena one last little duty.

An obscure impression slowed her steps. Disquiet. No other word for it. She examined the feeling, turning her attention toward the one who never left her. Their conversation was always in progress, even without wrapping words around it. She listened, but felt only his presence. *Give me wisdom, please*, she said within herself. *I don't want to say the wrong thing.*

Stay alert.

Hmm. Unexpected.

The door to the dining hall slid open as she neared it, and she scanned the room. Good. Almost everyone was seated and eating. She avoided eye contact, but she couldn't help noticing Inewin. His passing glance became a double take, encompassing the Grfdn table. At least one person was aware.

Rnl and Frdn sat before an array of dishes Hrndl would not eat from. They both faced the door with expressions of stone, watching Kena approach. She sat down opposite them, rehearsing the traditional Grfdn statement Hrndl had primed her with. Brief, direct, and cold. No doubt the best way to communicate with these men.

Keeping her voice low, she said, "Hrndl has chosen her mate: Dhgnr. You will cease courting her. You will not approach Dhgnr or Hrndl until her seclusion has ended."

Frdn began the formal acknowledgement. "I accept her choice and honor th—"

A growl vibrated within Rnl's throat, rising to drown Frdn's words.

So boorish! Now what? Hrndl had said nothing of what to do with such a response. Most likely, he would not have dared it before a Grfdn woman. Rnl stood, and Kena rose, eyeing his movements.

"I will not take this from you. Dhgnr twisted courtship law, and I will not—"

"Do you accept Hrndl's choice," Kena demanded, "or do you refuse her the right to choose her own mate?"

His throat worked.

"No answer?" Kena asked. "This will be so noted, should the matter need to be raised before a Grfdn khn. I repeat: You will not approach Dhgnr or Hrndl until her seclusion has ended."

Kena turned her back and strode for the door, listening for movement behind her. A heavy foot struck the floor.

Shouts erupted, all uttered at once.

"Rnl, stop!"

"Kena! Beware!"

"Duck!"

She snatched a quick look back.

Rnl's shoulder drew back as he raised his fist. A growl thundered from him. How fitting that he sounded like an animal.

Kena folded at the hip. His punch whiffed above her back as she jabbed a sharp back-kick to his right knee.

His growl faltered and he struggled for balance.

She straightened, bracing a fist into her hand and driving her right elbow back into his head.

The blow caught him beneath the chin and toppled him. Kena jumped away as he fell. His back thudded hard on the floor, his breath forced out as a grunt.

She glared down at him from a couple meters away. Chairs scraped as several men leapt up, but they were still too far away. Rnl shifted as if to rise.

"Do not stand!" Kena's order reverberated in the breathless silence of the hall. Her gaze pinned him to the floor. "Frdn, is Rnl's behavior legal on Grfdn?"

"No!"

"Nor is it legal on Earth," Kena said between her teeth.

Remlishos came to a halt near Rnl's head. Kena let out a deep breath and dragged her eyes up to his.

"I'll take care of it," Remlishos said. "Nice defense, by the way. You are not injured, are you?"

She shook her head.

"Get your rest, then. This need not concern you."

Kena left, adrenaline quickening her stride.

Footsteps hastened after her. Inewin said, "May I escort you?"

"If you wish, but I'm fine. It's not necessary to interrupt your meal."

"I'm in no hurry. If you're fine, why are you rubbing your elbow."

She huffed a wry laugh. "Because Rnl's chin is quite hard. Not to worry. A bruise maybe, nothing more." She walked in silence for a moment, pulling peace from within and slowing her stride. "Thank you for your warning. Were you watching the whole time?"

"I was. Hrndl's and Dhgnr's absence was—concerning, shall we say."

A couple minutes after they reached her quarters, Delatin

arrived with a container of food, which he placed on the table between them. He looked closely at her. "Are you all right?"

"Yes, of course," she said with her easy smile. "Thank you so much for bringing me dinner."

"My pleasure. Rest well."

Delatin hurried back to his kitchen, and Kena opened the meal container.

"Why the pensive look?" Inewin asked.

"Just thinking about how long it will take for the rumors to reach Hrndl."

She took a bite of bread and entered a message to Hrndl and Dhgnr on her computer. "Just to let you know, I've informed Frdn and Rnl. Frdn responded honorably. You may hear rumors of Rnl's idiocy, but all is well. You will not see him. Enjoy your evening. I'll see you in the morning."

Before she could finish her dinner, she received three messages asking if she was all right, and Jorlit, who had not been in the dining hall, stopped by her quarters.

"Really, I am fine, Jorlit," Kena said. "The rumors must be wildly out of hand."

"All I heard was that Rnl attacked you. How could you possibly not be hurt?"

Kena shrugged one shoulder. "He is slow. I am fast. Blows don't hurt if you aren't there when the fist arrives."

"You'd understand if you had seen it," Inewin said. "I hardly knew she was about to move before she stopped." The door chime sounded again, and Inewin stood. "You aren't going to get any rest at this rate. Shall I get rid of whoever it is?"

"That might be awkward. This one is Ghent." Kena touched the door control and stood.

Jorlit asked, "How do you know?" as the door slid open.

"I can sense him." She acknowledged Ghent as she returned dishes to the container. "Inewin," she said, "if you're going back to the dining hall, will you take these things?"

"Of course. I'll do what I can with the rumors."

Jorlit left with him, and Kena turned her attention to Ghent.
"Are you being inundated with—"

Her message signal interrupted him. Kena rolled her eyes, and
Ghent chuckled.

"Excuse me a moment," Kena said, "while I restrict messages."
She tapped her computer, indicating the few people whose
messages should be announced, and set her status to *sleep*.

"You are blessed with many friends," Ghent said. "Were you
referring to me a moment ago when you said you could
'sense him'?"

"Yes." Kena moved to the couch and sat against the curve of
one end so she could face Ghent.

He took the opposite end. "I didn't realize your sensitivity to
me remains. Is my emfrel still disturbing?"

"Not at all. I can feel every non-Human, but it's only a faint
awareness."

"Sounds distracting," he said.

"No more than having a person stand next to you."

His quick nod ended the subject, and his voice grew choppy.
"Let's get the annoying matter out of the way first. I've linked with
Remlishos. His formal report states that Rnl attacked you from
behind and you defended yourself. Rnl is confined to his quarters;
only Remlishos or I can release him. That will not happen for the
next few days, at the very least. Any concerns?"

Kena angled her head. "Sounds perfect."

"I thought you might approve." His speech smoothed. He ran
through crew and craft assignments and additional details of the
mission. "I am giving you command of the beta crew. That's a little
touchy, since Hrndl has several more years of experience than
you do."

He paused. Kena guessed at the question that troubled him. "I
still value her experience even though I have command," she said.
"We'll be switching tasks, anyway, and must pass command back
and forth in order to sleep. When we're both awake, we'll be
working as a team, as we always do." His expression hadn't changed

so she added a little more. "To me, the designation of command is for clarity of direction—for those rare moments when decisions must be instantaneous and unquestioned."

"Not everyone sees command in that way," Ghent said.

"True. Among Humans, as well. Are you concerned about my perception or Hrndl's?"

"Both," he said, "but I've already spoken to Hrndl about it. She doesn't take it as a slight."

"Are you afraid it will inflate my ego and turn me into a despot?"

Ghent leaned back and laughed. "In spite of your confidence, I have yet to find a delusional side to your ego." His expression grew serious again. "I am thinking of the future. You assume command readily. Be equally ready to relinquish it, for I will likely give Hrndl command of the next mission. Will that be a problem for you?"

Odd. Had she overstepped or been too foreward at some point? "Not at all," she said, shaking her head. "That is just not the way I think."

His intent gaze filled a silence. He slowed his words. "Even though we have spoken often, Kena, I still don't feel I understand the way you think."

What to say? It almost sounded as though he hoped she would offer to link with him. But for what reason? Plynteth linked freely among themselves and telepathic races, but surely he must know Humans did not link without significant purpose.

Ghent gestured toward the book on the low table by the couch. "Are you reading tonight?"

"Yes, I was planning to."

"Will you permit me to stay and listen?" he asked.

So intriguing that he liked to hear her read. "You are welcome to." She picked up the Bible and flipped to the ninety-first Psalm. "This poem is about protection and security in the midst of danger."

"How appropriate, considering what you're flying into tomorrow."

A smile sufficed to answer him. She read, letting the words unroll in their lyrical beauty, savoring their meaning, absorbing their promise. Her beloved was with her, embracing her.

When she finished, comfortable silence lay between them. How nice that Ghent didn't feel the need to disturb it. For a few minutes, she leaned back with eyes closed, drifting in the arms of her love.

Her beloved spoke within her. *He is so puzzled.*

She opened her eyes to Ghent's gaze. Yes, his fur-covered brow was puckered.

"Hrndl told me once," he said, "that she enjoys your quarters because it's so peaceful here. I thought she must mean the sights and sounds of nature, but—it's not that."

Her eyelids dipped then opened. "No, it is not."

Ghent turned his head, and his brow fur twitched into a vertical pattern. "You seem both relaxed and vibrant. Intensely so. How can you simultaneously be in such opposite states?"

She chuckled deep in her throat, pleased that he interpreted with such clarity in spite of the paradox.

Her beloved's words whispered through her spirit. *Let him see.*

Now? When I am so stirred by your presence?

His presence lightened. It did not leave; rather, it drew back from her mind, settling within her spirit.

"Kena..." Ghent licked his lips. "If it will not stress you...will you link with me?"

Her breath halted for an instant. He really did want to link. Strange—and yet, perhaps not. She would have avoided this, but the prompting a moment ago changed all that.

Concern flickered in his eyes at her silence. "I know you must control the link. I do not mind, at all. And I also understand that Plynteth are overwhelming to a Human. The link can be very brief. I don't want to tire you."

She prepared herself, breathing her words out gently. "You will not overwhelm or tire me. You think that you understand, but you don't. If you wish to link, reach for me."

"But—if you are to control the link—do you not prefer to initiate it?"

Her words were hardly more than a whisper. "Reach for me, Ghent."

S trange. How exactly was this supposed to work? Ghent held his telepathic energy in check as he extended his awareness ever so slightly. Then, he sucked in a breath.

She was all around him. Had been there before him. His mind reeled.

She contained him. Like hands surrounding a fluttering bird: touching only where the feathers brushed, slowly enfolding to still his reaction.

All is well, The thought swept through his mind like the hushing breath of a gentle wind.

The peace he had recognized—it was her! He'd thought he glimpsed its abundance, but that had only been a thin, outer layer. And even more surprising, she was restraining the revelation—only showing another layer. How deep could it be?

He absorbed her internal response. She smiled at his amazement. The expression contained fond pleasure. Not that he could see her face, but he knew what this smile looked like. His understanding pleased her. More than he would have thought possible. Yet, even this was restrained.

She was drawing back, now that his first reaction had eased. *Be still until you're accustomed.*

He was supposed to be remembering something. Oh, yes. Not to tire her. They laughed together at the absurdity of it.

Her silent words formed in his mind. *What do you wonder?*

Had there been something specific? *Ah. I have wondered about your range—how it could reach so far. I know that now.*

That brought a memory of Frethan to his mind and an answering memory in hers. Impressions touched his awareness: the moment when she had comforted Frethan and his reaction to her. So quick, barely there. As their sadness brushed past one another, the sting of his pain faded. Then, she took them beyond the memory.

What else do you puzzle over?

His words from before they linked came to mind. *So relaxed—I see that now—your peace. But I cannot see the vibrancy.*

Playfulness stirred through the link. He had heard it before in her laugh, seen it in the mischief of her tilted glance and quick smile. She teased. *Ah! I do not know if you really want to see that!*

But she let him see it, nonetheless. Or a sliver of what he termed vibrancy, for even that tiny glimpse was overwhelming. To correlate this indescribable experience, she led his thoughts to the nature of Plynteth, observed as he framed it within his world, resonated with the free flight and the power portrayed in his images.

Vibrancy didn't begin to describe this force. It was the cataract that burst from the cliff face and crashed down the canyon wall. It was the bird climbing to the crest of a thermal, diving, wheeling upward in great arcs, effortlessly powered by the momentum of its dive.

In a way, the insufficient analogies saddened him. Nature could not capture this feeling, for it wasn't truly a feeling. It was a flight of joy, powered by love. He longed to remember the nuances and depths of its majesty.

Not to worry, she assured him. *It will ever remain. Use the images to draw it back.* She followed the waterfall he had imagined, to the river it formed, and swept a stream aside to wind lazily into quiet shade. There, she left him in the peace he had first witnessed, watchful and careful until the link was no more.

Ghent let the moments stretch—let the memories settle. He could not speak yet, anyway. He knew better than to try to force words after a link so rich. It would have been pleasant to dwell in the images she left him with, but he still had duties to perform. He didn't even know how long the link had lasted. Probably longer than he had time to spare. This reverie must end.

"Thank you, Kena," he said. "That was...amazing!"

"You are most welcome." Her faint smile meant so much more to him now. The corners lifted higher and the teasing note crept into her voice. "It was not what you were expecting, was it?"

"Not at all! To think I worried about tiring you."

She chuckled. "Did *I* tire *you?*"

"No. Oddly enough, you didn't. How long was that?" He checked his computer to answer his own question. Another surprise.

She shrugged. "Only a few minutes."

"I would have guessed twenty. Or even more."

Kena's eyebrows rose. "Time is a rather interesting concept: no more significant than distance."

He suddenly understood what she meant, the reason why it had not mattered how far away Frethan was when she linked with him. The reason she could sense a person outside her quarters. So many other things. He remembered what Frethan had said about her skill in designing a dimensional slip course. Time no more significant than distance? That hinted at something he ought to realize about her, but couldn't quite grasp.

A sigh escaped as he stood. "Kena, I would love to stay all night and talk with you, but neither of us can."

"True. There will be another day."

"Rest well, Kena."

"I shall," she whispered.

If a sculptor sought to depict serenity, he would find no better model than Kena.

CHAPTER TWENTY-SIX

Ghent awoke at the precise moment he had chosen. A short sleep, but no matter. He would have time for more soon. Twenty minutes before launch, he entered the bay on the second-level walkway, which partially ringed the vast room.

Activity buzzed below him. Craft had been pulled from their storage positions. All three shifts of navigators were in the bay, as well as the scientists who would accompany them. Support crew scurried between them, completing final checks and responding to last minute orders.

The alpha command ship stood ready near the bay doors. A cylindrical payload module separated the paraboloid navigation module and the primary drive. The reflective surface of the nav module's transparent hull gleamed gold under the bay's lights. By comparison, the white payload module looked mundane. A section of its hull had been lowered to form an access ramp. Delf stood on the ramp behind Netlyn, head and shoulders above her. The entire alpha crew clustered around them, listening to Netlyn's instructions.

Below Ghent, Kena also stood on her command ship's ramp.

The white mesh and inner control ring of an EVA belt contrasted with her black navigation suit and emphasized the curve of her waist. Could she seriously be considering extra-vehicular activities? The beta crewmembers stood around her, preoccupied with securing their EVA belts. Support crew moved among them, distributing belts to those who didn't have their own and verifying that they were properly set. Hrndl jumped down from the ramp to assist a scientist who was having trouble getting hers configured for her race.

Krdn came to stand beside Ghent.

"EVA belts?" Ghent demanded. "Explain to me why the beta crew thinks they'll be leaving their craft."

"They don't. It's a precautionary measure. Most of them think it's unnecessary, but Kena has declared that she will fly no one to the large moon unless they are wearing life support field generators."

That made more sense. The shield of an EVA belt would deploy the instant pressure changed. Since they were designed for repairs, the field was configured to wrap the fingers individually. It was possible to use a console, even with the field deployed. Awkward to a novice, but workable.

A member of the beta crew lifted the belt he was still holding and called up to Ghent. "Captain, will you tell Kena and Hrndl we don't need these clumsy things?"

Ghent emphasized each word. "You will obey every order they give you."

The scientist made haste to fasten his belt.

"Any changes since I went to sleep?" Ghent asked Krdn.

"Plans are essentially the same. The command ships may do some collecting as long as they can keep data streams open with the secondary craft."

"Did Delf or Kena name any groupings of their craft?"

"Delf named pairs: red, green, blue, and yellow. Kena named quads." Disapproval crept into Krdn's voice. "Amethyst, sapphire, emerald, amber, and ruby."

Ghent shook his head. "I shouldn't have expected Kena to choose a common designation. Do the gem names have significance?"

"She says they are *fitting* names because of the crystals found in the beta crust sample she brought back. They are ordered according to the light spectrum from violet to red."

"I suppose that is a fitting choice for Kena. Any issues with the crew?"

"Not with these two groups," Krdn said. "Rnl is claiming cultural interference. He sends me incessant demands to wake you so he can issue a formal complaint." The contempt in his voice explained why Ghent's sleep had been undisturbed.

Ghent snorted. "You may tell him I will see him when I have time—which will not be soon. Is Frdn causing any trouble?"

"No. He's been on duty half the night doing comm device checkouts. There is concern over the effectiveness of communication through the debris field."

"Yes, I know," Ghent said. "You've kept minimal nav staff here, as I instructed?"

"There are two navigators in Nav command and one in ex op command."

"Then, we'd better get to ex op ourselves. It'll soon be time to open the bay."

K ena remained on her hatch ramp as her orders were carried out. Around her, hatch after hatch closed and sealed with a soft hiss. Netlyn and the alpha command crew had disappeared into their ship. Delf stood alone on the ramp, watching the last of his group seal their hatches.

Kena could just make out Netlyn's voice from within their craft. "Checkouts are complete. All craft have reported ready for launch."

"Acknowledged," Delf said over his shoulder. He raised his voice and called to Kena. "We're ready to exit."

He was way too serious. Kena drew on a couple Veet idioms, put her hands on her hips, and struck an attitude. "Well, hoist your sails, then. D'you think my thumbs want to jig while you paddle out of my way?"

This sally won her a lopsided grin, and Delf swung into his ship. The ramp rose behind him and sealed.

Kena entered her ship and slapped the hatch control. The ramp rose and embedded into the hull. She checked the seal then said over her shoulder to Hrndl, "Tell ex op all beta ships are sealed."

Kena grabbed a handhold on the hull's interior. While she waited for the gravitational field to release, she watched the eight scientists strapped into seats before their consoles. Good, they had all figured out how to re-form their couches to make room for the EVA units fitted against their backs. Remarkably small, those units were, but even a small pack would make acceleration painful if the couches weren't adjusted.

Thrayl answered a question from a colleague, already fulfilling the responsibility Kena had assigned him for coordinating the scientists' work. Calm and dependable; and, according to Netlyn, he could track an object as well as a navigator. A couple of the others worried her a bit, but Thrayl could manage that issue, if need be.

Within moments, Kena's feet floated away from the floor. A few seconds later, the hull shuddered. The bay doors had opened and the vacuum had snatched at the waiting ships, making them strain against their anchors. Six of her crew took these changes complacently. The faces of the other two betrayed shaky composures, but they kept their lips clamped.

Kena pushed away from the handhold. She pirouetted a turn and a half as she rose toward grips embedded in the high ceiling then propelled herself forward. She sailed through the navigation module's airlock, entering the cockpit with her knees drawn up to her chest. Hrndl was already strapped into the right-hand couch. Kena extended her legs toward the other and eased away from the transparent ceiling. Drifting down, she slid her legs under the console and grabbed the floating lap belt. She secured it the instant she landed in her couch.

"You make it look like a dance," Hrndl said, closing the door, which was really the inner hatch of the airlock, but now served only to block sound between the two connected modules.

"Zero G should always be considered a dance. Just as flying should be." Kena secured her shoulder straps and pulled her console down close to her legs. "Any problems reported with checkout?"

"None yet. Still waiting on two craft. How did our rookies take the transition?"

"Pretty well. Leelee and Presh looked nervous, but game. I think they'll do." Kena watched the alpha command ship head out into the black void beyond the bay doors. Smaller craft followed it, spreading out to fly a four-point formation behind it. "There, now. Isn't that as pretty as any dance you've ever seen?"

Hrndl gave her a Grfdn smile and said, "A few weeks ago, all this talk of dancing would have gotten you a sharp reprimand for taking your responsibilities far too casually."

Kena grinned. "Beyond doubt, you'd have refused to fly with me." The last checkout confirmation appeared on her display. She opened the comm channel to ex op and said, "Beta crew is fully checked out."

"Acknowledged. Stand by."

With very little to do at this point, Kena and Hrndl both gazed out of the transparent hull of the navigation module. The only obstructions to their view were four narrow struts. These served double duty, housing the module's field generator and supporting the forward nav jets. The interior layout was also designed to give them maximum viewing area. Even the airlock doors and the floor between the couches were transparent. Kena could pull the low-profile console so close to her lap, the direction and power control sticks rested beside her thighs. Power reserves were located beneath her and Hrndl's couches. Remaining systems were housed in enclosures directly behind them, on either side of the airlock. The three-dimensional scanning display was currently projected just above their feet, but it could also be superimposed on the hull, showing the long-range image in alignment with nearby objects.

The last alpha craft slipped out of view. With no visible reference point, the blackness of space closed in like an ebony wall. They awaited the next command from ex op.

Ghent's voice said, "Kena, you are clear to launch."

She released her anchor field. With minimal thrust, the ship rose from the floor and sailed into the void. Away from the bay's lighting, glittering sparks and misty streaks of dust spread across the panorama. Kena brought her primary drive on line.

After a moment, she asked, "Any surprises for me yet?"

"Scans match predictions," Hrndl said.

Kena opened the comm channel to her craft and ordered, "Amethyst units one and two, launch."

Two craft sailed out of the bay together. One rose, and the other descended into their formation positions.

As soon as they separated, she ordered, "Units three and four, launch."

This pair separated to the right and left.

A moment later, Hrndl said, "Amethyst quad is in proper position. Primary drives powering up."

"Sapphire units five and six, launch." Kena continued ordering each of the pairs out until five quads followed behind her ship. She altered course and curved away from the *Ontrevay*. Twenty craft followed in cone formation. When all were aligned with their planned course and fully powered, she announced, "Prepare to initiate programmed course. Synchronize to my countdown."

Kena opened a comm channel to her science crew and said, "Prepare for acceleration in ten seconds." The numbers counted down on her console. She spoke the last few aloud. "Three, two, one."

The force pinned her to her couch. The formation streamed after her like a banner stretched out by a mighty wind. Minutes ticked by, as the primary drive hurtled her ship toward the gap in the debris field.

Far ahead, the alpha craft approached the gap. Delf's voice came over a comm channel Hrndl had opened before acceleration. "Alpha command reporting status for all craft. We are on target. Near scans of the corridor are within prediction margin."

The *Ontrevay* responded. Kena toyed with giving Delf a little more banter, but it was too much effort to reach for her comm controls. The minutes continued to pass, and Kena's toes grew numb. The debris field rushed toward her, faster and faster. Finally, the primary drive completed its acceleration burn. Invisible weight released Kena's chest. She activated her navigational systems and checked scans, while Hrndl confirmed status with the other navigators.

Kena made her own status report to the *Ontrevay*, told Hrndl to take over piloting, and opened the module's door. She released her restraints, twisted around, and floated high enough to get a clear view of each face. "How are you all doing?" she asked.

They uttered murmurs of "fine" with varying degrees of believability.

Leelee asked with wide eyes, "What went wrong?"

Kena suppressed a laugh. "Nothing went wrong. We have a long trip, and we're short on time. The acceleration rate is much faster than on the brief trips you're used to. If you're queasy, close your eyes and take it easy for a while. We need to get a lot closer for your scanning, so you've nothing else to do, anyway."

Kena returned to her couch and resumed piloting.

Hrndl closed the door and asked, "Are they really fine or just lying valiantly?"

"Some of both, I suspect. Fortunately, none of them lost their breakfast."

"What a colorful phrase. Is it safe to assume that you mean none of them regurgitated?"

Kena grinned at Hrndl's rumbling tone. "Of course."

"Why not just say so?"

"*Regurgitate* is such an ugly word. It doesn't fit at all well into my dance." After opening a comm channel, Kena said, "Quon, why don't I have your status report?"

"Sorry, Kena. Had a little mess to clean up here. One of my passengers turned his stomach inside out. Everything else is just— oh, Hrndl's listening—all systems are operating within normal parameters."

Kena acknowledged and closed the channel, casting an amused glance at Hrndl.

"Turned his stomach inside out," Hrndl repeated with pinched nostrils. "That would be the Veet so-called euphemism for that horribly ugly word. I wonder why it's more acceptable than the real word."

Kena chuckled but focused on their tasks at hand. The three-hour trip required several course changes, but was otherwise uneventful. Arriving at a cluster of remnants from the large moon, the quads split up and began three hours of intense work. They scanned extensively for both navigation and composition purposes, and collected a significant amount of loose material. Leaving two of the emerald craft in the area to mine from large chunks, Kena led the rest out with their samples in tow.

When they'd hurtled past the riskiest areas, Kena drifted back into the aft section and ordered her crew to eat and rest. She ate her own meal with them, so she could get a better idea of how they were doing.

Hrndl had her chance to eat once Kena was strapped into her couch again. "Are they all right back there?" Hrndl asked.

"I've seen hardier appetites, but they're steady enough." Kena tapped the console to pull up a reverse view of her trailing craft. "They're immensely pleased with their new data, by the way."

"Good," Hrndl said. "Do you want to sleep first, or shall I?"

"You'd better. I can't sleep at will like you Grfdn can. I'm not nearly tired enough to sleep now."

"All right. Do you know how to wake me if you need me?"

Kena raised her brows. "Can't I just call your name?"

"No, I won't hear you," Hrndl said. "We all have a wake signal, well-established in our subconscious. I use the most common one. Just pinch one of my fingertips, and I'll be fully alert within seconds."

Kena occupied herself by preparing a report to send with the new scan data. She had it ready by the time they were clear enough of the debris field to send an unimpeded data stream. Then, she revised their next course plan and analyzed the effects of an explosion some way off. It didn't have much impact on their route, but it was an unpleasant reminder of what could happen without warning.

They arrived back at the *Ontrevay* right on schedule, completing the full trip in just under nine hours.

Krdn's voice came over the comm channel. "Beta crew, command is transferred to ex op. Kena, drop your load first and reenter the bay." He indicated a course for her and then started directing the other craft.

Kena flew beneath the hold, released the anchor of her sample containment field, and took her ship inside. The bay pressurized, and its gravitational field reengaged.

The instant the command ship's ramp came to rest on the bay floor, Dhgnr strode up it.

Kena left the navigation module and invited him in. "She's still asleep. I'll let you wake her." Turning to the rest of her crew, she said, "You can get out and stretch your legs, but don't leave the bay."

She ran down the ramp as though she hadn't just spent nine hours weightless. The others followed her more cautiously. Ghent awaited them, as well as several scientists, Metchell, and his reluctant assistant. Ghent and Piert drew Kena aside.

"How's the alpha team doing?" Kena asked, already aware that Delf's team was behind schedule.

"Not good," Ghent said. "They have to deal with a lot more

planetary material than you do, and there's been an explosion.
Both of the yellow craft were damaged. Also, they cannot find the
exotic material we're looking for in the small moon debris, only in
the planetary debris."

Kena raised her eyebrows and looked at Piert. "Isn't that last
part a good thing?"

"It does solve part of the riddle, but we must be certain it
contains no exotic matter. That means we need a lot more close-up
scanning."

Ghent said, "For all these reasons, we've delayed the alpha
team. They will only make two runs and will stay longer at the
target area."

Kena nodded and asked, "Do you want to reassign any of my
craft to alpha?"

"No. We thought about it but decided against it. How's your
team doing? Is there anything I should know that wasn't in your
report?"

"No, they're fine."

"Hrndl included?" Ghent asked.

"As far as I know. I had her sleep most of the way back, so I
haven't talked to her in a couple hours. Better ask Dhgnr or
Metchell."

Metchell was approaching, and Ghent went to meet him.

Kena would have followed, but Piert detained her. "There's
something else you may find interesting. Do you recall that we
believed this system once had a close encounter with another?"

She nodded.

"We have found that system, or rather, the remains of it."

He paused, and Kena tilted her head.

"It's at the heart of the nebula we passed on our way here," he
said. "From this side, we can get a better look at the central region.
There are at least four...*objects*, shall we say. We aren't sure how to
classify them yet, but there's easily enough matter to assume they
could have been stars. If so, they died in a manner never before
observed. The nebula appears to be the result of numerous

explosions. It's filled with debris. A large percentage has probably been ejected, but there is still a tremendous amount of matter, more or less orbiting the larger objects."

"That means..." Kena's lips didn't form the next word. Her eyes widened, and her brow tensed.

"Yes." Piert nodded as he drew out the word. "It means quite a number of very interesting things!"

CHAPTER TWENTY-SEVEN

Ghent strode back to Kena and Piert. "Metchell tells me Hrndl is still fit for duty. It's time to get underway."

Kena barely heard him. "Piert just told me—"

Ghent held up a hand to silence her. "I'm sure he has, and it's a fascinating subject. But right now, you are collecting samples, and we haven't much time. Take your crew back out."

"Yes, sir."

Ghent headed for the door. Kena turned and announced, "Beta crew, get on board. The rest of you, clear the bay." She strode up the ramp, and the crew hurried behind her. Hrndl stood in the airlock, facing Dhgnr. The corners of her eyes pulled so high that her cheeks stretched. Hmm. Delight, perhaps?

"Hate to spoil your fun, but it's time to go," Kena said.

Dhgnr's response was unintelligible to Kena, but Hrndl uttered a gargling laugh and turned him around with a little push. In a few minutes, the ship was sealed, the bay doors slid open, and they slipped gracefully back outside. The two navigators had switched duties, so Hrndl issued the necessary commands to reassemble the craft into formation. They were soon speeding back to the large moon.

Through all these activities, Kena uttered not a single unnecessary word. Once the course was implemented and stable, she stared through the long-range image overlaid on the hull.

After several minutes, Hrndl asked, "How long do you intend to stare into the void before you tell me what's wrong?"

"What?" Kena asked.

"*Stare into the void* is a Grfdn figure of speech referring to deep abstraction with a fixed gaze. I see nothing on that scan to hold your frowning attention. What's wrong?"

"Mm, well, it's not precisely that anything is wrong. It's just so —startling!"

"It must be," Hrndl said. "You just hummed. A sure sign of very deep abstraction."

Kena chuckled.

"Much better," Hrndl said. "Now, tell me."

Kena related what Piert had said, and it was Hrndl's turn to frown thoughtfully at nothing in particular.

Kena exclaimed, "Hrndl! You're staring into space." At Hrndl's puzzled look, she said, "That's the Human version of *staring into the void*."

"Really? It's virtually the same phrase. Is it commonly used?"

"Uh-huh," Kena said through barely parted, unmoving lips, much like a Grfdn would speak their native language.

Hrndl smiled with her eyes and said, "I never cease to be amazed by the minute similarities between our two very different races."

"Yes, it's almost as interesting as Piert's news."

"I wouldn't say that," Hrndl said. "Have you considered what this means about the debris we encountered on the way here?"

"First thing to cross my mind," Kena said dryly.

"We all assumed it was another PitKreelaundun device. But if that nebula is spewing out this mysterious matter—it could as easily be mere chance that debris exploded so close to us."

"Yes and no," Kena said, her voice even drier than before.

Hrndl looked at her with narrowed eyes. "I don't like that tone, Kena. What do you mean?"

"I recall speculation about the possible effects of gravity on this bizarre matter we're trying to identify." Kena took a deep breath then let it out. "Consider this: We go streaking along, generating a gravitational field all the way. In the vast emptiness of space, we hit a rock. How likely is that?"

"Highly unlikely, yet possible. That is precisely why we shield our ships."

"Ah, yes," Kena said, "and we shield them well! Yet this highly unlikely rock delivers a highly unlikely explosive force. So powerful, in fact, that the extended shield bows all the way in and crushes a sensor array. I'd say there is a pretty good chance we collided with the very type of matter we're searching for."

Hrndl's hand wrapped around a control stick, even though the computer was controlling their course. She exhaled a vibrating breath.

Kena tugged at her shoulder restraints. "Then, we reenter normal space, still generating a gravitational field. A cluster of debris changes course to a much greater degree than it should and heads straight for us. We think that proves it's controlled by an enemy. Disguised weapons, in fact. But what if our own gravitational field not only pulled it to us, but even triggered the explosion?"

Hrndl was silent for a couple minutes, her frown deepening. Finally, she shook her head and said, "I do hope you are wrong."

"Why?" Kena asked. Was Hrndl reaching the same conclusions she had?

"Because, if you are right, the same scenario could have happened many times before. Who knows how much of this matter is deep in PitKreelaundun space—and the ejection arms?"

"We certainly don't know, but it behooves us to find out." Kena's voice turned grim as she added, "And more important, to find a way to calculate trajectories."

"Now, what are you thinking?"

Kena fidgeted in her couch again. "I've spent plenty of time in the nebula's ejection arms between Prednia and PitKreelaundun space. They hold anomalies that no one can explain. How many so-called *attacks* from PitKreelaundun *disguised weapons* have there been? I'll bet it's pushing a hundred by now. If those were really natural phenomena, how many near misses have we overlooked? Thousands, perhaps. How many times have our gravitational fields altered the trajectories of explosive debris? Maybe even redirected into PitKreelaundun space?" Kena shook her head. "Probably not often, but if it has happened even once, it may have looked intentional to them."

"Slow down, Kena. You're extrapolating this pretty far. Bear in mind, they don't have the technology to understand generated gravity. Even if we did accidentally send some debris their way, they wouldn't necessarily connect its arrival with our activities."

"How do you know they don't have gravitation technology?"

"Because they don't use..." Hrndl's voice tapered off.

"If I lived where they do," Kena said, "the last thing I would generate is a gravitational field. They need them, too, with all the large ships they have. But instead, they build cylindrical ships and spin them to create centrifugal force. Ever had to maneuver a spinning ship?"

"Only in simulation," Hrndl murmured. "I admit, it's not my first choice for a ship design."

"Nor theirs, I suspect. The smaller ships are never cylinders. I begin to wonder why they have such vast fleets of large ships. What do we really know about their history? Are they really struggling for dominance, as we believe, or are they trying to ensure racial survival?" Her grim tone turned bitter. "I even begin to wonder about the Collaborative's stance on the PitKreelaundun conflict."

"All right, Kena, stop and listen to me for a few minutes," Hrndl said. "You're raising valid questions, but we don't have the

232

answers right now. The question of explosive debris, which may or may not be strategically placed, is one thing. PitKreelaundun fighters are another thing entirely. You should know that better than most of us. Whatever their motives, whatever they think of us, we still need to survive their attacks."

Hrndl slowed and emphasized her words. "More important right now, we need to survive the debris field we're flying into. Piert did not tell you about this so you could spend the next eighteen hours considering racial issues. If you want to use his information for analyzing trajectories, fine. But forget the rest of it until tomorrow. You and I are piloting a command ship, and that is *all* we are doing."

Kena's frown had melted away, and a grin replaced it. "Ghent really ought to make you chief navigator."

Hrndl's brow pulled back. It took her a second to clear the surprise from her face. "Where is your focus? Were you listening?"

"Beyond doubt!" Kena's voice acquired great enthusiasm. "Observe me running an unnecessary scan and double checking the display against it. Look! It matches. Oh, this is so exciting!"

Hrndl choked back a gurgling laugh and assumed a dignified pose. "Performing a routine task is an accepted method for reestablishing focus."

"You sound like a training manual."

"Why does every officer on this ship, and even me, let you get by with all this frivolity?"

"Don't you know, Hrndl? It's because I work best when I'm relaxed, and humor relaxes me. If Ghent does promote you to chief navigator, it won't be just because you can deliver a stern reprimand. It'll be because you know how to adjust your leadership style for diverse personalities."

Hrndl feigned offense. "Really? I don't suppose it would have anything to do with my navigational skills."

"Oh, no! If that were the case, he would promote me."

Hrndl laughed, but quickly followed it with a question about the alpha crew's status. Kena responded and let Hrndl guide both their conversation and activities.

Their trip back to the moon was uneventful, but once they arrived, the work became grueling. They had to mine several large pieces in a denser region on this run. Watching continuously for danger, directing the activities of the small craft, and collecting samples of their own, demanded constant vigilance and intense focus.

After a couple hours, Kena began to worry about Hrndl. She fidgeted, repeatedly adjusted her life support belt, and made uncharacteristic mistakes. As support navigator, Kena monitored and compensated as necessary, but Hrndl needed as much compensation as a junior navigator. Kena used her console to send a private message to Thrayl. When he responded with a trajectory analysis correctly identifying the greatest risks, she re-assigned him to navigational scanning.

"This may be hard for you to imagine," Kena said to Hrndl, "but I think we're getting too focused now. It's time to switch tasks."

"I hope you're right about the source of the problem. If I monitor and scan as poorly as I'm piloting, we're in trouble."

"You probably just need a change," Kena said, "but I've assigned Thrayl to watch for danger. Do you feel all right?"

"Yes. It's just—My back muscles are so tight."

Hrndl did a little better. With the added assurance of Thrayl's support, Kena was able to gather all the material she'd hoped for. As she reassembled the quads for the return trip, however, she began to wonder again. She insisted that Hrndl sleep on the way back. Hrndl tossed fitfully and woke often. Kena let out a long sigh when she at last completed deceleration beside the *Ontrevay*.

A support navigator's voice came over the comm channel. "Welcome back, beta crew. Kena, release your samples and re-enter the bay."

This time, only Krdn, Metchell, and Dhgnr were waiting for her when she disembarked. Kena frowned at Metchell and jerked her head toward the navigation module. He nodded and followed Dhgnr inside. Kena turned her attention to Krdn. "Where are all the samples we collected before?" she asked.

"We took the precaution of moving them farther out while you were gone. There are indications that the corridor to the moons may deteriorate earlier than expected. Ghent wants you back out immediately. We kept the navigators from alpha's yellow pair here to deal with your samples, so you can get your crew back underway at once."

"Where are they?"

"Still at the remote sample area," he said. "Your crew can drop samples at anchor here. We'll move them after you leave."

"Where is Ghent?"

Krdn's voice chilled. "Asleep. Do you doubt that these are his orders?"

"Not at all. Who do you have inside for support?"

"The same minimal crew."

"The least experienced navigators we have," she said, lifting her hands and letting them slap her thighs. "When did you last sleep?"

"A few hours ago."

Metchell returned and said, "I cannot guarantee that Hrndl can last another nine hours, though she insists otherwise."

"I will not accept the risk." Kena turned back to Krdn. "Wake Ghent. I need a proficient support navigator, and you appear to be the only one available."

She turned without waiting for an answer and hurried back to the navigation module. Dhgnr was leaning over Hrndl, speaking in his own language. He stopped when Kena entered.

"You're relieved, Hrndl," she said quickly. "We're in a bit of a hurry, so you need to disembark at once."

"Who is—"

"I'd love to chat, but I don't have time. Dhgnr, would you escort her out, please?"

"But there isn't anyone qualified to—"

"Come, Hrndl." Dhgnr's voice was quiet, but firm. He

unhooked both her restraint and EVA belt as he spoke. "You must realize that none of us will agree to launch this ship if you are in it."

Conflicting emotions fought for control of Hrndl's face. She let him lift her from the couch.

CHAPTER TWENTY-EIGHT

Krdn busied himself at a wall-mounted console, first dispatching someone to wake Ghent, then issuing orders to his limited staff. These actions were automatic. His mind grappled with a very different problem. Kena had asked him to join her. Inconceivable! What could come of it? Only two possibilities, disaster or redemption—The first, the most probable. One thing he must absolutely ensure; no action of his could be the cause of any mishap.

He kept his back to Hrndl and Dhgnr until they left the bay, then he sprinted to the command ship. More automatic actions. Check the bay. Close and seal the hull. Quick glance at the crew before entering the navigation module. They stared at him.

He closed the inner door and grabbed the EVA belt. "The hatch seal is confirmed," he said, snugging the belt around his waist then checking its life support functions.

K ena was already on an alternate comm channel, giving
orders to the outside craft. She had fit an audio unit into
her ear and now adhered its microphone to her cheek. "Krdn, use
the main channel to finish whatever you need to do." Without a
pause, she returned to her previous task, saying into her
microphone, "Amethyst, leave the sample area and align to the
departure course. I'll join you in a few minutes. Sapphire, drop
your loads."

Krdn adjusted his couch and strapped in while he spoke on the
main channel. "Ex op, we are sealed. Open the bay and release the
gravitational field."

"Acknowledged."

The two navigators each continued giving instructions as
though the other was not speaking. However, Kena listened to the
main channel, as well as her private one. The instant the words
"cleared to launch" came over the channel, she grasped the control
sticks beside her legs and piloted the ship out of the bay. She
aligned behind amethyst quad and sailed between them.

"Sapphire, assume departure position," she ordered and then
muted all comm channels.

Krdn spoke immediately. "I've completed instructions to the
remaining crew. Ghent will be in ex op at any moment."

"Good. Then, there is only one thing to do before we leave. I
fly with you only if it is clear who is in command of this ship and
crew. My strong preference is that I command."

"Then, you have command." He pointed at a flashing comm
light, which indicated that someone in the aft module wanted to
talk to them. "Do they always demand your attention this
insistently?"

"No. Get emerald into position," she said, opening the door.
"What is it?" she asked over her shoulder.

The voice had an odd squeak. Leelee, maybe. "Is Krdn flying
with us on this trip?"

This lame attempt to object to his presence struck Kena as

funny. The word *duh* came to mind. She made sure her crew heard only a pleasant tone. "Yes, he is. Hrndl isn't able to continue, so I asked Krdn to take her place. Sorry I couldn't explain earlier. We're a little busy."

Presh blurted out, "But he tried to kill you!"

All desire to laugh left Kena. Not bothering to suppress her irritation, she swung around and said, "Oh, I strongly doubt that!"

"Then who did?"

"No one. It was an accident. If I trust Krdn, there is no reason whatsoever for you to doubt him." She closed the door with a vicious jab at the control.

Ghent's voice broke in. "Krdn, I want Kena on the main channel."

"I am here," she said.

"Whose idea was it for Krdn to take Hrndl's place?"

"It was mine," she said firmly.

"Have you discussed command?" Ghent asked.

Krdn answered. "We have. Kena wanted it, and I agreed. Do you concur?"

"Yes. Krdn, are you aware that Kena has recorded her memory?"

Kena rolled her eyes, and Krdn's face tightened.

"Yes, but it is irrelevant," he said. "I have never tried to kill her. It would be beyond insanity to attempt it now."

Kena asked, "If everyone is finished irritating my support navigator, can we get underway?"

Ghent answered her in a soothing tone. "Yes, Kena. But before you go, I'm confirming the command structure to your navigators. Then, leave as soon as you can."

Within moments, Krdn said, "All quads are in position."

Kena opened the channel and, once again, ordered her craft to accelerate. While they were pressed into their couches, she filled Krdn in on everything they had learned during the previous two trips and her plans for this one. "Any questions?"

K rdn made a few inquiries regarding their mission. though a much different question puzzled him. How could she possibly have said she trusted him? Her answers were calm and natural—as though she were speaking to any other navigator. He searched for contempt in her voice but found none.

A pause followed her last answer. "Any other questions?"

"Not about the mission." He took another breath and made certain his tone was respectfully formal. "Will you permit me to ask you a personal question?"

"I permit."

"Everyone else believes—or at least suspects—that I tried to kill you. Why don't you?"

"Well, for one thing," Kena said, "if you had tried, I think you would have succeeded. If that fire was an attempt at murder, it was a very sloppy, haphazard one."

He nodded. "What else?"

"If I am murdered, you would be, by far, the most likely suspect. That would also make it appear as if you intended to kill Frethan and were simply waiting for a good opportunity. Why would you want two murder charges in place of one accusation of accidental death? Not the sort of strategy I would expect from you."

"All of this should be self-evident," he said. "Yet, few seem to perceive it. Hrndl does not. I expected you to be influenced by her reasoning."

A wry smirk touched Kena's lips. "Much as I like and respect her, this is not the time to rely on her reasoning—not in regard to you. Besides, Grfdn views of coordination are so different from mine. Sometimes you are coordinating and sometimes you are not. If you are, then no one may interfere." Kena shrugged. "But I am always coordinating with all navigators on duty. The command officer always has the right to interfere if deemed necessary. The fact that you choose to take action is not itself an offence. In my view, the only thing you're guilty of was your refusal to learn of my skills. If you had known what I'm capable of, you wouldn't have interfered."

Krdn stared at her, his brow puckered. "You are so different from other Humans."

"All Humans are different. All Grfdn are, too. I see very little similarity between Rnl and Dhgnr, for instance. It never works to rely on racial generalizations when dealing with individuals."

He shook his head. "I am still mystified. You have just pointed out a failure of my judgment. My actions injured you. How can you now say that you trust me?"

"You must have noticed my capabilities by now," Kena said. "In any event, I'm in command, so it doesn't matter a great deal if you haven't. Am I deluding myself? Will you counteract my maneuvers if you dislike my technique?"

"Certainly not!"

"I didn't think you would, Krdn. Ghent once told me how utterly committed to coordination the Grfdn are. We are sitting in the same cockpit on the same mission. In my view, we are coordinating. Do you see it that way?"

He had yielded command to her; now she asked for coordination, as well? After he had questioned her trust, she offered him more trust? Did she understand? She couldn't. How to answer her? He took a deep breath. "Grfdn are deliberate about coordination. It is stated, for the commitment is on both sides."

"I am already committed."

She gave her commitment before receiving his. Unbelievable. Especially after all that had happened. There was really no way he could refuse. Even simple agreement was inadequate. "I am honored to coordinate with you."

Kena only nodded, a slight furrow between her brows. Was that because of what he'd said, or because of the new scan data they were receiving? More debris misaligned with projections.

Several minutes later, she adjusted her couch to half-recline. She pulled her audio unit off and slapped it into its holder. "Set up to take over piloting, Krdn." Touching the comm channel button, she said, "Beta crew, you're looking good. I'm going to sleep now, so you'll be getting instructions from Krdn. If anyone hasn't slept yet, do so now. Consider that an order." She put up a hand to hide a cavernous yawn.

"Is this your first sleep?" he asked, as she pushed her control sticks into the console and moved it away from her lap.

"Yes." Kena released her shoulder straps, adjusted her couch, and pulled the sleep restraint around herself. "Wake me up about ten minutes before we arrive at the collection point."

"Is that going to be enough sleep?"

"It will do. I'll sleep again on the way back." She fit her personal earphones in place and selected a music track on her computer.

"Will those block all sound?" Krdn asked.

"No, but enough so I can sleep. Music will mask your voice."

"How do I wake you?"

"Call my name," she said. "If that doesn't work, move me back and forth."

Krdn held silence, and Kena met his steady gaze. She raised an eyebrow and asked, "What is it?"

He shook his head and looked forward again. "Sleep, Kena."

Soon, her breathing grew slow and rhythmic. Her hands floated before her chest.

Krdn looked over at her, noting every detail of her relaxed body, from her peaceful face to her long, curved fingers with their fine bone structure. So different from the times he'd seen them dart across a console. At rest, they looked like a graceful sculpture. He found her face in repose even more surprising. Gone were the quick expressions and exuberance. It struck him, now, that Kena always seemed to be in motion, even when she stilled in absolute concentration. There was an energy about her that never subsided. Seeing her asleep—so vulnerable—caused unexpected emotions to stir within him. If only he could diffuse his tension as easily as she released hers.

The three-hour journey was interminable. He forced himself to focus on analysis. The changes occurring around the corridor to their destination were too critical to ignore. Yet, again and again he found his eyes straying back to the still, unguarded figure beside him.

He'd allowed no one to see the damage his confidence had suffered—would barely acknowledge it even to himself. Now, she had placed complete trust in him. That unnerved him more than the contempt Dhgnr and Hrndl heaped upon him. Did she really trust him? Even in part? If so, she honored him. He grasped at the balm of her honor, but shame squirmed, weakening his grip. He did not deserve her trust. And yet, it was imperative he fulfill that trust. In this, flickered a spark of hope. His career might yet be saved if he succeeded. Perhaps not on the high-status, interracial ships, but among his own race.

He made himself wait until the exact moment Kena had specified and then said her name. No response. He said it again, louder. A fleeting expression passed over her features, but still she did not wake. He reluctantly reached for her shoulder and set her to rocking against the sleep restraint. "Kena, we'll be at the collection area in ten minutes."

Her arms rose above her head, the fingers intertwining. Her entire body stiffened in a long stretch. In silence, she stowed the restraint and brought her couch back to a sitting position. Krdn pulled the relevant scans up on display for her to review. She groped for a sealed container in her seat pocket then flipped open the tube with her teeth. Wrapping her lips around it, she sucked the contents while she studied the images before her.

The shifting muscles of her face grabbed his attention. She drank like a Grfdn. Beyond doubt! How foolish of him not to expect as much. It would be the instinct of every Human infant. Once again, emotion surged through him. He quickly suppressed it, irritated that something so trivial could remind him of how much he'd overlooked.

K ena finished her drink before she finally spoke. "Well, debris has shifted quite a ways from projection, but I suppose it could be worse. Do you think we need to leave early?"

"Only if the deterioration rate increases. The alpha crew will pull out in an hour. Since they have extra time, they're going to deploy probes along the way to send us short range scans and improve communications with the *Ontrevay*. That will provide us current information for our departure decision."

"Sounds good. How's the crew back there?" she asked with a jerk of her head toward the aft module."

"I haven't checked. I didn't want to disturb you. Nothing they've sent me indicates any problems. Have they had difficulties before?"

"Presh and Leelee have zero-G sickness, but they don't admit it." Kena released her lap belt, opened the door, and floated into the aft module. "Anyone having trouble?" she asked, scrutinizing each face.

They all shook their heads or murmured "no." A rather subdued response.

"We may need to cut this trip short," Kena said. "Prioritize your needs so we get the most important samples first. Thrayl, see that the rest of the scientists understand this as well. Once I decide to leave, nothing that any of you say will delay our departure."

Kena returned to her couch and strapped in.

Krdn asked, "What's their status?"

She pulled the console into her lap and said, "They look like gravity lovers who've been on weightless duty for twenty-one hours. They didn't even complain when I said we might need to leave early. Get the long-range display off the hull so I can see what I'm doing." After opening a channel, she said, "Amber and ruby, drop out here and head to your zones. Emerald units nine and ten, rejoin eleven and twelve to continue mining."

The ruby and amber quads separated and returned to their assigned areas. A moment later, the pair from emerald veered off toward a large, familiar chunk.

She selected a single comm channel to Emerald 12. "Hi, Jorlit. How's the mining business?"

"A little tedious," Jorlit said. "Navigating loses its charm when you're anchored in a hole in a rock."

"I can't argue that. Switch out with nine and ten. What's your sampling status?"

He reported, ending with, "We'll be finished in an hour."

"Sounds good. I'll join you then."

The command ship continued on, with the amethyst and sapphire quads following. Kena reviewed the sample requests she had for this untouched area. Dividing the craft into four pairs, she sent each pair a set of coordinates.

"Amethyst, load to your full capacity. Sapphire, your area has a lot of small material. Don't waste time with mining or breaking objects up, and don't load above 80 percent. I'll be gathering samples in the central area, which you will need to take out."

She turned to Krdn. "You watch for danger to emerald, amber, and ruby. They're in familiar territory, so they don't need much direction." Having said this, she ignored Krdn and his assigned craft. They were both using audio units now, so their one-sided conversations dropped to background noise in the nav module. Much like solo flight, even though they sat within arm's reach.

Kena selected the biggest void she could find and deployed a remote-controlled anchor. She synchronized its course to the prevailing orbit of the debris cloud then activated its containment field. She began capturing samples, anchoring them within the remote energy field.

All went smoothly for nearly an hour. Then, a rock exploded near amethyst units three and four. They took evasive action. Unit three was in the direct path of a dozen large fragments. It turned too slowly, hampered by the samples it dragged.

Kena ordered, "Unit three, drop your load."

Quick compliance saved the ship, but their samples scattered.

The pilot's chagrined voice came over her audio unit. "Great! There goes an hour's worth of work. Sorry, Kena."

"We could've done without that, but your crew is safe. Setbacks were expected. Just go back to collecting and don't waste a thought on the past."

Kena continued to listen in on the comm channel amethyst three and four used. In a little while, their voices grew calm and their work pattern routine. She turned her attention back to sapphire quad.

Addressing their lead navigator, she said, "It's time to come and pick up my samples. Get all of your craft fully loaded then lead them back to the *Ontrevay*."

"We could help sweep in more samples for amethyst before we go."

"The fewer craft I have to take into a collapsing corridor, the better. Head back as soon as you're loaded."

"Acknowledged."

"Amethyst, I'm going to join emerald. Continue here."

"Kena, we still have way more to collect here than we can manage without your help," the quad leader said.

"I know. I'll send you help in a few minutes." Kena muted the channel to talk to Krdn. "Leave emerald to me now. Analyze the exit route and sapphire's course."

"I've just reviewed the corridor. It's relatively stable." After a moment, he said, "Sapphire's course plan is acceptable."

"How far have amber and ruby gotten?"

"They have about half of what they need," Krdn said. "I'll send six of the craft out in an hour, and the other two can join the remaining quads."

"Good." Kena pulled into alignment with emerald. Three of the craft were collecting matter, and the fourth was just emerging from a hole that had been cut deep into a 50-kilometer chunk of the moon. "Jorlit, who has the lightest load?"

"That would be our last miner, Kena, unit nine. They've just finished blasting."

"Unit nine, I want you to join up with amethyst and gather for them. Load them first then pick up anything they can't haul. I'm sending you a course plan."

Kena watched the maneuver she had ordered, monitored ongoing activities, and planned a collection course.

After a couple minutes, Krdn asked, "Is this how you coordinate with Hrndl?"

Kena blinked and threw a quick glance his way. "No, of course not."

"How do you divide the tasks?"

"We each monitor two quads and jointly assist the fifth. One of us pilots and collects forward, while the other monitors and collects aft. We jointly plan the courses and collection strategy."

"A much more efficient division of work than what we are doing now," Krdn said. "I suggest we use that approach."

"Not a chance. I've trained and worked with Hrndl, but not with you."

"Kena, I have very little to do. You have more than necessary and are also tired. Please give me another task."

"Fine. Monitor amethyst."

"Acknowledged," he said. "If you're doing all the piloting and collecting here, I can easily monitor for you, as well."

"You can watch and report all you like, but don't correct. Wondering what you might do will wear me out much faster than anything else."

K rdn paused before answering. "Understood." He hoped Kena didn't realize how hard it was to control his voice. Her explanation for not allowing him full participation was reasonable—they hadn't trained together. Still, the rejection burned.

The next hour was worse than the interminable trip out. Krdn watched Kena incessantly, determined not to miss any need she might have. Her maneuvers were often difficult, but she never faltered. She seemed to know intuitively which courses would sweep in the greatest amount of matter in the least amount of time. Did she even consider difficulty factors?

Her skills were incredible. The realization emphasized how inexcusably blind he had been. His estimation of his own abilities fell ever lower. Even though Hrndl could coordinate with Kena, he doubted he could. Making the attempt wasn't even an option.

Krdn sent ruby quad and two of the amber units back to the *Ontrevay*. Amber thirteen and fourteen joined emerald under Kena's control, and amethyst was functioning smoothly. Even though he had less than ever to do, Kena didn't involve him in local activities. She had them so thoroughly—yes, coordinated—that he couldn't offer her assistance again. It galled him unbearably that he had never recognized her capabilities until now.

They were about 90 percent complete when their exit route grew even more questionable. Krdn checked that Kena wasn't focused on anything particularly critical, then he said, "Kena, I suggest you review the exit corridor."

"You review it. If you don't like it, just tell me how long till we leave."

"Not more than ten minutes until we should all be in the main corridor. I'm going to order amethyst out now and have unit nine rejoin emerald."

"Fine. You plan the exit course, and I'll finish up here." She opened a channel to the aft module and said, "We're leaving. Notify the other scientists."

Krdn plotted their exit course and also reviewed the rendezvous courses that Kena had given the six remaining craft. Each was to sweep straight through a separate area, indiscriminately gathering whatever fell within their range, and end at the corridor entrance. Emerald ten was on its way to the entrance and was drawing its collection into a tightly held pack.

Krdn spoke over the main channel. "Amber thirteen and fourteen, stop collecting. Pull your samp—"

Energy readings surged from the rock they had mined.

"Evasive!" he snapped.

The rock exploded with awesome force.

Kena was already twisting the ship away. "Activate EVA life support."

Debris exploded beside them. It jerked them hard to the right. Bangs and shouts came over the comm channel from the aft module.

"Get back there and tie down whatever is loose," Kena ordered. "They don't know what they're doing."

Krdn was in the aft module in seconds. An oxygen canister had broken free and was bouncing wildly through the module. He snagged and anchored it. His glance took in the crew's terrified faces but came to rest on the inward bulge of the hull. He'd never seen anything like it. That much damage through their hull shield couldn't have been caused by a simple collision.

He grabbed a ceiling handhold and headed forward. Powerful thrust pinned him back. He clung to the grip. Kena altered course, and Krdn's legs swung above the scientists' heads. Hand over hand, he struggled toward the navigation module. Another collision sent the ship into an uncontrolled spin.

CHAPTER TWENTY-NINE

Kena activated the module's independent shields and closed her airlock. She controlled the spin, but couldn't avoid the next collision. The rock exploded as it slammed into the side of the aft module, fragmenting its hull. The nav module's shield held. Kena snatched a quick look backward. There was nothing to see but debris spinning by.

The computer responded to the loss of aft thrusters, resetting the control system. Kena adapted instinctively, flying the nav module as a single-pilot craft. She flipped it and headed straight back to the center of the explosion, the only area in all this seething mess that was relatively free of debris. With her left hand on the control stick and her right skimming across the console, she initiated a broad sensor sweep, scanning for beacons and life signs. She read five on the first pass. Better than expected. They might all be alive.

Kena exhaled a shaky breath. Voices on the comm channel registered.

Someone said, "I've got visual of the nav module. Somebody's piloting."

Had she missed something?

Jorlit's voice came over, firm and clear. "Beta command, what is your status?"

"My aft module shattered. Krdn and eight scientists were in it with their life support fields active. I've read five signals from my crew, all with life signs. Make that six. I'm sending coordinate and trajectory data. All craft, scan and send me your data. Report your status while you're working on it."

Kena's chest relaxed as they reported. They'd been battered, but everyone else had escaped serious damage. Two more beacon signals with life readings showed up on her display, complete with trajectory data. Warmth spread down her arms. Only one was still missing.

Kena broadcast her main channel so everyone in a life support field would be able to hear it. "Jorlit, take over support for me until I get Krdn back. Collect the status info while I organize pickup." She dropped her voice to a soothing tone. "To my crew—who so suddenly parted company from me—please don't worry. We are tracking you and will pick you all up in a few minutes. Your comm channel control is at the very center of your belt. I want each of you to press it and give Jorlit your status. Other than that, there is nothing you need to do, so just relax. You are still safe."

Presh's voice, quivering on the edge of hysteria, shouted across the channel. "You call this safe?"

Jorlit answered him firmly. "You are perfectly safe inside your life support field. What is your—"

"There's at least two rocks heading straight for me!" he screamed back.

Jorlit's pitch held steady. "We've tracked your position. We'll rescue you long before anything can hit you. Now, control your panic. State your name, whether you are injured, and nothing else."

Kena released another worry at Jorlit's masterful use of tone to quell or encourage each of her crewmembers.

A quiet voice spoke within her. *I've given my angels charge concerning you, to guard you in all your ways.*

She absorbed the comfort even while she dispatched craft to

rescue her free-floating crew. She assigned each of them to retrieve one or two specific people. Some of the maneuvers were tricky, but navigators executed without mishap.

Kena searched, ever mindful of the brief window still available for a stable exit corridor. When three craft had welcomed half of her crew inside, she ordered them back to the *Ontrevay*. In a few more minutes she'd be able to send the others back, but still no signal appeared from Krdn. His field had been active—she was sure of it. Why couldn't she find him? She altered her position for the second time to scan from a different angle.

All the while, voices spoke over the comm channels. Jorlit had sent a status message to the *Ontrevay*. Perhaps they'd been able to decipher it, for Ghent's voice responded in bits and pieces, not much more than syllables and occasional words. The communication systems were set to repeat long-range messages, while the receiving computer filled in more and more of the words as it replayed.

Kena ignored it. Her position wasn't getting her significantly more data. She headed farther out.

Jorlit's voice came over her comm channel. "Kena, you need to alter your course back around toward the exit corridor. I have one person left to pick up. We can accomplish full rendezvous within another forty-five seconds. We'll just barely be able to make it into the corridor in time."

"Quite right," Kena said. "I still have someone to pick up, too. Don't wait for me to rendezvous. Head for the *Ontrevay* as soon as you've got Thrayl inside."

"Kena..." The strain in his voice matched her own tension.

"I know, Jorlit. You're no more willing to leave me than I am to leave Krdn. But I have to draw the line somewhere. You, and all the craft with you, are returning to the *Ontrevay*. The next word I expect to hear from you is, *acknowledged*. Then, I want confirmation that you have Thrayl and all three craft are heading out. That is *all* I want to hear."

When the hull shattered, debris hit Krdn and swept him away. The impact stunned him, and it took a few minutes to recover his senses. He blinked several times. What? Where? Oh, yes. Oh, no! Pinned in the cavity of a rock? His pulse raced.

He glanced at the rock at his back and then ahead. The region looked particularly lethal. Collisions occurred as he watched—five already. The rock that carried him jerked several times. Unseen objects must be pelting it. The cavity that held him was little more than an indentation. It could not protect him.

Krdn groped at his EVA belt, pulled the control module up, and spread it out for use. He accessed the spatial display. His own position was pinpointed on the short-range scan. No other man-made object registered. No wonder he couldn't hear the others. He was on the far side of this rock from the rest of the beta crew.

Options? He was all but helpless. Still, he was a navigator and, therefore, responsible for his crew. Could anyone's life depend on his actions? Slim chance of that, but he must confirm it. He deployed the simple jets, designed for EVA maneuvering, and deactivated his homing beacon. Brief thrust nudged him away from the rock, and he veered off to one side. When he cleared the rock's horizon, the voices of his crew reached his ears, choppy but intelligible.

He listened carefully and soon deciphered that all of the scientists from his ship had been located. Another minute was enough to reveal Kena's rescue plan. She directed the others to pick up all eight while she herself kept scanning.

Conflicting emotions warred within him. It was her duty to search, but part of him was amazed that she did so. Even as her own risk increased, she continued to search. The hope that he would not be left to die tried to rise within him. He suppressed it.

Using his miniature console, he confirmed what he already knew. He had been swept far from the escape corridor. The rock, which bore him away, must've been impacted by the mysterious, volatile substance that wreaked such havoc. It had propelled him from the collection area. Kena was at least ten minutes away, probably more. Not enough time to reach him and get out again. Worse yet, flying this region was far beyond the safety margin for any navigator, even Kena. If she took the time to rescue him, the escape corridor would be almost as bad.

Krdn made his final decision. He would not turn the homing beacon back on. There was nothing left for him, but to watch the craft complete the rescue and head for the *Ontrevay*. And to compose himself for death.

He'd read this phrase in Grfdn literature. It had sounded fitting, even courageous. Could anyone actually do such a thing? Regret and grief swirled to the surface. *Maintain control. Focus on the idea that my silence enables my partner to escape death.*

The thought failed to console him. Beyond doubt, such a claim of noble self-sacrifice also belonged in literature. Literature of the dead, where the subject of grandiose eulogy could no longer refute it.

Perhaps he should get it over with, lest bitterness consume his final moments. His life support belt contained a simple emergency medical unit. It could induce sleep, thereby slowing oxygen consumption. The intent was to increase time for rescue when things went wrong. Not very useful for someone trapped in a maelstrom. The drug could serve another purpose that no one spoke of.

Ahead, Kena's craft shifted position again. Krdn welcomed the distraction. As he watched, his brow tightened. Kena drew farther from the corridor. What was she doing?

Her voice came over his comm channel. "Krdn, I can't pick up your homing signal. Respond verbally."

No. He couldn't let her. She'd leave if she couldn't locate him— wouldn't she? He maintained silence while Kena addressed him repeatedly. Her voice grew pleading, almost desperate. Krdn's worry increased with every word. Then, she ordered Jorlit to leave without her. *No!*

Kena uttered a passable imitation of a Grfdn growl and declared, "Krdn, I know you're in that swarm, and I don't have time to waste looking behind every rock. You've turned your beacon off, or I would have found it by now. That means you're alive, and I am not leaving without you. So answer me, now!"

Krdn's thoughts sped. She had likely realized he could only be in the dense region. She couldn't know for certain that he was alive, but she did have reason to assume it. If she came looking for him, it would ensure her death. After a few seconds of indecision, he finally opened his comm channel. "Kena, you cannot possibly reach me. Return to the *Ontrevay.* That is an order."

"You forget, you gave command to me. Now, turn your beacon back on. *That* is an order."

"I will not. My death is already certain. Your attempt to rescue me cannot succeed. It will only cause another unnecessary death."

"I know what I'm capable of better than you do. Turn that beacon on and let me decide."

"Kena, your flying today has convinced me that you are, by far, the best navigator I have ever seen. But this area is too dangerous, even for you."

"I will not leave my partner."

Krdn sighed and said quietly, "Then, you must go back. Hrndl is your partner, not I."

"Krdn—"

"No more, Kena. I'd prefer to have a few more minutes to live, but if you don't head back immediately, I'm going to deactivate my life support field. I'll turn the homing signal on so you can pick up my life signs and see when they stop."

"No! Wait!"

"I suggest you set your initial bearing for 74.18.331. I'll give you a count of five to initiate. If you don't, I'll shut down my field. One..."

Her anguished whisper reached him. "No!"

SHARON ROSE

"Two."

"Please don't make me leave you."

"Three."

"Krdn, please!"

"Four."

Kena shouted. "I'll do what you ask. Just don't die that way. It's worse than you know." Her tiny craft flipped and thrust away.

Oh, no! Why had he mentioned death by vacuum? If she had a relapse now, she'd never get out. He changed to a soothing tone. "I won't. My medical unit is functioning. I'll die in my sleep before the field fails."

Kena gained control of her frantic voice. At least no one would see her tears. "I—I really wanted to bring you back."

"I know," Krdn said. "Focus on navigation. It will make this easier."

He was right. In fact, she had no choice. A cloud of debris had almost reached the corridor opening. "Jorlit, what's your fuel status?" she asked, her voice dull.

"I have plenty for both of us."

"Send the other craft in first then follow them into the corridor. Keep your load high, so I can come in beneath you. I'm going to burn my fuel fast."

Jorlit confirmed courses with the other navigators, while Kena rocketed toward them. Insane to speed through that much debris, but she managed it. She was soon in position beneath his craft, well within range of his energy beam.

Jorlit murmured, "Wish I could pull you inside."

"Now, that would be cozy. Trust me, I'm much better off out here. I've got precious little power left; you'd better engage the field now."

Kena settled herself for the trip home. She soon had nothing to do. Her tiny module was helpless, and she was so tired, she yielded to Jorlit's request to take command.

Her thoughts bounced like jostling debris. What bothered her most? Exhaustion or despair over leaving her partner behind? She didn't even like him. That only made her feel worse, for his final act was above reproach. Tears pooled in her eyes. She felt so alone, isolated more by grief than by space. Yet, this could be nothing to the loneliness Krdn must be feeling.

———

F ar away, he floated, no longer tracking the others. He set himself slowly spinning. The chaotic power of this bizarre and deadly area revealed itself before his eyes. He didn't allow himself to consider when he should inject the drug that would send him to permanent sleep. When he was ready, he would simply do it. Suppressing memories of the last few weeks proved much harder. He focused on the kaleidoscope panorama, trying to block them out.

When Hrndl's voice reached his ears, he thought it was an errant memory. But no. The words were broken, with long pauses. Comm interference on a live message. Amazing. A woman didn't send messages during her seclusion. Why would Hrndl send him a message anyway? He silenced the audio and waited. The computer continued to receive, to assemble the pieces into a full, smooth message. Finally, the display flashed a completion signal. He hesitated, then played it.

"I hope I'm not too late," Hrndl's voice said. "I know you forced Kena to return to us. She would otherwise have died trying to save you. Instead, it is you who have saved her. I...I will not insult you by pretending to approve of recent events, but...in the end...you are as you were when I first knew you."

Quietly, he answered. "Thank you, Hrndl. Goodnight."

The words transmitted through the cold void then slowly

reassembled for Hrndl. She would comprehend his last word. It could have only one meaning.

"Goodnight, Krdn," she whispered.

Her fragmented words came to him, replaying again and again, as he drifted in slow motion through a dense fog. His eyelids drooped, and memories fell away. His thoughts turned into a dream of Hrndl, beautiful and desirable, whispering in his ear as he slept beside her.

PART TWO

CHAPTER THIRTY

Kena sat cross-legged on her bed with a pillow shoved between her back and the wall. Ten hours of sleep, breakfast, a bath, and the coffee she sipped had returned her to a sense of normalcy. It did nothing to change the facts.

Navigators sometimes died. They had a high-risk job and knew it. That didn't make this any more pleasant. She'd been one breath away from death herself. More than once. The idea of her own death didn't trouble her nearly as much as that of a non-Human. Physical death was not the end for a Human—her creator loved her and would draw her to himself. But what became of those of other races?

They were so different. Much more so than they realized. No race but Humans wondered much about God. Others held a general assumption that some creating entity existed, but so few strived to describe him or to know him. No race mentioned an afterlife—at least not openly. Their deaths seemed so final and tragic. Krdn's last moments had seemed not merely lonely, but a devastating isolation. How could they endure it?

Kena's beloved spoke within her. *I did not abandon him.*

She sought for deeper answers. *Does that mean they do have an afterlife?*

His assurance remained steadfast, but nothing more was added. When she stopped struggling to hear what he was not saying, the reason for his silence became clear. He was waiting to comfort *her*, not to speak of another.

She settled more fully into his presence. She needed it. "As a deer pants for water, so my heart longs for you." She quoted the words slowly, welcoming him nearer.

Most of her people advised against a single Human living among non-Humans. For good reason. One's own kind provided an intangible connection. Its absence could produce isolation stress, even for a person with strong alien friendships. Kena understood these warnings, even agreed with them. But she had also found the only way to relieve the isolation. It lay in the knowledge—the deep knowing and understanding—of her creator's love for her. A rich mixture encompassing and surpassing a parent's love, spouse's love, any kind of Human love. It sustained her when far from home.

She quoted words from her favorite Psalm. "If I ascend to the stars, you are there. If I ride the wings of the dawn into brilliant light, even there your hand guides me and your right hand supports me."

How wondrous that David, flowing with the Spirit of God, had penned such words thousands of years ago, so long before star travel was imagined. Before the nature of light and time were known. What more elegant way to describe her travels than riding the wings of the dawn? *Even then you were thinking of me.*

I am.

She savored his choice of words. Not *I was.* Not past tense. Rather, a statement that filled the past, present, and future. The fullness of time where he dwelled. The one who fills all in all. She rested in his presence.

A faint awareness of Ghent penetrated her thoughts, along with a Grfdn. They neither approached nor withdrew. The message Ghent had left her—to contact him when she was awake and refreshed—needed to be answered. It felt like a summons, even though it contained no demand. What would his reaction be? *Why ponder it when you can know it? Is there anything that I cannot turn to good for you?*

No point in arguing that. Kena reached for her computer.

Ghent joined her a couple minutes later at the table in her sitting room. Kena inhaled the steam from her coffee and returned Ghent's steady regard.

"Have you ever been forced to leave a partner before, Kena?" he asked.

"No."

"A disturbing experience."

"True."

Ghent's fingertips brushed across the table in a slow arc. "I'm regretting bringing only one Human to the *Ontrevay*. It leaves you with no support during a difficult time. If there's anything you need that I'm capable of providing, please tell me."

"Thank you," Kena said, "but I need nothing. I assume you've investigated the event?"

"As much as I can without talking to you. I've reviewed the scan, navigation, and communication records. I've talked with other navigators, particularly Jorlit. Is that what you mean?"

She nodded. "I'd like to hear your observations."

"I would rather hear yours."

Kena swallowed and took a deep breath. "I did everything I could think of to find Krdn. When that failed, there was no choice left but to return."

Ghent leaned back in his chair. "You sound a little defensive. What have you heard from others who've had a partner die?"

"From one extreme to another." Kena flipped her hand from side to side. "I've heard of a senior navigator demoted all the way to junior, even though there was nothing he could have done to prevent the accident or save his partner. I've heard of another navigator who was demoted for risking his own life, even though he successfully rescued his partner. And I've even heard of a captain who didn't bother to investigate the circumstances surrounding a death."

Ghent shook his head. "I am none of those captains. Were those navigators Human?"

"Only one of them."

"Which one?"

"The one who saved his partner's life."

"I'm not surprised." Ghent leaned forward, folding his forearms on the table. "One of the challenges on a multi-racial ship is to determine what is possible for a given race, or even a given person. Some captains use a single standard for everyone. I find that...unrealistic, to put it mildly. Instead, I expect every crew member to do what he or she is capable of. Not less, not more.

"Your leadership, Kena, and your piloting were exemplary. Your recovery after collision was nothing short of astonishing. I cannot fault you for any of this." He nodded to one side. "It's possible that you stayed too long. Since you succeeded in returning, I cannot definitively fault you in this, either. Still, I know your tendency to push your limits. Please understand that I do not want them pushed so near to the point of death."

She ducked her head. "I understand."

"When you look away from me like that, I wonder if you infer more than I intended."

Kena lifted her eyes to his in question.

"I am not reprimanding you. Nor do I want you second-guessing your decisions when you're in the cockpit. I merely want you to understand that I value *your* safety as much as I value the safety of others."

"I see."

He gave his quick nod, like the ending of a paragraph. "There are still a few things I'd like to know, which only you can tell me."

"Such as?"

"How did you know Krdn had turned his homing signal off?"

"I didn't." She gave her head a little shake. "It was a guess. There was too much debris to find him by scanning. I needed another way. Voice was the only thing left to me. Frankly, I'm surprised he answered."

"Did you try to reach him telepathically?" Ghent asked.

"There was no chance of that. It was much unlike my link with Frethan, if that's what you're thinking. Krdn could have been anywhere. I had felt Frethan before; he wasn't shy with telepathy. But Krdn never so much as extended his awareness in my presence." She lifted her shoulders. "I knew of no identity to search for. Nor would he have been able to recognize me."

"From comments you've made before, I understood that you always have awareness of those around you."

"I do, but it's indistinct. I can differentiate non-Human races, but not individuals." She tilted her head. "Do you think I should have been able to find him?"

"No, but I'm wondering if you think so."

She shook her head. "I thought at first I'd be able to. The others were all moving in concurrent trajectories. But he wasn't among them. I still don't know why, or where he was."

"A lot of debris passed through the strike zone. Something must have hit him. We did eventually find the signal from his EVA belt. His location is beyond what you could have reached."

She nodded, staring into her coffee cup.

"Kena, I was hoping you might be relieved to know that there really was nothing else you could have done for him."

"Mm. I suppose I already knew that, but thanks for the confirmation."

"If it's not that," Ghent asked, "what does trouble you?"

It took her a moment to form the words. "To be so isolated. So completely alone. I've no idea how long he endured that, or even if..." She swallowed hard.

Ghent answered what she was unable to ask. "The signal from his life support belt confirms that he died before oxygen depletion or field failure. There're a lot of gaps in the reception, so we don't know the exact time of death. Hrndl sent him a message, to which he replied. She believes he died by the sedation drug not long afterward. Probably less than an hour after your decision to leave."

Ghent's percipience was a relief. He'd given her as much as she would ever be able to know. It would have to do. Only one part surprised her.

"You've spoken with Hrndl?" Kena asked. "Already?"

"No, with Dhgnr. She's still in seclusion. Does knowing about Krdn comfort you at all?"

"It helps."

"What do you need most, Kena—time to rest or something to do?"

"Something to do. I'm certainly not expecting time off when we're so short staffed, particularly with leadership."

"Good. Netlyn is spread too thin. Come."

"Join us," Quon said to Kena.

She turned from the buffet, about to follow. The sight of Frdn, alone at the Grfdn table, stopped her. "In a moment, perhaps." She paused by the conspicuously bare table. "What will irritate you the least, Frdn, to eat alone or to eat with a Human?"

He startled. "T-to eat with a Human, beyond doubt!"

She slid into the chair across from him. He shifted, not meeting her eyes. Had he felt compelled to say the opposite of his true opinion?

His voice tensed. "Have I done something that you object to?"

Her hand stilled as she reached for her glass. "I've hardly seen you. What could I object to? Do I still have some Grfdn obligation that I'm unaware of?"

"No," he said. "I mean, you could—if I tried to interfere—but I won't."

"That, I can easily believe of you. Thank you so much for relieving me of further duties." She hoped her humorous inflection would ease him. The formal inclination of his head made that seem unlikely. "What disturbs you?" she asked.

"Nothing. I am just...surprised that you would join me. You could sit anywhere." A Prednian sauntered by, sucking a large piece of sopping fruit from his bowl as he walked. Frdn averted his gaze. "Almost anywhere."

"Ah! You see?" she murmured. "You would not condemn me to eat with him, and I will not condemn you to eat alone."

"It's not the same." He grasped a whitish piece of cooked vegetable in his tongs. "I am rejected."

"Hmm." Kena tilted her head. "I think I would phrase that as you were not chosen. If she had picked Rnl in preference to you, then you'd have reason for humiliation. Her choice of Dhgnr does not reflect badly upon you."

"He only courted her for a day, whereas I could not win her favor in many days."

"It's not as though she didn't already know him well." Kena sliced a strawberry. "He also spent her courtship period placing her needs above his own preferences."

Frdn stared. "Is that a trait Human's seek, or do you know that Grfdn females value it?"

"Humans value it; I can see why a Grfdn would also. Every race should, though it may be more obvious to some than others." Kena took a sip of water. "How old are you, Frdn?"

He shifted again and frowned. "Younger than Hrndl. I know my courting her could be deemed presumptuous, but there were so few of us."

"Giving her a choice is not presumptuous," Kena said. "That's not what I meant. You will have other opportunities. Experience is nothing to disdain, even when acquiring it is unpleasant."

Again, he inclined his head, almost bowing.

Dhgnr strode to their table with a stack of food containers. Frdn bowed and pushed back to leave.

"Stay," Dhgnr said, sitting down. "You may view me as khn

rather than rival. Kena stated that your behavior was honorable, for which I commend you."

"Thank you."

Dhgnr turned to Kena. "I have no time to converse, but wish to know...is it well with you?"

"All is well. How is Hrndl?"

Both men sucked their breath in. Dhgnr drew back, his nostrils pinching.

"What is this?" Kena asked. "Do I still stumble?"

"The inquiry is rude," Dhgnr said. "You imply it's doubtful that I am caring for her."

"Such a thought would never occur to me."

Dhgnr paused. "Graceful recovery. What is the Human meaning of the question?"

"Merely a courtesy toward someone I value."

His expression softened. "I cannot speak of her directly. Permit me to quote you. All is well." He left with those words.

Kena ate in pensive silence until Frdn broke it.

"Do you realize that Dhgnr is not angry over your mistake?"

"I think he was," she said, "but chose to disregard it."

Seconds passed while he seemed to consider her. "You are... intrepid...in racial matters. It's not the best word, but as close as I can get in Prednian."

"Thank you." A smile hovered on her lips. "May I ask what prompted that?"

"Most people get along with other races by avoiding known offences and maintaining some distance. Considerable distance from the Grfdn. But you came into our midst, in spite of all the pitfalls that would certainly trip you. What Dhgnr said is true: You are graceful. It preserves you when you stumble. But even so, I don't understand how you succeed so well."

"I seek to know individuals, rather than races. I look for similarities, rather than differences."

Days crammed with activity rushed by Kena. Navigators ferried samples for scientists and stabilized the collection in the wake of an explosion. Much of the benzlium they'd collected was lost, but Netlyn had her eye on additional sources skirting the nebula. A good thing she'd found another source, considering how much energy their containment fields were sucking down.

Hrndl emerged from seclusion and behaved as though nothing had happened.

When Hrndl first walked into the astro section, Kena leaned close to Netlyn and whispered, "Have you seen that thing they wear when they're carrying a fertilized ovum? Would we recognize it?"

Netlyn's eyes followed Hrndl for a moment. "She's not wearing it." She shook her head and kept her voice soft. "I didn't think they'd fertilize the first one. It's common for Grfdn to wait on children. And wouldn't this be a terrible time?"

Hrndl's return to calm professionalism was a relief to Kena— and to others, if the looks they exchanged meant anything. Within a day, Ghent announced her promotion to chief navigator. No one was surprised when she appointed Netlyn as second navigator.

The three senior navigators; Delf, Jorlit, and Kena, joined them for an end-of-shift meeting that Hrndl had instituted. A few other navigators stood nearby and joined in the light-hearted banter that spread from Kena's exuberance.

"We should have a celebration," a Prednian said.

"What for?" Hrndl asked.

"Promotion, of course!" His round eyes lit up. "Say the word, and I'll arrange it for you."

"Are you seriously expecting me to order some enormous celebration of myself?" Hrndl demanded.

Kena laughed. "We could make it a little more general than that. Netlyn and Jorlit have been promoted, too. We have a new team. Is that not worth a little celebration?"

Delf grinned. "What would we do to celebrate on Earth, Kena?"

"The five of us would go out to dinner together."

"What does that mean?" the Prednian asked, leaning toward her.

She held back a laugh. "We'd go to a restaurant and eat a fine meal."

The subject turned, and nothing more was said. However, the matter was apparently discussed elsewhere. Later, Ghent sent a message to Hrndl to have her next meeting in one of the common rooms.

"Odd," Hrndl murmured to Kena. "I suppose he must want to talk with us about something a little more privately."

The real reason for Ghent's message became clear the next evening, when Kena and the other navigators entered the designated room. They found a table spread with a white cloth, five place settings, and even a bowl of flowers. A soft instrumental played in the background. Delatin and one of his staff waited by a side table with covered dishes.

"What's all this?" Jorlit asked.

"A Human-style dinner," Delatin said. "I have prepared traditional cuisine suitable for each race, but will serve it in the Human style." He turned to Kena. "I researched as best I could. I hope it's at least close to what you are accustomed to."

Kena's smile scrunched the corners of her eyes. "It's really quite delightful. Come, sit down, my friends."

Delf eyed the bouquet with apparent concern. "Are these...edible?"

Kena burst into laughter.

Delatin replied with the reserve of an English butler. What had he researched? "They are for decorative purposes. It is called a *center piece*. A more common choice would be something called"—

he paused to enunciate the English word—"candles. However, I'm unsure what they are made of, and they must be set on fire. I felt flowers would be a better choice."

"On fire?" Delf exclaimed.

Kena's laughter was no longer audible. Even her chair shook.

"Enough of that, or Kena won't be able to eat," Hrndl said, controlling the mirth that glowed in her eyes.

Delatin served suitable drinks for each race. Kena sipped hers and dabbed tears from her eyes. He set a plate before her, and she took up her napkin as she caught the scent of subtle herbs on the rising steam.

"What is the little cloth for?" Netlyn asked.

"Spread it across your lap to catch anything that may spill. You may wipe your fingers or lips on it. At the end of the meal, it's folded again and placed on the table."

"Is there something special we should know about the utensils?" Hrndl asked. "I've noticed before that you lay your knife across the edge of your plate."

"Yes, once it's been used. Also, the knife is never, ever put in the mouth. But don't bother with all this Human etiquette. This is a celebration!"

Hrndl's eyes tilted up. "So it is. Yet, I will not miss this opportunity to learn your culture."

"I've seen Humans touch glasses together," Delf said. "What does that mean?"

Toasts followed, good food, and banter. By dessert, their camaraderie was all that Kena could have wished for on Earth. She and Delf were the only two off duty after dinner. He escorted her on an energetic walk around one of the hallways that ringed the circumference of the ship.

Later, Kena stretched out in bed. "Thank you, my beloved," she murmured. "You are all I need, yet you bless me even more with friends and touches of home." His sweet affection surrounded her in the darkness. He would be with her when she woke and on the excursion planned for morning.

CHAPTER THIRTY-ONE

Kena frowned. No matter how she tried, she couldn't make sense of the anomaly within the nebula.

At least their primary mission was complete. The benzlium had been scattered and challenging to collect. Worse yet, one of the three craft with her was having trouble with its primary drive. In spite of all the problems, they'd gathered enough benzlium to call it a success.

She knit her brow. Still one science task left. With the benzlium collected, they'd have no reason to venture this far from the *Ontrevay* again, and Piert would be disappointed, to put it mildly, if she didn't bring him information on whatever lurked within the gas cloud. For that matter, she would be, too. These energy signatures did not belong together under any circumstances. They defied explanation.

"It doesn't make sense," Quon said. "What could possibly behave that way?"

"Nothing." Which was exactly why she wanted to see it. Kena let out an audible breath and responded to a status update from the damaged craft.

She missed Hrndl in the other couch, but Quon was skillful

and quick with short-range course design. She could leave local activities to him while she focused on the other craft and plotted their return course.

Quon glanced at her plan. "What? Aren't we going for a look at Piert's anomaly?"

A question that still plagued her. "We've got a craft on the verge of failure. It may require towing at any moment. With all that benzlium to drag, I can't send them back to the *Ontrevay* without at least two craft for escort. That leaves no support for us."

Kena pressed the comm control and said, "Elna, run a diagnostic on the extended fields and make sure you're not losing energy there."

A few minutes passed before she answered. "Extended fields are stable, Kena. It's only the primary drive that's draining power."

"I've got it!" Quon exclaimed, his smile as big as Delf's, but not so lopsided.

"Got what?"

"An aperture. Won't take that long to reach the opening. We'll be able to scan uninhibited. Here, take a look." He pointed at the display, his long arm extending past the console. "If we swing around through here, the route is completely clear."

"Hmm. Nice choice," Kena said, "but we still don't have a support craft."

"We don't need one with risk factors that low. We won't be any more than twenty minutes behind the others, in case we get desperate—which won't happen."

Kena feigned an uncertain tone. "I take it, you're game for this?"

He rose to her bait. "Game for it? We have to! We'll be kicking ourselves forever if we don't go see what that is."

She chuckled and sent their course plan to the *Ontrevay*. "Oh, fine then. If you insist."

Kena gave final instructions to the other craft then closed the comm channel. She grinned at Quon and said, "Initiate course."

Twenty minutes later, Quon reversed thrust and synchronized motion with the gap in the thick, dusty cloud.

"Now then, what have we here?" Kena magnified the image and sucked in a breath.

"Thias! It's a craft!"

"Comm silence," Kena ordered. "Scan broad range."

She studied the cluster of spinning objects in orbit around an irregular, high-density rock. Rather than a single item, they had been scanning several, which eclipsed one another. But it was the one unnatural object that now consumed all of her attention.

It emitted a faint energy signal. Was that even enough to maintain life support in a craft of its size? She targeted her scans to the craft and increased visual magnification. Just as she feared. "It's PitKreelaundun," Kena said, her tone grim. "At least it's not fully powered."

The craft was larger than any the *Ontrevay* carried. What was the purpose for all that space? A hold? Living quarters? They were a long way from any planet.

"Are you picking up any other ships?" she asked.

"Nope. No unnatural matter or energy at all."

"Keep looking," she ordered.

"Oh, believe me, I will!"

The craft gradually turned as it orbited, revealing another side —and the reason its power was so low. Twisted, scarred metal gaped open.

"It's severely damaged," she said. "The primary drive will never fire again."

"Guess we won't have to worry about outrunning it."

"Why does it have any power at all?" Kena murmured.

"It would've had reserves. Must have happened recently."

"But it's not transmitting any comm signal—not even automated distress. What's the very last system to remain active when power is near failure?"

"Life support." Quon's voice sharpened. "What are you thinking?"

"That I want a closer scan. Stay on long range. If you see even the slightest oddity, I want to know on the instant." Kena took over piloting and brought her craft through the aperture.

Quon uttered a disbelieving laugh. "Is there anything you wouldn't dare?"

"Approaching a dead ship isn't the most daring act of my life."

"What if it's not as dead as it looks?"

"It hasn't even scanned. At this range, we would know." After reconfiguring her own scan, she followed a precise gap in the hull. She kept her next words slow and soft. "There's a shield still active within the craft." She fell silent.

"Kena?"

She couldn't answer. Her telepathic search was too intense, for she didn't actually know what she was looking for. Seconds slipped by. Her breath caught. "Someone's alive. Distraught."

Quon gasped. "Don't tell me you linked with him!"

"No. He—or she—didn't sense me."

"Then, how do you—Oh, never mind that. What are you going to do?"

Kena cut thrusters and let her craft drift nearer. She laid a couple fingers against her mouth as she frowned at the disabled hulk. "Quon, can you bring us in, match orbit with that craft, and hold position?"

"Sure, but—"

"I don't want a casual 'Sure.'" She released her restraints as she spoke. "Take a good look at that orbit and spin. I need to know for certain you can maintain a stable position." She pushed back and glided through the aft section. She grabbed a handhold near the airlock and detached one of the EVA belts. A quick twist and kick brought her to his side again. "Can you do it?"

"Yes." His gaze rested on the EVA belt in her hand. His tone flattened—more statement than question. "You're going outside."

"I am."

"How will you get through the craft's energy shield without breaking the seal?"

"Back in the days when they and the PitKreelaundun were tentative friends, the Prednians gave them our shielding technology. There's a good possibility my life support shield will merge with theirs. I won't know unless I try."

"What if there's more than one?" he asked. "What if they attack you?"

"There's only one. I think I sensed a child."

"That doesn't make any sense."

"I know," she said, "but that was my impression. What's your entry and exit plan?"

K ena watched from within the airlock as Quon positioned them between orbiting bodies, giving her a safe route to the other craft.

"Position is stable, and the area is clear," he said.

She opened the external airlock door. EVA nav jets carried her across the gap and through the rent hull. Her light revealed a grisly sight as its beam moved through the wreckage. Blood spattered the inner hull. A tethered body floated, the shoulder sliced open. Male, if she judged his size correctly.

She grabbed a twisted bar and propelled herself through an open doorway. A dead shield-ring surrounded it, marked in blue just as they were on Collaborative ships. Promising. She passed a compartment full of unfamiliar equipment and another dead shield. Living quarters came next. Across the dark chamber, her light reached into the nav section. The pilot was strapped into a couch, which had swung around to face the living quarters. Golden brown hair floated around a face frozen in anguish. The body was smaller than the other. Female, no doubt.

Kena averted her eyes from the haunting face and focused on sleeping compartments outlined in blue. She had never seen so many separate shields in a single craft. These PitKreelaundun must have known they were in dangerous territory. Only one of the shield rings glowed. She moved closer and directed her light within the compartment.

A child squinted at her, cringing from the light but desperate to see.

Quon's voice spoke in her ear. "I sure would like to hear more than your breath, Kena. What's going on?"

"Sorry. Two adult corpses and a living child." She tapped her shield controls as she spoke. "I'm through the shield."

The child thrashed in its sleep harness and stretched out trembling arms.

Kena's shield blocked the sound of the child's cries, but the damp, sobbing face told her everything. She opened the soiled harness.

The child grabbed for her, then jerked back from the unnatural shield. Its mouth opened wide in a frantic wail.

Kena tore open supply containers and grabbed a cloth that floated out. She wrapped it twice around the squirming child and drew it tight against her left side. A few touches to her controls, and her shield enclosed the child.

Kena clamped her teeth and endured the child's raspy wail.

"Tell me that's not you, Kena," Quon's voice said.

"You may want to turn the volume down for a bit." She grabbed at some floating clothes and headed aft. "I'm on my way out. Shush, baby. Sh-shush."

The child's cry subsided to a whimper, its squirming to shaking. Kena doubted that had much to do with her soothing voice. This baby was too weak to maintain exertion. By the time they passed through the airlock, the child made no sound except rapid, hoarse breathing.

Kena deactivated her shield in the aft section. "Take us out, Quon. A smooth ride, please, until I can get this baby cleaned up."

"Whew! That can't happen soon enough."

"At least you weren't trapped inside a shield with this smell."

Kena stripped off the child's filthy clothes and did what she could with water and a rag. All the while, the little—girl?—

clutched at Kena's arm, trying to pull close to her again. Kena dressed her in mismatched pants and a shirt that looked much like a miniature robe. She looked around in vain for a place to safely secure a child. The baby found her own spot: arms around Kena's neck, legs gripping her sides. Kena rubbed her back and took her into the cockpit.

"Shouldn't you put it in a restraint somewhere?" Quon asked.

"See if you can peel her off me. I'd say her emotional need is more critical than a personal safety restraint."

"Her?"

"That's my guess. Not that I've ever seen pictures of PitKreelaundun anatomy."

"It's as good a guess as any, until Metchell examines her. How old do you suppose she is?"

Kena positioned her lap belt and pulled part of a sleep restraint around to hold the child against her chest. "By Human measurement, I'd guess about a year-and-a-half."

Quon gradually increased acceleration, turning their course back toward the *Ontrevay*. "Poor little orphan. She doesn't even have a name."

Kena looked over the long-range scans. Still clear. "That's easy to take care of." She cupped her hand against a little damp cheek. The child gazed up at her. What striking eyes she had. No white showed. Wide, brown irises generously flecked with gold. Her skin was the color of dark honey, her hair nearly white. "Pearl. Your name is Pearl."

Quon gave her a quizzical look. "If you say so. What are your plans for Pearl's future?"

"I haven't quite reached the point of mapping out her entire life." Kena snapped open her water bottle and squeezed a few drops into Pearl's mouth. The child quickly proved she knew how to drink in zero G.

"Are you sure that's a good idea?" Quon asked.

Kena took the water away, despite Pearl's protest. "No, but I'll only give her a little at a time. I'm sure she's dehydrated, and we're hours from the *Ontrevay*, especially with this gradual acceleration."

"Do you want me to pick it up?"

"Better not," Kena said. "I don't know what she can—" A spark of light pierced the void on the display. "Oh, no! Shut everything down. Drift."

They both jabbed at controls. Even the cockpit went dark. Only a faint reddish glow from the console illuminated their faces.

A dimensional rift was forming. The spark expanded into a tunnel-like diagram of the invisible dimensional features. Perfectly symmetrical, as only an artificial rift could be. It opened and disgorged a ship.

Kena shut down the scanning field, a silent prayer forming in her mind.

Quon's voice was hushed. "We aren't going to look like a piece of debris if they run a detailed scan, Kena."

"I know, but I'll take any hope or time I can get. Quiet, now."

A hundred thoughts raced through her mind, even faster than her pulse. *What do I do?*

The eternal voice within resonated with the strength and love of a perfect father. *Rest.*

Her lips twitched. How typical that her father would tell her to rest in the midst of disaster. She took a deep breath then let it out. And then another.

"Right. Here's the plan," she said. "The first part, anyway. Most important, do not make a sound if I have to talk with them. I want them believing I'm alone in this craft. Be ready to bring everything back on line. Start with communication and scanning. Wait for my signals."

"If we're going to have any chance of outrunning them, we need a head start."

"I know. A bigger head start than we have right now. Stay calm, Quon."

"Yeah, I get it. Do you want to record a message for the *Ontrevay*?"

"The PitKreelaundun won't permit a signal through. Their communication technology is really quite brilliant."

"How do you know?" Quon asked.

"I've been near them. I've also studied what little information was gathered before they freaked out and started hating us."

"I didn't even know they were ever friendly."

"*Neutral* may be a better word," Kena said. "The Prednians were friendly. Hard to know the PitKreelaundun views."

Their receiving sensors picked up a scan sweep.

"Time's up," Quon said, his voice grim.

Within seconds, a harsh PitKreelaundun voice spoke over the comm system in heavily accented Prednian. "Identify yourself."

CHAPTER THIRTY-TWO

"Get me comm and scan, Quon." Kena ordered. "Keep quiet."

She waited a few seconds before opening her comm channel, so she could see what she was dealing with. The scan revealed an enormous cylinder, which Quon magnified. It was slowing, but still on fast approach and heading straight for her. No escort craft—yet.

"My name is Kena Talgarth." She kept her voice slow and calm, hoping to buy time.

"What race?"

"Human."

"What are you doing here?" the voice demanded. "You're violating the treaty."

"I'm on a science mission. Primarily, I'm investigating matter and energy phenomena we have never before witnessed. At present, I was investigating an anomaly within the nebula. Like you, I'm aware of the borders specified in the treaty. We both know I am not violating it."

"You must have, in order to get here."

"Assumptions are so rarely accurate," Kena said. "What brings you here?"

"It is not your prerogative to question me."

Was he trying to intimidate her? She kept her tone mild. "That's a pity," she said. "Conversation will serve us so much better than demands. I have information that might interest you. I'm willing to participate in a peaceful exchange. If you want to threaten, I'll be off now."

"You can't possibly outrun us."

She chuckled. "True. Forgive me if this sounds arrogant, but I am considered a skillful pilot. Follow me into the nebula if you like. Or you can keep a reasonable distance, and we can talk. What brings you so far from home?"

Distant voices in another language drifted over the speakers. Kena waited. The ship's reverse thrust engaged.

A softer voice spoke, without the heavy accent. "I am Pernanyen of Frayunomen. Please forgive my colleague. We are concerned about some friends who have ceased communicating. It is...disturbing to find an enemy craft so near their last known location."

"I am not your enemy," Kena said. "I am Human. We are not at war with you. I would be happy to demonstrate our peaceful intent."

The ship's approach continued to slow, but she suspected she might already be in weapon range. Kena played her first card.

"About an hour ago, I found a damaged craft while investigating the anomaly I mentioned. If you follow my trail back, you'll see an aperture in the dust cloud where you can get a clear scan. The ship was already severely damaged when I found it."

The man spoke again. "We have located your trail. It leads all the way to our missing craft. We will soon know how it was damaged and what you did there." Even as he spoke, a craft exited from the end of the cylinder.

"Please consider my circumstances," Kena said. "If you're going to deploy craft, I must leave."

"Do not be alarmed," Pernanyen said. "It is only one. They must make haste to our craft, for its power is dangerously low."

Another voice spoke, choppy and nearly squeaking. "Enough. End the suspense. Tell me what you found."

Kena gentled her voice. "I offer you my condolences. The hull was breached. There were two adult bodies."

Murmured voices uttered unintelligible words.

The choppy one spoke again. "There was"—she drew a ragged breath—"a little girl with them. Did you..." Her voice broke.

Quon shook his head and mouthed the word *no*.

What point in delaying? They would soon find the empty, soiled sleep harness within a sealed chamber. "Do not grieve for her," Kena said. "She is safe in my arms."

Strained breathing filled a pause. "You—you have her?"

"Certainly. I had no way to know that anyone was coming, or how long the shield would hold. I couldn't leave a child to die."

"What have you done with her?" the frantic voice demanded.

"Done? Cleaned her as best I could, and dressed her. Also gave her a little water. There has been no time for more."

"What—what are you going to do?"

Was it really necessary to be so frantic? Kena kept her voice neutral. "I think it may be time to give her a little more water."

"You must know that's not what I mean!"

"There is no cause for alarm. My only intent is to keep her safe." Kena dribbled water into Pearl's mouth.

Rapid breathing came over the channel, but at least the voice tempered a little. "Is she—does she seem to be...well?"

"I have no medical training," Kena said, "so I can only guess. She seems weak and dehydrated, but she can still cry. She clings to me."

Pearl gulped at the water. When Kena attempted to turn her, Pearl abandoned the water and grasped Kena even tighter than before. Kena resigned herself to a wet nav suit and let the baby drink with one cheek pressed against her chest. The instant she pulled the water bottle from Pearl's lips, the child began whimpering.

"What are you doing? Why is she crying?" the choppy voice demanded.

"She disagrees with me on how much water she should have at one time." Kena stroked Pearl's hair and murmured in English, "Sh-shush, little Pearl. All is well. You are loved."

"The communication is unclear. Repeat."

"I am only soothing her," Kena said.

"You aren't bonding with her, are you?" The voice asked, tense again.

"That is a Prednian word with no counterpart in any Human language. We are not natural telepaths. I doubt it's even possible for me to bond with her. I wish I could convince you that I intend no harm to this child. What is her name?"

"You need not know."

"As you wish. I'm tired of calling her *child*, so for the time being, I will call her by the name of Pearl."

"You've no right to name her. You have no idea what you're doing. Do you really think you can keep her and care for her? She is mine!"

Pernanyen murmured in the background, "Gwillenin, you must calm yourself. This will not help."

"What do you mean?" Kena asked. "I assumed she was the daughter of the couple in the craft."

"Her mother is my sister. Now that her parents are...are dead, I become her mother. You don't understand what she—"

"Gwillenin." Kena waited for silence. "I have a sister. She has a little daughter, three years old. If my niece were orphaned, I would raise her as my own child. In this, we are much alike. I would gladly place Pearl in your arms, but that is much easier to say than to do. Let's discuss how it may be accomplished."

The first rough voice spoke again. "If you meant that, you would already be in our hold."

"*Your hold* is what concerns me. Do you command the ship, or is there another?"

"Where is all this peaceful intent you wanted to demonstrate? Bring us the child so we may see it."

Quon's chest heaved ever faster with his carefully silent breath. He swung his head from side to side.

"My peaceful intent," Kena said, "is waiting for even a hint that you will return it. Permit me to be blunt. No Human has ever attacked a PitKreelaundun. The reverse is not true. I have been chased by your fighter craft. Their determination to kill me was quite clear. I will not approach until I know who holds authority and what their intent is."

"If so, you must have been in our space, violating the treaty. The fault is yours."

"Another false assumption. It was a PitKreelaundun fighter that broke the treaty. Who holds authority?"

"So you say. You could have been mistaken."

"I was there. You were not. I'm an experienced navigator. I don't make mistakes with spatial coordinates."

Another deep voice spoke clear Prednian. "Enough. You are dismissed." A brief pause. "Kena Talgarth, I am TarKeen, commander of this ship. Though I have just arrived in this room, I've heard this entire conversation. I have no interest in debating your past encounter with us, but would like to confirm a point. Was it only one fighter craft that pursued you?"

"It was."

"You may already know our fighters do not travel alone. If one chose to pursue, there were others who chose not to. I make this point to assure you that not every PitKreelaundun is so antagonistic as the watch officer I just dismissed."

"I see."

"You enquired about authority. I have command of this ship, known as the *Epri7*, and all of its support and fighter craft. A member of the governmental ruling families may countermand my orders. On this ship, Pernanyen of Frayunomen represents the

PitKreelaundun government. You spoke with her a few moments ago. Pernanyen, would you care to confirm what I have said?"

"I confirm it is so. I will add, TarKeen has never given me reason to countermand his orders. Kena Talgarth, I request that you bring the child to us. I commit that you will be permitted to leave in peace. TarKeen, do you concur?"

"I agree with your choice."

"Then, I entrust the details to you," Pernanyen said. "Gwillenin, know that we will recover your daughter. I will send for you when she arrives. Leave us, now, to arrange it."

"Permit me to stay with you."

"No, my friend, for grief disrupts your normal gentleness. Too many voices will invite dissention. Only TarKeen and I need to talk with her."

During the brief silence, Quon shook his head and mouthed the words, "Don't trust them."

TarKeen spoke again. "Kena Talgarth, will you accept our assurances?"

"In conversation my name is shortened to Kena." She turned her craft and realigned its drift toward the *Epri7*. With only nav thrusters, she gave it a little nudge along its new course.

"As you wish, Kena. A more definitive answer would be appreciated."

Kena licked her lips. "All that you say *sounds* acceptable."

TarKeen paused again before answering. "I have never spoken with a Human before. It is difficult to know what I should infer from that."

"You have given me only words. I still bear all the risk. Once you have Pearl, you no longer have a motive for ensuring my safety. It would be well if your arrangements for receiving Pearl demonstrated that your assurances can be trusted."

"I cannot imagine how we can prove our commitments until after you have given her to us."

"I can," Kena said. "How far can you extend an energy field to capture a remote object?"

He was slow to answer—perhaps reluctant to reveal their capabilities. "That would not be an acceptable solution. The child was deprived of contact for too long. She should pass directly from your arms to Gwillenin's."

"That may not be possible. Would you prefer that I guess the distance, or would you like to tell me your range?"

He drew an audible breath. "I realize this requires considerable trust on your part, but it is possible to bring your craft into our hold and safely depart again."

"Ah, yes." Kena drew her words out. "Considerable trust. I'm trying to determine how much trust to extend, and you decline to answer a simple question."

"We do not have technology to extend fields," TarKeen said. "An object must be at the plane of the hull before we can engage it."

"Unfortunate," Kena murmured.

Pernanyen tried again. "Perhaps I should explain that the PitKreelaundun government is dissatisfied with the high degree of tension at the borders. The treaty was supposed to help, but it did not. We have been seeking a means to improve relations. Such encounters as you have described live in memory for decades. As you pointed out, words alone are inadequate. I view this as a rare opportunity. When you leave our hold and continue on your way, we will have demonstrated the truth of our words. Not just to you, but to all who will learn of this. So, we do have strong motivation to let you depart in peace."

"I see." Kena let the silence stretch.

"Do we have a complete impasse?" TarKeen asked.

"No."

"At your current approach rate," he said, "you should arrive in a week. Is there a problem with your primary drive?"

Kena chuckled. "Oh, surely not more than five Prednian days. You must have short weeks." She nudged the ship a little faster. "You may consider that an indication of my plans. My drive is fully operational. For now, grant me a little patience. I occasionally must respond to physical needs, which some races consider unmentionable. Pearl is not making that any easier for me. You'll need to endure some minutes of silence, and then I would like an explanation of docking maneuvers."

"Certainly."

Kena cut communication and let out a long sigh.

Quon looked too appalled to speak. After a moment, he asked, "Do you really need to relieve yourself?"

"Not nearly as bad as I needed an excuse to talk to you."

He opened and closed his fist. "Please tell me you're not planning to take us into that ship."

"I won't, but I want them to believe I will."

His hand stilled. "How do you intend to convince them without getting so close that all hope of escape is gone?"

"We approach fast, reach the highest speed we can manage, release what they want, veer away, and head for safety. They'll need to decide whether to pick up Pearl or chase this craft. I believe they will opt for Pearl. By the time they have her safe, you'll have that head start you wanted."

He frowned at the console. "It might work."

Kena squirmed out of the awkward restraint. "Start planning the course, while I go aft. I'll be back in a couple minutes."

Out of Quon's view, Kena released the guard on her demeanor. Her shoulders heaved. Automatic, physical motions could not claim her attention. Her thoughts churned, lurching back and forth. *Oh, God, help me! If I had left her, she would have been safe with her own race by now.*

Stewing over if-only regrets was pointless, but this one stabbed tangible pain through her chest.

I was doing good. Oh father, maybe I should have asked you, but the choice was so obvious! I was rescuing a child. Now I'm on the verge of capture by the *PitKreelaundun.* She'd jeopardized Quon, too. If the PitKreelaundun got this craft, they'd get additional technology, which would make them even more dangerous to the entire

Collaborative. *Please, father, show me some other way out of this mess. Please!*

She'd started shaking. Her trained navigator's mind snapped an order at her fears. *You do not fall apart in danger!* She took several calming breaths. It was so hard to hear God when focused on fear.

He spoke the instant she turned her attention to him. *I love you. I work all things together for good. I have promised: I will never, never, never leave you!*

Kena wrapped herself in his words. As an energy shield protected her body, so his words protected her mind. She let herself drift in mid-air for a moment, rubbing Pearl's back. If only another idea would come to her. But it didn't.

She took a deep breath, grabbed her EVA belt from its anchor, and returned to the cockpit.

Quon eyed the belt. When he spoke, his voice was subdued, echoing her unspoken fears. "There are your acceleration and release options."

Kena touched the console to select one then made a slight alteration.

"That's getting awfully close, considering the speed."

"I know, but I'm not sure how fast we can accelerate with Pearl on board. We'll just have to adjust as needed."

He eyed the belt again. "That needs to contact the body all the way around, and the closure must be engaged correctly."

"Yeah. For some strange reason, there's no baby-sized EVA belt on this craft." She'd meant it to sound light, but sarcasm edged her words.

"You're planning to go out with her, aren't you?"

"I don't see any other way."

"No, Kena. Do not do this!"

"I can't let them have this craft," Kena said. "It needs a pilot. I made the decision to rescue Pearl. It's my responsibility to salvage what I can out of this disaster."

"I can't just fly off and leave you here."

"I was hoping you'd feel that way." She tightened her lips to keep them from trembling. "I'm going to ask them to let me out of their hold and withdraw. If they do, you can come back for me. If not, you will return to the *Ontrevay*."

"Kena..." His hands clenched and extended, the fingers arching as though he longed to grab something.

"I'm open to better ideas, so long as they keep you and this craft out of PitKreelaundun hands. They must also keep the PitKreelaundun from chasing us all the way back to the *Ontrevay*. I will not start a war."

Silence stretched. Kena wiggled her computer from between her belt and Pearl's leg and anchored it to the console. She uploaded a recording of the conversation she'd just had with the PitKreelaundun. "If they don't let me go, give my computer to Ghent and ask him to get it to my family on Earth."

"Understood." His voice was barely audible. He forced confidence into it. "But it will be here waiting for you when I pick you up."

"I expect so." Kena got the EVA belt around herself despite Pearl's objection to any movement that interfered with her grip. She settled into her couch. "Engage the primary drive. Let's get this over with before I get peed on."

TarKeen's voice came back on the comm channel with a description of docking procedures. Kena listened and questioned as though she intended to use them. Another tidbit of information to return to the Collaborative, assuming Quon escaped. She had never docked within a spinning cylinder, and the method the PitKreelaundun had developed intrigued her. Rather than the chambered bay of the *Ontrevay*, they had fashioned a receiving bay interlaced with a web-like version of energy shielding. A relief, since she and Pearl would be propelled toward them with all the momentum of her craft.

TarKeen was silent for a few minutes then returned with the statement, "The captain of the *Ontrevay* has contacted us."

"I'm sure he has," Kena said.

"We have given him a summary of the situation and assured him that you will be permitted to return."

"I see. Would you care to explain why I have not received communications from him?"

"They have sent several requests for your status," TarKeen said. "We are blocking the communication signal."

Pernanyen rushed into speech. "I would like you to understand our reasons. You offered peace to us as a Human. We are dealing with you as a Human. However, we understand that you are a member of an Interstellar Collaborative crew. This presents possible contradictions. We do not wish to destabilize an already sensitive situation."

Quon made a derisive face at the ship in their display screen.

"I perceive your concern," Kena said "However, withholding communication is likely to increase distrust. I assume you have recorded our conversations. If you will not let me speak with Ghent directly, I request that you send him the recordings."

"We will consider your request," Pernanyen said.

When Kena closed the comm channel, Quon rudely parroted Pernanyen's last sentence.

Kena smirked. "You would never make it in a diplomatic position."

"Believe me, I will stay with navigation. Do you really think we'll ever be able to trust them?"

"I'll let you know in an hour," Kena said. "Pearl is breathing hard. You'd better level off the acceleration rate. Keep an eye on the craft that went into the nebula. And let me know if the *Ontrevay* changes position."

Kena kept their attention on navigating, determined to ignore the feeling in the pit of her stomach. Increasing detail of the *Epri7* came into focus. "Look at this!" she said. "It's not a single cylinder. There are several...kind of like separate decks nested inside each other, all spinning at different rates."

"Wonder how they move from one deck to another?"

"I'm reading considerable shielding between decks. They could enclose airlocks and let them rotate." When they drew a little closer, she said, "Look at the way the shield is configured over the flat end. It's not flat at all, but stepped in. Every deck is completely self-contained in its own shield."

"Redundant to the extreme," Quon said.

"Not a bad design if you fly around explosive debris all the time. Failure of the outer hull would have no impact on the decks within. See that all this data gets to the *Ontrevay*."

TarKeen addressed her again. "Why are you still accelerating?"

"First, you complain that I approached too slow; now too fast. I would like to hand Pearl to her new mother and be on my way as soon as possible."

"You're more than halfway here," he said. "Additional speed is both inefficient and concerning."

"Perhaps, but it is possible. Reverse thrust can compensate during final approach. I know my craft better than you do. It is— shall we say, unnecessary for you to tell me how to operate it."

She closed the channel. "Time is about up. I'll wait by the airlock. Be sure you're out of range before you slow down."

A few more minutes passed. TarKeen's voice grew adamant.

No other option had presented itself to Kena. She enquired of her beloved one more time, listening deep within. The only response was quiet assurance. She felt more like vomiting than continuing, but she had no choice.

The EVA shield enveloped her and Pearl. She entered the airlock and passed through the opposite hatch. Her craft lingered between her and the *Epri7*. It continued on course for a moment, increasing separation from her.

Father, protect me.

I work all things—all things—together for good. Even the things that look bad.

Quon swung away and fired the primary drive to maximum.

CHAPTER THIRTY-THREE

"What are you doing?" TarKeen's voice demanded.

"I have exited my craft. I'm still on the same course, heading straight for you. Can you scan in enough detail to locate me and Pearl?"

After a brief pause, he said, "Confirmed. Who is piloting the craft?"

"His name is Quon."

"Quon, turn the craft back to original course." TarKeen sounded like he was used to being obeyed.

"He is under my orders," Kena said, "not yours. Since you tend to restrict communication, I have already given him full instructions."

"This is madness. How can we fulfill our commitment when you have sent your craft away? We did not agree to provide you with PitKreelaundun transport."

Time to keep her voice calm. "Nor did I agree to bring my craft within your hold. I bring you Pearl; that is all. It's really quite simple for you to honor your commitment. You need only release me in the same manner that I arrive and withdraw from the area. Quon will return for me when you are beyond intercept range."

"Are you seriously asking us to cast you adrift in the void?" TarKeen asked. "Alone?"

"Why so shocked? My EVA belt will keep me safe."

"Apparently, you have never been alone."

She laughed. "No, never, but our perceptions diverge. I doubt we understand one another. My approach is the immediate concern."

"True." His voice turned grim. "I told you before, you were approaching too fast."

"Yes, and now I have virtually no ability to slow down. You will need to compensate."

"And if we cannot?"

"I can think of at least two ways. You probably know more. Why are you so angry with me, TarKeen? Did you want more than Pearl?"

His voice leveled again. "You misconstrue my tone. I am not angry with you. I am concerned for your wellbeing. If you withhold information, it's harder to ensure your safety. You intentionally hid that there was another pilot on board and what options you have."

"True. Do you not also conceal information from me?"

"To what do you refer?" he asked.

"Is there not a captain as well as a commander on PitKreelaundun ships? Does not the captain outrank the commander? Yet you did not mention this when you explained the authority structure. I wonder what options the captain may have that are hidden from me."

TarKeen paused before speaking again. "I did not mention him because I didn't want to complicate the issue while he was unavailable to talk with you. His name is Leonfir. It is currently his sleep time. I have served with him for several years, and I'm convinced that he will agree with what Pernanyen and I have committed to. Even if he didn't, he cannot countermand Pernanyen of Frayunomen. If I had realized you have knowledge of our command structure, I would have told you this before."

"Such a reasonable explanation. Do you care to tell me how you plan to receive Pearl and me?"

"In a moment," TarKeen said. "Pernanyen, please talk with her. It may help ease isolation stress."

Their concern seemed excessive, but hardly worth debating.

Pernanyen spoke again, her voice calm and gentle. "You have more information than I would have expected. Where did you learn of our ships' command structure?"

"The Prednians who first made contact with your race distributed a racial profile. I included cultural studies in my formal education. Your race was one of many I studied."

"We interacted with them for such a short time."

"I know," Kena said. "There wasn't much to study. And with only one perspective, it's bound to be skewed. Still, it was better than nothing. It included the names of the seven ruling families, so I recognized Frayunomen. It also mentioned two non-ruling families, which we find puzzling. If they are non-ruling, why are they designated with the ruling families?"

"There is a time when each ruling family must relinquish authority for one generation. It enables change and lowers the risk of stagnation within the government." Pernanyen paused, then said, "TarKeen has the information you requested."

"We will alter configuration of our shields," he said, "to absorb some of your momentum. Unfortunately, we cannot absorb it all without risking damage to your shield. We must also move the ship away from your approach to lessen the speed difference. You will need to be outside longer than you realized."

"I was aware of this possibility."

"Has the child shown increased stress during isolation?" he asked.

"What do you mean? Since I left my craft?"

"Yes."

"She didn't react," Kena said, caressing Pearl's head. "She is aware of me, so I doubt she perceives isolation. As long as I don't move her away from my chest, she's calm."

"Perhaps we again misunderstand one another," TarKeen said, "so we will leave this. I'm concerned that you will surprise me again. Is there any possibility that you will use maneuvering jets?"

Kena smiled. "Not unless you tell me to."

"Thank you." He went on to confirm the details of her shield specifications then finally asked, "Do you have any questions for me?"

"Did you send the recording to the *Ontrevay* as I requested?"

"We did," TarKeen said. "Also, our following communications."

"I expected to receive a status report from Quon by now."

"Just a moment."

A half-minute passed. Quon's welcome voice sounded in her ear. "I'm receiving all this, Kena. Probably near real-time. I am on planned course. The *Ontrevay* has not moved, and the PitKreelaundun craft has just left the nebula with the disabled craft in tow. How are you doing?"

"I'm fine," she said. "Carry on."

"Yes, ma'am."

After a brief silence, Pernanyen's voice returned. "You can talk with him more, if you like."

"Constant conversation is not necessary for my peace of mind."

Pearl whimpered and turned her head, seeking something. Kena responded with soft murmurs, stroking her hair and back.

"Can you tell what distresses her?" Pernanyen asked.

"Thirst or hunger, most likely. She opens her mouth. I didn't bring the water with me. Shush. Hush, my little Pearl."

"Why do you give her a name?" Pernanyen asked. "You know she has another. Are you planning something other than returning her to Gwillenin?"

"I will do as I have said," Kena answered. What importance did this race invest in names? She couldn't pass up an avenue to explore their culture. "I named her before you arrived. She is not an object; she is a person and should have a name. Gwillenin won't disclose it, so she is Pearl to me. It's common for Humans to have multiple names. I understood that you do, as well. An additional name will not harm her. It wouldn't even hurt you to pronounce it."

"Our names have significance. We do not know what Pearl means."

"It's a Human word for a gem that symbolizes purity and innocence. When used as a name, it means *treasured one*."

Pernanyen drew a deep breath. "Why did you choose such a name for her?"

What did her whispery tone signify? Stunned surprise, perhaps? Hard to be sure, but Kena wasn't about to waste this moment. "A few reasons, I suppose. In ancient times, pearls were rare because they could only be found by diving underwater to search for and extract them. It strikes me as similar to finding a child in a nebula—rare, indeed—and then passing through the vacuum to extract her from a dead craft. Also, it is my nature to treasure children. A child is innocent of any wrong-doing, regardless of what other members of her race may have done. And so, I named her Pearl."

Pernanyen exhaled a soft *Oh*. It took her a moment to speak again. "We appreciate that you have bestowed such a fine name on her. I would like you to understand why Gwillenin wouldn't reveal her name. PitKreelaundun parents often use a child's name when they are teaching her how to establish a link. If you call her by that name, she may reach for you and be distressed when you do not respond."

"Then, I agree that I should not use it," Kena said. "She does, at times, search for someone."

"Do you mean...telepathically?"

"Yes."

"I—don't understand. You said Humans are not telepaths."

Kena committed the rising pitch of Pernanyen's puzzled tone to memory. "True, yet I live among them, so I've learned to sense telepathic energy. I can recognize and avoid an attempted link, which may be necessary to prevent injury."

"How very odd." Pernanyen said. "Again, we may not understand one another."

Kena chuckled. "I'm glad you noticed. It is well to remember that when a Human speaks of telepathy, there's a very strong chance you do not understand what they really mean. Will Gwillenin try to establish a link with Pearl immediately?"

"Most certainly."

"Then, I would much appreciate it if no one but she approaches me."

"As you wish," Pernanyen said.

"It will take me a moment to release Pearl from my shield. Gwillenin will need to be patient."

"I will tell her." Pernanyen's voice quickened." I know she sounded harsh, but it's only because she's distressed over her sister's death and Pearl's long isolation. She is normally a gentle woman."

"I understand." Kena marvelled. The conversation had changed so much from that first demand to identify herself. She was completely dependent on them already. They no longer had any real need to treat her with courtesy, yet they did. The *Epri7* filled her view but no longer seemed so ominous. As long as nothing went awry, there seemed to be a good chance that they would let her go.

TarKeen's voice spoke again. "Kena, are you able to turn without risk of altering your course?"

"Easily."

"I suggest you turn 180 degrees to face away from the ship. The loss of reference point may be disorienting, but it will be brief."

Sheesh! This was one race that could not stand to be outside their ships. She executed the simple maneuver. "The nebula is really quite lovely, TarKeen. I'm sure I'll be fine with the change of scene."

"The first field you contact," he said, "will cause the hardest jolt. Your momentum will diminish with each field you pass through."

"I would appreciate a final countdown."

"Five, four, three, two, one."

Kena's organs compressed against her spine. Pearl's body jammed into her chest. Air was forced from her lungs. Then, she broke through the first shield. Pearl let out a wail.

"Three, two, one," TarKeen said.

Again, though not as bad, she collided with a wall that resisted then burst.

"Three, two, one."

More like a rubber wall, this time. Pearl's cry silenced at each impact, then resumed.

Counting down, then crying. Counting, crying. The stepped walls of the *Epri7* enclosed them.

"How many more?" Kena asked.

"Two more. Three, two, one."

This impact wasn't bad at all.

"The last one will be gentler but longer," TarKeen said. "Three, two, one."

More like plunging into an enormous marshmallow. Pearl's cry barely faltered.

"You'll feel a slight rebound," TarKeen said. "You can relax now."

Blue lines marked the inside of the receiving bay, flashing past Kena's vision as the cylinder spun. They began to slow.

"Your respiration sounds rapid. Are you injured?" TarKeen asked.

That was nothing compared to the hammering in her ears. "No. Just a little dizzy."

"We're aligning you with the spin rate of the receiving bay. Where is your balance organ located?"

"Ears." Kena closed her eyes, steadied her breathing, and murmured soothing sounds to Pearl. Weight returned to her body, pressing toward her toes. When she opened her eyes again, the blue lines of the bay were barely spinning in relation to her motion. They had adjusted her position so that her head was exactly centered in the bay. Nice.

Her motion stabilized. The bay appeared stationary. She glanced around the inner cylinder. Panels filled the spaces between the blue lines. Doors to many holds, by the look of them.

"We're bringing you toward one of the access tubes," TarKeen said. "It will take you to the chamber where Gwillenin is waiting with Pernanyen and one of our doctors, Freltenloe."

The energy field drew Kena through an opening in the wall, which was now beneath her feet, and down into the chamber. Five people, not three, waited there. Her stomach tightened.

She swept her gaze across them. The photos she had seen of PitKreelaundun had accurately depicted their appearance variations. Of the black-haired, brown-skinned variety, only one was present. Taller than Kena, he stood against the wall to her right. The others had honey-brown skin, much like Pearl's, with hair ranging from blonde to dark brown. Their softer features lacked the prominent chin and cheekbones of their darker companion. They wore tunics over their trousers, the women's fuller with a trailing side.

Kena glanced around as TarKeen's voice spoke in her ear, but none of their lips moved. "The field is releasing you, now. The impression of gravity may be less strong than you're accustomed to."

She took a short step to test her weight. Just a bit light.

"We'll broadcast your voice to the chamber until you release your EVA field."

A small woman approached, her golden-brown hair reminding Kena of the dead pilot's. "I am Gwillenin."

Kena nodded and looked to the other woman. Her brown tunic glittered with coppery flecks as she moved, and a beaded chain lay across her chest. The front locks of her blonde hair were caught up in a complex twist, but it was her eyes that held Kena's attention, much like amber encircling ebony.

"Please do not regard us," the woman said. "We will wait."

"I would like to know who is in the room," Kena said.

"I am Pernanyen of Frayunomen." She gestured to the man at her side. "This is Freltenloe, the doctor TarKeen mentioned."

Kena's glance flicked to the men who stood to either side against the walls. They wore belts with various devices clipped to them. Tools? Weapons? Kena looked back to Pernanyen.

"These men?"

"They attend me when I am with a member of an alien race. They need not concern you."

Gwillenin spoke again. "I wish to offer you an apology for the manner in which I addressed you earlier."

"Your apology is accepted."

Pearl still uttered little sobs. Kena shifted her higher in order to extend the controls on her belt. Pearl clung tighter than ever to Kena's neck.

"Jennellee," Gwillenin said.

"She can't hear you through the shield," Kena said. "Can you link without touch or sound?"

"Not with a child who has never shared a link with me."

Too bad. This poor little girl was going to scream. Kena grasped Pearl's hands and pulled them from her neck. The child let out a shriek.

Gwillenin's face contorted and trembled. Not a pretty way to cry, if that's what it was. "Don't do that!"

Kena let go, and Pearl flung herself back in place.

"Gwillenin, stay calm," Freltenloe said. "Kena, it is likely that Pearl will turn to Gwillenin as soon as they link. Please deactivate your shield."

"No."

"It's no longer necessary," he said.

"This is not open to debate. I asked for one of you, TarKeen said three would join me, but there are five. My shield stays. Gwillenin, please come near."

She hurried closer. Kena extended the shield to surround her then gasped and turned her face away. The woman's intensity was much like Ghent's, but far less controlled. Did she really need to spray that much telepathic energy to create a link?

Gwillenin drew back. "I am so sorry!"

"Yeah." Kena steadied herself then drew back the faint, tender presence she had used to soothe Pearl. "Focus on your child."

"Jennellee." Gwillenin caressed her child with both voice and hands. She repeated the name and spoke a few words in her own language.

Pearl turned her face away from Kena's chest.

Gwillenin repeated the same name and words several more times. Pearl let one arm slide from Kena's neck and clutched Gwillenin's fingers. Their link formed. Pearl's body relaxed. The two women eased the child around, her legs releasing Kena's waist and wrapping around her new mother's. But during the exchange, Pearl's fingers laced into the hair above Kena's ear. Something she clearly intended to keep.

Kena peeled the tiny fingers open and worked her locks free. Pearl turned and leaned back toward her, while keeping a tight grip on Gwillenin's hand. Her palm pressed against Kena's face. The child's tender longing brushed her awareness.

Kena pressed a quick kiss into the little palm and placed it on Gwillenin's shoulder. "Go home now, little love."

Gwillenin stared at her. "You *are* a telepath!"

"Not like you think." Kena used her belt controls and stepped away, drawing the shield back to enclose only her.

Pearl—once again Jennellee—snuggled in and laid her head on her new mother's shoulder. Her eyes drooped.

Freltenloe held a device near the base of the child's head.

Gwillenin's mouth dropped open then slowly lifted into a bemused smile. "She is not injured!"

"No," he murmured. "She doesn't seem to be. She needs food and water. Take her to the medical facility nearest your home. You may need to spend the night there with her."

Gwillenin stared at Kena. Her voice grew husky. "I don't know how you did it. There is no way I can ever tell you of...of all the thanks I feel for..." Her mouth worked without sound.

"You already have," Kena said. "I wish you peace."

Gwillenin turned and hurried out.

A tangible silence filled the room. Kena stowed her belt controls and ran a hand through her disheveled hair.

Now, would they keep their word?

CHAPTER THIRTY-FOUR

Pernanyen stepped nearer. "Please forgive me for causing you stress with too many people. I was too fascinated. I could not bear to wait—to meet the woman who would risk so much for the child of an enemy. I did not even know for sure I would have a chance to talk with you. Will you grant me a few minutes?"

"As you wish. Has the *Epri7* returned to its earlier location?"

Pernanyen shrugged. "It is somewhere near the *Ontrevay*, which has also moved away from the nebula. TarKeen and your captain, Ghent, agreed on the location and distance. Quon is now in contact with the *Ontrevay*, but is still waiting between our two ships. I hope this contents you, so we may talk of more important things."

Kena nodded.

Pernanyen swayed to one side and licked her lips. "I found a little, a very little, information about Humans. I think you must know more of us than we know of you. It was in with many other racial profiles that the Prednians gave us quite some time ago. It seems, they are fond of distributing information."

Kena's chest tightened with suppressed laughter. She managed a calm response. "They have that reputation. What did they say of Humans?"

"Your planet is called Earth, the third planet of a yellow star. Quite remote from us—on the far side of the Collaborative's reach. You have colonies on the fourth planet, Mars, and your rather large satellite, Luna. They don't sound like very friendly habitats."

"They're not. The colonies have mining and scientific purposes. What else did you find interesting?"

"The Tenelli were the first race to contact you. The profile said you have only recently joined the Collaborative, though we realize the information is old. Your robotics technology is of interest to the Collaborative. There were several references to navigational skills. That puzzled me. They made it sound like it's a racial trait."

Kena couldn't stop the laughter this time.

Pernanyen smiled up at her. "Your laugh is so pretty—almost like music."

"Thank you. Not many of us are navigators, but those who pursue that career tend to be quite good at it."

"You certainly seem to be. TarKeen searched for records of encounters and found one in which the Collaborative navigator was addressed as Kena. We don't know whether Humans are a race that reuses names."

"We do." Kena omitted just how unique her own first name was. "Did he mention anything else about it?"

"Yes. Three other craft recorded scans, so it's very clear what happened. He published a bulletin to the ship." She walked the fingertips of one hand across her other fingers as she made each point. "It states that the fighter which pursued did so against the advice of the others; the actions of the Collaborative pilot were evasive; the PitKreelaundun pilot died by crashing into an asteroid; and the ruling families chose not to raise a charge of border violation."

"I see."

"If you were the pilot, you may not want to say so here. I will not ask you directly, but I wanted you to know the PitKreelaundun view."

"Thank you. What else did the Prednians say of Humans?" Kena didn't really care—anything to change the subject.

"Referring to culture, they said, 'Humans have long been separated by oceans and barriers to travel. Consequently, there are many cultures, which are not yet fully blended.' I find that difficult to interpret. Are they implying that such travel barriers have only been overcome recently? This would seem odd for a race that colonizes other planets."

"Indeed," Kena said. "A profile will tell you as much about the race that wrote it as the race it describes. Prednians have one culture. As far as we can tell, this has been true for quite a long time. Since they cannot imagine a reason why cultures should vary, they assume physical barriers caused it on Earth. Perhaps these contributed, but they are neither the cause nor the reason distinct cultures persist."

"Why, then, do the cultures not blend?"

"To some degree, they do," Kena said. "If I may turn the question, why should they blend?"

"For unity," Pernanyen said, as though it should be obvious. "To include all. Is that not desirable to a Human?"

"It is, but sameness is not unity. Different cultures can achieve unity, if they are willing."

"You intrigue me so!"

What an odd intonation. How could she respond to such a statement? Kena tilted her head and asked, "Was there anything else?"

"The profile included some taboos and sensitivities." Pernanyen shook her head as she spoke. "Which we will avoid. There was some mention of social behaviors. Humans like music and have a great variety of styles. Your dances are vigorous. Social events typically include food. You can eat sweet/sour, but not freth/prin." Pernanyen's shoulders swayed forward and back, as though talking were like walking. "Unfortunately, that only tells me how to avoid making you ill, not what flavors you actually like. Apparently, food must be consumed in accordance with certain rules. That part was oddly emphatic, yet vague."

Kena lifted a shoulder. "Prednians say that about every race. In reality, we don't much care, so long as cleanliness is maintained."

Pernanyen smiled. "I'm sure we can accommodate that. I invite you to join me for a meal so we may talk more."

Kena ensured that her expression remained pleasant. "Thank you for the invitation; however, I must decline."

"I realize food from an unfamiliar race may pose a concern," Pernanyen said. "I offered a meal in an attempt to match your culture. But if you prefer, we can converse without it. I would be pleased to take you to a furnished room. Perhaps you would prefer to sit while we talk."

"I find our conversation interesting," Kena said, "but we must remember broader concerns. Commitments were made by you and TarKeen. It's time for me to return to the *Ontrevay*."

"We will honor our commitments, but I see no need to hurry. Please do not be concerned. We are most grateful to you for your care of Jennellee Pearl. I promise you, we will do nothing to harm you."

Kena's stomach tightened. "It's your relations with the Collaborative that you are about to harm. Is this conversation still being transmitted to Ghent?"

"No, it was necessary to interrupt communication while you passed through the shields. I told TarKeen not to restart it until I had time to review it."

"Please consider the results of your actions. A silence this long will cause concern."

"How rushed your life must be," Pernanyen said. "TarKeen knows what is happening; I'm sure he is informing your captain. If there were a serious concern, he would tell me. Please, I so much wish to know more of you and your race. Come."

She turned toward the door, but Kena didn't move. Freltenloe stepped aside but kept his eyes on Kena. The other two remained as statues.

Pernanyen paused at the door then walked slowly back to her. Kena could feel her telepathic energy carefully extend. At least she knew how to control it. Kena yielded no access.

"You are a telepath," Pernanyen said.

"Not like you think."

"The Prednians said Humans aren't natural telepaths, but that you can be trained. Clearly, you are one of the trained."

Kena shook her head. "Prednians do not understand what telepathy means to a Human. None of the races do, though they all think otherwise."

"No race understands another," Pernanyen said. "Particularly if they do nothing but talk. They speak from their own perspectives and hear from their own perspectives. Neither has any idea whether they understand or were understood."

Where was she going with this?

Words spilled from Pernanyen like waves surging through a cracked dike, and her shoulders swayed faster. "This happened when we first met the Interstellar Collaborative. It happened again when we established our treaty. We thought we were being very specific and clear. Yet the Collaborative interprets the borders in a way we never envisioned. We would have stated them differently if we had known."

Not good! Kena concentrated on listening. She'd have to be careful if she was going to talk her way out of this.

Pernanyen's words flowed so fast she didn't seem to breathe. "Most PitKreelaundun believe the Collaborative purposely misinterprets the borders. The Collaborative accuses us of contradicting our own words and trying to extend our reach. Perhaps they really believe the things they say. Perhaps it is all show. We have no way to determine how to communicate with any of your races and be certain of what is really meant."

Pernanyen leaned forward, and her pace slowed. "The little you have said shows that you comprehend perspective. If I could have a few days with you, perhaps we could learn enough to start communicating. But you will not give me even an hour. And it seems that your captain would not, even if you were willing."

Kena let another breath pass to make sure the tirade was over. "I would love to assist in a dialog between our races," she said. "It needs to start with small steps. Send me back, now. Let me convey what you desire. Let us arrange a meeting where none of us will feel forced or vulnerable. Then, we will talk more."

For a time, Pernanyen was silent, staring up into Kena's face. "If the *Ontrevay* were a ship from Earth, then what you suggest might be possible. But it is not. You do not trust me. They will trust me less. They will not take the small steps you speak of, so only one is available to me. If it is small, it is wasted. Therefore, I will take a single, big step."

Freltenloe watched Pernanyen with narrowed eyes and parted lips.

"What, exactly, does that mean?" Kena asked.

"You will stay for a short time; I will make it as brief as possible. We will link in order to learn of each other quickly."

"I could not possibly!" Kena declared. "I am not acclimated to your race."

"We understand the need. Freltenloe will acclimate you first."

Kena abandoned diplomatic phrases. "No. I can tell already that it will be harsh. Several days must pass before I could link with you, even if I wanted to, which I don't."

Pernanyen heaved a sigh then straightened her posture. "The Prednians only used one form of acclimation. We know of other forms. Freltenloe will have you fully acclimated within a day. Since you are constrained, I will submit to the same after you have time to rest."

"What is that supposed to mean?" Kena asked.

Pernanyen jerked as though Kena had slapped her. "Perhaps my words sound meaningless to you, but I will not be able to withdraw from my obligation. It is law. Else, I forfeit my life." She looked to one of the men. "FarNon, disrupt her shield and remove her EVA apparatus."

The black-haired guard pulled one of those ominous devices from his belt and stepped behind Kena.

The other guard drew near and faced her. "Please, do not panic," he murmured. "Be still."

Freltenloe spoke rapidly in his own language.

Kena felt the shield release and inhaled the tangy scent of alien air. Her stomach muscles twitched, as FarNon's hand slid between her waist and the belt.

"Pardon. I intend no disrespect, ma'am." he said, tugging at the clasp.

Instinct demanded action—spin, jab, kick, drop him—but she was trapped. A sealed chamber, with three men and hundreds more beyond the door. All of them ready to hate her.

The belt released. It brushed against her leg as the guard stepped back with it. Electricity tingled from her spine to fingertips. Her stomach turned in on itself.

"I have made my decision," Pernanyen declared, cutting Freltenloe off. "There will be no more discussion."

Freltenloe widened his stance and made one more statement in Prednian. "Let my statement be heard, ma'am, that I advised against this course of action."

"It is heard and witnessed," Pernanyen said. "Guards, stay with them until they reach the medical facilities."

Then, she strode out the door.

Kena could barely breathe. *Oh, my father, this is not good! All things, Kena. I love you.*

Freltenloe turned to Kena and regarded her through several loud beats of her heart. Two vertical lines between his eyebrows marred his smooth honey-brown skin. Dark brown hair swept back toward the nape of his neck, hiding his ears.

He licked his lips. "I am now responsible for your wellbeing."

"You don't look very pleased about it," Kena said between her teeth.

"It would not displease me," he said, "but it's difficult to reassure you since Pernanyen ordered rapid acclimation. I will not pretend that you'll enjoy it, but I will monitor you closely to ensure you are not harmed."

Kena sought for words that could turn the course of events. She found none.

Freltenloe shifted his weight and drew another breath. "Before we go farther into the ship, I'd like to give you a temporary emfrel shield." He withdrew a device from the pack he carried over one shoulder.

Four simple bands joined together at the ends, similar to the external emfrel shields of any other race—in appearance, anyway. Harmless...probably. In addition to the shield, such devices usually contained simple medical sensors, for heart rate and such. Whether this one contained anything else, she had no way of knowing.

"Will you permit me to fit this to your head?"

Pressure built in her chest. She clamped her lips. No, he did not have permission for anything. But he would do it anyway.

When she didn't answer, he stepped nearer and fit it over her head. The upper and lower bands followed her hairline. The other two, he threaded through her hair. He stepped back, giving her space again, and adjusted the control from a device he held.

She felt nothing but the mental equivalent of silence. Much like a door being closed to block out the sound of a crowd she hadn't even noticed till now.

He motioned one guard toward the door. "Please walk beside me, ma'am. We will not touch you if you do not try to flee."

As though there was a place to flee to!

They walked—one guard behind, one leading—through featureless hallways, which soon changed. Alcoves in the walls held trellises and plants, each one different. Light glowed from them, casting patterns on the floor, as though sun shone through windows. An oddly cozy setting for dread.

311

A voice Kena recognized spoke overhead in a language she did not know.

"Is that TarKeen?" she asked.

"Yes."

"What's he saying?"

"He is giving orders to ensure your safety."

He had to give *orders* to ensure it? Kena shuddered.

CHAPTER THIRTY-FIVE

They entered a reception room with hallways branching from it. Fabric swathed the walls: variegated greens pulled aside in graceful folds, exposing a soft beige background. A half dozen PitKreelaundun, black-haired and brown, turned to stare at Kena. Why did their coloring seem so significant?

"This is Kena Talgarth, a Human," Freltenloe said. "Pernanyen has ordered me to acclimate Kena to our emfrel. I need an assistant, preferably a volunteer."

A black-haired man curled his lip. "Ah! So, we'll get some entertainment, after all. I volunteer. It will be a pleasure to watch her squirm."

The PitKreelaundun drew a collective gasp.

"Get...out!" Freltenloe demanded through clenched teeth. "You are confined to quarters for the duration of Kena's presence on this ship. No communication." To the guards, he snapped, "Bind DrenVid, take him to his quarters, and seal it under my orders."

One of the brown-haired women hurried forward. Tiny lines rayed out from her tense lips. "I offer to assist you. I will tend her needs gently."

"Kena," Freltenloe said, "this is Shannandi. Come."

They led Kena down one of the hallways. A glance over her shoulder gave her a glimpse of a livid PitKreelaundun and impassive guards. What a confusing, unpredictable race.

The next room contained medical equipment. Her pulse quickened anew.

"This is predominantly physical scanning equipment," Freltenloe said. "I would like more knowledge of you in order to care for you effectively. Shannandi, lie down in the scanner to show Kena what to expect."

Freltenloe demonstrated the scan. Trying to reassure her, she supposed. It didn't. Her gaze traveled the room.

"Please lie down," he said, gesturing to the place where Shannandi had lain.

Kena ignored him. Which of these devices was used for acclimation?

"Kena, nothing in this room will cause you any discomfort," he said. "Please lie down. This will take several minutes. You may rest."

She did as he asked, for she had no real choice. Reason fought with fear. It was only a scan—yet one step closer. Panic edged in. She mustn't let it. She should use this time to calm herself. Easier said than done. Pernanyen's obscure words echoed through her mind. What sort of acclimation could be accomplished in a day? They didn't understand! What damage would they do? Constrained link? It couldn't be what it sounded like. But Pernanyen would try whatever it was she meant.

All Kena could get out of Freltenloe were calm non-answers. "Do not speak now. Rest." He wouldn't let her get two words into a sentence. Her first opportunity to speak came when he said, "I'm finished with the scan, but I want to record a sample of your emfrel so Pernanyen can be acclimated."

"I'm Human. We don't project emfrel."

"Pernanyen will still encounter it when she links with you. A brief sample will be adequate."

"There is nothing more I can give you," Kena said. "The sooner you realize that I am not like other races, the better."

"I'll record it later," he said. "You may get up. I want motion scans next."

"Please let me explain."

He ignored her. Instead, he described the next scanning device, again having Shannandi demonstrate. She walked back and forth within a framework structure the size of a short hallway.

"Go in, please," he said to Kena.

At least it delayed the inevitable. And yet, another step closer.

A black-haired man entered as Kena walked. He went to Freltenloe's side, where he stood by the scanner's console. As soon as he spoke, Kena recognized TarKeen's voice.

"I passed DrenVid on his way to his quarters," TarKeen said. "He had the audacity to demand that I override your orders. I confirmed them."

"Do you know the details?" Freltenloe asked.

"I do. FarNon showed me his memory. Let me know when you've had time to submit your charge. I want to endorse it."

Freltenloe nodded. "Have you spoken with Pernanyen?"

TarKeen's voice dipped and slowed. "I have."

"I take it, you were no more successful than I. Did you wake the captain?"

"She forbade it before I even met with her. Our golden girl is not stupid, in spite of her appalling absence of wisdom. It makes little difference whether I wake Leonfir. She will not listen to him either."

"Kena, stop there and turn around." Freltenloe asked for a few more motions. "That will do. I'd like to see any other movements that come naturally to you."

Nothing with agility or speed for you! She lifted her hands overhead then slowly lowered them to her sides. It was the calming start and end of her exercise routine. One more attempt to still her mind.

Her beloved directed her attention to the two men. They seemed so dissimilar.

What was it? True, the physical differences seemed more pronounced than in the photos she had seen, but why did that matter? Her own race accustomed her to far greater variations. But the feeling of significance lingered. Enough of this scanning. She left the framework and approached the two men.

"I am TarKeen."

She nodded. His hair was as black as the void, thick, and a little shaggy—as though it grew no longer than ten centimeters or so and had never met a blade. His eyebrows matched his hair, and his brown skin seemed more substantial than Freltenloe's—like the difference between suede and cotton.

"I have recorded my objection," he said, "to Pernanyen's decision to keep you here after your request to depart. I'm sure you realize, by now, that will change nothing."

She looked back and forth between the two men. "Are you the same race?"

Both men shifted backward. Whatever they may have expected her to say, that was not it.

Freltenloe replied. "We are both PitKreelaundun."

TarKeen gave him a look impossible for Kena to interpret. "That's the answer you will always hear from his race. I will answer that I am PitKree and he is Laundun. We share the same planet and government...and to a degree, the same culture. Jointly, we are called PitKreelaundun."

Why was this not published anywhere? There was no point in asking them. Instead, she asked, "What does *golden girl* signify?"

"Young and inexperienced. The Laundun have white hair at birth, like Jennellee's." TarKeen nodded toward Freltenloe's dark brown hair. "It darkens as they age. Golden hair is only found on very young adults."

"I see." Was there some way that she could get TarKeen to prevent what she dreaded?

"Come here and sit down, Kena," Freltenloe said. "I want to get a blood sample."

She lingered by TarKeen, but he must have noticed her delay. He followed Freltenloe to the side of the room. "Ma'am, I came here to ask you something that may be of importance." He motioned toward the chair.

He wasn't going to continue until she sat. Would his question be useful? Her stomach clenched so tight, it made lowering herself into the chair awkward.

Shannandi came near with supplies. They quickly prepped Kena's arm, and the area went numb.

"What question?" she asked TarKeen.

"You said you were investigating phenomena never before seen. What, precisely?"

"Two planets used to orbit the nearest star. They broke up. No one knows why. Someone had a telescope trained on them, so we know there wasn't a collision."

His brow gathered, and he used the same rising tone Pernanyen had. "No one knows why?"

Kena shook her head. "No. We've gathered some samples of matter from them, but there hasn't been much time to study it yet. It's unstable, which makes study harder."

He just looked at her.

"Don't you understand the imperative to learn the cause?" she asked. "Something that can break up entire planets. Have you no interest?"

"We already know what causes it," TarKeen said. "This is not the first time it's happened. There are a few remnants of such breakups in PitKreelaundun space." He paused and his words slowed. "The last was a few hundred years ago. A planet in our own system. PitKreel, by name."

She sucked in a breath. Her words came out in a whisper. "Your planet?"

He nodded. "That is why we share a planet, now named PitKreelaundun."

Kena closed her eyes as a shudder ran through her body.

TarKeen regarded her intently. "I can see why Pernanyen is intrigued." He left without waiting for a reply.

Kena glanced down at her left arm. Two tubes had been inserted. Shannandi detached a blood sample from one and capped it. Freltenloe wrapped Kena's arm, perhaps guessing that she would pull the tubes out, given the opportunity. Control of her body was slipping away. Soon their emfrel would disrupt her ability to think. And then, what would Pernanyen do?

"You do not have any comprehension of what you're about to do," Kena said. "I am not like other races."

He ignored her yet again.

Shannandi tried a soothing tone. "Don't be alarmed. Freltenloe has a great deal of experience in studying alien races. He knows what to watch for during acclimation: both how to protect you and how to be sure it's effective."

"I'm less concerned about acclimation than about the link Pernanyen intends."

Shannandi drew back and blinked several times. "Oh! You needn't be. She is skillful. I'm sure she has no intent to harm you."

"Intentions mean nothing. It's ignorance that worries me. I must control the link."

"You will have that opportunity," she said, sweetly reassuring.

Kena ground her teeth. She licked her lips and tried again. "Throughout the entire link."

"Tha—"

"Shannandi." Freltenloe pointed at the display behind Kena. "Have you noticed yet that your responses do not calm her? The reverse, in fact. Stop responding." He switched languages and added a sentence.

Shannandi reached for something on the counter. They stood on either side of Kena, now. Harder to watch. Freltenloe wrapped something around her upper arm.

"What are you doing?"

"One last test. It won't take long."

Her bicep relaxed—without her permission.

At Shannandi's touch, Kena jerked her right arm away.

This distraction must have been what Freltenloe intended. He pressed something against the base of her neck.

Kena's muscles released, beyond her control. Her body slumped in the chair.

"It will only last a few minutes," he said. "I'm just relieving you of the decision whether to fight me or walk into the next room."

She could only watch. How purposeful their motions were. He lifted her body, which seemed to be a foreign thing under someone else's control. Her pulse hammered in her head as he carried her to another room.

"Raise the table," Freltenloe said. He positioned her limp body. "Support her neck."

His simple dispassionate statements increased her sense of vulnerability. Kena couldn't even shudder.

Their words switched to their own language. They removed the temporary emfrel shield and fit something more elaborate over her head. A network of bands. Shannandi gently pulled Kena's hair through the gaps, so the device fit snug to her scalp, all the way from the base of her skull to her eyebrows.

Freltenloe wrapped a restraint around her waist. An energy field anchored her elbows to it.

A muscle quivered in her arm. She tried moving her fingers, but got only a sluggish response.

It seemed strange how little the PitKreelaundun said to her while they worked. None of the repetitive descriptions she was used to. Would she lose memory? Would they even tell her when it was time to start her relaxation technique?

"You have muscle control again," Freltenloe said. "Use it."

What a strange thing to say. "Why?"

He secured an IV tube to her arm. "You're under minimal restraint. Just enough to keep you on the table. I've activated fields around the sides. Explore how far you can move."

It seemed pointless, but she moved enough to touch the walls of her transparent cage. "Will you at lea—" Then it struck. A cry forced its way through her constricted throat.

Acclimation emfrel always felt like an engulfing wave. This was like a firehose spray twisted down to narrow focus. Staccato bursts. Pause. Repeat. Beating one place, then another, and another. Cycling back through them again. And again.

She writhed, dragging her head along the padded table to dislodge the cap from her scalp. Futile. She curled up, straining her head toward her hands. The restraint held them a centimeter apart. Panting breath forced spit through her clenched teeth. "What're you…doing?"

"Rapid acclimation."

"This…isn't…accli…mation!"

"The doses are high, so it must be administered in small areas. Your shield is responding. The acclimation is highly effective."

"Stop!"

Her scream met silence.

She threw herself against the side field and tried to bring her legs up to kick through. They wouldn't respond correctly. Every burst of emfrel made her jerk and falter.

Her stomach revolted. Vomit spewed out.

The emfrel stopped.

Her damp cheek rested on the table, her hair tangled and wet. A suction tube cleaned up her vomit. She was shaking and crying. Hot. Cold. Shuddering. Shannandi wiped her face.

"Kena, some motion is useful," Freltenloe said. "It prevents disorientation, but too much could harm you. I'm increasing restraint a little. It's not possible for you to break through the fields. Move, but do not fight."

The extreme doses of emfrel resumed. On and on, endless. Her body thrashed. Pernanyen's words echoed in her mind. *He'll have you acclimated within a day.* A day? Not a whole day!

Pauses were few. Once to remove the lower half of her nav suit and clean her. She hadn't been aware of losing control. Even the feeling of humiliation was beyond her. Another pause to wipe away bloody froth from her mouth and restrain her jaw. Her tongue hurt, like all her muscles. She was allowed less and less space to move. The agony continued. Interminable.

CHAPTER THIRTY-SIX

Ghent sat with his officers in the visual communication room. Not the most convenient place to meet. The chairs all stood along one side of the curved table, facing the blank view screen. There was space for pacing, though, and some officers took advantage of this.

Hours had passed, too many of them in silence. After Pernanyen's last message, the PitKreelaundun would not even acknowledge communications from the *Ontrevay*.

Several officers continued to study the old Prednian profile of the PitKreelaundun race. That, along with records of the treaty negotiations, which had been brief and clearly inadequate. They'd even sifted the information Quon brought back.

Ghent rubbed a shurg back and forth over his knuckles. In all this study, nothing of value emerged. He could devise no method to extract Kena from the *Epri7*. He couldn't even communicate with the PitKreelaundun—or anyone else.

Ghent stretched and relaxed his tight shoulders, then touched the control console. PitKreelaundun communications replayed while the officers listened, searching for any hint they could use to reestablish a dialog.

In the recording, TarKeen's voice gave Kena the countdown she requested. He made a few more statements; first that Pearl had been given to Gwillenin, and later that Kena and Pernanyen were conversing. The replay reached the last message. Pernanyen had recorded a formal statement, both visual and audio.

She sat at a table with her hands laid one atop the other. In the background, a textured column and arch motif framed her. Was this décor or an emblem of authority? Her amber eyes seemed to look into Ghent's from the screen.

Her voice, smooth and calm, flowed in rehearsed cadence. "I am Pernanyen of Frayunomen of PitKreelaundun, addressing Ghent, captain of the *Ontrevay*, of the Interstellar Collaborative. I wish to reassure you that my commitment to Kena Talgarth of Earth will be honored. Kena will be returned to you safely. I have enjoyed conversing with her and wish to continue. To ensure that she is not harmed, we are acclimating her to our emfrel."

Ghent's shurgs tightened around his fists while Pernanyen's voice purred on.

"As I'm sure you know, this will take some time. I understand you may have inferred from earlier conversations that Kena would return to you within minutes of giving Pearl to Gwillenin. When I gave my commitment, I did not realize such a brief time constraint would be applied. This is an example of the miscommunications that so often mar interactions between our races. We long to find a way to alleviate this recurring problem. This may be possible through Kena.

"Such a rare opportunity should not be passed over, even though it causes inconvenience or concern. Please grant me your patience. Perhaps you would like an estimate of duration. Though it is difficult to predict the exact time, I would expect her to stay with us approximately three days."

Much longer than Kena had intended. Of that, he was certain.

"Until I have opportunity to learn from Kena," Pernanyen said, "I would prefer to avoid communications that are all too likely to produce confusion. Again, I assure you, we will provide every possible care to Kena and return her to you safely."

Silence followed the end of the recording. Ghent broke it. "I would like to hear suggestions."

More silence.

Remlishos finally spoke. "When Kena couldn't communicate with us directly, she convinced them to send us a recording of past conversations. They followed that by transmitting communication for a time. We could ask for more recordings."

"You don't look like you have high expectations of success," Ghent said.

"I don't. I still suspect that something went wrong after she arrived. Otherwise, they would have continued communication."

"Knowing Kena's interest in culture," Hrndl said, swiveling her chair toward Ghent, "it's conceivable that she would agree to stay for a few days, perhaps even agree to acclimation. However, she would've tried to tell us. If she did agree, they would have already sent that recording. If she refused, they won't let us hear it."

Metchell paced. "The acclimation procedure should have been completed hours ago. Maybe they wouldn't want to reveal her condition under a high-stress acclimation; but, by now, she should be recovering." He faced Ghent, resting his hands on the table. "Perhaps we could ask for a feed of her vital signs. It would tell us whether she is asleep or awake, calm or stressed."

"How easy is that to fake?" Ghent asked.

"Unless they have actual Human medical records, a convincing fake would be difficult."

Ghent looked up at him. "I would far rather hear Kena's voice than her heartbeat."

Metchell straightened. "Much as I hate to defend their silence, it's possible that Kena is still sleeping after the acclimation. Letting her sleep would indicate that they're taking appropriate care of her."

"The challenge, then," Ghent said, "is how to word this request for non-verbal information into a message that prompts them to converse."

TarKeen entered the small waiting room where Pernanyen paced. Her fingers gripped one another and twisted, as though fighting an endless battle.

"It is advisable to rest before a stressful link," he said.

She flipped her hands apart. "I slept. This is taking so long. I can't sleep the whole time."

"Was your acclimation to Human emfrel stressful?"

She glared at him. "You know it wasn't. Her emfrel is so insubstantial, I didn't even need acclimation."

"Convenient for you."

"But not for her? Is that what you really mean? With emfrel that simple, she's bound to have a terrible time acclimating to us."

"You must have realized this when you first met her. Why so disturbed now?"

Pernanyen looked down as her fingers resumed their battle. "I checked on her a while ago." She drew an unsteady breath. "A mistake, perhaps. I've never heard of anyone needing so much physical intervention. She's braced everywhere—even her mouth! They've put in a breathing tube and—and others. I can't imagine what they're all for."

Was she going to make this disaster even worse? "Are you reconsidering your decision?" TarKeen asked.

"I don't see how I can. To put her through this and then not link..." She raised uncertain eyes to his. "Is that what you think I should do?"

"The time for my advice has passed. You created this situation. It is yours to resolve."

Pernanyen lifted her chin.

"This is not a time for you to falter," TarKeen said. "It is time for you to link with her. To be sure of what you are doing. To remain calm throughout."

"Kena is ready?" She stepped nearer the door. "Why didn't Freltenloe tell me?"

"He cannot leave her. She is deeply exhausted, but her sairital recovery is quick. You will need to initiate at the precise end of an emfrel sweep."

Again, she moved for the door, but he sidestepped to block her.

"Did you hear me, Pernanyen? She does not look good. You cannot let that unnerve you again. Are you able to calm yourself and maintain stability?"

She looked up at him, finally showing comprehension. She closed her eyes and took several slow breaths while her posture and expression neutralized. "I am ready."

The beating stopped. The emfrel intensity diminished as the strikes broadened. Kena's resistance, instinctive now, pushed back. Wave after wave. Resist, release, resist. Why did Freltenloe continue? How could she become any more acclimated than she already was? Exhaustion wrapped her, so complete she couldn't lift her eyelids. Sleep captured her in the seconds between each wave.

Her body seemed distant, insignificant. She didn't want to be bothered with it. She was dressed in only her camisole now, though she couldn't remember when her nav suit had been removed. Shannandi had sponged away the clammy sweat and wrapped her in a warm blanket. Why wouldn't they let her rest?

She fell into sleep during one of the intervals. The pattern changed. The waves stopped. Instead, a strong presence remained.

I am Pernanyen.

The words carried no sound, for they were spoken within her mind.

Kena woke on the instant. Painfully awake. Her body shook as she violently tried to force Pernanyen out.

Pernanyen suppressed Kena's instinctive response.

She flailed mentally, as effective as grass beating a rock in a storm. The rock didn't flinch. It settled on the grass, holding it. Gently conquering. Waiting.

When Kena continued her struggle, Pernanyen formed words in her mind. *Be still. You're only exhausting yourself further. It's not possible for you to break the link.* She paused again then tried once more. *It will be easier for you if you just let this happen.*

Impossible. Kena sensed a puzzled regret. Very faint, for Pernanyen was holding her own reactions in check. Then, the invader moved through her recent memories, searching for something tangible she could relate to. Kena pushed her need to explain Human telepathy toward Pernanyen, but so much frustration mingled with the memory, Pernanyen didn't grasp its meaning. Instead, she subdued the distraction.

Pernanyen found TarKeen's brief conversation. She keyed in on his voice and statement, "I came here to ask you something that may be of importance." The conversation played out in Kena's memory. Not just the words, but Kena's emotions, as well. Pernanyen inspected the depth of Kena's feelings when she'd heard that the planet PitKreel had been destroyed. Kena cringed to have something so personal touched.

Pernanyen moved on, exploring Kena's perception of their conversations. Then, she eavesdropped into Kena's conversation with Quon. The discovery and rescue of Pearl was next. She seemed to stare at Kena's tenderness—the love she extended to an orphan.

To have such an intimate emotion inspected and judged! Kena couldn't even react. The more she tried to, the more Pernanyen suppressed.

Pernanyen searched farther back and found the memory of Kena's encounters with PitKreelaundun fighters. She inspected Kena's feelings and opinions then listened to what other crew members had said of the events. She moved forward again and found which ships Kena had been assigned to, then skimmed over memories until she came to the briefing where Kena first learned of her current mission. The quick glances at memories ceased. Now, she dove into relationships, watched them develop, considered Kena's perceptions of the people around her, wondered over her emotions.

Twice, she showed some compassion. When she discovered Frethan's and Krdn's deaths and the pain Kena had felt, she left the memory paths and moved on. All else incited a detailed study, invading Kena's dearest feelings.

Pernanyen moved slowly through the mission to collect samples of the two shattered planets and listened to what Piert told Kena of the exotic substance. She examined all the nuances of the ensuing conversation with Hrndl. Then she studied the intricacies of a friendship between two such different races, violating places she had no right to enter.

Amidst it all, Kena suffered exhaustion beyond any she had ever imagined. She could not abate her struggle. Pernanyen was swift and delved deep. At any moment, she would go too far—and then they would die. At least, Pernanyen would. If Kena survived, Pernanyen's death would destroy her from within. Death would be better.

Pernanyen almost pierced the entwined boundary of mind and spirit when she tried to understand Kena's conversation with Jorlit after Frethan's death. For some reason, she drew back before satisfying her puzzlement. She pried into the nights when Kena was alone in her quarters, singing and lifting her heart to the one she loved. Kena cringed and struggled away. She could not let Pernanyen see that depth. Pernanyen held back but looked for other opportunities.

Then she discovered the evening when Kena had linked with Ghent. Pernanyen had veered away from other memories of links, but not this one. So intrigued, she was. But Kena had been with her beloved both before and after. Pernanyen would touch

one of those contacts, both so intense. They would lead
Pernanyen from Kena's mind into her spirit, where God dwelled.
Worse yet, Pernanyen was in the act of violating a Human's will,
something even God wouldn't do. She would never survive
contact.

Kena turned her mind away. Pernanyen brought it back. Twice
more, Kena tried. Pernanyen was relentless. Kena's resistance
faltered. Pernanyen pressed deeper. Despair welled up. *Impossible to
stop her. She will die within me. It's over.*

Pernanyen drew back at the last instant. Confusion swirled in
Kena's mind. Her thoughts separated, disassociated, like leaves
stripped from branches in a storm.

"It's over. I'm ending it now," Pernanyen's voice said, both
inside Kena's mind and in her physical ears. The woman's hands
smoothed over Kena's face. She nudged Kena to notice the
sensation—to remember her body—to focus on the sound as she
spoke. "It's over. It's over."

Kena fell adrift. Alone. Her mind grew numb and confused,
registering only despair.

TarKeen stood in the monitoring room, staring at Kena's
inanimate form. A doctor, YefRon, paid more attention to
the medical monitors.

Freltenloe and Shannandi returned to Kena's room. He
motioned Pernanyen to leave and bent over Kena, running his
hands from her shoulders to fingertips and back again.

Freltenloe's voice sounded distant as it came over the
monitoring room's speaker. "It's over now, Kena. Focus on
sensation. It's over."

Kena stared at nothing.

Freltenloe brought his hand swiftly toward her eyes. No flinch.
Not even a flutter of an eyelid.

"What is he doing?" TarKeen asked.

"Testing her response," YefRon said. "It didn't register in sairital activity."

Freltenloe spoke again. "Shannandi and I will remove medical devices that are no longer necessary. You need do nothing. I'll remove the breathing tube first."

Kena's body displayed no reaction whatsoever. Not even a twitch.

"Is this normal," TarKeen asked, "that she doesn't move at all?"

"No." YefRon drew the word out, his voice low. "Physical sensation registers in her brain, but she is not showing any sairital reaction."

"We're removing the acclimation cap, now," Freltenloe said. "It will take a few minutes."

YefRon pointed at a physical scan where a foreign object moved at the base of her head. "He's inserting a sensor, just inside the skull. It will give us continued sairital readings even when she's off the table."

Shannandi worked the bands free of Kena's tangled hair. Every minute or so, she reassured Kena that this was removal of the cap.

The monitors revealed what little impression their words made.

YefRon pointed to an image of Kena's brain, where symbolic colors extended and receded. "The activity in this area is the sound reaching her brain. Over here, is where her sairital responses indicating comprehension should be—but aren't."

Disturbing. TarKeen studied her still form as Shannandi smoothed Kena's messy hair back from her slack face. "Is it possible that she's asleep?"

"No," YefRon said. He pointed up at one of several brain images that had been recorded earlier. "That is the onset of sleep. No sign of it now. Still no reaction to stimuli."

The brain images all looked similar to TarKeen. He could only rely on the doctor's interpretation. It seemed consistent with Freltenloe's, for he frowned at monitors near Kena and increased his efforts to elicit a response.

Shannandi lifted one of Kena's hands into her line of sight and described the manner in which she was massaging each finger. She let the limp hand drape over hers. "Squeeze my fingers." She waited, shifted position, and tried again. "Kena, grip my hand."

"They're trying multiple, concurrent stimuli," YefRon said. "Visual, audible, and tactile. Still nothing."

Freltenloe and Shannandi attended Kena's every physical need, assuring her, all the while, that it was over. At last, Freltenloe supported her as Shannandi wrapped her in a silky robe.

"I'm going to carry you to another room where you can sleep," he said.

Kena's body hung limp in his arms.

Several monitors went blank, and TarKeen paced across the back of the room. Could this get any worse? Monitors lit again, and he returned to them, gripping the back of a chair as he watched.

The camera showed Freltenloe laying Kena on a bed. The room's décor mimicked a bedroom, with no visible medical equipment. Freltenloe reconnected the IV, running the tube to an aperture in the wall.

Movement beside the far-right monitor caught TarKeen's attention. YefRon explained it. "That's the IV station. We can change the fluid bags from this side without disturbing her."

Freltenloe spoke again. "We'll give you privacy, now. Sleep."

No reaction. TarKeen adjusted the camera to get a better view of Kena's face. Her eyelids remained half closed, her gaze fixed, her lips parted and loose.

Freltenloe and Shannandi left Kena and joined TarKeen a moment later. They sank into the empty chairs.

TarKeen moved so he could watch Freltenloe's face. Shadows surrounded his eyes, and his mouth formed a grim line.

Minutes passed. Freltenloe suppressed a yawn while he studied the monitors.

TarKeen waited, giving privacy some time to return Kena to a more normal state. At last, he broke the silence. "I need an explanation of what's happening."

"Nothing is happening," Freltenloe said through tight lips. "Absolutely nothing. There has been no change of any sort since Pernanyen ended the link. Kena is exhausted beyond measure but does not sleep."

Freltenloe leaned his forehead on his fingertips, working them in circles. No surprise his head would ache. He was long overdue for sleep. It would be longer still.

"Leonfir and Pernanyen are waiting for your report," TarKeen said. "Come."

Freltenloe stood. "Shannandi, her condition must be monitored continuously." His gaze lifted to YefRon. "She is not to be disturbed unless it is necessary to maintain her life."

YefRon turned to him. "Make no mistake, Freltenloe. I understand the gravity of the situation."

CHAPTER THIRTY-SEVEN

arKeen took Freltenloe to the communication chamber. Freltenloe slowed as they neared it. "Wait. Why here?"

"Leonfir intends to contact the *Ontrevay's* captain soon." TarKeen touched the door control. "They are not transmitting yet."

TarKeen motioned Freltenloe to the center of the room, while he remained to one side, where he could observe all faces.

Leonfir's full lips, usually in a soft curve, clamped in a rigid line. The brown and gold entwined rank bands on his shoulders rose and fell with each breath. The captain, ever calm and collected, for once let his anger be seen. Not that TarKeen blamed him.

Pernanyen sat next to him with her head lifted high and her eyes downcast. She had taken time to change her clothing. The amber and topaz chain of the Frayunomen ruling family lay prominently across her chest. She looked like a cross between dignity personified and a scolded child.

Leonfir glared at Freltenloe. "State the condition of Kena Talgarth."

He startled at the abrupt demand, but responded with equal

firmness. "Her pulse and respiration rate are stable, but slow. All other measurements indicate that her condition is grave. Recovery has not begun, nor is there any indication that it will."

Pernanyen's eyes widened.

"What did you do to her?" Freltenloe demanded.

"I was gentle throughout." Her voice caught on the last syllable.

Not a muscle shifted in Freltenloe's stern face, stating disbelief as surely as if he spoke it.

Pernanyen gripped the table's edge. "She fought me the entire time. I tried to persuade her to relax control, but she wouldn't relent."

"You've told me she is a weak telepath," Leonfir said, his voice harsh. "Her acclimation caused extreme exhaustion. How could she have fought you?"

Pernanyen jerked her chair around. "I didn't say she was successful—only that she tried. Continuously! I thought exhaustion would soon stop her, but—it's hard to explain. Even when she was completely spent, her strength returned. If she had just stopped fighting, it wouldn't have been so hard on her."

Leonfir slapped his hand to the table, fingers splayed. "You're babbling contradictions. Is this what you intend to say to her captain? She is weak, but she is strong. She was exhausted, but she was fighting. And the crowning insult: You imply that her injury is her own fault because she fought. The fault is yours!"

"I am not shifting the blame." Her shoulders heaved. "I'm just explaining why I didn't foresee what would happen."

"What are the chances," Leonfir asked, "that you can explain this to her captain without senseless contradictions?"

TarKeen's low voice ended the ensuing silence. "Kena stated several times that she is not like other races, and that telepathy means something different to Humans than it does to others. It's time someone paid attention to what she said." He stepped nearer. "Freltenloe, you have observed her through acclimation and a constrained link. Do you have any idea what she meant?"

Freltenloe took a deep breath and relaxed his shoulders. "Measurements of her sairital energy have been low throughout. However, she has incredible resilience. It's as though she can be crushed in one instant, and in the next, her energy returns—almost as strong as before. I suspect we're not measuring her full sairital capacity."

"A reserve of some sort?" Leonfir asked.

Freltenloe flipped a hand. "A reasonable guess. I have no idea if it's correct."

"If she is highly resilient," Leonfir said, "explain why she is not recovering now."

Freltenloe released a long exhalation. "I don't know. That's why I'm so concerned. She no longer shows any sign of resilience. She was falling asleep between emfrel doses at the end of her acclimation, but now that stress is removed, she does not sleep. It appears damage was done during the link." His gaze swung back to Pernanyen, and his voice firmed. "I need to know the cause and nature of the damage."

"I didn't touch anything to do with physiological processes," she said. "I only viewed her memories."

"Her condition worsened at the end. I know you can't tell me the content of the memories, but you must tell me what was happening."

"I found a memory of her linking with Ghent." Pernanyen shifted forward then back. "She was frantically trying to stop me from seeing it. There were other times she did so; mostly memories of times when she was alone. I thought perhaps the moments were too private, so I didn't look, but I wanted a glimpse of Ghent." She looked between TarKeen and the others, as though searching for understanding. "She was so determined to stop me— I thought she was trying to hide something. I wanted to know what. But then..." She licked her lips. "There really was no way she could stop me. As I was moving into the memory, she realized it and...I sensed utter despair. She believed I was about to die within her mind."

Leonfir shook his head. "You were strong and rested. She was weak and exhausted. Yet, she believed *you* were about to die. Not her? *You?*"

Her voice pled. "I know it doesn't make sense, but her despair was real. She did believe I was going to die." Pernanyen shifted again. "I thought it was too stressful for her, so I ended the link."

"Did you just withdraw," Freltenloe demanded, "when you felt her despair?"

"Of course not!" Pernanyen spread her hands on the table. "I'm not a novice, and I'm not cruel. You know me better than that. I told her it was over—that I was ending it. I made sure she could hear and feel before I withdrew."

"Can she hear and feel now?" Leonfir asked.

Freltenloe shook his head. "Only in the physical sense. There is no sairital reaction to stimuli."

Leonfir leaned toward her, relentless. "Then clearly, Pernanyen, you did harm her."

"I trained her myself," Freltenloe said. "She is skillful and has ever been gentle."

Leonfir turned a glare upon him.

"I'm as angry with her as you are, sir," Freltenloe said, "but my statement is true. We do not know what caused harm or if it is permanent. You must do what is lawful in regard to Pernanyen. I must do what is necessary to restore Kena to health."

"Your point?" Leonfir demanded.

"Even if I knew the cause and nature of the injury, I could do nothing to repair it until Kena is thoroughly rested. The woman must sleep!" He spread restless hands. "Sleep alone may even restore her natural resilience." He took a deep breath and shifted to a wider stance. "Before I request what neither of us will like, will you permit me a moment to check on her condition?"

Leonfir nodded and remained silent, listening. The frown that etched his brow deepened while Shannandi's voice responded. "There is no change. She is still awake. She has not moved at all."

Freltenloe turned back to Leonfir. "I need something that will induce sleep. I have no idea what will work for a Human. I must ask a doctor on the *Ontrevay*."

The expression that passed over Leonfir's face spoke volumes. His voice was equally grim. "This question must be phrased in such a way that Ghent does not learn how severe her condition is. There is to be no mention, whatsoever, that anyone has linked with her."

TarKeen let out the breath he now realized he'd been holding. Leonfir had covered the crucial points.

"What have you told them, so far?" Freltenloe asked.

Leonfir motioned him aside. "Go listen to the recordings. It won't take long. Then, decide exactly what and how you will ask their doctor." He turned. "Pernanyen." He held her gaze. "Do you have any idea how close you are to starting a war?"

She lifted her chin. "I am aware of the sensitive nature of this encounter. There are several possible outcomes, some of them highly desirable."

Leonfir's nostrils quivered. His hand struck the table again. "My tolerance for your political statements has ended. Ghent does not have the patience you want to believe he should have. Stop clinging to fallacy. Grasp the fact that they do not have any way to know whether Kena is still alive. The moment they believe we have severely harmed or even killed her, they will fire on us. That is the beginning of war. Once it occurs, it is irreversible. One misstep, and it will be...too...late. Do you understand?"

Pernanyen's rigid body vibrated at the reverberation of his voice "I do. I will—"

"Then do you understand why you cannot be the one to talk with them at this moment?"

"Captain Leonfir, you are usurping my authority."

"On the contrary," he said. "I'm attempting to give you counsel. Are you willing to listen yet?"

TarKeen took a step toward Pernanyen. Time for a calm counterpoint, an option she could favor rather than a battle for authority. "Consider the value of your absence, Pernanyen.

Nothing can be decided or changed if you are not in the room. If Ghent were to make a demand, we must defer our answer."

Pernanyen's eyes shifted to his, and her brow lifted.

Quick understanding—that, he could grant her. With a few more words, he got her out of the communication chamber.

When she was gone, Leonfir looked up at TarKeen with the first hint of a smile to touch his lips in the entire day. "That was well done."

TarKeen inclined his head.

"Considering your opinion of her judgment, I would have expected you to push for her arrest."

"I think it would be unwise to disrupt the authority triad at this moment."

"True." Leonfir held his comm device to his mouth and said, "Send a message to the *Ontrevay* that I wish to speak with Ghent and the doctor who is most knowledgeable about Kena." He motioned Freltenloe to join him at the table, and TarKeen stepped back from the camera's range.

They had not long to wait. Two dissimilar people faced them on the screen: one with short hair in varied shades of brown, and the other with dark fur covering most of his upper body. So, that was what a Plynteth actually looked like.

"I am Ghent," the Plynteth said.

That was brief. True they knew the captain's name and race, but no greeting of any sort?

"I am Leonfir, captain of the *Eprij*. Please accept my greeting and pardon the length of time it took to respond to your request for information." He gestured to his side. "Freltenloe is the doctor who is responsible for the care of Kena Talgarth. He was attending her, and I felt it would be better to wait until he was available before replying to you."

Ghent copied Leonfir's gesture and said, "This is Metchell of Dantokrell. He is our chief medical officer. What is Kena's condition?"

Freltenloe answered. "The acclimation exhausted her, which is not surprising. Her condition is stable. However, I'm concerned because she does not sleep. I request that you provide me with the chemical composition of a drug that will induce sleep."

Metchell's brow lowered. "She has not slept yet?"

"That is correct."

"What, exactly, do you mean by *stable* condition?"

"She is physically relaxed," Freltenloe said. "Her pulse and respiration are regular and appropriate for an inactive state."

"Forgive me for doubting your words," Metchell said, "but this sounds most unlikely. I've performed a high-stress acclimation for Kena. If you wanted to wake her, you would need a drug, but not to get her to sleep. It's possible for Humans to sleep with their eyes open. Are you certain she is awake?"

"I am judging her consciousness based on sairital data, not outward conditions." Freltenloe's shoulders began a rhythmic shifting. "I witnessed her sleep between emfrel doses near the end of acclimation. After the final contact with PitKreelaundun emfrel, she remained awake. I also find it surprising, but I am certain that she is not asleep. We are familiar with the chemical notation used by the Prednians. If you use that format to define a drug, I will be able to duplicate the substance."

"I would like to talk with her first."

"That is not advisable at this time," Freltenloe said. "I am unable to continue conversing, due to Pernanyen's directive. Will you provide me with a sleep-inducing drug?"

Metchell looked away, a couple of fingers sliding back and forth beneath his chin.

"Are you going to answer me?" Freltenloe demanded.

Ghent responded. "Considering the amount of patience you demand from us, can you not give him a moment to decide what is best for Kena?"

"Certainly," Leonfir replied for Freltenloe. "I regret that this conversation is limited. The difficulty of communication is already evident. We hope to improve this soon."

"I suggest," Ghent said, "that it will improve more quickly if conversation is not limited. Kena and Pernanyen spoke of general, non-controversial topics without difficulty. We can do the same to learn of each other."

Leonfir spread his hands. "I must defer to the directive of a ruling family member. I realize this may be frustrating to you, so I greatly value your patience."

Metchell used his computer to send a chemical description through the communication channel. Freltenloe studied it as Metchell spoke.

"From what little you've told me, I suspect that her sleep process has been disrupted. Most likely by stress. This is the substance that her body naturally produces to initiate her sleep cycle. The dose suggested is considerably more than she would need under normal circumstances, but it will not harm her. You should see results in half an hour or less. You can give her another dose if she is not fully asleep in that time. Please let me know the results."

"Thank you." Freltenloe inclined his head.

"We will talk more later," Leonfir said and ended the transmission. An audible breath escaped his lips. He propped an elbow on the table and leaned his forehead against his hand.

CHAPTER THIRTY-EIGHT

TarKeen strode through the halls, careful to keep his irritation from his face. *Urgent,* the message had said. Doubtful, but he couldn't ignore it.

The specified chamber was well removed from the command areas of the ship. For good reason. When, at last, he reached it, he swept his gaze over those scattered through the chamber, assessing who had felt this meeting was worth attending. People sat on tall stools or stood around the high tables, pretending to be occupied with their own concerns. One could never tell when someone uninvited might chance to enter.

VanDar, however, made no attempt to feign casual posture. His pacing ceased mid-stride as his eyes darted across the room to TarKeen's. He lifted his square chin. "What kept you?"

"I have a profession that consumes my time. Are you not familiar with the concept?"

How would he react? As a member of the PitKree non-ruling family of Kell, VanDar was expected—required, in fact—to have occupation. His token profession and meddling in government could bring him under investigation. Not that anyone present would report him. They were all PitKree.

VanDar ignored TarKeen's jab. "You have confirmed an order
to keep DrenVid confined to quarters when you should have
reversed it. I sometimes wonder where your loyalties really lie."

"DrenVid is an idiot. I do not tolerate fools. Particularly when
secrecy is required."

"He could be useful to us."

TarKeen enunciated each word. "Not after he opened
his mouth."

A voice from the crowd said, "DrenVid is a problem waiting to
happen." The man drummed his knuckles against the table. "He's
been in trouble before. To use his word, he *forgot* to numb the arm
of a Laundun man before setting a broken bone. He'll give false
impressions of our intent and harm our cause."

"Secondhand stories are not proof of wrongdoing." VanDar
shifted his glare back to TarKeen. "Nor is one man's overreaction
to a few poorly chosen words. Have him released."

"Are you taking on the role of judge, now?" TarKeen asked.
"The duty of ruling families? Interesting." He shook his head. "Do
not think that DrenVid is committed to our cause. He's only
committed to a warped delight in vengeance. He will have the
hearing he's entitled to, though you will not preside." TarKeen
swept the room with his gaze. "My concerns are far more practical.
A man who cannot follow orders for five minutes will not be
granted opportunity to participate in our endeavors."

"What orders?" VanDar demanded. "You weren't even there."

"Did you not hear what I announced to the entire ship?"
TarKeen strolled the room. Unlike VanDar, he did not need to
raise his voice. His words carried the ring of command, no matter
how loud or soft. "Let this be clear in your minds; being a member
of this company does not exempt any of you from compliance with
my orders. Treat them with contempt, and you guarantee that no
authority will ever be granted you. We are a minority. The risk is
great, and timing is crucial. My orders must be followed with
precision. I will maintain discipline. If this disturbs any of you,
withdraw."

TarKeen judged their reactions while VanDar ranted.

"Pernanyen seems not to have heard your orders. Oh, that's right: she's the one who kidnapped the alien, ordered her tortured, and then attacked her." VanDar spread his arms. "Our kind and caring Laundun government at work." He slapped a hand down on a table. "Their hypocrisy is revealed. This is exactly the opportunity we have needed. Now is the time to act!"

"Now?" TarKeen stretched the word.

"Certainly. Pernanyen is vulnerable. Even the Laundun condemn her."

ShenLee made a dismissive *p'fuf* sound without looking up. "They will soon *commend* her if she is successful."

The timbre of her voice eased TarKeen. Pity that he must listen to VanDar instead of her.

"We must not allow her to be successful. This Kena Talgarth..." VanDar seemed to spit her name. "She is injured already. Her death would be easy to accomplish and surprise no one. DrenVid could—"

"You want to murder her?" ShenLee demanded, swinging around so fast, the trailing side of her tunic flared out. Graceful as a dancer, even when startled.

"Not murder." VanDar jerked his head to the side, discarding her objection. "Even though it must be done subtly, the word is *execute*. Have you forgotten the PitKree who died because of her?"

"That is true," another woman said. "There could have been others we don't know of."

"Judging again?" an older man grumbled. "Conviction without a hearing,"

TarKeen noted the stirrings within the group, but addressed VanDar. "Do explain how Kena's death will help our cause."

"There will be outrage among the Laundun. They'll blame Pernanyen for her death. Everyone knows she constrained that alien to link and has not yet submitted to the same. Leonfir is still supporting Pernanyen. We will arrest both of them. You will take Leonfir's place, and I will take Pernanyen's."

"Ah! I see." An unpleasant smile lifted TarKeen's lips as he drew near VanDar. "This is not about the PitKree cause. It's a method for you to claim power. And you questioned *my* loyalties?"

VanDar's voice rose. "Not so. It will give us opportunity to take control of the ship without any hint of mutiny. We won't even be challenged when entering PitKreelaundun orbit. We'll be able to take over the communication complex and move against the Laundun fam—"

"Enough!" TarKeen's voice shattered VanDar's rant and sent a charged hush through the chamber. "If Kena dies, a war starts with the Interstellar Collaborative. Are you actually proposing to challenge the Laundun while we are under attack from the Collaborative? Do you not realize what havoc that will create? If we are battling one another, who will defend against the Collaborative? Both Laundun and PitKree will...lose...everything!"

As the view screen flickered to life, Ghent motioned for Metchell to join him at the table, and Remlishos moved out of the camera's range. Leonfir sat at the corresponding table in the *Epri7*.

"I had hoped to hear an update on Kena's condition by now," Ghent said.

Leonfir's brow twitched, then smoothed. "Freltenloe has been summoned." He glanced aside as someone else moved into view. "This is TarKeen, with whom you have spoken before. He is commander of the *Epri7* and is authorized to speak on my behalf when I am unavailable. We link regularly, so we are both equally aware of events."

Ghent considered TarKeen. Direct gaze. He remained standing. Did that mean something to his race? Could useful information, or maybe even leverage, be obtained from him? "The last time we spoke," Ghent said to TarKeen, "Kena was talking with Pernanyen. Did you join them?"

"No."

"Have you spoken with Kena since she arrived?"

"Briefly," TarKeen said.

"When was that?"

"Before acclimation began."

"What did you speak of?" Ghent asked.

"I asked her for more detail about the phenomena she said you had come to study. There was little time for discussion. We remain curious about why you are here."

At last, an opening to conversation. Ghent leaned back in his chair. "Two planets broke up not far from here. This wasn't caused by collisions. Something that devastating warrants study."

"We're aware that they broke up," TarKeen said, "and also aware of how dangerous that system is. Are there no remnants of such events closer to home that you could study?"

"None." Ghent leaned forward. "Are there such remnants in PitKreelaundun space?"

"There are. Kena mentioned gathering samples of unstable matter, but she didn't say the Prednian name for the substance. What word do you use?"

"We've not named it yet. What do you call it?"

That pause before TarKeen answered—what did that mean?

"The semi-stable form is called trazine. The volatile, catalyst substance is called pentazine. The words are sometimes combined to tra-pentazine." TarKeen shifted, though his face still revealed nothing. "We've identified the samples you left behind when you followed us away from the nebula. A very lethal collection, you have assembled. Yet another curiosity for us to ponder."

He stepped back as Freltenloe joined Leonfir at the table.

"What is Kena's condition?" Leonfir asked.

Freltenloe directed his answer to Metchell. "There is no change. She is still awake."

Metchell frowned. "Did you give her the full doses?"

"I did," Freltenloe said. "I could describe their impact as a suggestion that she should sleep. She needs something stronger that actually *induces* sleep."

Metchell shook his head. "I need to understand what is wrong before I can tell you how to treat her. Please give me all of the medical data you've recorded."

Freltenloe stared. "What we measure and the format in which we record are certain to be different than yours. Converting it is problematic. The data would need to be thoroughly tested by doctors from both of our races who actually understand each other. Kena needs to sleep now, not months from now. Do you really doubt she's exhausted and needs sleep?"

"No, I do not. However, I do know that exhausted Humans sleep. Something must be preventing it. I need to know what, so the cause of the problem can be resolved."

Ghent listened intently. The frustration in Metchell's voice was no surprise, but the increasing emphasis in Freltenloe's was still an unknown. Probably not good.

"Her medical data does not indicate a cause," Freltenloe said. "It does indicate a need for sleep. Again, I request that you provide me with the chemical description of a drug that will induce sleep."

"I cannot." Metchell shook his head. "I need to examine her first. You need to return her to us, now."

The two seated men twitched back. TarKeen didn't move, but all three of them appeared too stunned to speak. Ghent was no less surprised, but waited to see how they might respond.

Seconds ticked by before Freltenloe managed to ask, "How could we possibly do so?"

"If you won't bring her to us, then return her as she specified. Her EVA belt will protect her. Release her from your ship and withdraw. We will pick her up."

Freltenloe turned to Leonfir. "I heard that the ships are far apart. Is this not so?"

"It is so." Though he answered Freltenloe, Leonfir's eyes fixed on Metchell. "She would be isolated for hours. I have not calculated the exact time; for, such an unacceptable solution never occurred to me."

"It appears," Metchell said, "that you have a high aversion to activity beyond the protection of your ships. Kena does not share that trait. Review what she said about it. She chose that method of travel. It didn't bother her."

TarKeen rejoined the discussion. "At that time, she was rested and alert. She also was not isolated; she was interacting with Jennellee Pearl. We've discovered that she was even providing the child with a light sairital presence, apparently to comfort her. She was conversing with us and active. None of this would be true if she were put out of our ship now."

"I assure you, she will survive the trip," Metchell said, tight-lipped.

Freltenloe shook his head, his upper lip raised. "Survive? Is that all that matters to you? She's endured acclimation stress and exhaustion. Now, you want to add hours of isolation stress? She is one of yours, but you would treat her with such cruelty? You are nothing like Kena."

Metchell leaned across the table and drew a rapid breath to speak, but Ghent shot a hand out and gripped his arm before hasty words could escape.

Freltenloe strode out of view.

Leonfir said, "Perhaps Pernanyen is right. Nothing good came from this conversation."

The screen went blank.

Metchell's arm shook in Ghent's grasp. Ghent released him, but ordered, "Do not speak until your anger is under control."

Metchell swung away and paced between the table and screen.

In truth, Ghent needed time to still his own ire. How could that have turned bitter so suddenly? The idea of being accused of cruelty toward Kena galled him, even if it was directed toward another. The PitKreelaundun had brought her to this state. How dare they now..."

347

He stopped himself. Anger, so counterproductive. He needed understanding. Alternatives.

Once Metchell's pacing slowed, Ghent said, "I need to know why you won't give them the drug Freltenloe requested."

"There is something wrong that they're not telling us," Metchell said. "It must have sairital implications. Any drugs strong enough to put her to sleep can worsen certain types of sairital injuries and make them much harder to heal. They could make her vulnerable to additional injury. Even small alterations in these drugs can have devastating effects. It is because I am *not cruel* that I cannot give them these formulas. They could cause much more harm than good."

"I know you have Kena's best interests in mind. Don't Humans have anything less dangerous?"

"Of course, they do. I've already given them the preferred method. There are a couple of mild drugs, but I doubt they would bring her to sleep."

Ghent stared at the blank screen. The silence stretched.

Metchell finally said, "I cannot help her if I cannot examine her. Will it really take as long as they say to retrieve her?"

"We are staying out of weapon range," Remlishos said. "It would take a few hours to get a craft from the *Ontrevay* to the *Epri7's* location. We need to allow time for them to get beyond intercept range, as well. That's harder to predict."

"Can't they do that while we approach?"

"They will need to begin with only navigational jets," Remlishos said. "If they engaged the primary drive of a ship that size, we wouldn't even be able to find Kena's corpse."

"Oh. I suppose that should have been obvious."

Remlishos gave him an understanding nod. "To some of us. I gather, it's not covered in medical training."

Metchell didn't even smile at the mild jest. "Is there any way to shorten the period she would need to be alone?"

Ghent rejoined the conversation. "Not enough. I know she sounded unconcerned about extended EVA time, but she had no other option. She shared her view of isolation when we talked about Krdn's death. I don't want her alone when she's in a weakened state."

Metchell's lips parted then closed.

Ghent stood. "Remlishos, choose the simplest craft we have. It only needs to hold two people. Strip it of all but the most rudimentary technology. No extended shield or integrated robotics. No communication encryption or decryption. No ability for remote control. Remove all but the simplest scanners. You'll need to strip the computer, too. No security identifications for them to decipher. No navigational programs. Nothing that isn't used to keep the craft functional under manual control."

Remlishos nodded. "I understand."

"Once you have the final specs, feed them to the simulation computer."

"Any navigator on the ship could already operate such a simple craft. Who will be piloting it?" Remlishos asked.

"I don't know. Maybe no one. But I want it readied in case it's needed."

CHAPTER THIRTY-NINE

"We got the design specs from Remlishos," Hrndl said to Ghent as she pulled simulation records up on a screen in nav section. "Here's the list of navigators who have—"

Inewin's voice came over the comm system. "Communication request received from the *Epri7*."

Ghent touched a console. "Relay it to me here."

TarKeen's recorded voice said, "I request to speak with a Human. Preferably one who knows Kena well."

"What did you respond?" Ghent asked.

"Just an acknowledgement," Inewin said.

The fur on Ghent's brow puckered as he lifted himself from his chair.

Hrndl also hurried to her feet. "Will you let me talk with him?"

"What do you have in mind?"

What did she have in mind? Better decide quick. "I could... speak as her friend, instead of as an officer."

"I'm open to any new approaches," he said. "Come."

I n the visual communication room, Hrndl sat down at the table
and opened the channel. Ghent stood to one side, out of view.
TarKeen was waiting—the only one at the table. He took one
look at Hrndl and said, "You do not appear to be Human."

"No, I am Grfdn. My name is Hrndl. There are no other
Humans on the *Ontrevay*, so I came because I'm Kena's friend.
What do you wish to speak of?"

"I wanted to hear what a Human would do to draw someone
toward sleep when no medical assistance is available."

Painfully aware of her ignorance, Hrndl said, "I will find
answers for you. Kena has many friends here. Some of them have
served with Humans before. They may know some details that I
do not."

He nodded and began to reach for a control on his table.

"Wait," Hrndl said. "Please don't end communications yet."

He leaned back but said nothing. This man was hard to read or
even study. His expression revealed nothing, and he seemed to use
no unnecessary motions. Unlike the others, with their swaying
shoulders.

"I'm so worried about her," Hrndl said. "May I see her?"

"There is nothing to see. She simply lies there, unmoving."

"Even so, I would like to see her. I may notice something that
would not seem significant to you."

He pulled a device of some sort near himself, and his hand
moved over it. After a couple minutes, he said, "This image is from
a monitoring camera in the medical facility where she's cared for.
Medical equipment is hidden; the room is intended to look like a
bedroom."

The screen split to show another image beside TarKeen's.
Hrndl stared at it. The camera provided an overhead view. Kena
lay on her side, mostly covered by a sheet. Her hair lay neatly in
place, as though it had been combed. Someone sat beside her,
massaging one of her hands.

"Kena normally sleeps alone," Hrndl said. "I don't think she'll sleep if someone is touching her."

"We have given her privacy, quiet, and a darkened room. It has not helped. We've reached the point of searching for anything that may bring about a change. Gwillenin offered to tend to her basic needs, hoping to soothe her."

"Gwillenin? The woman who mothers Pearl?"

"Yes," TarKeen said. "Kena's pulse increases when medical personnel tend to her. We have wondered if she is still expecting more acclimation. Kena would know that Gwillenin will never harm her. If you've heard their first conversation, you may be skeptical, but when Gwillenin realized how Kena had cared for Jennellee Pearl, their interaction became...appreciative and friendly."

"How like Kena to make a friend among the PitKreelaundun."

TarKeen turned his head. "What do you mean?"

"She makes friends among every race, no matter how different. Grfdn and Humans are not well suited to one another, and yet Kena has become a valuable friend to me. She could well be named Pearl herself, for she is a treasure."

TarKeen leaned farther back in his chair. "So I would have thought, but our last conversation with your crew did not leave the impression that she is treasured by all."

"No, but I think you misunderstood. I know Metchell, and I've seen him care for Kena. My opinion of his concern for her is far different from yours. I cannot quite make out the words from Kena's room. Is Gwillenin repeating 'It's over'?"

"Yes."

"Why?"

"Whatever went wrong," TarKeen said, "happened at the end of contact with PitKreelaundun emfrel. When acclimation is long and stressful, it's common to give the person assurance that it's over. Do you think Kena should be set adrift alone?"

"I find the idea disturbing, but my race has some difficulty with lengthy isolation. The Human view is different."

"Apparently, the Dantokrellie view is different, as well."

Ah. His voice dropped at the reference to Metchell. Not a good change, but discernable, at least.

Hrndl shrugged. "I don't know. Perhaps I should mention that, even though Metchell is a well-qualified doctor, he's never experienced EVA, and he has a poor grasp of navigational concepts. If Kena were rested and healthy, she could manage it. Be certain that several of us would be ready to talk with her for more hours than the trip would take."

"Unfortunately, she is not rested and healthy. Now that you've seen her, do you have any suggestions?"

"Sound—but it needs to be the right sort. I'll get a recording for you, but it might take a little while. If I send a message to you, will you respond?"

"I will." The corners of his mouth lifted slightly.

The screen went blank, and Hrndl let out a pained breath. She looked over at Ghent. "Did you see her face?"

He nodded.

"It's so...still! Almost like she's..." Her voice caught.

"She's breathing," Ghent said. "I watched the sheet."

So, he had noticed the deadness in her slack expression, too.

"I'll have Metchell review it, of course. Well done, Hrndl."

Absently, she murmured, "Thank you."

"Do you know how much you've changed since Kena arrived?"

She thought of their early days, and of realizations that had come over time. If they couldn't recover Kena, or if she had suffered permanent sairital damage...Hrndl brushed a hand across her forehead. "I suppose I have," she said, standing. "Excuse me; I need to figure out how to get a restful recording for Kena." She walked to the door, then turned back. "I think you have changed a little, too."

He smiled. "I take that as a compliment."

Hrndl used her officer's override to open the door of Kena's quarters. The lights came up, and woodland sounds greeted her. Memories—Kena's face at rest, so different from the vacant stare she had just seen.

Kena's computer lay on the table. So, Ghent had been here, too. Hrndl picked it up and searched through the few public files. The room configurations were public, of course, because they had to be available to the ship's computer. But it was music she really wanted. Kena often played instrumentals over the forest sounds. Hrndl found a short list of selections. Their names were gibberish to her, Human words written with Human letters. All she could do was select them and listen.

She paused to contact Frdn from her own computer.

A moment later, a voice responded. "This is Frdn."

"I want you to meet me in Kena's quarters. Bring whatever equipment you need to record sound. Do you have any information on the Human language?"

"On English, yes."

"Bring it."

He joined her in a few minutes. "I heard the latest transmission," Frdn said, "where you spoke with TarKeen."

"Good. I want the woodland sounds recorded from her room configuration. Can you do that?"

"Easily. I can get it from the interface."

"Do we need to let it play through?"

He was already using his communication systems. "No, the file is stored with the configuration."

"Can you get this music, too?"

"That's going to be harder. Humans use sophisticated sound files for their music. There's a lot of nuance to capture." His eyes traveled over the holographic display projected from his computer. "It looks like I can't get the file directly. I'll need to record in our format."

"All right. I think, maybe, this one." She pointed at a selection on Kena's computer. "I've heard her play it a couple times."

He nodded and sat at the table. After detaching an audio unit from his computer, he fit it into one ear. Colored bars rose and fell in a 3-D graph on his display. He watched and listened with the intensity of a navigator reviewing astro scans.

She gave him a few minutes and then asked, "What do you know about English?"

He slid the volume control down and looked up at her. "I can pronounce the basic phrases. Things like *yes*, *no*, courtesy words, *message received*, and *stand by*. For anything more than that, I have to use the translation system." He pulled up the English interface as he spoke. "This is for written language." He leaned over to look at the letters on Kena's computer, then entered them into his.

The computer announced, "Antonio Vivaldi. The Four Seasons." It gave the English pronunciation and Prednian translation, followed by a description of the piece of music.

"Oh," Hrndl said. "Well, I didn't know that, but there should be no problem with letting the PitKreelaundun hear it."

"The description would have told us if copying or transmission was restricted."

Humans restricted their music? But that didn't matter now. "What can your system do with translation?" she asked. "I need more than just literal meaning; I want implications and subtleties."

"I have two audio files for Kena," Hrndl said to TarKeen. His expression remained as still as ever. At least he'd responded quickly to her communication request.

"This first one I'm sending is a recording of forest sounds from Earth. Kena lets it play continuously while she's in her quarters. The volume should be low, like distant sounds."

TarKeen looked down at the table, and his fingers moved over a device. "I've received the file."

"The second one is Human music," Hrndl said. "She sometimes listens to it in the evening. Play it over the forest sounds, but don't let it repeat. The volume should be moderate."

"Will these cause her to sleep?"

Hrndl shifted. Did he think she could answer such a question? "Perhaps, particularly the forest sounds. According to Human-authored information, some of them habitually go to bed with music playing. If it's absent, they can have difficulty falling asleep. I don't know if Kena does this, but music may give her a feeling that things are—or can be —normal."

The forest sounds, then music, played second-hand over the comm channel as TarKeen listened to each recording for a moment. "We'll play these for her and analyze the results. Did you find anything else that will draw a Human to sleep?"

"Some, but it mostly pertained to children. There seems to be no need of it in adults." She drew a breath and tightened her brows. "I did find that a rocking motion can cause a Human to feel drowsy."

"Rocking? What do you mean?"

She mimicked it with her hand. "I believe it's a side-to-side, or backward and forward movement. Apparently, they even have furniture that produces such motion."

TarKeen turned his head. Was he as puzzled as she?

Hrndl moved on. "I checked on the phrase *it's over*. I don't think it should be said any more."

"Why not?"

"It has a negative connotation beyond its literal meaning. It can imply hopelessness, or that something has been destroyed. Something of great value, like a relationship or an endeavor."

His eyes grew a little wider. Was he finally taking her seriously? "I will tell those who care for her. Is there anything that should be said instead?"

Hrndl frowned at her hands for a moment. "I cannot give you exact words. When things go wrong, Kena doesn't focus on the past. She looks toward the future. She speaks of the goal—of what to do next."

TarKeen leaned back in his chair. "The Prednian description of the Grfdn does not seem to be accurate in regard to you."

How unexpected. Would it have seemed accurate on the day she'd met Kena? Probably. Still, Hrndl had no idea what he had read. "The Prednians have difficulty comprehending our race."

A hint of a smile lightened his dark features. "How is it that you are a friend of Kena? Why do you seek to help her?"

The word *help* grated on Hrndl's sensitivity. She suspected he had chosen it intentionally, but couldn't guess whether he was testing her, or insulting Kena, or something else entirely. "What I have done has cost me very little. Kena has done much more than this for me, and would do more again without thought of the cost. I will do nothing less for her, if I can just find a way to do it."

He nodded. "I will let you know, ma'am, if any of your suggestions are successful."

B ird song. Wind in the trees. A brook.

The sounds filtered into Kena's awareness. She didn't want them. She only waited to die. Why was it taking so long?

A squirrel chattered. Water gurgled over rocks.

The sounds wouldn't leave. They prompted earlier memories— contrasting past joys with present devastation, creating anguish beyond her strength. She could not bear to think.

Sounds of quietness persisted.

She sought emptiness. That place where she was oblivious to the death of hope.

Footsteps.

Not now. She must hasten to that distant place.

"I am TarKeen," a low voice said.

His legs stopped within her line of sight. She willed herself not to see.

He knelt, bringing his face within her view.

Oh, she needed to close her eyes. To command the body she wanted to shed. No, she would not make use of it.

TarKeen spoke again. "All of the difficult moments are past. They will not repeat."

Her pulse quickened. *Stupid heart. Stop.*

"You will recover now. It's time for you to sleep."

Her breath copied her pulse. She rejected his voice.

"Hrndl sent music for you. We will play it. Sleep."

Hrndl. Dear one. Kena's eyelids squeezed. She had other dear ones. If only she had never known their friendship. There would have been so much less for Pernanyen to sift.

Footsteps receded. Light dimmed. Vivaldi called to her from the past, lilted through vibrant nature, bursting with life. The melody emphasized the seared wasteland in her mind.

A ragged sob scraped through Kena's unwilling throat. Her body demanded air, would not let her refuse it. Stubborn body that wouldn't let her leave. No sooner did it have the breath it wanted, then it sobbed it out again.

Kena pulled the sheet over her head and curled into a ball. Wracking sobs shook her body. All the while, Vivaldi declared the joy of life.

Bouts of crying ebbed and flowed, her body no more capable than her mind of sustaining so much grief. Though tears soaked her pillow, they brought no relief. No calm after the storm. No sleep. They only merged into exhaustion.

The final notes of Vivaldi faded into the woodland's hush. Kena faded into numbness.

Eventually, rising light announced Gwillenin's approach. She washed Kena's face and combed her hair. She spoke of new things, of how well Pearl was adjusting. Kena tried not to hear. At least the baby was all right.

Barely realizing it, Kena swallowed the water Gwillenin carefully squirted into her mouth.

CHAPTER FORTY

TarKeen listened but didn't join the discussion. Doomsayers, every one. Obsessing over problems that had not begun to form. Granted, tra-pentazine protectors had to consider worst-case scenarios—unfortunate that it turned them into such pessimists. Leonfir pulled them back to discussion of probabilities when the pessimism got too extreme, but he continued to question the protectors.

They detailed dozens of predictions for every possible scenario; whether the *Ontrevay's* crew abandoned the sample collection, took it back across the nebula, or—worst of all— developed weapons from it. The wall screens around the room showed one projection after another. This went on for hours. TarKeen strolled the chamber's perimeter. He pitied the PitKree among the protectors—obliged to sit for so long.

At last, Leonfir issued several orders and dismissed them.

TarKeen turned for the nearest door.

"TarKeen, stay," Leonfir said.

He joined the captain as the others left.

When the door closed behind the last of them, Leonfir leaned back in his chair and stretched. "I'd like to hear your observations."

TarKeen leaned against a table's edge. Leonfir often used this sort of discussion to organize his thoughts. "If we can persuade Ghent to leave the samples behind," TarKeen said, "we can likely persuade him to set them on a course away from us. With their extended field technology, that should be a simple matter. Therefore, all scenarios of this sort have little risk to us; they need not be solved."

Leonfir nodded.

TarKeen rested his hands on the table's edge. "If they take them between the nebula and our domain, we are at risk, since they're likely to lose control of some or all of the samples. However, the debris will be easy to locate. We know how to neutralize the risk. The biggest problem to us is that we'll once again need to reassign ships to clean up another of their messes."

"True."

"In this group of scenarios, there is one possible outcome that was not mentioned."

Leonfir's nostrils pinched. "I thought they were exhaustively explored!"

TarKeen let a sympathetic smile form at Leonfir's rare acknowledgement of impatience. "I refer to the possibility that the *Ontrevay* will be destroyed if they lose control of the trapentazine."

A shadow crossed Leonfir's face. "In which case, we will be blamed, and the Collaborative will declare war." When TarKeen did not reply, he asked, "What have I missed?"

"I don't know if they'll declare war. It would be advisable to keep our distance until the *Ontrevay* is well beyond our domain. The greatest risk is not to us." TarKeen glanced toward one of the screens, which displayed the *Ontrevay*. "If it happens, I would guess some three or four hundred lives will be lost."

Leonfir gave him a long look. "After all the years I've known you, there are times you still surprise me. Since when do you care what becomes of the Collaborative's members?"

An interesting question. Did he care? He'd be loath to kill Kena; that much was certain, be it ever so strange. To Leonfir, he said, "I wouldn't wish them ill if they'd stop stirring up tra-pentazine courses with their gravity ships."

"What are your thoughts on the likelihood of the Collaborative making weapons of trazine?"

"Probability of success is low," TarKeen said. "We cannot do it, and we have plenty of material to experiment with."

"True enough," Leonfir said, "but we don't have extended energy field technology. They do. Have you seen the energy levels on their containment fields?"

"I have." Both men stared at the screen where the sample collection was displayed. "I would give much for that technology," TarKeen said.

"As would we all." Leonfir sighed. "What do you suppose the possibility is that Pernanyen will have gained such information for us?"

"I try not to think about it. I suspect her idealism will have stopped her short of extracting technology secrets." He dropped his voice. "I suppose that must command my respect, in spite of how infuriating it will be."

Leonfir laughed. "You see—this is what I mean. Most will mix disdain with their fury, yet you mention respect."

TarKeen let his expression soften. "What's your view?"

"I can't get beyond frustration." Leonfir rested his arms on the table in front of him. "If Kena does not recover enough to perform her side of the constrained link, Pernanyen will be executed. Not only will we lose all the information she obtained, but we lose a young woman who could have matured into a fine leader. A tremendous cost with no value gained." He shook his head and sighed. "Even worse than no value, since the Collaborative will have another reason to hate us."

"Are you arguing that the law should be set aside based on circumstance?"

"Never!" Leonfir squared his shoulders and clasped his hands on the table. "Even if that seemed acceptable now, abuses would be certain to follow. Pernanyen must bear the consequences of her decision." He raised his eyes to meet TarKeen's. "Speaking of Pernanyen, I heard that you dismissed one of her guards and assigned another in his place. Why?"

TarKeen shrugged. "His contempt for her was blatant. Not useful in a guard. Have you received an answer yet from the ruling families?"

"Apparently, they're still debating the matter." Leonfir waved a dismissive hand and leaned back. "I also heard that you restricted a certain medical technician from entering the facility where Kena resides."

TarKeen maintained his composure, but his every sense sprang to alert. "True. Freltenloe has forbidden *spectators*, to use his word. I agree with him. She's not an object to be stared at, and the disruption in the monitoring room could interfere with medical care."

"Agreed, but this was a medical tech."

"He's assigned on level six," TarKeen said. "There was nothing to bring him to level one except...to give him the benefit of doubt, I will say *curiosity*."

"What would you say without benefit of doubt?"

"A desire to gloat."

"That makes three, counting DrenVid," Leonfir said. "Not that I disagree with your decisions, but I can't help noticing your discipline is more severe than usual."

"Perhaps so. Recent events seem to have reduced my tolerance of fools."

"I also can't help but notice that all three men are PitKree."

TarKeen considered turning this aside as well, but Leonfir had never used that race name alone. He suspected something, but what? TarKeen chose his words with care. "They are. I'm in a

362

position to hear things that will never be said in your presence. I make use of the opportunity. Do not misunderstand; other than DrenVid, these men have made no threats. They have committed no crime. If Kena were not on this ship, if Pernanyen were not on the verge of arrest, then I would only reprimand them. As it is, I will take no unnecessary risks."

"What else will I never hear?" Leonfir asked.

"Probably not much that would surprise you. The most common themes center around disillusionment. Planetary exploration that can benefit every race...except PitKree."

"Are we referring to the viable, uninhabited planet designated for Harnon colonies?"

"Of course," TarKeen said.

"Their native planet has as much tra-pentazine as PitKreel had. The race's survival is doubtful if they do not colonize elsewhere."

"And so, the Harnon have two planets, while the PitKree have none."

"I suppose it's pointless to say that you have PitKreelaundun," Leonfir said, with a faint sigh. "The decision about Harnon's second planet cannot be revoked. It's been a decade. How can this still rankle so badly?"

"It's not the Harnon decision alone, but viewing that decision in light of our ancient memory."

"I sometimes wonder," Leonfir said, "whether it's wise to pass memories from one generation to the next. Particularly, a memory as devastating as the loss of your planet."

"You're not alone in wondering this," TarKeen said, "but, whether wise or not, we do possess those memories. We're also convinced that the Laundun ruling families would force a similar decision if we find another planet suitable for habitation. It will be given to some other race for colonization." He crossed his arms over his chest. "In other decisions of our government, race makes little difference. But this matter forever divides us. Laundun ruling families will always hold the majority, so PitKree can never benefit from exploration."

Leonfir let out a long breath. "And you agree with them."

TarKeen let his arms fall. "No, sir. I certainly do not agree with everything I hear. On the other hand, I understand their viewpoint better than you do. I make no attempt to convince anyone that their opinions are wrong. Instead, I listen. Occasionally, I point out...I think I will call it *distorted reasoning.*"

Leonfir laughed but seemed to take little enjoyment in it.

"Do not be overly concerned, my friend," TarKeen said. "Such grumbling has sprung up among the PitKree for the past decade. I only spoke of it because you asked."

"What else won't I hear?"

TarKeen turned his head. "You puzzle me, sir. If there's something specific you're looking for, tell me."

Leonfir leaned his elbows on the table and pressed his palms together. "Someone walked in on a gathering of PitKree. The instant the door opened, the speaker stopped, mid-sentence."

"When was this?"

"Several hours ago."

Tangible energy pumped through TarKeen's limbs; relief that he had not been present, fear of what had been said. He allowed his voice to reveal none of this. "What did he hear?"

"Only a few words. No meaning can be determined from them. But he felt that his entrance caused inordinate tension."

"Already, I suspect that VanDar was speaking. Am I right?"

"You are. How do you know?" Leonfir asked.

"If ever a man was fascinated with his own voice, it's VanDar. All who are present must listen to his rants. Since all do not agree, tension follows him. I've seen it often."

"Is there risk, TarKeen?"

"If I thought there were no possible risk, I would not spend my off-duty time in his vicinity." TarKeen furrowed his brow. "Believe me, that is no pleasure. I have yet to see him commit any crime. He rants but takes no action. I can do nothing but listen." He waved his hand aside. "That is really all I can tell you."

Leonfir leaned back. "Then there is nothing for me to do, but express my appreciation."

TarKeen's brow remained furrowed. "I hope you remember your appreciation if VanDar ever turns to action."

"What do you mean?"

"I am often seen in his presence. I even permit him to think I agree with him at times. My position would be vulnerable if he commits some act of stupidity."

Leonfir dismissed TarKeen but sat staring at nothing for several minutes. His brow tensed. He had relied on TarKeen for years and come to trust him implicitly. Now, this strange conversation where TarKeen said much but committed to nothing. Was he over-analyzing this? TarKeen had said nothing wrong, but those final comments—He could draw two very different interpretations from them.

TarKeen turned over those same two possibilities as he strode through the halls. So far it had progressed, this dangerous game he played, slipping ever closer to critical mass. A decision was nearing. There was no longer a question of whether he would become a traitor, only a question of who would call him traitor.

Kena lay in a recliner with her eyes closed, but rest was beyond her. They had fed her a thick drink, followed an hour later by a bland pudding. After removing the last two tubes from her body, they had lifted her into a standing position. She'd found it less troublesome to put her weight on her legs than to hang between their shoulders. She'd taken the few steps toward the recliner as they insisted, only so they'd let her sink back into lethargy.

She knew what they were doing; trying to get her to use her body again. The sounds, the food, the movement, even the flowering plant that filled the air with exotic perfume.

Then, they'd left her alone again. Alone with thoughts she didn't want to think.

She dodged between painful memories. Her mind invaded. Her private thoughts and feelings inspected. Was this what rape felt like? It wasn't physical, but her treasured places were violated.

And now they expected her to return to normal?

How deluded they were. Normal would never exist again.

Some literal portion of her mind pointed out that she was closer to normal now than she had been.

She examined those earlier thoughts; the confusion, the estrangement from her body. How convinced she'd been, during all those hours, that death was only moments away. Even the belief that she could refuse her body. She still wished that were true, though there was no longer a way to convince herself it could be. No amount of limp inactivity made it so.

She supposed she would have to bestir herself, but motivation was non-existent.

She tried to think of seeing friends again. Barren. Emotion refused to rise.

She imagined flying. Hollow. No excitement. No pleasure.

How would she endure this? People said life was short. Hers loomed as an eternal void.

Pernanyen's silent voice returned to her memory. *I want to know how you view us—both you and the Collaborative. I want to know if you speak the truth; if you really don't know what tra-pentazine is. I want to know if you are as you seem.*

Wow, what an insane way to get to know someone. Torment them while you learn of them. But Kena couldn't deny the realization that had come with those silent words. Pernanyen was comfortable in telepathy. To her, it was not so different from verbal conversation. She was well trained. She'd believed she could soothe Kena, that the link would be gentle. Oh, how wrong...how terribly wrong she'd been!

She even seemed to think Kena would want to do the same to her. Kena shuddered. Revulsion twisted her stomach, while her overwhelmed mind invented fears. Would they find some means to coerce her into such a link? Or inflict some other horror she had yet to imagine?

What if she never slept again? The exhaustion grew painful. Cold shivered through her body in spite of the warmth radiating from the recliner. Her thoughts, never rational for long, gyrated through impossibilities. She was lost, couldn't find her way, didn't know what she was looking for.

Vivaldi began to play again. There was order in the sounds. Rhythm. Predictability. She grabbed hold and hung on.

TarKeen made an abrupt entrance to the meeting chamber—a long, narrow lounge this time.

VanDar broke off mid-sentence, swinging around to the door, then opened his mouth to continue.

TarKeen spoke first. "How predictable. Just like this morning."

"What do you mean?" someone in the gathering asked.

ShenLee answered. "A Laundun walked in while VanDar was speaking inadvisably." She looked to TarKeen. "Is that it?"

"Yes."

"You weren't here. How do you know?" she asked.

TarKeen kept his eyes locked on VanDar. "Leonfir asked me about it. What did the Laundun hear?"

VanDar shifted his weight, his voice quiet for once. "Not more than a couple words. Nothing was revealed."

TarKeen wove between the tables toward VanDar, his firm steps at odds with his casual pace. "Then why did Leonfir hear of it?"

"I have no idea."

"How careless of you to have no idea." TarKeen let his sharp words hang for a moment. "The man perceived inordinate tension. As though you were saying something you didn't want a Laundun to hear."

Murmuring rose from the crowd.

"VanDar will destroy everything."

"His tongue is dangerous."

"They'll assume that we're party to anything he says."

"Don't over-react," a calm voice said. "Nothing was compromised."

One spoke louder than the rest. "TarKeen, how did you respond?"

TarKeen drew near VanDar and held his gaze. "I laid the blame for tension where it belongs. I said that VanDar rants, and everyone present cannot help but listen. I said that tension follows him because there are many who do not agree with him."

The murmurs behind him eased.

"No harm will come of it," the calm voice said.

"We must continue to plan," another said. "We will simply need to be more cautious."

TarKeen continued forward, forcing VanDar to step back. He read the anger in VanDar's eyes. The man wanted to strike but knew the consequence. Pity. It would be a pleasure to arrest him. Not today, apparently.

TarKeen taunted him. "Have you any objection to taking the blame, VanDar?"

"I have strength to bear the results of my words."

"Strength." TarKeen spat the word. "Strength impresses me far less than wisdom. Of that, you have no more than Pernanyen. She, at least, had authority for her decisions. Something else you do not possess. Or have you forgotten that yours is the generation of your family that will not rule?"

VanDar's face worked, but he did not speak.

"You have a profession, do you not?" TarKeen demanded.

"Something to do with communication research, though I've never heard you speak of it. I believe it's time that you give attention to whatever it is you supposedly do. Something other than stirring up contention and damaging the PitKree reputation."

VanDar's lips darkened and twitched. "You cannot command my silence. I have as much right to speak as anyone."

"You speak *far more* than anyone. Do not imagine I will assist you in usurping Frayunomen authority. Speak one word, take one action that is treason, and I will arrest you myself."

VanDar's breath blew hot against TarKeen's face as he shouted, "Are you PitKree or PitKreelaundun?"

In that instant, the door opened.

TarKeen relaxed his posture immediately, leaving only VanDar in the pose of aggressor. TarKeen matched his voice to his mild stance. "Both, of course. What a ridiculous question." He turned a casual glance toward the door. A Laundun couple hesitated there. "Don't be alarmed. It's only VanDar who shouts; the rest of us are far more hospitable."

They advanced through the room's open center, which permitted a shortcut across the long chamber. The man threw a disapproving glance around the room. "Why do you PitKree gather like this?"

"You must know," TarKeen said, "that PitKree families are bountiful. We're comfortable in large gatherings. Feel free to join us, if you have no other plans. We have no intent to exclude the Laundun."

"PitKreelaundun," the man corrected.

Someone else answered, keeping his voice as mild as TarKeen's. "Even though you noticed that we are all PitKree, you seem to have forgotten that you are Laundun. How odd."

"It is not we who maintain division," the Laundun man said.

ShenLee responded as the couple neared her. "There is nothing to maintain or disallow. The only way to be PitKreelaundun is to be either PitKree or Laundun. Why pretend it is otherwise?"

"Centuries have passed! Will you never accept our welcome?"

"Are we not here?" she said with a smile. "Can we not acknowledge that we are PitKree at the same time as we acknowledge the union of PitKree and Laundun?"

"But you don't. VanDar said 'PitKree *or* PitKreelaundun.'"

Another voice rose with a touch of ire. "That was VanDar's opinion. He does not speak for all of us."

A snort was the Laundun man's only answer.

As the couple neared the opposite door, the woman spoke for the first time. "Be fair, my dear. No one else echoed his opinion." She inclined her head to TarKeen. "We must decline your invitation; our own, much smaller family is waiting for us."

The door closed behind them.

"Again, your tongue stirs up trouble!" someone said to VanDar.

"It is nothing," he declared. "All know that we call ourselves PitKree. Enough of this. We need to plan and act. Take advantage of opportunity."

"It is not time for action," TarKeen said. "This opportunity that you perceive is only useful if the goal is to place you in power. Acting now will cause war, which will prevent us from getting PitKree ships for PitKree exploration. Do not think that I will support you in this, VanDar." He dropped his voice, but flared the emphasis. "And do not imagine that you can control this ship without me."

CHAPTER FORTY-ONE

Leonfir scanned the faces on the screen. Three he recognized, one he did not. How would Ghent react, since his primary request had not been granted? Ghent had matched the number of PitKreelaundun attendees Leonfir specified. An indication that he knew something about negotiation protocol—more promising than his oddly brief greeting.

"I requested a meeting with Pernanyen of Frayunomen," Ghent said, emphasizing her name.

Leonfir stated his planned response. "I must inform you of a directive we have received from the ruling families of PitKreelaundun. Pernanyen's authority has been suspended until her actions have been investigated and judged by the other families. It will take at least fifteen days for one of them to reach us. She is no longer permitted to make decisions or to speak with you."

"How convenient for her."

Leonfir's eyes widened. "I doubt she would describe her situation as convenient. She has lost her authority, but is still responsible for her actions. If Kena Talgarth does not recover, Pernanyen will be executed."

"That may satisfy your sense of justice," Ghent said, "but it will not help Kena."

Leonfir acknowledged the point with a nod. "Fortunately, Kena has shown some signs of improvement. Pernanyen's suspension does provide a benefit to us. I now hold highest authority on this ship and can speak with you freely. Permit me to express the hope that communications will improve."

"Any improvement would be appreciated." Ghent's fingers swept an arc on the table. "Do your goals differ from Pernanyen's?"

"It is my firm intention to return Kena to you in the best possible health. Pernanyen hoped to improve relations between us and the Interstellar Collaborative. While I *do not* endorse her approach, I do agree with her goal."

"Pernanyen said that, but her actions suggest the opposite."

Apparently, Ghent was not going to make this easy. Of course, negotiation never was. Leonfir ensured his voice remained calm. "You may understand better," he said, "if I describe her. She is young, barely an adult. She is on this ship to continue learning, not because we expected contact with other races. Her father, Travannesal of Frayunomen, is the family member active in government. Pernanyen's idealism and inexperience led her to an error of judgment. If she had foreseen what would occur, she would have chosen differently. It's not her nature to intentionally harm anyone. However, she is still accountable for the results of her decision. As a race, we do not take this lightly."

Ghent's expression remained fixed.

Leonfir leaned forward. "Others will decide what comes to Pernanyen. You and I, Ghent, will decide what comes to us now. My desire is that we strive toward improving relations."

"I am willing, but to be blunt, I'm skeptical. I need more than words. I need actions. We requested recordings of Kena's conversations. Pernanyen did not provide them. Will you?"

Leonfir perceived his unspoken meaning. *If you don't, I won't believe you any more than I believe her.* "I'll review what was recorded. I'm sure some can be given to you. Please understand that there will come a point where that is no longer appropriate."

"Why not?"

"You already know Kena's acclimation was harsh. We do not reproduce what anyone says under stress. Nor will I transmit what I deem to be private. If you have concerns after you've heard the recordings, we'll speak of this again." Leonfir leaned back. He needed to return this conversation to plan. "For now, there are other subjects I wish to discuss. I propose that we first give you the latest information on Kena's condition, then agree on how communication will occur. Last, I would like to open a discussion of your plans after Kena returns to the *Ontrevay*."

"This is acceptable," Ghent said.

Leonfir glanced toward Freltenloe, who was waiting for this cue.

"Kena has shown some degree of improvement," Freltenloe said, "although not as much as we would like. Her muscle tone is approaching normal. She drinks and eats. She can sit up and walk a short distance. None of this was true when we last talked. Unfortunately, she still has not slept. She is lethargic, probably due to exhaustion."

"Has she spoken?" Metchell asked.

"No, but we have not encouraged that. We speak to her only in brief, simple statements. We find that it is better to wait for other sairital systems to normalize before prompting speech."

Metchell nodded. "Agreed. What is her reaction to the sound files Hrndl provided?"

"Reaction to the forest sounds is too subtle to draw conclusions. We can tell that she gives attention to the music." Freltenloe shifted and licked his lips. "My impression was that her brain activity indicated dissonance the first time she heard it. I suspect, she experienced an emotional release that was inconsistent with the music. It was played again a few hours later. Strong synapses were active. Her earlier intense emotional response was not evident. My interpretation is that she was listening to the music in a more normal way."

Metchell frowned as though considering this.

Freltenloe shifted again. "I'm reluctant to use the word *normal* since I have no experience with Humans. The Prednians gave us medical and sairital information on several races. They did not include any that pertained to Humans, perhaps because Humans had only recently joined the Collaborative. I realize, now, that you may have assumed we already had such information, but we do not. Will you provide me what is commonly available?"

Metchell started shaking his head, even before Freltenloe finished. His lips pinched into a thin line.

Freltenloe hurried back into speech. "It need not contain drug specifications. I am only asking to understand what constitutes normal responses for a Human. Particularly sairital responses."

"That is not possible," Metchell said. "Nor is it necessary. Sairital intervention is completely out of the question. I would have thought you would understand this."

"I do." Freltenloe's voice held rigid restraint. "I only seek a way to judge the impact of the things we are trying. We want to ease her back into a normal state, but we don't have baseline information. We cannot be sure whether she approaches it or digresses."

"There is nothing I can give you."

Freltenloe stared at Metchell's image. "I see two possibilities. Either you don't know how to care for her, or you want us to fail in caring for her. The latter, I suspect."

Hrndl darted a look at Metchell's livid face and said, "Pause." She turned back to the screen, her guttural voice utterly calm. "You have injured her and yet you blame Metchell? By association, you blame all of us for something that happened on the *Epri7*. Please understand that we find this both absurd and infuriating. Your captain says he wants to improve relations. Do you?"

Freltenloe's lips quivered.

Before he could speak, Leonfir said, "*Pause?* An interesting word choice. Useful. Freltenloe, vent your anger at Pernanyen, not Metchell. I do not want to hear what you are unable to do for Kena. Only what you can do. You have forty years' experience and have been the first to study multiple alien races. You were successful with them. I expect you to be successful with Kena."

Ghent rejoined the discussion. "It's a mistake to believe that anything you have learned of other races can be applied to Kena. Sairital information was once published on Humans. Misinterpretations of it resulted in injuries. Attempts to correct it did not help. Humans finally insisted that all copies be destroyed." He spread his hands wide on the table. "It concerns me greatly that you ask for sairital information. I expect you already know what I'm about to say, but I must be certain." He stressed each word. "You absolutely must not link with Kena!"

Leonfir took care to hide his feelings and speak only of the future. "Now that I hold authority, my permission would be required for anyone to link with her. I, most certainly, will not grant it." He looked aside. "Freltenloe, you're dismissed."

Ghent motioned to Metchell with the same result.

After the two doctors left, Leonfir said "I believe this next subject will be far less contentious."

Ghent resumed a neutral tone. "So I should hope. I would like to introduce Remlishos to you. He is second in command. His position is similar to TarKeen's, although we do not use the title of commander."

"What race are you?" TarKeen asked.

"Meklehon," Remlishos said.

Light skin, hair a sort of pale, brownish hue, not much darker than his skin. Leonfir searched his memory of the racial profiles.

Apparently, TarKeen did as well. He bowed from the hip and asked, "Is this the appropriate greeting?"

Remlishos returned the bow. "It is."

Leonfir offered the gesture as well.

"I understand," TarKeen said, "that both Meklehon and Plynteth are strong telepaths. Is this correct?"

"It is so," Remlishos said.

"If it's permitted that I ask," TarKeen said, "please tell me whether you and Ghent link regularly."

Remlishos nodded. "As often as convenient or needful."

"He has heard every conversation between us," Ghent said, "and is in full agreement with my goals. You have met Hrndl, but her position was not mentioned. She is an officer: chief navigator."

TarKeen inclined his head to her. "You described yourself as Kena's friend. Is she also an officer?"

"No," Hrndl said, "but she is one of the senior navigators, so she does have leadership authority. When I met Kena, we were both senior navigators. We've flown many missions as peers and also spend off-duty time together. I suspect that your authority structure is more rigid than ours. Perhaps it seems odd that we would be friends while one of us holds authority over the other. Kena and I are comfortable with it."

Leonfir gestured to the man beside him. "This is Rialmerray, another of my officers. He is chief of tra-pentazine protection. That is his sole responsibility. It keeps him and his staff fully occupied."

"Naturally," Ghent said, "we do not have a similar, dedicated role. The tracking of objects falls within the chief navigator's responsibilities. I believe, it may be useful to include our chief scientist, who has led our study of trazine and pentazine."

"As you choose," Leonfir said.

The scientist, Piert, soon joined them. Notably taller than the others, with a mouth as broad and mobile as Hrndl's was tiny and still, He addressed Rialmerray. "I was intrigued when I heard your role mentioned. Will you explain it further?"

Rialmerray nodded, a stiff motion. "My team locates and tracks trazine and pentazine. We analyze risk of explosion in projected paths. When appropriate, we neutralize the risk."

Piert smiled. "I look forward to a long conversation with you."

Rialmerray's rigid expression held, but he said, "I hope it will be mutually satisfying."

Leonfir leaned forward and pressed his palms together, letting his fingertips interlace. "Ghent, there are things we need to discuss. It is possible we will have opposing views and probable that misunderstandings will occur. Yet, it's imperative that we reach agreement. Are you willing to make the attempt with me?"

Ghent seemed to take a longer breath than necessary. "We may already be misunderstanding one another. I don't know what agreement you seek. We desire a peaceful conclusion to our dealings. Does that satisfy you?"

Leonfir struggled to understand Ghent's expressions, but he seemed less than pleased. "Yes," Leonfir said. "I would prefer to keep a small consistent group involved in all communications. Do you believe this group we have now includes the right people to engage in discussion?"

"That depends on the subject. Is this related to tra-pentazine?"

"It is."

"Then, these are the members of my crew who should be involved."

"Let us proceed, then."

<hr />

"Piert, this is your opportunity," Ghent said. Between the arguments and the lengthy preambles to actual conversation, his hopes were not high. What did they want that they would not state?

Piert dove in, clearly untroubled. "We're fortunate to have contacted a ship with a staff focused on tra-pentazine."

"All PitKreelaundun ships," Rialmerray said, "are staffed to neutralize tra-pentazine."

How stiff the man was, without the gentle shoulder movement Ghent attributed to the PitKreelaundun.

"Surely you do more than that with your fleet!" Piert exclaimed.

"Of course we do. But we're all prepared for reassignment when the need arises."

"I see. Is this area unusually rich in tra-pentazine?"

Rialmerray stared. "Rich? What do you mean?"

Piert shifted a bit at the odd tone. "An unusually large concentration."

Rialmerray's dark eyebrows pressed together. "I understood that the word *rich* had a connotation of *desirable* or *prized*."

"I...suppose so." Piert nodded. "But, pertaining to matter, it can simply mean a high concentration. Is that the case?"

Rialmerray's shoulders twitched, and his voice sharpened. "I would phrase it differently. It *was* moderately contaminated. Your sample collection increases it, and the continued presence of your gravity ship will increase the concentration further. We must *now* treat it as *highly* contaminated with unknown risk of future explosions. Does that answer your question?"

"In a most unexpected way," Piert said. "Please understand that we have only just discovered the existence of these substances."

Rialmerray's voice remained sharp despite Piert's attempt at a soothing tone. "That discovery was prompted by the destruction of two planets, was it not? How you could overlook that tra-pentazine is dangerous rather than valuable, is beyond comprehension."

Piert drew a breath and held his tone steady. "Could you comprehend that my poorly chosen word was only intended to mean high concentration?"

Leonfir turned to Rialmerray and said in an acidic tone, "The answer is *yes*. You can comprehend that."

Ghent became aware of his own forward movement and eased back when Leonfir corrected his officer. Was this the best they could do?

Rialmerray's voice lost all expression. "I will not refer to the misunderstanding again."

"Thank you," Piert said. "I would like to better understand what can trigger explosions."

Rialmerray' shoulders jerked again as he turned to Leonfir. "Did you not say that we would discuss the sample collection?"

"There is time," Leonfir said. "Let conversation flow."

Rialmerray listed potential triggers and replied to questions concerning trigger thresholds and energy output.

Piert's posture relaxed. He followed every answer with more questions. His eyes glowed, and his wide lips curled.

Suddenly, Rialmerray swung back to Leonfir. "He is like a child with a new puzzle. Are we never to speak of the death trap they've collected?"

L eonfir cringed inwardly as four gasps sounded over the communication channel.

Ghent spoke with a strong cadence. "Piert is an intelligent adult with an appetite for knowledge. It is through knowledge that risks are identified and death prevented."

"That is why—"

"Rialmerray!" Leonfir snapped. "Stop talking and listen. Learn to recognize anger."

To Leonfir's relief, TarKeen spoke, his low voice calm and unhurried. "Hrndl, will you tell us what the reference to a child means to all of you?"

It seemed to take effort, but she also managed a calm tone. "It's an implication that the person is uneducated and lacks understanding. An absurdity in relation to Piert."

"Thank you," TarKeen said. "Among the PitKreelaundun, *child* implies exuberance or great energy. Adding the word *puzzle* implies intelligent curiosity. I can perceive why you inferred an insult, but that is not our connotation." His voice developed an edge as he turned to Rialmerray. "But for one who is offended by the word *rich*, it's remarkably sloppy communication."

Rialmerray licked his lips and returned to the formal tone so common to his race. "I apologize for my poor choice of words. My concern over your sample collection has compromised my patience."

Piert nodded as Ghent replied. "Do not be alarmed. We will not leave them here."

"What do you plan to do with them?" Leonfir asked.

"Take them back with us to the Collaborative's area."

Rialmerray spun away from the camera, likely to hide his expression.

Leonfir tightened his interlaced fingers over his knuckles. "Would you like to know what I just heard?" he asked, his eyes on Ghent.

"Certainly."

"You told me not to be alarmed about a moderate danger because you are going to do something far more dangerous than leaving the tra-pentazine here."

Ghent leaned back and shook his head. "Not my meaning. We have the technology to contain the samples."

Perhaps Ghent meant that mild tone to calm, but it sounded nonchalant. Leonfir firmed his voice. "I'm sure you understand your technology, but you don't understand what you've wrapped it around."

"Fortunately," Ghent said, "you've just given us more knowledge, which Piert and the rest of our scientists will combine with what we've already learned. When Kena is safe within the *Ontrevay*, we will speak more of this."

Silence followed the end of the transmission. Leonfir rubbed his fingertips in circles against his forehead.

TarKeen dismissed Rialmerray and paced, waiting for Leonfir to speak.

He broke the silence with heavy words. "He'll use the samples to bargain for Kena's return."

"We intend to return her, anyway."

"True," Leonfir said, "but her full recovery is doubtful. They will very soon know that Pernanyen forced her to link. If you found anything comforting in their description of Humans and telepathy, you are alone!"

TarKeen made no reply.

Leonfir's frown began to hurt. He ran his hand upward over his brow. "I think it unlikely that she'll recover enough to perform her side of the constrained link. That means, we'll not be permitted insight into whatever Pernanyen learned. Likewise, Kena will learn nothing from us—beyond torturous memories, that is. Her own people will be convinced that we are worse than they thought us before. If the persistent tension between Metchell and Freltenloe is any indication, we'll never get useful communication between Rialmerray and Piert."

TarKeen shook his head. "That may not be a reliable indicator. Perhaps we erred in having Freltenloe converse with them. They believe he is the one who injured Kena, and we cannot tell them otherwise. I suggest appointing a different doctor to discuss her condition, for what little that's worth."

"I gather Hrndl lost her tolerance, too." Leonfir shifted. "Not that I claim to be able to interpret her rigid, little mouth and mobile brows."

TarKeen appeared to subject this to careful consideration. "I would guess that she longed to project her body through the camera and slit Rialmerray's mouth open from ear to ear."

Leonfir uttered a bitter laugh.

"At least Hrndl and Ghent continue to speak," TarKeen said. "Particularly Ghent."

"Yes, he seems to be our best hope. Though, how I will convince him, I cannot imagine. So much to convince him of—and all of it before he knows what happened to Kena."

CHAPTER FORTY-TWO

Ghent listened to the recording of Kena's arrival in the *Epri7*, while Leonfir watched him from the screen. It ended with Pernanyen inviting Kena to a more comfortable room.

"Come," she said and turned toward the door.

The ending seemed abrupt to Ghent. Or was he too suspicious? They wouldn't have cameras in the hallway, after all. "What was Kena's response?" he asked.

"There was no direct response," Leonfir said. "They spoke of the need for acclimation, and Freltenloe escorted Kena to a medical facility. The conversation Pernanyen asked for never occurred."

The meeting went downhill from there. Against his better judgment, Ghent yielded to another request to discuss the sample collection. It was now brutally clear that the PitKreelaundun did not want the Collaborative to have even one tiny sample of either trazine or pentazine.

The cost of obtaining those samples—so high. Not just time and work. Not just a large craft. Two lives had been lost—one of them a close friend. He halted the reflexive tensing of his shurgs.

And now the PitKreelaundun wanted everything given up? If they had their way, the Collaborative's research of this dangerous substance must stop. It was all for nothing.

Interventions of *pause* became ever more frequent.

When Rialmerray said, "The treaty was supposed to protect us from—" Leonfir stopped him once again.

Piert ignored the halt. "Let me guess: When you said in the treaty that your border was the side of the nebula, you meant the far side, not the near side."

"A longer pause seems to be necessary," Ghent said and closed the session.

His body and mind demanded exertion. So much frustration— it had to be vented. Ghent headed for the bay, the only place in the ship with adequate height. The exercise rooms the others used could not fulfill the activity he missed from his home on Plynteth. Using struts and anchors for hand holds, he scaled the three-story walls. Up, down, sideways—all around the bay at high speed. This was nothing like climbing in a canyon, but it felt good to stretch his limbs and use his strength. It also prompted memories of his wife and son.

How long before they began to worry about the silence the PitKreelaundun enforced? He was too far for direct communication, but they exchanged messages every four or five days. A common practice for many of the crew. Sooner or later, someone would notice that no communication was coming from the *Ontrevay*. The Collaborative would send a ship to search for them. It wouldn't arrive before more PitKreelaundun ships gathered.

Multiple ships worried him. The possibility of outright war was never far from his mind. He needed to get beyond the impasse miring them, but how?

The PitKreelaundun were a confusing race. Leonfir and TarKeen seemed capable of reason, but no one else. Rialmerray clearly hated anyone and everyone associated with the Collaborative. The attitude must be widespread, or Leonfir would have chosen someone else to join their meetings. Even Gwillenin, who seemed to have the best possible intentions toward Kena, did not reassure him. The woman had assumed the worst, and was not persuaded otherwise until after Kena had given the child into her arms.

There was something odd in that exchange, as though Kena had helped Pearl in some profound and inexplicable way. It seemed impossible, and yet Kena so often surprised him. The depth of her commitment. How much she would invest, even risk, on behalf of someone she had no reason to care for. Ghent swung beneath an anchored craft and continued around the bay, pondering her compassion.

And now, she lay injured and helpless, wholly under the power of people who cared nothing at all for her. Even if he could think of a way to rescue her, he could put no navigator at risk of capture. Nor could he leave her to her fate. He could think of only one way. The risk was so great. If he failed...He'd never even have the chance to explain it to his wife and son.

He paused, allowing his gaze to rest on the small, stripped craft below him. A couple technicians left it and headed for the door. Ghent climbed down the wall. The craft both beckoned and alarmed him. He circled it, inspecting the hull, then stepped inside. Most of the interior panels were back in place. Test equipment, which still ran diagnostics, displayed no faults. He studied the navigation console.

Remlishos stepped through the hatch. "Hrndl tells me you've been flying simulations configured for this craft."

"True. Did she mention that it's well within my skill level?"

"Yours and many others."

Ghent nodded. "Hrndl has received several volunteers. Quon even approached me—argued at length that he should be the one to go. But if anyone goes, it will be me. Are you surprised, Remlishos?"

"*Concerned* would be a better word. Kena needs rescue, but the *Ontrevay* needs its captain."

"I will not leave my crew without a captain," Ghent said. "Did you come here to talk me out of a decision that cannot even be made?"

"No, to tell you that we've received a most unusual message from Earth."

"Received a message?" Ghent left the craft as he spoke. "How?" Remlishos matched his rapid pace. "Inewin is still puzzling over that. I suppose, if anyone could pierce PitKreelaundun comm disruption, it would be Humans."

"How would they even know it was necessary?"

"We can only guess. Perhaps they tried to communicate and received no response. This message isn't in standard format. It didn't go directly to Kena's computer. It has a brief instruction to the *Ontrevay* communication staff, as well as the content for Kena."

"What's it say?"

"It's from her father. He stresses that the message is to be delivered to Kena immediately. Strangely, it's in verbal format rather than text."

As they entered a lift, Ghent pondered the oddities. Her father? How would he have access to comm technology sophisticated enough to penetrate PitKreelaundun disruption? Connections, perhaps. But their silence really hadn't been long enough yet to cause alarm. Did Humans even have such technology? Why verbal format? It might make sense to record speech for his daughter, even though it made for fat transmissions, but why transmit voice to strangers?

Ghent strode into the communication section, convinced that he was missing something important. Several members of Inewin's staff were present, as well as Hrndl.

They all looked as puzzled as Ghent felt. Inewin didn't even wait for a request before playing the initial instructions. Ghent listened to the voice, lower pitched than Kena's, but enriched with similar inflections.

"I am Andrew Talgarth, the father of Kena Talgarth. I request

SHARON ROSE

that you give the attached content to Kena immediately. You will
not understand why; but, I assure you, it is of *utmost* importance."

Ghent was still pondering the words, when a PitKreelaundun
voice demanded communication.

"Just acknowledge," Ghent said, scowling at the interruption.
"So, Andrew Talgarth is her father. I suppose that shouldn't be a
surprise. Inewin, what's Human protocol for an urgent message if
the recipient's not available? Would they expect an officer to listen
and pass it on verbally?"

"That's not even possible," Inewin said. "It's music."

"Music?"

He nodded. "Twenty-four files in the music format Humans
use. Hours of music! Nothing else. Even her father's message was
in the same format. It's possible that's the reason it got through
to us."

"Why would music be of utmost importance?" Ghent asked.

"I suppose it could contain a message," Inewin said, his brow
knit. "They do have that alternate music voice."

"*Sing*, you mean? Or is it *song*?"

Frdn answered. "*Sing* is the verb; *song* is the noun. They don't
use song for messages. The words are a form of poetry. Even if he
embedded a message in a song, it wouldn't take that many files."

"Music," Ghent murmured. Urgent? It was almost as if her
father knew something of what was going on. But he couldn't.
Kena did have a strange concept of distance—that it was
insignificant. But that made no sense either. Humans never linked
with other Humans. Inexplicable, since some of them would link
with other races. Ghent shook his head. "The man definitely knew
what he was talking about when he said we wouldn't understand!"

Those surrounding him uttered varied sounds of agreement.

"It's hard to believe," Remlishos said, "that Andrew Talgarth
would make a statement like this for something trivial. Hrndl,
what has Kena said about him?"

She looked up from the computer in her hand. "Very little. I'm
just now realizing who he is. I know family is important to her—

386

she communicates with them often. As for her father, the only thing I can call to mind is her commenting that he is wise. I suppose his accomplishments already prove this."

She stepped closer to Ghent. "I don't understand his message any better than you do, but we can't doubt his expertise or comprehension. I think we should send it to the *Epri7*. They played the other music. I don't see any reason why they wouldn't play this, as well." She paused looking around at the others' negative expressions. "Why not? Can't we convert it into standard format?"

Inewin said, "As far as we know, this is the only format the PitKreelaundun cannot block or interpret. That means, it could be useful for encoded messages. They probably recorded the signal. If we send them the message contents, we'll be giving them the key to the code." He swung his head from side to side. "I can't imagine anyone in the Collaborative, Human or otherwise, commending us for that!"

Hrndl vented a guttural sound. "What if her father does know what's happening here? It's conceivable that the ruling families have contacted the Collaborative, or even Earth. We don't really understand why Humans are so enamored with music. What if this is something that Kena actually needs?"

Ghent remained silent, his brow fur deeply puckered.

Remlishos said, "We still cannot give them the key. Get creative. Other options, please."

Ghent considered strategy while they tossed ideas around. He would so much rather bring Kena to the message than send the message to her. The little craft that awaited him was no answer. He could take it right up to the bay of the *Epri7*, but he could not force them to grant him entrance. Of course, it wasn't really entrance that worried him. Departure was the problem.

He could ask them. They would promise to let him take Kena and leave. He just couldn't trust them. He needed leverage. Some reason why they would need to release Kena and him.

Music played in the room amidst discussions of how to slightly alter it. A challenge, since the changes could not be obvious to the PitKreelaundun or repulsive to the Human ear. Opyera knew enough about Human music to preserve the essential sound. They altered a clip and converted it to a common file format.

When they played back the test clip, Ghent could tell no difference. Multiple instruments created the music, none of them familiar to him. He couldn't even differentiate where Human voice was included.

When he said as much, Opyera grinned. "The vocals are still clear, but if you don't recognize them, what chance do the PitKreelaundun have? There's no need to mention this contains words."

Inewin shook his head. "It's not good enough." His eyes remained fixed on his computer. "It'll take them a while, but they'll eventually find correlations between the two transmissions. We won't get past that without destroying the music."

"We can't transmit," Frdn said. "We need to use hard storage with only audio output. If they access the music any other way, the files will be destroyed."

"How will we design and test that in a reasonable amount of time?" Opyera asked.

"Destroying files is easy. Humans use audio units all the time, and they encrypt everything. We already have the synthesizer specs. Using such a unit will be second nature to Kena."

"We still have a big problem," Inewin said. "There's no way to get a physical device to her."

"You may leave that problem to us," Ghent said. "Get it ready." He turned to the door, but stopped at the sound of another transmission from the *Epri7*.

"Captain Leonfir requests to meet, alone, with Captain Ghent alone."

"Interesting grammar," one of the technicians murmured.

"Give it a moment," Ghent said, "then tell him I'll meet with him in five minutes. Hrndl, nav command. Remlishos, with me."

The visual communication room was only a few paces down

the hall. The moment the door slid shut, Ghent said, "This will likely be about the message from Earth."

"I expect so."

"That may place some pressure on them. We'll have to see if we can make use of this. It's time I formalize your position." He used his computer as he spoke. "You are hereby promoted to primary officer."

Remlishos also extended his computer to enter the necessary acceptance and promotion of Dhgnr to chief engineer. "I can't even thank you, for it means you intend to leave the ship. I've never imagined being this unhappy about a promotion."

A faint smile touched Ghent's lips for the first time in days. "I'm not surprised. If all goes well, I'll return. You will be endlessly bored."

"I can tolerate that far better than losing you as well as Kena. I still advise that you send one of the navigators. They are willing, after all."

"True. It would be a viable option, if only we had a way in and out of the *Epri7*."

"I don't see why you would consider any other option."

Ghent gave some thought to his answer. "To some degree, it's because I would like to meet these people. Granted, it would be too brief, so that's a trivial reason. More significantly, most navigators know someone who has been attacked or even killed by a PitKreelaundun. Including Quon, by the way. Not the best choice, if negotiation skills are needed. But we have yet to find the opportunity to send anyone. In the meantime, get familiar with Hrndl's suggestions for maneuvers and get that craft—Ah, I have a habit to break. Inform Dhgnr of his new responsibilities and tell him I want that craft ready."

Leonfir's image appeared on the screen as Remlishos turned to leave.

CHAPTER FORTY-THREE

G hent nodded at Leonfir's formal greeting. "Why alone?" he asked.

"It seems that more voices only create more tension," Leonfir said. "Somehow, we must begin to establish trust. Let us speak of a new subject."

"Such as?"

"The *Ontrevay* received a substantial communication. I'm told that it was from Earth."

So, they could pinpoint the source. "Yes. Have you given the content to Kena?"

Leonfir's full lips curved. "What an interesting way to ask whether we have a conversion algorithm. We do not. If you would like to translate it to common format and send it to us, I will certainly give it to her."

"I must give you the obvious response: No."

"Hardly a surprise, since it appears to be designed specifically to bypass our communication block."

"Unlikely," Ghent said. "I believe Humans were using this format before they were aware that the PitKreelaundun existed."

"So, the message is pure coincidence, then?"

"That is also unlikely. It's from Kena's father, with instructions that it be given to her immediately."

Leonfir's eyes widened. "If you're willing to give it to me verbally, I will convey it to her."

"I cannot translate it. I suspect that only a Human can comprehend the message's significance. It's music."

"Music?" Leonfir's voice seemed to contain even more surprise than Ghent had experienced.

"Indeed. Music is more pervasive among Humans than any other race we know. It seems to have a purpose we don't comprehend. I can only assume her father believes she has need of it. And that makes me wonder what he knows." Ghent studied Leonfir's expression and dared to hope that he was concerned.

Leonfir's words slowed, as though his thoughts traveled elsewhere. "An interesting race. And such an intriguing woman. We had hoped to learn from her. It grieves us that she is injured."

"Us? Not very many of you, I gather."

"Yes, many. Why do you doubt that?"

"I see no indication of it," Ghent said. "Rialmerray, for instance. He's never mentioned Kena, but he so clearly hates the rest of us. Why would he feel any differently toward her?"

Leonfir stared long at Ghent. "Rialmerray has dedicated his entire life to protecting others, many of whom are not even PitKreelaundun, but other races we protect. Some don't believe they're at risk. One primitive race doesn't even know we exist. Yet Rialmerray, and other protectors like him, continuously redirect tra-pentazine away from their planets. They monitor and stabilize the ejection arms of the nebula. And after your gravity ships pass and destabilize them, they go back and do it all again. He will do it many more times, because there does not seem to be a way to convince the Collaborative to stop putting every system in our space at ever greater risk."

His shoulders had taken on the swaying motion that seemed to come with long speeches. Ghent made no attempt to interrupt—hardly possible anyway, since Leonfir didn't pause for breath.

"When we discovered, Ghent, that there was a member of the Collaborative who actually cared about a PitKreelaundun life..." Leonfir shook his head. "I cannot begin to describe how stunned we were. If one such person exists, perhaps there are others like her. Rialmerray admires Kena. He perceives her as one who protects others. Yes, he is saddened that she's injured. And disappointed, as well. If we had a chance to know Kena, maybe we could get her to understand what the Collaborative is doing to us. Maybe we could find others like her. If your own people could help persuade the rest of you, maybe someday you would stop scattering the tra-pentazine along our border."

Ghent gave the air a moment to clear. "We have no desire to place any of you at risk. I studied the treaty negotiation records. Never once does it mention why you did not want our ships near the debris in the ejection arms."

"It was so obvious." Leonfir's hand rose and fell. "I know...you'll say it wasn't to the Collaborative, because tra-pentazine was unknown. We find it hard to believe that it could be plentiful in our domain, but non-existent in yours. I would like to believe you're telling me the truth, but too many lives hang in the balance. I must *know* the truth of your words."

"Now we are aware of it. The more knowledge we gain, the easier it will be to avoid redirecting the debris into your space."

"Again, I would like to believe that the Collaborative would use this knowledge to protect us. But I don't know if that's true, either. The alarmists within this ship are appalled that we have given you any information about tra-pentazine. They believe you will weaponize it and use it against us."

"I'm familiar with the concern." Ghent rested his forearms on the table's edge and leaned on them. "Please do not take this amiss. Objects have often been redirected toward Collaborative ships. We had no way to know the extreme effect of gravity on a substance that we'd never identified. Many in the Collaborative believe that disguised weapons are placed and directed in order to damage our ships. Even now, it could be speculated that tra-pentazine is strategically placed."

Leonfir shook his head. "Review the locations where your ships have been hit. Always near high concentrations. There would be no purpose in adding tra-pentazine, even if we had the technology to do it."

"You freely express your distrust of us. Do you, then, expect me to trust your statements?"

"Not...at...all." Leonfir swung his head back and forth with each word. "Distrust is mutual. It feeds on itself, ever growing. It contaminates every conversation, even this one. Pernanyen sought to interrupt the cycle. Two individuals, both determined to seek peace. It could have worked if they'd had time to know one another." Regret crossed his features. "Instead, the very woman we placed our hopes on was injured while under our care. Pernanyen can no longer act. I would make the same attempt that she did, but two people are required. I've yet to discover anyone else on the *Ontrevay* who is willing to seek peace."

Ghent leaned back and spread his hands on the table. "We all want peace, Leonfir. I wish I could persuade you to approach this in terms acceptable to the Collaborative."

"That has never worked before, but what do you have in mind?"

"One step at a time. Return Kena."

"Even that is a challenge." Leonfir shifted to one side. "Kena sent her craft away, I assume, to keep our eyes from your technology. I'm no more willing to share our technology than you are to share yours. TarKeen made it clear immediately that we would not provide her with transport. Nor will we eject her into the void. How do you plan to overcome this dilemma, Ghent?"

"We've prepared a craft with only rudimentary technology. That obstacle has been removed."

"So, you intend to send someone for her?" Leonfir asked.

"I do," Ghent said. "All that is required of you is to bring Kena to the craft and let it depart. There is no risk to you."

A tight smile stretched Leonfir's lips. "And then you will return to the Collaborative, where all will expound on our horrible treatment of Kena—injuring her after she rescued a PitKreelaundun child and returned her to us. Tensions at the border will greatly increase. There is much risk to us. Forgive me, Ghent, but I see no value in 'terms acceptable to the Collaborative.'"

Ghent suppressed a sigh. How could he reach this man? "What alternative do you propose?"

"No more distant communication. Come and meet with me face-to-face, Ghent. To be clear, I do not suggest a few minutes only. I mean a day or more. I want candid conversation, without recording, without wondering how others will interpret our words. You and Kena will then return to the *Ontrevay*."

Ghent looked into Leonfir's eyes on the screen. He had at least one thing in common with this alien captain. He *hoped* that his words were true, but he needed to *know*. "This reminds me of Kena's first conversation with TarKeen. The risk is entirely on my side."

Leonfir nodded. "I, too, perceive the similarity. Naturally, we do not want the same outcome as with Kena." He rested his palms together. "I've had extensive conversations with the most experienced doctors on the *Epri7*. We have information on the Plynteth race, both physical and sairital. You are far more compatible with PitKreelaundun than Humans are. Every one of these doctors assures me that you are not at risk of injury among us."

"Did they think Kena was at risk?"

"They were not consulted, although Freltenloe did warn Pernanyen. We are now very much aware of the gap in our knowledge of Humans. That same gap does not exist with the Plynteth. We have the specifications of your emfrel. One of our doctors has even acclimated to your race in order to confirm our understanding. If you would like additional information for your own medical staff, we will provide it."

"It's not sairital risk that concerns me, Leonfir. Forgive me for questioning your integrity, but I have no certainty that you will permit either Kena or me to leave. As with TarKeen and Pernanyen, you give me only words. Will you grant me a more tangible gesture?"

"What do you desire?"

"That our ships change relative position," Ghent said.

Leonfir paused. "I still feel that it's wise to maintain adequate distance, beyond weapon range."

"Agreed, so long as you do not attempt to return to PitKreelaundun space." Ghent traced an arc on the table. "The *Ontrevay* will swing around the *Epri7* and take up position between you and your own domain. You need only to rotate your ship in order to keep your receiving bay within our view. In case the implication is not clear, Remlishos will have my orders to attack if you attempt to leave with Kena and me on board."

Leonfir passed that off with a jerk of his head. "We will not leave with you on board. The *Ontrevay* may take the position you've described when you are ready to come to us."

G hent ordered Remlishos to arrange final details. Within minutes, Leonfir followed suit, ensuring that TarKeen conversed with Remlishos. The two men maintained efficient, amicable relations. Ghent completed his trip to the *Epri7* without incident. The course was simple; he had only to enter the receiving bay. The PitKreelaundun crew performed the actual docking procedure, bringing his craft to rest within a pressurized hold.

Leonfir met him as he disembarked. "Welcome to the *Epri7*, sir. It is a great pleasure to meet you directly."

Ghent took in Leonfir's smiling face. His honey-colored skin and gold-lined, brown eyes were a striking combination. Ghent returned the smile, which he didn't really trust. Having come, he had no choice but to assume the best until proven otherwise. "It also pleases me to meet you." He hoped this would end the courtesies.

"Come," Leonfir said. "Let us not waste the little time we have."

Ghent stepped over the blue markings on the floor and walked with him toward a door. The hold contained little. Tubes and cables were anchored to a wall. Metal lattice doors secured servicing equipment. Two of the walls sloped together as they neared the ceiling, which was really the hold's door to the receiving bay. The hum of field activation caused Ghent to glance over his shoulder. An energy field ringed his craft. "Is there a reason for that?"

"TarKeen has command of the ship while I am with you. I told him no one was to approach your craft. That's his method of ensuring my order is fulfilled."

"What's to stop someone from deactivating it?"

Leonfir raised his eyebrows. "If TarKeen did not bind the controls to his or my order, I would be very surprised."

The door slid open at their approach, revealing a small control room.

Beside a woman seated at the console, TarKeen stood tall and dark, with the serious face Ghent found hard to read. His voice revealed no more than his expression. "Sir, I've informed Remlishos that you have disembarked and joined Leonfir. He told me of the music device you've brought for Kena. I can take it to her."

"I would rather give it to her myself."

"We must talk first," Leonfir said. "It cannot wait."

Not what he wanted, but not surprising, either. Ghent pulled the device from his belt and handed it to TarKeen.

He turned it over, inspecting it. "Will she know how to use this?"

Ghent nodded. "It's designed by her race. I should mention that Humans are fanatical about encryption. If you try to access the files, they'll be destroyed."

TarKeen inclined his head. "I'll deliver it to her at once."

They left the control room, the two PitKreelaundun flanking Ghent until TarKeen turned down an intersecting hallway. Plants filled alcoves in the corridor. Ghent counted them, memorizing the route.

Leonfir escorted Ghent to a room where rich fabric decorated walls, couches, and chairs. "These quarters are yours while you're here."

TarKeen strode into the observation room, where Shannandi was again on duty. One of the many screens displayed the camera feed. Kena sat in the recliner.

"Is there any change?" he asked.

"Nothing significant."

"I'm going to give her a music device that her captain brought for her. Let me know how she responds to it."

A few steps took him into Kena's room. She did not react.

"The *Ontrevay* has received a message for you," he said. "They tell us it contains music that was sent by your father."

Her brows twitched.

"They put it on a device, which has been delivered to us."

He held it above her hands, which lay limp on her thighs. One turned to take it from him. It was the first movement she had initiated in days. So much for the theory that she'd lost the ability to comprehend language.

With trembling fingers, she touched a button. Music flowed, gentle, lifting. Her face changed with the sound. More instruments joined the first in complexities inexplicable to his ears. He watched her chest heave as her breath quickened. The pathetic sagging of her face morphed into rapt attention. Her parted lips almost reached a smile.

Relief swelled within him. What was in these sounds that

stirred her so? It didn't really matter, though—it had worked. Silently, he turned to leave.

"Tar-Keen."

Her weak voice arrested him as surely as a containment field would have. In an instant, he squatted by her recliner, bringing his eyes level with hers. "What do you desire?"

Her lips struggled with the word. "P-privacy."

Disappointing, but at least she had spoken. "I will leave you... and tell others not to enter. Is that what you're asking for?"

She nodded but frowned. Her lips still worked.

"I can wait. What else do you desire?"

Her thumb brought the music to a whisper. Her eyes roamed the walls and ceiling, fixing on the camera above her bed. "No... watch. No...listen."

Not good. Still, he couldn't deny her. "Are you saying you don't want the medical staff to see or hear what's in this room?"

She nodded. "No one. No...record."

"I'm concerned that we won't be able to hear or see if you need help. You must be able to use the communication controls before we stop visual monitoring."

She nodded.

"Bring your hand along the side of the armrest." He waited for her to do so. "Touch here. It sends a signal. Someone will reopen the audio channel to talk with you."

Her fingers found the control. A voice spoke. "What do you need?"

"Pri-va-cy." Kena's word emerged slow and stilted, but understandable.

TarKeen said, "Turn off the visual and audio monitoring."

"But, sir," Shannandi's voice said, "I must—"

"Turn it off, now."

"Yes, sir."

TarKeen softened his voice, revealing emotion even he hadn't expected. "I will ensure that your privacy is maintained. Enjoy your music."

A sigh eased through her lips. Still no eye contact. He dared to hope that would come soon.

He spent a few minutes in the monitoring room. Freltenloe hurried in, as well. Medical monitors confirmed the change. She was physically and mentally active. Areas of her brain that had been dormant now pulsed with energy. TarKeen pointed at a display. "Is this normal?"

"She used that area when she first arrived," Freltenloe said. "Levels are elevated right now, but variances are common during recovery."

"Keep me informed."

K ena restarted the song and turned the volume up. She let the words—the voice—encase her. A familiar song, but new. Her dad's tenor sang with the soundtrack. It held a double meaning; for, this was a love song from her eternal father to his children. Her mind leapt beyond the pain. He was there—waiting for her—in that realm where he could be so easily found. She flung herself into him. Surrendered all her effort to hide from reality, from her fear of emotional pain, from hopelessness. His strength permeated her mind, stilled her.

The music went on and on. Some, she recognized. Other songs were new. All perfectly choreographed into a message of love and peace, strength and mercy, hope and love. Always love. Without conscious decision, she stood and swayed with the melodies. A slow dance in the arms of eternal love. A heavenly scent filled the room. Her thoughts drew together into this moment. She was only now. She was only loved.

CHAPTER FORTY-FOUR

Leonfir pointed out a few basic controls in Ghent's room, ending with the wall mounted display. He touched a control on the low table, and a frozen image appeared. Ghent glanced between Leonfir and the display. It showed the end of the conversation he'd seen between Kena and Pernanyen. Interesting. He settled on the couch, as Leonfir took a chair.

"It's time that you learn what has happened here," Leonfir said. "I would really rather not show you the rest of this conversation. I worry that it's enough to trigger war, which is why I didn't want you to record it for the Collaborative at large."

Ghent said nothing. Energy surged down his arms; he just barely kept his shurgs from snapping out.

"Before I show you," Leonfir said, "just allow me to emphasize that Pernanyen made an individual decision. It was within her authority, but it should not be viewed as the consensus of our government." Leonfir touched another control, and the images played on.

Ghent listened in growing concern as Pernanyen tried to persuade Kena to link with her.

The recording reached the point where Kena said, "Several

days must pass before I could link with you, even if I wanted to, which I don't."

Leonfir paused the recording. "That statement has legal ramifications. Naturally, Kena didn't know that, but Pernanyen did. You'll better understand what's coming if I explain."

Ghent nodded, not trusting his voice.

"Once Kena said she didn't want to link, even if she later changed her mind, it would be considered a *constrained link* under PitKreelaundun law. This places strict obligations on the initiating party and confers additional rights to the one who is constrained. This law is intended to protect someone from an undesired link. For instance, if Kena later agreed to link because she thought it was the only way we would allow her to leave, we'd view that as no different from being forced into the link."

"Do you actually force people to link?" Ghent asked.

"Under very rare circumstances, yes." Leonfir shook his head. "Your expression tells me nothing good. I don't ask you to agree with our viewpoint. All I ask is that you let me explain it and attempt to understand. This will make the rest of their conversation easier to follow."

Had someone linked with Kena? Ghent longed to demand an answer, but Leonfir would take the circuitous route. If he was to maintain any chance of success, he would need to listen—and at least try to understand. "Your explanation, please."

"We use telepathy more than any other race we've encountered," Leonfir said. "Children link before they speak. Learning occurs through links. Even trivial information may be exchanged, simply because it is quick or clearer. Telepathy is as natural to us as speech. Various forms of it are taught and practiced. We realize, of course, that all races use telepathy in different ways. The only thing we have trouble grasping is the complete absence of it."

Ghent nodded. This much, at least, made sense to a Plynteth.

"Unfortunately," Leonfir said, "great ability can open the door to problems. Forced links were more common up until a few hundred years ago. Around that time, laws were enacted to prevent abuses. We've never outlawed it entirely, because there are times when it's necessary. Instead, we control it. That's the reason even a voluntary link may be considered a constrained link under our law."

"I comprehend what you're saying," Ghent said, trying to maintain a diplomatic tone, "but I think you should know our viewpoint. All races within the Collaborative consider a forced link to be both illegal and unethical. Appallingly so! Even what you term a voluntary constrained link is unethical. Only one of our races permits it, to a very limited degree."

"Which race?"

"Grfdn."

"Interesting," Leonfir said. "When Kena said she didn't want to link, Pernanyen knew that she would be under the obligations of a constrained link if she chose to proceed. The penalty for failing these obligations is death. This is what's in Pernanyen's mind through the rest of the conversation." Leonfir resumed the recording.

Pernanyen rejected Kena's right to choose, and the guards removed her EVA belt. Kena's lips and nostrils twitched. Even the way she jerked showed the tension of her muscles, but she was outnumbered. Ghent's shurgs snapped into the grooves of his fists. How had she felt? Livid? Terrified? Both? He longed to voice the scathing words that marched through his mind, but they would destroy what he came to do.

Freltenloe stated his objection to Pernanyen's decision, and she left him to carry out the deed. Ghent noted his reluctance, his measured gentleness, as he put the emfrel shield in place. He seemed no more willing than Kena. This didn't exonerate him, but the scales grew heavier on Pernanyen's side.

The recording ended, and Leonfir said, "After this, Freltenloe escorted Kena to the medical facility. He performed some scans and tests in order to gain basic information—or perhaps to buy time for TarKeen to dissuade Pernanyen. Kena didn't seem to object to the scans too much, though she was concerned about the acclimation and proposed link. The next recording is audio only. It's recorded from TarKeen's memory, so the voices—particularly his—will sound different. We give it to you partly because you asked about it, and partly because we find it puzzling."

The words played out in the room. When Kena asked, "Are you the same race?" Ghent startled and glanced at Leonfir.

Leonfir nodded but let the recording continue.

Ghent listened to the explanation and then to TarKeen's question. Realization formed. This was the very first time a PitKreelaundun discovered that the Collaborative knew nothing of tra-pentazine. Leonfir's gaze was fixed on him.

Then, TarKeen identified the planet destroyed long ago: PitKreel. Ghent sucked in a breath and did not exhale until the recording ended. Even then, it was hard to speak. "I can't—This is too shocking to grasp quickly. Please confirm what he just said."

"Two habitable planets once orbited our star," Leonfir said. "PitKreel, which was nearer the sun, contained several concentrations of trazine and enough pentazine to trigger a reaction. It broke up a few hundred years ago."

"How did the—the other planet survive?"

"Elaundun, which is the old name for our planet, contains a negligible amount of trazine and only traces of pentazine."

"But the debris—"

"The breakup of PitKreel wasn't nearly as dramatic as the one you've been studying," Leonfir said. "Its major remnants are still in orbit. It took some time to clear the scattered debris, but we knew how. Predict, prioritize, neutralize. We are proficient at that, you know."

Ghent still struggled with the ramifications. "How did the PitKree race survive?"

"Neighbors visit," Leonfir said, with a turn of his head. "Travel between the two planets has been common for centuries—long before we even imagined non-standard dimensions. There were a few PitKree settlements in the equatorial region of Elaundun.

Those who were in space or on Elaundun survived. Around
fourteen thousand of them. Shock waves stripped PitKreel's
atmosphere. Everyone on planet died."

"The aftermath..."

Leonfir nodded, his eyes lowered. "Suffice it to say, the
surviving PitKree were devastated. Over the next few years, we
changed our planet and race name and assigned the full equatorial
region to them. Not that they're required to stay only there; they
simply appreciate heat far more than the Laundun."

How strange that Kena had stumbled upon this information.
Or had she stumbled? Why had she asked in the first place?

Leonfir's posture relaxed as he moved beyond the tragedy. "We
combined the governments, which were already similar, and jointly
built the PitKree's earliest cities. Even though our cultures are
integrated, you can still see signs of this. My lightweight clothing,
for instance, compared to TarKeen's much heavier, darker clothes.
Laundun rarely have more than two children. PitKree often have
around ten, although the number has been dropping in the last
couple decades. They currently make up almost 30 percent of the
PitKreelaundun population."

"I'm stunned," Ghent said, "that the Prednians did not publish
any of this. We had no idea."

"They never came to our system," Leonfir said. "Our only
contact was at the border. I'm not surprised they didn't know. It's
very rare to hear the divided race names. We are PitKreelaundun.
I've only used the separate names to describe our distant history.
In anything you may publish, please make it clear that the race
names should not be used separately."

"As you wish." Ghent inclined his head. Was any of this related
to Kena's injury? "How similar are you at the sairital level?"
he asked.

"Very."

"Which of your races was Kena acclimated to?"

"Both," Leonfir said. "The emfrel is almost indistinguishable."

"To you, perhaps. Humans are very sensitive to alien emfrel. The Prednians didn't notice the difference, but Kena must have." Leonfir angled his head. "Most perplexing! We cannot understand this. She obviously noticed something—appearance, perhaps—but it couldn't have been the emfrel. She was wearing a shield."

He looked no more convinced of his own suggestion than Ghent was. "If you'd ever seen Human variations, you'd realize appearance couldn't have caused her to question your race. But we stray from the point. No matter how tragic the past, only the present is under our control. I'm still waiting to hear what happened to Kena."

"She was acclimated. Freltenloe and an assistant named Shannandi attended her. Even though it was highly stressful, it was effective. She was exhausted but not harmed. They monitored her constantly in every possible way. I've had other doctors confirm from the records that she was *not* injured during acclimation. Freltenloe took the blame, because we did not dare tell you the actual cause. This brings me to the reason I so desperately wanted to talk with you in person, without recording. We believe this incident has pushed us to the brink of war. I will do almost anything to avoid that outcome."

Ghent closed his eyes and summoned patience yet again. "You spend a lot of time talking about what you're going to talk about. Just tell me what happened."

"Pernanyen forced Kena to link with her."

Hardly a surprise, at this point. Still, Ghent had clung to a scrap of hope that Kena had been spared this. He drew in a long breath then let it out with equal deliberation. He could not allow emotion to drive their future. Not while they teetered toward war. Ramifications began to form in his mind.

Ghent finally broke the long silence. "I assume that we have not been *allowed* to speak with Pernanyen because she is dead. Is Kena accused of murder?"

Leonfir stared, the hair at his temples drawing backward. "I

have no idea why you said that or what you mean! Pernanyen is not
dead. I've said nothing of the sort. Why anyone claims that verbal
communication is better than telepathy is beyond
comprehension!"

Ghent squelched a bizarre urge to laugh. Not so hard,
considering his grief and confusion. "Pardon me, then. You said
Pernanyen forced Kena to link. Was this what you'd term a
voluntary constrained link? Was Kena controlling the link, or
Pernanyen?"

Leonfir seemed confused, but answered. "Pernanyen
controlled."

"Then, she holds the distinction," Ghent said, "of being the
first person to survive such a link with a Human. How did she
accomplish that?"

Leonfir lifted his hands, palms up. "I don't even understand
why you would ask such a question."

"That's difficult to believe for someone who passes trivial
information telepathically. Surely you have linked with Pernanyen
since the incident."

Leonfir shook his head. "No, that is strictly forbidden by law.
Kena has the right to link with Pernanyen and completely control
that link. No one else may link with her until after Kena has done
so. Kena even has the right to destroy Pernanyen's memory of
their links."

Ghent stared at him. They did take this seriously—he could no
longer doubt that. But that wouldn't reconcile a Human to forced
telepathy. He kept his voice calm. "The Human viewpoint is more
restrictive than the rest of the Collaborative's. Humans never link
with members of their own race. Very few of them even learn
telepathy, as Kena has. They have *no* tolerance for a forced link! It's
possible that Kena will refuse any further links. What then?"

Leonfir dropped his gaze and sighed his words out. "Pernanyen
will be executed."

He regretted that, did he? No such emotion echoed within
Ghent. It was what she deserved. Still, he needed to keep this

conversation positive. His and Kena's lives might depend on it. "Is she a close friend?"

Leonfir shifted his gaze back to Ghent. "I think you misinterpret my expression. I'll try again. We saw compassion in Kena and then empathy. We hoped to gain understanding from Humans. Maybe even friendship, someday. Instead, we have made them bitter enemies. If you knew how desperate we are for change, you would understand the depth of my disappointment. The border situation will become war if we cannot find a way to gain real understanding from the Collaborative."

Ghent's brow fur shifted. He hoped Leonfir would see and hear how earnest his words were. "I have every intention already of bringing your concerns to the Collaborative's leadership. You don't need to keep convincing me."

Leonfir closed his eyes and swallowed. "Ghent"—he locked eyes again—"do you remember a collection of tra-pentazine, which you intend to drag across our space into yours? This tells us you don't care at all about our concerns. You don't need to repeat your reasons. Whether your intentions are good or bad, you will say what is necessary to secure an uncontested journey home. As you and Kena have both pointed out, words go only so far. You and Kena will soon return to the *Ontrevay* and know that our words were true." He gripped the arms of his chair. "How long will it take until your words are proven true? Likely, not until it is too late. I need to know today, with certainty!"

Ghent shook his head. What did this man want? "What do you think you can possibly know within a day? Time and communication are required for trust."

"We have had decades. We have had words. No trust has formed. Think about it, Ghent. I am not the only one who needs certainty. You also need to know if our words are true."

Ghent held his silence. These very thoughts had passed through his mind on the *Ontrevay*.

"It isn't really your words I care about," Leonfir said. "TarKeen is convinced that Kena felt deep empathy when he told her of

PitKreel's destruction. Others say expressions vary so greatly between races that it's impossible to interpret her reaction." He leaned back. "I was curious whether I would see the same reaction in you. I saw shock." He flipped a hand. "Empathy, perhaps. But I don't truly know if you care about us or the races under our protection. And just as much, I want you to know what we feel when the Collaborative disrupts the ejection arms of the nebula."

Realization formed in Ghent's mind. Leonfir's many words pointed to only one thing. He wanted to link. It stilled Ghent's breath for a moment. "Are you planning to repeat Pernanyen's folly?"

Leonfir swung his head side to side. "Certainly not! Under no circumstances would I engage in a constrained link with you. If that is what you think...Do not answer me yet. You must know, we'd gain no advantage in keeping you or Kena here."

Ghent remained silent. No advantage? Would a race that would force a link have any qualms about extracting information from him whenever the need arose?

"You do perceive this, don't you?" Leonfir asked. "You and Kena *will* return to the *Ontrevay*."

If he didn't understand the possible advantage, Ghent wasn't going to point it out. "Could you just simply state what you are proposing?"

Leonfir rubbed his forehead and shifted position. "Really, I am trying to communicate as clearly as I can."

In the midst of the insanity, Ghent suppressed another urge to laugh. He was no less frustrated than the captain across from him. "And I am equally trying to understand. We will try again."

Leonfir took a deep breath. "What I suggest must be entirely voluntary. If you do not wish to do it, then it will not happen. I am *inviting* you to know me. I am *requesting* the privilege of knowing you. Through a telepathic link...that we *mutually* control. I hope that is correctly stated. We have distinct words for telepathic control, but I can find no counterparts in the Prednian language. I don't mean transferring control back and forth between us. I mean that we both control throughout. Either of us can withdraw at any time. Is this explanation clear for your culture?"

"I believe so." Ghent closed his eyes for an instant then said, "I begin to understand why Kena laughs at odd moments."

Leonfir's eyes widened. "Does she?" His brow contracted. "Yes, she did on the trip here. Why?"

"It's a Human form of stress relief. Are you under the impression that we can do this without acclimation?"

"No. If you are even tentatively willing, I will explain that part."

Ghent ignored the embedded question. "Explain."

Leonfir settled back into a faint sway as he talked. "The Prednian method is called gradual acclimation here. Sweeping, low doses are administered—just enough to cause recognition of the alien emfrel. Complete acclimation occurs through subsequent contact." He shifted. "Rapid acclimation uses higher levels, but they are focused to smaller areas and repeated until full acclimation occurs." He licked his lips. "You look appalled. Our doctors are convinced that you'll be able to tolerate it."

Ghent couldn't keep the heavy cadence from his words. "I am thinking about what Kena experienced and how much damage was done. Humans lose memory from traumatic acclimation."

Leonfir waited a few seconds before replying. "Emfrel does not engulf the mind during rapid acclimation, so there is no disorientation or associated memory loss. We have developed yet another form of gradual acclimation that we use for races that have difficulty with alien emfrel. It may work better for Humans than your current approach. We'll provide the information to the Collaborative, regardless of whether you choose to link with me."

Ghent tamed his anger. This was the first time a PitKreelaundun had offered anything to the Collaborative without direct benefit to themselves. "Thank you."

"I don't want to appear to mislead you," Leonfir said. "Rapid acclimation is unpleasant and exhausting. You will hate every moment of the procedure. It must be all or nothing. Once the doctor starts, he will not stop. If you cannot agree to that, then we will not do it."

"I understand," Ghent said.

"I will also undergo acclimation at the same time as you. We should both sleep before we link. Is there any difficulty we should know of in waking a Plynteth?"

"None at all."

"Good." Leonfir paused. "I don't know what else you may wish to hear. Do any questions trouble you?"

"I'm curious why the Prednians never linked with the PitKreelaundun. They're not strong telepaths, but they still would have wanted to. Do you know?"

Leonfir met his gaze with a wide-eyed stare. "It was planned. You don't know what happened?"

Ghent shook his head.

Leonfir appeared to collect his thoughts. "Gradual acclimation had been completed. There had been several meetings. A ruling family member, Kendimarron of Shennasee, and a doctor went to the Prednian ship for the link.

"Kendimarron was the son designated to inherit his father's position in government. He was about ten years older than Pernanyen is now. They had just completed docking, when the Prednians moved their gravity ship with no notice at all." His voice trembled. "They actually came through the ejection arm toward our ship."

Leonfir swallowed and firmed his lips. "Debris was disrupted. The PitKreelaundun captain notified Kendimarron. He was both shocked and furious. He demanded to be permitted immediate departure and that the Prednians vacate the area. Both demands were met. While his craft was returning to the PitKreelaundun ship, trazine exploded nearby. At that time, none of our craft had the energy shields we use now. Kendimarron's craft was hit. Everyone on board was killed."

Ghent rose and paced.

Leonfir kept silent for a full minute. "Did you really not know that this happened?"

"No one in the Collaborative knows this."

"Are you suggesting," Leonfir asked, "that the Prednians hid it from everyone else?"

"Unlikely. Prednian ships typically have other races on board. If you had spent much time with them, you'd know that nothing is hidden among Prednians. It's documented that a message came from the PitKreelaundun ship, but it was not translated. The PitKreelaundun left and demanded that the Prednians also leave. The Prednians were dumbfounded, but hurried to comply. There is no record of a PitKreelaundun craft being destroyed."

"How could they not know?" Leonfir demanded. "Do they not monitor the ejection arms?"

"Not like you do!" Ghent said, shaking his head. "I'm sure they get fresh scans whenever they come in to gather benzlium, but they wouldn't monitor it when departing."

"Another example," Leonfir said. "We have completely different understandings of what happened. Imagine if we each could truly know what the other believes and why. Imagine if we could verify this with such complete certainty that our leadership could not reject it. Could we not resolve differences and approach peace? Is that worth it to you, Ghent?"

Ghent looked across the room into those brown and gold eyes. He thought of the price they had already paid on this mission. He thought of the lives lost in skirmishes with the PitKreelaundun. And he thought of the risk Kena had taken to save an enemy's baby. "I need to talk with Remlishos before we start. He must know I do this willingly."

L eonfir had spoken no less than the truth. Ghent did hate every moment of acclimation. He dived for the oblivion of sleep with a relief he'd never before imagined. If only he could have stayed there and awakened naturally.

A voice...TarKeen's...demanded otherwise. "Ghent. Ghent, you need to wake up."

Ghent struggled onto an elbow. Leonfir sat across the room, and a doctor stood staring at a monitor.

"I know it is too soon," TarKeen said. "You don't need to speak. Just awaken."

Ghent identified where he was in his sleep cycle and made the appropriate sairital adjustment to end it. He swung his legs over the side of the bed and locked his arms to hold himself upright. Alert but exhausted, he nodded, unwilling to waste thought on words.

TarKeen spoke slowly. "We have received a message that Travannesal of Frayunomen is on his way. He'll arrive in an hour. If you and Leonfir are to complete your link before he arrives, you must start it now."

Ghent met Leonfir's gaze. He slumped in his chair, lips closed and face slack, He looked as tired as Ghent felt, but his eyes never wavered.

"I must have a clear answer," TarKeen said. "A gesture will be adequate. Do you desire to link with Leonfir?"

This was not how he wanted it to happen, but it would be far worse to have interference from some unknown member of government. Ghent nodded.

CHAPTER FORTY-FIVE

TarKeen took a chair in the communication chamber as he planned out what he would say. Hopefully, Remlishos would not overreact to change. The screen came to life, and the men exchanged formal greetings, which seemed to flow more easily from Remlishos than Ghent.

"I wish to update you on events," TarKeen said.

Remlishos leaned back in his chair. "I appreciate that."

"All is proceeding as expected with Ghent and Leonfir. They were both acclimated, slept for a while, and are now linked. They are monitored, since this is the first link between a PitKreelaundun and Plynteth. There is no sign of any problem."

"Good to hear."

"Freltenloe reports encouraging change in regard to Kena. As I told you before, she desired no visual or audio monitoring. He continues to monitor brain activity and key physical indicators." TarKeen let his smile appear. "She fell asleep a few hours ago. Our doctors interpret her brain activity as indicating very deep sleep."

"More good news!"

All courtesy and goodwill so far. Now to see if he could keep that going. "Yes. We are very pleased." TarKeen paused. "There is also an unexpected development. It is unrelated to Kena and Ghent, but I want you to be aware of it. Travannesal of Frayunomen is approaching. His craft will come out of slip in about twenty minutes. Since he comes from our domain, he will need to pass the *Ontrevay* to reach us. There is no need for concern. I just didn't want you to be surprised."

Remlishos raised his brows and tapped a finger against the table.

"Feel free, sir, to voice your concerns," TarKeen said. How he hated to invite that!

"I assume that if Travannesal disagrees with Leonfir's commitments, they become meaningless."

"No." TarKeen emphasized the word. "He has ultimate authority, but he's also bound by law. Pernanyen and I made commitments to permit Kena's departure—they must be honored. The only question has been when and how to return her. Leonfir's commitment to Ghent must likewise be honored. Further, there is no reason for Travannesal to disagree."

"Can you tell me," Remlishos asked, "why Leonfir said, yesterday, that it would take fifteen days for a ruling family member to arrive?"

TarKeen nodded. "He was referring to the charge against Pernanyen. She cannot be judged by a member of her own family. However, the primary members of government want one of their number here, because they are concerned over relations with the Collaborative. Pernanyen cannot fill that role now. Travannesal was the only one near enough to reach us quickly."

Remlishos leaned against the armrest of his chair. "The lengthy silences between our two ships have increased tension. How long do you think it will be before Travannesal contacts us?"

"I can speak for myself," TarKeen said, "but not for him. I will meet him at the hatch of his craft and request an immediate link. I'm sure he'll grant it and will take time to learn what has occurred. I'll tell him you desire communication."

"What sort of craft does he come in, and how many craft escort him?"

"His craft is similar to the one Kena and Quon found in the nebula, but about twice the size. He normally travels with two escort craft, but has instructed them to remain a considerable distance behind him."

Remlishos bowed. "Thank you for the information, TarKeen. I look forward to future conversations."

As TarKeen strode from the chamber, he assessed the conversation. That wasn't so bad.

Several minutes later, TarKeen watched the command room's view screen. Consoles and ship operations staff surrounded him, more than half of them PitKree. An artificial dimensional rift formed and released a craft. Successful exit.

A technician spoke. "Sir, they're broadcasting a message."

"Play it aloud," TarKeen said.

"I am Travannesal of Frayunomen of the PitKreelaundun government, addressing the crew of the *Ontrevay*, of the Interstellar Collaborative. We greet you and wish to assure you that we pursue a peaceful conclusion to this encounter between our races. If any damage or harm has occurred, I will ensure that justice is accomplished immediately. I will contact you again when I have reached the *Epri7* and obtained full knowledge of the situation."

TarKeen's brow gathered, and his eyes narrowed. Justice? Immediately? What did he intend?"

Kena startled awake. Had someone called her name? The only sound was music playing softly from the device she still clutched in her hand. She propped herself up on one arm and glanced around the room—and actually saw it this time. Textured walls and a curtain. Her navigation suit hung neatly over the back of a chair by a small table. The rich presence of her beloved enveloped her still. She enquired without words. *Was it you who called?*

Yes, my child. Eat and dress.

Kena rose and touched the communication control.

A familiar voice responded. "What do you desire?"

"Food."

Kena snatched up her clothing and headed behind the curtain that screened a bathroom. When she came out, Shannandi was setting a tray on the table.

Kena strode to the chair, sat, and took up a strange utensil. Two prongs on one end, spoon on the other. It would do.

Shannandi stared much like she beheld the impossible.

Kena scooped up something thick and soft. "TarKeen?" she said, and consumed her first mouthful.

"He is—uh—he may not be able to come at once."

"Tell him I asked for him."

TarKeen inclined his head to Travannesal and left to fulfill his order. He walked slower than usual, for Pernanyen's suite was not far. He could use the time to prepare himself. Few tasks could be less pleasant.

She would be distraught by now. Days without any telepathic contact. Fully aware that her father was on board and refusing to see her, not even responding to her messages. Her information access had been blocked. Her hope of Kena's recovery must be all but extinguished. Would she guess what was about to happen?

Perhaps not. This was so rarely done. Not once in his lifetime.

She'd likely ask questions. He needed to prepare a response. It must keep her calm and neither reveal how dire her situation was, nor give her false hope. A little breath huffed out his nose. Impossible.

Would she wonder at the deserted route they took? Travannesal had ordered one hallway restricted so she would meet no one on the way to the chamber. He didn't want her losing control in the hallway.

Her two guards looked to him as he approached.

TarKeen pointed to the far side of the doorway. "Take position there. I will escort Pernanyen of Frayunomen to the trial chamber. You will follow us, ten paces distant. You will not speak to her." He could have entered without permission, but he touched the call button and waited for her to grant him entrance.

She stood in the midst of her elegant reception room. The trimmings of authority were everywhere, even draped across her chest. Pernanyen fingered the chain of topaz and amber beads that hung from shoulder to hip.

Her hopeful—or was it desperate? —gaze fell at the sight of him. No doubt, she longed for her father. She worried the beads back and forth between restless fingers. "What news do you bring me, TarKeen?"

"Travannesal of Frayunomen has summoned you, ma'am. I will escort you to him."

Her eyes held his for several seconds. She calmed her expression and held her posture erect as she moved toward him. Self-contained. Brave, even. Memories emerged of past days when the budding traits of a good leader had shown through her actions and words. It made this task all the harder.

"Please tell me Kena's current condition," she said.

He turned for the door to keep her moving. "Would it not be better to let Travannesal answer your questions?"

She was silent for a moment as they started down the hallway. "Such a gentle tone of voice you use, TarKeen."

She knew something was wrong. "You've been without a link so long. I prefer to keep you calm."

She abandoned her attempts to converse. They reached the side entrance of the chamber, and he opened the door. A crowd filled the room. Pernanyen's breath fled her lungs, and she staggered.

TarKeen gripped her arm to steady her. It went limp, and he

cupped the elbow in his hand to give the impression of escorting her rather than dragging her forward. She took a deep breath and drew her features into a mask-like expression.

A gap led from the door to Travannesal, standing at the front, center of the chamber. He wore formal attire: the wide, gold band of his office spread across his chest from shoulder to shoulder, set off by his rich, night-brown tunic.

TarKeen took Pernanyen through the crowd.

She stopped in the open space before her father, and TarKeen stepped aside. Most of the furniture had been removed from the chamber, but Ghent and Leonfir occupied two chairs off to one side, with a couple doctors standing behind them. Pernanyen's eyes widened as she looked at Ghent.

Travannesal stated her family title. "Daughter of Frayunomen."

She dipped her upper body in respect then straightened.

His voice rang loud in the silence, though he did not raise it. "The captains Ghent and Leonfir have just completed an extensive link and are not ready for interaction. They choose to listen. You will not address them."

She nodded.

Travannesal's voice filled the room as he addressed Pernanyen again. "The ruling council has monitored this situation, to the extent possible from such a distance. We have determined that it is too sensitive to proceed without our presence. None but I could reach this location in time. I have accepted the commission to investigate, judge, and act." He let seconds pass.

Pernanyen's face sagged. TarKeen's chest tightened.

"I cannot judge my own daughter," Travannesal said. "I shall dissolve our relationship."

She inhaled a ragged breath. "P-permanently?"

"I taught you to control your emotions. Do so now."

She closed her eyes, pulled the mask back in place, and stared at his chest.

"If I find you guilty of an illegal constrained link with Kena Talgarth of Earth, the sentence will be execution. Yes, death is permanent. If you are not guilty, the question of reinstating our relationship will be considered by the ruling council. Place no dependence on that possibility. Act in this moment." He pointed at the floor. "Kneel."

She stepped forward and dropped to her knees at his feet.

He unfastened the clasp at her shoulder as he spoke and removed the amber and topaz chain, symbol of the ruling family of Frayunomen. "Pernanyen, you are not my daughter. You have no family. You are forbidden to call yourself by the name of Frayunomen. In a moment, I shall link with you to complete the separation. You will not call to mind the link with Kena Talgarth. You will remain passive. Prepare yourself."

She closed her eyes. Seconds slipped by. "I am ready."

TarKeen wished to look elsewhere, but could not.

Travannesal's hands gripped her head.

For an instant, relief spread over her face as the link ended her telepathic isolation.

Travannesal's eyes nearly closed. He would be seeking the bond he had formed during her infancy. The bond he must sever. His lips tightened, then he released her head.

Devastation. No other word could describe her expression. Her hips gave way. She barely kept her torso upright, bracing herself with one arm. Agony contorted her face, but she uttered no sound.

Travannesal stated somber words. "The trial will now proceed. Pernanyen is charged with initiating a forced, constrained link with Kena Talgarth of Earth. The link has not yet been completed. We will begin by establishing the—"

A tone sounded. Travannesal stopped, and TarKeen stiffened. Only certain messages were allowed during the proceedings. TarKeen moved to read the message then showed it to Travannesal.

"Go to her," Travannesal said. "Be prepared to link with me when you return."

TarKeen inclined his head and left.

T arKeen halted inside the door. An energy field couldn't have stopped him any quicker.

Kena finished her drink and set the glass down. She met his eyes—as aware of him as in their first meeting. How long ago, that seemed. "Thank you for coming to me," she said. "I gather, it may not have been convenient."

His eyes widened and lips parted, even before they formed words. "I am...delighted to see you so much improved." He took the chair across from her as she clipped the music player to her belt and eased the volume down to a whisper. "Did music accomplish this?"

He sounded so puzzled. "Not really. It just...reminded me."

"I don't understand."

"The non-Human languages lack words for certain concepts." She shrugged one shoulder. "It doesn't matter right now. I need to know what's happening."

"You will be returned to the *Ontrevay*."

She blinked. "Yes, but that isn't what I asked. Recent past and now. That's what I want to know."

TarKeen seemed to emerge from his intent stare and look inward. "I will summarize for you. There were several conversations between our two ships, but they were...no more satisfactory than other interactions with the Collaborative. Pernanyen's authority was suspended because you were injured during the link and your recovery seemed unlikely. Ghent has come to the *Epri7* in order to take you to the *Ontrevay* and also to meet in person with Leonfir. They chose to link, which lasted a considerable time."

Her forehead tightened. "Was Ghent put through the same thing I was?"

He shook his head. "It was entirely voluntary. The acclimation was not as difficult for him. He slept for a while before they linked. It was not constrained at all." He waited a moment but continued when she did not respond. "The ruling families wanted a representative present because of our prolonged encounter. Unfortunately, Travannesal of Frayunomen was the only one close enough. He arrived about an hour ago."

"Why is that unfortunate?"

"He is Pernanyen's father."

Kena emphasized her words. "So, why is that unfortunate?"

"Because Pernanyen must be judged. Her trial has started."

"Trial for what?"

TarKeen stared at her. "For performing a constrained link that could not be reciprocated."

Kena stared back, remembering Pernanyen's obscure words before the horrors began. There was way too much that she didn't understand. She stood. "Take me there, now, please."

He hurried to his feet. "Ma'am, you have been unwell and have not slept nearly long enough. You should rest."

Exhaustion did lurk beneath the surface. But her beloved wouldn't have awakened her without reason. "True, but I am capable. I will attend this trial."

He hesitated, frowning, but said, "I'll escort you. Is there a manner in which Humans provide honorable escort?"

Did that matter so much? Still, she'd been a limp rag for days and had no idea how far she was about to go. "Walk beside me." She used a simple demonstration to get him moving. Holding her palm against her navel, she said, "Hold your arm nearest me like so, and I'll rest my hand on it." The urge to hurry grew strong within her.

He matched her pace. After a couple minutes, he said, "May I ask you a question?"

"Of course."

"How did you recognize that Freltenloe and I are different races? Had you already noticed a difference between FarNon and the others before you had an emfrel shield?"

"No, I can't detect emfrel until I'm acclimated."

"That didn't seem possible to me either," he murmured, "and yet...you noticed something."

Kena sighed. "There are no Prednian words to describe this. Sometimes Humans know things that there is no physical means for them to know. It's infrequent—or perhaps just so subtle that even we aren't aware how often it happens. Like when I found Pearl. I felt a distressed child's presence before I entered that craft. It's the only reason I went in. But now when I think about it, I realize it should have been impossible."

He grew silent for a while, his gaze inward until he needed to speak again. "We're nearly at the trial chamber. I will introduce you to Travannesal of Frayunomen. Leonfir and Ghent are there in order to listen. They have only recently completed acclimation and linking, so they're not participating. Pernanyen is there, of course, and also Freltenloe. There are about fifty others who may participate if they choose. You're not required to say anything."

"Understood. May I speak if I wish?"

"You may. It is my right to protect you. If you need something, or if anything at all disturbs you, tell me."

His right? Interesting choice of words. They crossed an antechamber, and someone hurried to open the door for them. It looked to be carved from wood and swung on hinges. How strange to see such a thing in a ship.

A woman's voice carried from the opposite side of the next chamber. Heads were turned in her direction. "How is it that you know enough about Human law to be sure they will approve your demand for judgement and sentence?"

A murmur of agreement passed around the room as TarKeen escorted Kena through the crowd. A gasp silenced the voices, and every eye turned to them.

Kena froze and gripped TarKeen's arm. Universal surprise swept over her from the crowd, but what stunned her was the sharp contrast between consternation and gladness.

TarKeen demanded something in his own language. She felt the emfrel settle. He'd misunderstood, but no matter. They could use a little practice in controlling all that emfrel. Voices rose again. Comments revolved around why she'd been brought here when she was injured.

"Shall I take you out?" he whispered.

A simple *no* would not work. They needed to hear her capacity for speech. She answered loud enough to be heard by all. "I am quite capable of participating."

CHAPTER FORTY-SIX

Kena walked at TarKeen's side as he escorted her toward an open space at the front of the opulent chamber. Half-columns of marbled stone jutted from the walls and appeared to support carved arches. Some of them framed ornate doors, others a fabric like watered silk.

Pernanyen slumped on her knees, isolated in the midst of the open area. At the sight of her, fire leapt within Kena, tightening her chest and heating her lips. She turned her eyes away, compelling her lungs to release a cleansing breath.

A brown-haired Laundun man faced her. A golden band, the width of her palm, hung heavy from his shoulders. Its narrow plates interlaced in a fishbone pattern and reflected altering shades as they shifted with his movement.

Two people sat at the edge of the central space: Ghent and one other. Leonfir?

"One moment, please." Kena squatted beside Ghent's chair and looked up into his face. His brow fur puckered. Was he as worried about her as she was about him? She extended her presence and waited to see if he would link.

More comments filtered through her concentration, from

DIVERSE SIMILARITY

doctors this time. They fretted over whether she was trying to link with him. She ignored them.

Ghent joined with her. He made no attempt to form words. She felt his deep exhaustion, but a calmness lay behind it that hinted at—was it completion, or success, perhaps? Concerns also lurked. To ease his worry, she let her peace drift toward him on the lazy stream they had once imagined together.

"True, but no link has formed," Freltenloe said to someone. "She is not telepathically active."

Ghent smiled at the same time that Kena uttered a small laugh. It provided an easy release from their link. She stood and moved into the open space.

TarKeen stepped back from Travannesal. Apparently, they had also linked. Just as well. TarKeen stated the formal introductions while Kena looked into amber eyes much like Pernanyen's. How surreal. From rescue of a stranded child, to torturous invasion, to audience with a primary member of government.

Guide me, Father.

His presence stirred, bringing her awareness to him.

Travannesal said, "I am honored to meet a representative of the Human race. And relieved, as well, to see you so much improved from the latest report I received."

"It's a pleasure to meet you, sir," Kena said.

"May I ask what caused you to laugh a moment ago?"

Odd, but no matter. "Statements pertaining to Human telepathy are often ironic; for, it's poorly understood. It seems much has happened that I'm unaware of. Also, these proceedings are unfamiliar to me. I wish to link with Pernanyen so I may quickly learn of these things."

It took Travannesal a few seconds to answer. "Are you asking to perform your side of the constrained link?"

"I don't even know the meaning of that term. Please give me a moment to learn. It won't take long. I'm only asking for simple, public facts. I want no opinions or observations—a surface link only."

Travannesal nodded, but said, "You have not slept very long. Are you certain you're able to tolerate the link?"

Tolerate? Did he mean what she heard? Probably not. The anger deep within was her concern, not his. "Yes," she said.

He angled his head, frowning. "Freltenloe, your opinion?"

"She is not adequately rested."

As though he could know. Kena met Freltenloe's eyes. "I am not a sairital being. You have no idea where my rest or my strength emanate from."

He averted his eyes from the challenge in her gaze.

She turned back to Travannesal and tilted her head in silent question.

"We'll wait for you to link with her." He glanced to someone else. "Bring a chair."

Kena looked down at Pernanyen. Her hands gripped her knees as though she needed to prop up her bowed shoulders. She didn't even raise her eyes from the floor. A mixture of anger and pity swirled through Kena. She maintained her stillness, necessary if she was to get the information she needed.

"Pernanyen of Frayunomen," Kena said.

Pain contorted her features.

Travannesal spoke. "It is no longer permitted that she be addressed by the name of Frayunomen. I have disowned her."

Kena stared at him. A quiver ran through her. "I certainly hope you didn't do that on my account."

Again he paused. "I did it because she must be judged before you and Ghent leave. I'm the only one with that authority, but I cannot judge my own heir."

So much, she didn't understand—and must understand. Immediately! "Pernanyen, are you willing to link with me and permit me to control the link?"

"Yes! Completely. The entire link." Her voice squeaked. Desperately willing, it seemed.

Someone placed a chair next to Pernanyen.

Kena pointed to it and said, "Sit there."

Gasps sounded around the room. Now what?

"The chair is for you," Travannesal said.

"Thank you, but I don't need it. She does."

"It's appropriate in our culture that she kneel. It need not disturb you."

Kena turned to him, her words firm. "But it does. It has meaning in my culture, as well. I cannot link with her kneeling at my feet."

A barrage of comments surrounded her from the crowd, some in Prednian, some not. Why was there so much contention?

Someone declared, "If the accused presumes to take a seat, she disresp—"

Travannesal silenced the crowd with a single word. Pernanyen's eyes pled with him. "TarKeen, put Pernanyen in the chair."

He picked her up by the shoulders and placed her there.

No sooner had he done so, than another interruption occurred, this time from two men. Unsought awareness filled Kena. Her eyes darted back and forth between them. PitKree, both, with murderous intent. They side-stepped, changing position, for Pernanyen was no longer in their line of sight. Their movements were subtle—no one else paid attention. Yet, the intensity within her was almost painful. *Father, why do you show me this? What do you want me to do?*

Her face must have revealed something. TarKeen came to her side. "Who is disturbing you?"

She pointed. "That one—and that one."

She sensed realization and tension within TarKeen. He spoke in his own language, and guards moved into the crowd.

One of the men objected, but Travannesal cut him off. "TarKeen has authority, both as commander of the *Epri7* and as protector of Kena Talgarth. You know our law. Are you asking *me* to undermine it?"

The man glared but submitted to the grip on his arm.

"It is noted," Travannesal said, "that these two have not spoken throughout the proceedings. Anyone else who has no intent to speak, or who is unable to control their emfrel, leave now. You can watch from elsewhere."

The two men were removed, and some others left. The room grew very still. Kena found her gaze on another PitKree. All she felt was restrained intensity. Why?

TarKeen followed her gaze. "Does he trouble you?"

The man looked to Travannesal, his voice perfectly calm. "Sir, I am certain that I am projecting nothing at all."

"That is a true statement," Kena said and turned back to Pernanyen.

Kena drew on her awareness of her father, ready to differentiate mind and spirit. She paused, for he was showing her his view of Pernanyen—love extended to an injured child. The words from both song and scripture echoed in her mind. *I delight in mercy.* The anger Kena harbored was rendered ugly in comparison to his love and everlasting compassion.

Understanding formed. He wanted her to forgive Pernanyen. *Oh, Father, must you ask that of me now? It is too much for me!*

You need only permit forgiveness. I will do the rest for you.

I permit it. She surrendered the anger and turned her mind away, knowing how quickly her own pain would snatch it up again. Kena took a slow breath, reestablishing her focus on Pernanyen, while her father withdrew from the portion of her being where spirit and mind intermingled.

Kena moved nearer, spreading her presence around Pernanyen, and gentled her voice. "Reach for me."

"But...you said you wanted to control."

Kena kept her voice soft. "I will. Reach for me."

"I—I don't understand."

"You will understand once we are linked."

"But if I—"

Kena threw her hands up and took hasty steps away. It was so hard to maintain patience! She licked her tight lips and turned back to Pernanyen, forcing herself to remember love toward an injured child. "Pernanyen," Kena said, "it is not possible for me to establish a link with you unless *you* reach for *me*. I know this seems strange to you, but it will work if you do it."

Travannesal said, "It seems that you request a contradiction."

"*Seems*. Accurately stated, for it only *seems* contradictory. I can stand here and wrap words around this for hours, but none of you will grasp it. She will understand as soon as she initiates the link."

The man whose intensity Kena had noticed before spoke. "It is currently not legal for Pernanyen to initiate any link, particularly with you. Only you have that prerogative."

Stubborn people! "Who are you?" Kena asked.

"I am VanDar."

"Do you believe you have the right to dictate how a Human performs telepathy?"

"No, ma'am." VanDar inclined his head. "I speak because I'm concerned for you. You've already been unjustly injured, and I do not want it to happen again. You are under no obligation to link with her. Please don't open yourself to further harm by letting Pernanyen control any portion of a link."

"You may have the purest of intentions, but you know nothing of Humans." Kena turned away from him.

"Pernanyen is PitKreelaundun and is bound by our law," VanDar said. "It's illegal for her to initiate the link."

Now it was TarKeen's intensity she felt, even though his face showed nothing as he stared past her at VanDar. What was going on between these people?

A woman spoke, the same voice Kena had heard when the door first opened. "It seems, we place unnecessary impediments. We object to Pernanyen's name. We object to her sitting in a chair. Then, a couple of people interfere. Now, there's an objection to a telepathic technique. Kena isn't even asking for the constrained link. Only for basic information. Certainly, she has that right. Not only is she the one who was injured, but she is the only one who knows Human law. Since we desire justice, we should enable her, not raise objections."

Kena smiled at the woman. "Your name, please?"

"I am ShenLee."

"Thank you."

Travannesal said, "I decide in favor of ShenLee's argument. Pernanyen, are you willing to link with Kena, follow every direction she gives you, and let her control the link?"

Her voice squeaked. "I am willing."

Kena stilled her mind again. She surrounded Pernanyen with comfort. "You'll be surprised. Don't let it disturb you. Reach for me, now."

Pernanyen finally did so. Then, she thrust back in the chair, quivering.

"Easy. All is well." Kena said the words both aloud and within Pernanyen's mind—slowly—letting seconds slip by between each sentence. "Let yourself settle. I will wait for you to grow accustomed. Be still."

It took her a couple minutes. Pernanyen's eyelids fluttered, and her shoulders twitched. When she calmed, Kena requested information that pertained to herself.

Indeed, Pernanyen was skillful. She set emotion aside and called specific memories to the surface. The recorded meetings with Ghent and others moved from Pernanyen's mind into Kena's. She heard reports of her own condition and of Ghent's arrival. She listened to Travannesal, a beloved father, disown his daughter. This memory was too raw. Kena had to resist the heartbreak. Then, the law on constrained links flowed into her mind. This was not good. Last, she asked who VanDar was. Pernanyen recalled a circular chart of the ruling families and showed his position. Interesting. And ominous.

Draw away from me and rest, Kena said through the link. She, too, withdrew but stood quite still.

The room was silent, waiting. They could wait a little longer. Kena needed time to think.

There were really two problems: an incomplete constrained link and a collection of tra-pentazine. Had Ghent been able to resolve the latter?

The PitKreelaundun would not know she could link with Ghent without approaching him. She extended herself to Ghent and waited to see if he would join another link. When he did, she again felt the exhaustion within him. Still he formed no words.

Samples? she prompted, keeping the thought in his perception, but entirely within her own mind.

Must remove from... That was more concept than words, really. An image appeared, much like a display. It included all the Collaborative and PitKreelaundun areas.

That would place them too far away for study.

Another mixture of concepts and images came from him. *Need provisions—access route.*

Ah. Leonfir did not have authority to commit to something with such far-reaching implications. Kena would have withdrawn, but felt there was more Ghent wanted to tell her. She waited, not knowing what to ask.

Ghent slowly formed words. *Leonfir convinced.*

Of what?

A long pause. *What Pernanyen sought.*

The exhaustion was too much for him. She focused on what he needed. *Peace. Rest by still waters.* Again, she kept the words within herself, where he could glimpse the imagery. She waited a few seconds then withdrew.

Why had he put so much effort into telling her this?

CHAPTER FORTY-SEVEN

Kena drew a deep breath and turned to Travannesal. She was about to tell him to proceed, when the doctor behind Ghent's chair said, "Sir, Ghent just attempted to project telepathic energy. This is the second time he's tried."

"Has he recovered enough to link?"

"No, but I'm concerned that his attempts will tire him further. Either we should determine if he has some need to communicate, or we should take him to privacy, where he may sleep."

Kena held her laugh in and looked to Ghent. "Do you want to leave?"

He shook his head, as she'd expected.

"He's fine," she assured the doctor. "How do you know when Ghent is telepathically active?"

"I placed an internal sensor—the same type the Prednians use."

She asked Freltenloe, "Do I have one as well?"

"Yes, ma'am. Please don't be alarmed. They're not disruptive. They're very simple to remove."

Kena tilted her head. "I'm not alarmed. I'm amused. Don't place any reliance on what it tells you. Travannesal, you may proceed."

Instead of continuing the trial, he asked, "Have you linked with Ghent since you came into this chamber?"

She nodded. "Yes. Twice, in fact. But not really." She stepped nearer to him. "This is where the words break down. It would be more accurate to say that I made myself available to Ghent, and he chose to telepathically communicate to my awareness. But as Freltenloe says, *I* was not telepathically active."

He frowned, as if mulling over that. "Pernanyen, did Kena link with you a few moments ago?"

Gaping at Kena, she nodded.

"Freltenloe, what did Kena's sensor indicate during the link with Pernanyen?"

Freltenloe looked almost as stunned as Pernanyen. "That she was telepathically active."

Kena met Travannesal's eyes. How would he phrase his next question?

As he watched her, a voice rose above the murmurs in the crowd. "Why do we delay while she mocks? Is this not a trial of Pernanyen? Put the—"

"Silence!" Travannesal quieted his voice and said, "Kena, will you explain why your telepathic energy could be detected during your link with Pernanyen, even though it wasn't with Ghent."

"Because I was telepathically active with her. It's the only way Pernanyen can communicate with me. Ghent knows me, but Pernanyen does not."

His eyes widened.

Kena slowed, emphasizing her words. "There is a huge difference between extracting facts and knowing a person. Some knowledge cannot be taken. It must be *received*."

Still, he stared. "I gather that you employ two forms of telepathy. You used a different form with Ghent than with Pernanyen. Is that correct?"

She shook her head. "I would never phrase it so. You're focusing on telepathy, which is the same mistake all the races of the Collaborative make. It will not give you the understanding you need."

"What, then?"

"Telepathy is a concept of sairital beings," Kena said. "Humans are not sairital beings, so we cannot be telepathic in the same sense that you are."

"What are you, then?"

"I will use two words from my language: *spirit* and *mind*. I am a spirit. I have a mind. I live in a body. For comparison, I would say that you are a sairit, and you live in a body."

"So, you differentiate two aspects of what we call sairit?" he asked.

"No. That is a common misconception." How intent, he was, as one who truly sought understanding. She shifted position and tried again. "A Human mind does have some similarities to portions of a sairit. Sairital beings perceive the similarities and conclude that we are essentially the same as them. Our mind contains memory, emotion, reason, and part of our will. It does not contain our life energy, as a sairit does. That is part of the spirit and is available to the mind as it is needed. I have learned how to convert some of that into telepathic energy."

She glanced toward Freltenloe. "That is why readings of Human emfrel and telepathic energy are so low. You only measure what is currently in use."

Freltenloe nodded, but his frown held many questions.

Travannesal asked, "What, besides life energy, is included in spirit?"

Kena spread her hands. "It is the essence of who I am."

He only looked more confused.

"What non-Human words could I use for this? There are none. It's not important right now, anyway."

"Did Pernanyen sense your spirit?"

"Oh, no! She got close, but didn't contact it. She would have died if she had."

Travannesal paused, so intent on her. "You said that Ghent knows you, but Pernanyen does not. I do not yet understand this."

He wasn't going to give up. She had to come up with something. And if that something could prevent them from forcing a link on a Human ever again, so much the better.

"Right, then. I will try a different approach." She paced slowly while she thought. "Do your races ever use analogies to describe abstract concepts?"

"We are all one race, Kena, but yes, we use analogies."

She sensed ire in the crowd, much like a molten thing bulging up from crevices. She looked around the room as she walked. The heat came from the PitKree, some more than others. The Laundun showed no awareness—not even Travannesal. She couldn't deal with that now. It had subsided, anyway.

She drew on analogies she'd heard related to mind and spirit; like joints, or like marrow enmeshed in bones. No, too dependent on Human anatomy. She needed something more visible. Her lowered gaze suddenly focused on her hands—she'd interlaced her fingers as she walked. That would do.

"Suppose," she said, lifting her hands as she spoke, "that my left hand represents my mind; and my right hand, my spirit." She interlaced them, laying the fingers of each hand along the back of the other. "Then, my mind and spirit fit together like this, tightly enmeshed."

She slid her fingers in and out. "They're not really distinct like physical objects. We rarely think of which we are using, because we always use both. When we train for telepathy, however, we must learn to differentiate."

"When I link, I draw back." She separated her hands until her fingers lay only between each other. "In a surface link"—she tucked her fingers into her palms and brought the back of her left hand forward—"only the mind is available. Perfectly useful for exchanging information. That is mostly what Pernanyen saw.

"The very first time I linked with Ghent, he didn't want facts, he wanted to know me. And he, of course, was willing to let me control." She laid her fingers beside one another again and wiggled those of her left hand. "I was able to show him this: the part of my mind most deeply impacted by my spirit. It's not the same as seeing my actual spirit, more like a reflection of spirit.

"When Pernanyen delved for deep understanding, it was like she forced her way down these paths." Kena traced a fingertip down the back of her left index finger. She was silent for a moment, no longer able to look around at them as she walked back and forth. "As Pernanyen did so, I drew farther and farther back, trying to protect her. In the end, I was in a state somewhat like this." Kena spread her fingers, tensed and widely spaced, only the center fingertips barely interlaced.

"A terribly unnatural state. Even humans don't have a word for it." Kena swallowed. "Fortunately, she stopped forcing her way in, because I was spent. An instant more, and she'd have breached the barrier and touched my spirit. A sairit is incompatible with spirit— no chance of survival."

Travannesal spoke slowly, as though puzzling through a train of thought. "This is why you believed she was about to die."

Kena nodded, then stressed her words. "And this, Travannesal of Frayunomen, is why no sairital being must ever attempt to control a link with a Human." She turned to Pernanyen. "That is also why I had no choice except to fight you throughout that entire, excruciating link." Kena stopped to let them ponder. She'd given them more than enough to puzzle over.

After a moment, VanDar said, "It appears that we now have sufficient understanding of Human law pertaining to telepathy. We may proceed with the trial of Pernanyen."

Kena's brows nearly merged with her hair. "That was a non-sequitur, if ever there was one. I am quite certain I did not state any laws."

He seemed to shift under the force of her words. "You said, 'no sairital being must ever attempt to control a link with a Human.' I don't know your process for formalizing a law, but it certainly sounds like an inherent law."

"No," Kena said. "That was an explanation with a warning, so all of you would recognize the danger and avoid it. Saying it's a law makes as much sense as saying that it's illegal to inhale water. It's stupid, it's potentially fatal, but it's not illegal."

Travannesal stilled a smile that tugged at the corners of his mouth. "I will convey this information to the other ruling families, so we may decide on appropriate measures to prevent future injuries. In the meantime, I do need to proceed with this trial. One difficulty has been that we do not know what laws Humans may have pertaining to telepathy."

"None, of course." Kena shrugged a shoulder. "Humans don't link with other Humans, so there is no reason to create laws. Very few Humans can link with other races."

"For those of you who can, what laws govern?"

"My spirit governs what I do when someone else's mind is open to me. It is not a matter of law. It is a matter of knowing."

His speech quickened, and he took a step nearer. "According to your *knowing,* then: Do Humans consider a constrained link permissible if both parties are able to perform their sides?"

He was getting frustrated, by the sound of it. Too bad. She wasn't about to state a position that Humans didn't have. "I would consider it impossible, rather than permissible. Humans do not engage in forced links, and sairital beings don't survive forced links with Humans. How can I state a law, or even an opinion, for something that never before occurred?"

The vehemence of her reply hadn't hurt. He smoothed his expression and gentled his voice. "Can *you* judge, by *your* knowing, whether Pernanyen's forced link was—" He broke off as she shook her head.

"I—my spirit—can judge only my actions. Never another's."

Travannesal seemed drawn to her, stepping nearer yet.

Kena tried to grasp his intent as she had sensed the others', but a wave of hatred overwhelmed her. She swept her eyes around, seeking the source. Once again, she found herself staring at

VanDar. He looked puzzled by her sudden attention. What was this she was feeling? She backed up a step, and it subsided.

Travannesal also stepped back, his brow furrowed.

TarKeen studied her. "Kena, do you need—"

She shook her head. "Travannesal, there is nothing more I can explain."

He resumed the proceedings, and Kena listened. There were no lawyers here. Anyone in attendance could raise accusations or argue them. Kena followed them easily, so long as they were in Prednian. Unfortunately, not everyone could speak that language. Interpretations became disruptive and led to a request that Kena be removed.

She said, "I don't like translation delays any more than you do. Pernanyen, will you let me hear your understanding of the PitKreelaundun words?"

She nodded, looking uncertainly at Travannesal.

Someone objected. "No, she'll learn our language."

"Why," Kena asked, "would that be a problem to a race that wants to improve relations?"

"We can use Prednian for that."

"Ah. You want to understand our every word, but you want to hide your own? I wonder why there are communication difficulties between our races."

A mixture of grumbling and soft laughter answered her. Travannesal seemed inclined toward the latter and said, "You may link."

Another wave of hatred hit Kena as she drew near to Pernanyen. What was with that man? Yet, VanDar looked innocent as ever.

The link was no shock to Pernanyen this time. She eased into it, and Kena absorbed language—structure, grammar, meaning, and nuance—all from a native-speaker's perspective. An unexpected treasure trove. Oh, dear, she would be in high demand among the Collaborative's linguists.

The trial, which seemed to be more of a debate, continued.

DIVERSE SIMILARITY

Things were not going well for Pernanyen. That was really no surprise, yet Kena's very presence weakened the accusations. Before she'd entered the room, they had pointed out the severity of the injury Pernanyen had inflicted. Now, the injured party stood before them, fully capable. She was not only lucid and speaking, but even linking.

How little they understood of what she had suffered. Kena let that particular ignorance persist.

Some asserted that Pernanyen shouldn't have forced a link upon a member of an unknown race. Kena's recovery weakened this point as well. Others defended Pernanyen. She had acted within her authority. Her goal was admirable, and the need was great. Kena absorbed the meaning and intent of PitKreelaundun values and their decision-making processes. Most enlightening!

Eventually, Travannesal said, "I am hearing no new arguments. The only accusation which requires execution is non-completion of the constrained link. Kena, this reverts to you."

CHAPTER FORTY-EIGHT

Kena released her link with Pernanyen and moved away from her. The flow of hatred she had been resisting eased with each step she took, only to resume as she approached Travannesal. She stepped back to find a respite. Her own exhaustion was becoming a problem. *Sustain me, father.*

Travannesal said, "Kena Talgarth, you have the right to a constrained link with Pernanyen. You will completely control such a link. We have a minor issue with timing. I will not delay your and Ghent's departure. You have the choice of completing that link now, before you leave. If you prefer to sleep first—and I encourage you to do so—you may rest on the *Ontrevay*. I will permit you to return for the link and guarantee your subsequent departure when you wish it. If so, my only request is that you confirm whether you intend to return to complete the constrained link."

Before she could answer, VanDar said, "Why do you place this added stress on her? Has she not suffered too much already? Ma'am, you are under no compulsion, whatsoever, to link with Pernanyen again."

The gentle compassion of his words set Kena's teeth on edge.

TarKeen said, "How unusual to hear you speak with such

consideration, VanDar. It almost sounds like you wish to prevent her from choosing."

VanDar addressed his reply to Travannesal. "I would spare her a decision that may not actually be open to her. It seems unlikely, based on her previous statements, that she is capable of fully controlling the link. She cannot even initiate it."

ShenLee asked, "Pernanyen, when you linked with Kena this day, did you permit her to control after you initiated the link?"

"I did. Within an instant of forming the link, she was controlling. In a way, she was controlling even before. It's…it's very hard to describe…almost as though my action was necessary for *me* to realize the link, but not necessary for *her*."

"An unconventional manner of initiating the link," ShenLee said, "can hardly be deemed proof that Kena is not capable of control."

VanDar didn't let an instant pass. "Pernanyen's statements cannot be considered. She has an obvious, all-compelling reason to persuade Kena to link with her."

Kena tilted her head. "Do you not also have a compelling reason to prevent the link, VanDar of Kell?"

His shoulders jerked. He obviously hadn't expected that.

"Do you not gain a position in government if Pernanyen is executed?" Kena asked. "Is that why you try to prevent my linking with her? So that the constrained link will never be complete, and her death will grant you authority?"

His chest heaved while she spoke, but he'd controlled it by the time she finished. Once again, his voice was calm. "That is not my reason. Any position I might gain could only commence many years in the future and is not even certain, for Travannesal is still in mid-life. I speak as an ordinary citizen—as VanDar only." His smooth words sweetened even further. "It is for your protection that I speak on your behalf, to prevent further harm. That is my only motive. If Pernanyen is executed, justice will be served. You need not concern yourself with her."

Nauseating! Kena could tolerate no more. "Justice? What you

want is her death. You're simply hoping justice will bring that
death about. I went through agony to keep this woman alive, and
now you seek to kill her." Kena's voice deepened with each word,
reverberating through the chamber. "Do not claim that you speak
on my behalf."

His eyes held steady through a heartbeat. "As you wish, ma'am,
but I still insist on justice." He turned to Travannesal. "There is
more to consider than initiation. Kena said Humans do not engage
in forced links. Yet, that is exactly what she must do if she is to
complete her side of the constrained link."

Kena's stomach turned. This very thought had tormented her
sleepless days and nights—that she would somehow be coerced
into this very link. Every fiber of both spirit and mind rejected
even the idea of it. They weren't really forcing her, of course. And
yet, Pernanyen would be executed if Kena did not forcibly link
with her. Why did she struggle with that? In a way, it shouldn't
matter. It wasn't as though she was killing Pernanyen. The
PitKreelaundun would carry out the execution according to their
own law. But this was not...could not be her path. *Father, show me!*

*I take no delight in judgement or the sacrifice of her life. My delight is
in mercy. Mercy triumphs over judgement.*

Someone else, a Laundun woman, was speaking at length,
pointing out the goal of understanding and peace between the
races. She asserted that Kena's suffering would be in vain without
completion and politely encouraged Kena to pursue the benefits of
forcibly linking with Pernanyen.

Perhaps Kena's face revealed her revulsion, for VanDar again
launched a defense of her right to decline. How manipulative he
was—as willing to control her with his words as Pernanyen had
been to control her with telepathy.

Travannesal interrupted him. "Desist. Kena has rejected your
advocacy. I will not have her further annoyed. You're monopolizing
the discussion. Restrict further comments to new arguments only."

A wave of anger and hatred flowed from VanDar. Kena glanced
around. No awareness registered on any face. She drew on her

father's love for strength. *Must I see this?* His power infused her, and the unwelcome feelings evaporated like mist in sunshine.

"Kena," Travannesal said, "I don't want you over-persuaded by any argument, either for or against completing the link. Part of the arguments in favor of doing so may no longer be significant, since Leonfir and Ghent have linked." He turned to Leonfir. "Can you tolerate a superficial link?"

Leonfir nodded.

Travannesal went to him. Their link lasted only a moment. He moved away, saying, "Leonfir is convinced that Ghent knew nothing of the existence of tra-pentazine before coming here. As a captain, he would have been informed of such a substance if the Collaborative knew of it. Leonfir will share the reasons behind his belief with me after he has rested. It is probable that I will also find them convincing. Pernanyen sought this knowledge from Kena, but it no longer needs confirmation."

Someone in the crowd said, "There is still a possibility that select individuals could know, while the majority do not."

Kena rolled her eyes. Why were there always people so determined to hang onto their beliefs? "The only way to prove that no one knew is for you to personally link with all the billions of people in the Collaborative." With a quick shake of her head, Kena said, "A rather burdensome form of proof, that. It's hard to imagine any motive for concealing the knowledge. I assure you, navigators demand to be informed of all known risks. Captains, no doubt, have the same expectation. The fact that we would go to so much trouble to obtain and study the material, supports both that we didn't know and that we very much want to know."

"What you say is reasonable, ma'am," the man replied, "but we still really only know what one person of one race believes. And, apparently, the Plynteth are barely active within the Collaborative."

Pernanyen fidgeted. "Uh...with permission, I could..." She looked back and forth between Travannesal and Kena.

When Kena didn't respond, Travannesal said, "You may speak,

but remember, you may not state anything you learned from your link with Kena."

"I...um...I think it would be obvious that I would have wanted to know the opinions of as many races as possible."

Travannesal stopped Pernanyen with a gesture, his eyes fixed on Kena.

Her heart pounded as the memories surfaced. All those conversations Pernanyen had pried into. Heat suffused her face and hands. Impossible to keep her lips from trembling. "Are you all expecting to become privy to everything she..." Kena's throat seized. No, she could not say it.

Travannesal softened his voice and gently emphasized each word. "We will know nothing that you do not permit us to know."

Kena took a few calming breaths. "If Pernanyen lives...what will prevent others from accessing her memories of the constrained link?"

"The only way Pernanyen will live is if you constrain her to link," Travannesal said. "During that link, you will have full access to her memory. Not only will you be able to see it, but you can restrict or even destroy memories. If she is to be executed, she will not be permitted to even speak of what she learned from you, much less link with anyone."

"So, only I choose what is revealed?" Kena asked.

"That is correct."

"I wish to ask her two questions that may be answered with *yes, no,* or *I don't know.* Is that acceptable?"

"It is your choice," Travannesal said.

"Pernanyen..." Kena paused to frame the question. "Based on all the knowledge you have of me, did I know of tra-pentazine before coming to investigate the shattered planets?"

"No."

"Do I have any desire to harm any PitKreelaundun?"

Pernanyen seemed to search within herself. "No."

Kena turned back to Travannesal. "Is that the crux of what you really want to confirm?"

"It is." His voice was strained.

Finally, Kena sensed something from Travannesal. He had seemed emotionless. Now, she perceived his feelings, all gripped in tight control. But mourning slipped out as if he despaired. Did he think she had asked those questions so Pernanyen could now be executed?

She murmured, "I did say *any* PitKreelaundun."

Someone began to speak, but Travannesal stopped her when the gist became clear. "Nothing more will be said in persuasion. Kena will decide as appropriate for herself. Ma'am, do you have adequate information to make your decision?"

Did she? How could she bring this around to satisfy their sense of justice and still allow mercy? "Not really. I know my desire, that Pernanyen live. In this, my decision is made. But the practicalities are...problematic. The very nature of how I link is different from yours. If I cannot link in the same manner as she did, will you say that I have not fulfilled my side of the link?"

"We will allow for differences. The only requirement is that you completely control."

"When I say 'control the link' it only means that I am controlling the interaction. It does not mean that I control what the other person chooses to reveal. Which do *you* mean?"

"The latter. Please remember, the goal is that you become as convinced of our intentions as she is of yours. She wants you to understand both our desire for peace and our need to protect ourselves."

Kena licked her lips and swallowed. "I cannot forcibly extract from another person's mind against their will."

Pernanyen spoke in a voice as little as a child's. "It would not be against my will. I permit it. In fact, I request it. I still really want...want you to know..." Her lips worked in silence.

She reminded Kena of Pearl. Orphaned, heart-broken, and desperate. It seemed odd that this was the same woman who had ruthlessly probed her mind. So strange that compassion and rage could coexist. She tried to envision searching through Pernanyen for those stolen memories and somehow restricting them. Tears filled her eyes. She didn't even know how to do that. Could she bear to see them in Pernanyen's mind? And on top of it all, exhaustion was overwhelming her. Kena put a hand over her mouth to cover a yawn that she could no longer suppress. *Oh, Father, I'm a mess. I shouldn't even be making a decision like this. Not in this state.*

"Tomorrow," Travannesal said. "Please don't link with her today."

"No, not today." Kena said, her voice listless.

"Do not be concerned about how long you need to sleep. Take as much time as you need."

He had no idea. *Father, I don't know what to do.*

I know, my child. You will find counsel among your own. Rest. Heal. Then, return.

She became aware of conversation around her. They were already talking about taking her and Ghent to their craft. She held up a hand to stop the flow of words. "You don't quite understand. Not today or tomorrow or even the next day. I need more time."

Silence stretched.

"That's a problem," Travannesal said. "The PitKreelaundun cannot endure extended isolation. We need to link. I know most races can get by with just emfrel, but we cannot. We must link every four or five days, at the very least."

Oh, would they ever quit coming up with objections? "So, link with her."

"She is forbidden to do so until she completes the constrained link with you. It needs to happen soon."

"You linked with her when you disowned her. I asked her about it."

His head twitched back as surprise jerked another wave of mourning from his grip. So, disowning his daughter had cost him something, after all. He grieved over the separation as much as Pernanyen did. A price he would be paying for months to come. And now his daughter would pay it also. Kena did not want to return to find the woman wracked, perhaps maddened, by isolation and grief.

Travannesal cleared his throat. "True, but that was necessary to sever our bond. I saw nothing of her link with you."

"This is also necessary. She kept you from seeing. You did not seek for the knowledge. If both of you could do that once, can you not do it many times over?"

"Yes, but...it isn't truly necessary. You need more rest than normal, but a few days should be sufficient."

Kena shook her head. "No, Travannesal. You don't actually know what happened within me, and you don't know what I need. I cannot link that deeply with Pernanyen until I have counsel from my own people. Your law guarantees me the right to complete the constrained link. This is the only way your law can be fulfilled. I need her to be healthy when I return." She moved nearer as she spoke, holding his gaze.

The crowd held its breath, waiting for his words.

He looked down into her eyes for a long moment. "I will do as you ask."

A wave of hatred, more putrid than the others, hit her. She quivered and swung her gaze to the side. Her father swept it from her, but she understood his reason for revealing it.

Travannesal's gaze followed hers to VanDar.

She looked back up at him, held her lips as still as a Grfdn's, and whispered, "You're in danger."

He responded with an infinitesimal nod.

She stepped back to the center again. "I want three-fold assurance from your authority triad that Pernanyen will be kept healthy, comfortable, and safe until I return."

"I ensure it," Travannesal said.

She turned to TarKeen.

"I ensure it," he repeated.

She turned to Leonfir and said, "Are you able to understand and make a commitment?"

His eyes were heavy, but he nodded and said, "Ensure."

Travannesal let out a long breath, his face somber. "I would appreciate an estimate of when you will return."

"Yes, I suppose so." Kena spoke her thoughts aloud, for calculating time was beyond her. "Assume about a month on Earth. Perhaps more. I'll need time for the journey there and back. And you may recall that I am on a science mission. Ghent indicated to me, as best he could, that our collection of tra-pentazine cannot be left where it is or taken to the Collaborative's area."

A sigh floated through the gathering, and their relief lingered, echoing the sound.

Travannesal moved one foot back and bowed toward Kena then to Ghent in a fluid movement. "I extend our thanks on behalf of all PitKreelaundun."

Some formal response was probably expected, but Kena only managed to incline her head. "I believe we must take the collection in the opposite direction, which will require more time."

"Obviously," Travannesal said, "I cannot object to that delay."

"It will also take longer than we planned for the mission. We need provisions."

"Is there something you want us to provide?"

"No," Kena said. "It must come from the Collaborative. That means, we need communication and an access route."

"I am hoping," Travannesal said with measured emphasis, "that you are not asking to bring another gravity ship between the nebula and PitKreelaundun space."

"No, a large craft will do." She massaged the center of her forehead. "My guess is that you will have ships nearby."

"We must reassess the area and neutralize any problems we find."

Kena nodded. "Can you speak for your government? Can you guarantee safe passage?"

He gave her a long, steady look. "I can speak for the PitKreelaundun government. I will guarantee safe passage for a craft that is commanded by a Human or a Plynteth."

"Hmm. It will most likely be a Human. Other races will be in the crew." Her frown deepened. "I do not want direct contact between any of you and any Human until I return. And frankly, I've heard some rather untrusting talk from PitKreelaundun. What are the chances that these other ships' captains will accept the commander's assurance of being Human or Plynteth?"

Travannesal glanced at Ghent. "Make sure they can send a live image during communication. That should work for the Plynteth. The Prednian profile of Humans said that you resemble the Tenelli. Do you have any visible traits that we'll be able to identify remotely?"

"No. In fact, be prepared for a great deal of variation in Humans. My skin tone is called white, but there are black skin tones as well, with many shades between." His brows shot up and lips parted, but she refused to let him stop her. "The shape of eyes and other features vary, as well. Some males even have thick facial hair. I think you'll have to rely on voice."

He looked even more taken aback. "But...your voice is not particularly unique."

"You haven't heard it all yet. We have an alternate voice, one to speak with and one to *sing* with."

"Sing? Please explain."

Kena was beyond explanations. She opened her mouth and let a series of notes rise and fall.

Exclamations filled the chamber.

"Can any of the races you've contacted do that?" she asked.

His mouth moved a couple times before he got words out. "No! That was...beautiful!"

She was used to amazement over Human voice, but this was the first time she'd ever been complimented for singing a scale. "Can we use that to identify a Human?"

"Yes, I think so."

She turned to Ghent. His face was sagging. She didn't even want to try for a link. "Do we need anything else before we leave?"

He shook his head.

She took a deep breath. "Right. Travannesal, I'm about to

request departure, and I only want to ask once. So, before I do, is there anything more to discuss?"

Seething reached her again from VanDar. *Father, what is it? What are you trying to show me?* In a way, she really didn't want to know. She was just too tired to deal with it.

"Only one," Travannesal said. "Would you be willing to sing again, so we may record it for identification? It's just not possible to describe with words."

Good point, actually. She'd given them so little, and her voice had cracked, besides. "Yes, I probably should. This won't be the best, because I don't have time to warm up my voice, but it'll have to do." He looked puzzled. Oh, well. "There are words and a melody in a *song*. No two people will *sing* it exactly the same."

Her mind cast around for something suitable. She had just listened to so many. Any of them would do, but somehow, that didn't seem right. She needed something common that any Human could repeat. Why couldn't she think of anything? Was she even awake enough to pilot a craft?

The first line of an old song popped into her mind. She cleared her throat and began. "My eyes have seen the fury of the raging, vengeful horde." *Where did this come from?* A melody first written for an old civil war, later reworded for the seven-year war that had engulfed Earth. And then, suddenly, she knew.

Her gaze swung to VanDar as she sang the next line. "As they trampled dying brothers and released the dogs of war."

Civil war screamed from every nuance of his being. She smelled death. Images flashed in her mind as she sang. It wasn't just VanDar's hatred of the Frayunomen family. Streams of tension pulsed through the room. Those two men had contemplated assassination. And it wasn't just here. That strange disparity between Freltenloe's and TarKeen's explanations of race came back to her.

But these revelations did not change the fact that she was singing of war and death. Someday, they'd be able to translate the

English words. Could she have picked anything worse? And yet, every eye—no, every sairit—was wholly fixed on her. Mesmerized.

She couldn't stop. Nor could she leave them with words of judgement.

There was another verse, the last one. It held hope. She turned to Travannesal and sang it to him. "In the beauty of the dawning, grace and truth returned to us..." Could she remember the rest? Wait. Why was she doing this alone? She cast herself into her beloved's embrace and turned the song to worship. The words flowed. She didn't even know if they were the original, but they worked.

The final notes echoed through the room, rich and strong, like the presence of her beloved. It was a pity no one else could sense that. Or had they, perhaps, felt something? They stared with mouths agape. Ghent wasn't shocked, but even he seemed spellbound. She focused on Travannesal and waited.

It took a full minute for him to find his voice, and even that sounded breathless. "That was...lovely beyond words. Can you... translate it?"

Kena shook her head. "It's figurative poetry, so it wouldn't make sense. It's remembered for historical reasons. People from my culture would likely be able to repeat at least part of it." She hoped that was enough to prevent a future uproar.

"Ah. Thank you, ma'am." He couldn't seem to say anything else.

Kena turned to Pernanyen, whose mobile shoulders trembled with shuddering exhalations. Kena prepared within then squatted by her chair. "Reach for me." A whispered invitation.

Pernanyen's quivering soon stilled in the comfort that Kena extended.

I will return. Kena waited for her to accept that. *You will show my memories to no one.*

Pernanyen returned those words as a solemn oath.

Be at peace. Kena withdrew.

The atmosphere had settled, and Travannesal stood waiting.

Kena neared him. "Travannesal of Frayunomen, I request departure for Ghent and myself."

He inclined his head in formal acknowledgement. "Commander TarKeen, escort Captain Ghent and Kena Talgarth to their craft and arrange their departure. Ensure a clear course to the *Ontrevay*."

TarKeen inclined his head. "As you order, sir."

Ghent lifted himself to his feet. He didn't bother with words, but managed to exchange that formal inclined head gesture with both Travannesal and Leonfir.

Permission to leave—at last. Now, what surprises did the hallways and bay hold?

CHAPTER FORTY-NINE

Kena and Ghent walked on either side of TarKeen through empty hallways. When they crossed the first intersection, she cast furtive glances to the side. TarKeen looked at her. "You are safe."

"I'm not so sure."

"I secured the route before the trial started," he said. "You *are* safe."

So, he'd felt the need. "Is VanDar a threat?"

"Probably not to either of you, but he's being watched."

Ah, he felt the need for that, too. His words confirmed at least some of what she had perceived in the chamber.

"How did you know," TarKeen asked, "about VanDar being a member of a non-ruling family?"

"I asked Pernanyen who he was when I linked with her."

"What else did she tell you?" he asked.

"That hers is the last generation of her family to rule. Frayunomen will then become non-ruling, and Kell will again take their position as a ruling family. VanDar is older than her, so it won't be him, but one of his children will probably be in the primary position."

"Did she tell you that if she dies young and Kell takes their position early, it will change the balance of power in the government?"

"Not really," Kena said, "but I saw an image of the cyclic diagram of ruling families. It's not hard to see that the PitKree would become the majority if the cycle is advanced."

Ghent stumbled, and TarKeen gripped his arm. "Sir, do you need more assistance?"

Ghent shook his head, but TarKeen maintained his grip as they continued walking.

TarKeen, apparently, could not be distracted from his questions. "Did Pernanyen believe that VanDar wants her position?"

"Not that I know of," Kena said. "Remember, it wasn't a forced link. She decided how much to reveal."

"How, then, did you...draw the conclusion that he seeks rule?"

She sighed. "I can't explain. It's like I told you before."

TarKeen didn't respond. She glanced sideways at him. His black eyebrows jutted low, and his lips were compressed. Should she tell him the rest? The knowing within herself insisted that she should. Must.

"There's something else, TarKeen. Can we be overheard or recorded here?"

"We're almost to the hold. We must go through the control room where a couple people are on duty. May I enter your craft?"

"You may."

TarKeen looked toward Ghent, perhaps expecting confirmation from him, but Ghent didn't even look up. His exhaustion called forth an answering yawn from Kena.

In the control room, TarKeen motioned a crew member aside and used the controls himself.

Only a few more steps took them past a doorway and blue lines. Kena put a hand out to touch their little craft—her chance to see home again. A long sigh slipped between her lips.

TarKeen stooped to pick up her EVA belt, which lay near the

hatch, and handed it to her. It prompted memory—the unnerving sensation of its removal, how it had slid down her hips and across her leg. How long ago, that seemed. She pressed the hatch release on the craft and stepped inside. TarKeen helped Ghent in and supported him until he was seated in one of the two couches.

TarKeen turned to Kena in the small space, his hair brushing the ceiling. "What else?" he asked.

"TarKeen, are you on the verge of civil war?"

His entire face tightened, and his voice grated. "Why do you ask me that?"

"Partly because...I feel that VanDar wants the Frayunomen family dead. Not just Pernanyen, but Travannesal, as well."

His nostrils shifted down.

"But it's more than that," she said. "There is a tension I can't describe between the PitKree and the Laundun. When I was singing, I had the impression that war was approaching—soon. Like an automated countdown that's already started. It won't stop on its own. Someone must abort it."

He stared into her eyes, his face rigid.

"Have your races ever had a civil war, TarKeen?"

He shook his head.

"Mine has. Even if one side claims victory, both sides lose. They both pay a tremendous price. It brings only death and devastation. Families are destroyed. Bitterness rages for generations. If you love anyone at all, if you have any friends—either PitKree or Laundun—don't let it happen, TarKeen. Abort that countdown before it's too late."

TarKeen's gut twisted so tight, it hurt.

If only he could link with her, to learn what she really knew and grasp the truth of it. He couldn't, of course. Then, he sensed her presence surrounding him. Just a breath, it seemed.

"I will not link," she said, "but you may reach to feel me."

An invitation he could not refuse. He quivered at that touch—
then it was gone. He reached out a hand to steady himself. No
wonder Pernanyen had been shaken.

TarKeen took a deep breath. "You must go."

Kena nodded. "It's time. You have fulfilled your commitment
to me. Thank you."

He inclined his head and stepped from the craft. The hatch
closed behind him as he strode to the control room.

Her words were balm. He had not fulfilled his commitment as
originally intended; but, if she would thank him, then at least she
recognized his attempt and determination. How she could, was a
mystery. Their contacts had been so brief. Another indication of
how much she knew that she couldn't know. Civil war? Would it
come to that? All the PitKree needed was a few ships and the right
to seek a planet on their own...not control of the government.

TarKeen gave orders and watched their execution from the
control room, but his mind remained riveted on her words. Civil
war? What if she was right? He could not let that become true!

K ena secured the flight restraint around Ghent then
strapped herself in. TarKeen's voice over the comm
channel gave her notice of the craft's move into the receiving bay.
False gravity slipped away. Zero G mirrored an internal release that
washed through her mind. Her craft was ejected past the blue-
lined walls into open space. She magnified the view until the
Ontrevay filled the screen. Her home away from home. She looked
over at Ghent.

He stared at it, too, and let out a long breath.

TarKeen said, "You are clear to engage primary drive. Safe
travels."

Wow, a phrase Humans used. "Thank you. I'll see you in the
months to come."

The habits of a navigator kicked in. She reviewed the empty

scan of the straight route to the *Ontrevay* and brought her craft's drive online. She couldn't program the course. Yes, this was definitely the stripped craft that Ghent had mentioned in one of the recorded messages.

A welcome voice came over the comm channel. "Ghent or Kena, report status."

"Hi, Hrndl. Sure is sweet to hear your voice."

"I feel the same about yours. How are you, my dear?"

"I'm okay," Kena said. "Pretty tired, though."

"Beyond doubt. Ghent, how are you doing?"

He didn't answer. His eyes were closed, and his breathing slow.

"He's fine, but he just fell asleep."

"Not good," Hrndl said. "He was supposed to pilot you home."

"Mm. I guess we're on plan B."

"Can you pilot that craft?"

"Yeah, what little there is." As she spoke, Kena slid her hand over one of the console panels—it failed to illuminate. "Quite a bit seems to be missing." She fiddled with an unusual device. "Oh, look at this. There's a manual lock for the control sticks. High tech!"

The comm system picked up Veet laughter in the background. The overdone sort that came from relief.

Kena let out a yawn that wouldn't be denied then asked, "Do you know what's been happening on the *Epri7*?"

"We've had multiple status reports," Hrndl said, "and they gave us visual and audio of the trial."

"Good. I'm really not up for explanations at the moment."

"That's fine."

Another yawn demanded release, so cavernous it felt like it would detach her jaw.

"Was that a yawn?" Hrndl asked.

"Yeah. You might want to talk to Metchell about how sleep deprivation affects Humans."

"I'll do that," Hrndl said. "Right now, we're going to talk

through shield levels, setting the burn duration on the primary drive, and locking down your controls."

"It's like you think I might fall asleep or something."

"Yes, it is, isn't it? Quon is on his way to meet you. He'll capture your craft and take over navigation as soon as you rendezvous. Tell me what your shield levels read."

Kena talked through the details. Hrndl was clearly getting her set up to reach the *Ontrevay*, even if she was unconscious on arrival.

"All right, Kena," Hrndl said. "You'll get here, and we'll take care of everything else. Don't change anything without talking to me first."

"Okay."

"Do you want to chat with me, or do you prefer quiet?"

"Prefer music, actually. I'm gonna mute the channel."

"That's fine." Hrndl's voice was so gentle. "If you're awake, give me status reports. That way, I won't have to interrupt a song. Even I know that's rude."

The music alternately soothed and sustained Kena. The halfway point arrived sooner than it should have. Even though she had vague knowledge of a craft approaching, it seemed suddenly close. Quon's and Hrndl's voices were discussing capture of her powered craft. Why hadn't they asked for her status? Or had they? Asleep while piloting. Pathetic. Time to show some sign of life.

"Hi, Quon. You got to come back for me, after all."

"So I did, Kena." Emotion deepened his voice. "How are you doing?"

"Um...I'm awake." An abrupt exhalation reached her ears. Was that suppressed laughter or disbelief?

"How is Ghent?" Quon asked.

Kena looked over at him. No change. "Still asleep."

Hrndl's voice came over the comm channel. "Kena, I know it's earlier than we planned, but I want you to shut down your primary drive."

Kena reached for the controls. "Am I doing that bad?"

"You're doing well, considering sleep deprivation. I had that conversation you suggested with Metchell. Consider this payback for the day you forced me to disembark before our mission was complete."

A tired smile pulled at Kena's mouth. Interesting double meaning for the word *payback*. "Shutdown complete."

"Shutdown confirmed," Quon said.

"All right, Kena," Hrndl said. "Quon has command now, and you are relieved. You don't have to fight to stay awake anymore. Just go to sleep."

That went against all instinct, but Kena had no doubt her craft was secure.

Her next realization was of the *Ontrevay* filling her window. Almost there. Longing and trepidation swirled to the surface. She desperately needed the touch of her own, yet she feared that emotions—theirs or hers—would plunge her into a sobbing meltdown. *Hold me together, father.*

I am your strength. Your safety and peace in the storm.

An unwelcome correlation surfaced from the tired, hurting side of her mind. He had comforted her when she was about to set herself adrift with Pearl. And then she had suffered agony. This comfort he offered her now—?

Ghent uttered an audible breath and stirred.

She glanced over at him. His expression changed from vague to alert in a couple seconds. How did he do that?

He looked at the *Ontrevay* and then her. "This is a pleasant sight to wake up to."

"That, it is!"

"I was trying to get a couple words out before sleep caught me. Well done, Kena!"

She blinked. "I, uh, didn't do much. Just laid there in a daze most of the time."

His eyes half closed then widened. "Kena, you have initiated *friendship*—with the *PitKreelaundun!*"

459

"So have you," she said, shrugging one shoulder. "With a lot less fuss, apparently."

He groaned. "Perhaps you are just despondent from exhaustion, but I'm not letting another moment pass with you thinking like this. Did you rescue and return an enemy's child?"

"Well, yes."

"Did your actions and words suggest to them that we are far different than they believed?"

"I suppose."

"Did you preserve Pernanyen's life?"

Kena made a sound in her throat. "Sort of. She's still in really grim circumstances."

"Did you, by chance, learn her language?"

"Yeah."

"And you learned it telepathically during active dialog. I'm guessing you picked up a lot of cultural nuances. Am I right?"

"Yes." Really, it was impossible to deny the value of that.

"You also gained enough influence with a primary member of government to negotiate safe passage for a supply vessel, and I'm guessing quite a bit more, besides."

"Mm."

"Even though you didn't intend it, you brought about a meeting between captains of the PitKreelaundun and the Collaborative. Yes, I will take some credit for its success, but I wouldn't have met him without your selfless and courageous actions."

Kena licked her lips and tried to figure out where to look.

"And last, there is the part I have yet to understand. That seems more profound than the rest. Not only have you decreased the chances of the Collaborative going to war with them, it appears you may even be preventing a civil war among the PitKreelaundun."

Kena let out a breath. "Oh, I do hope so."

Silence hovered for a moment, then he reached over and swept a finger across her furrowed brow. "No more frowning. I can only guess at what it cost you, but even the good we've seen already is priceless. We'll be recording the benefits of your last few days for years to come. You...have...done...well!"

A little breath huffed between her lips. She managed a shaky smile. "Thank you, Ghent," she whispered.

Another success crossed her mind—one that would never occur to Ghent. The PitKreelaundun had grasped that Humans were not sairital beings—crucial if Humans were to deal with such an intrinsically telepathic race. Her beloved's promise from days before whispered through her mind. Good had come in spite of Pernanyen's horrific decision. Kena still had a hard time with part of it, but she drew on the strength and peace he promised her now. It moved within her, so tangible she could almost smell the sweetness of his spirit.

Hrndl's voice came over the comm channel. "Kena, are you awake?"

Ghent reached across the console and tapped the control. "We both are."

"Ah, good. May I have your status?"

"I'm fine—no injury. Just a little tired. Kena still needs plenty of rest. Keep the welcoming party small."

"Yes, sir."

"I need to talk with Remlishos."

"I'm here," he said.

"Do we have communication to the Collaborative yet?"

"No, sir. TarKeen says they will cease blocking after you are on board."

"Good," Ghent said. "Announce an order that personal outgoing messages can only state that we have experienced communication issues—not the cause. No mention may be made of PitKreelaundun contact until after I inform the Collaborative leadership. Set up to record a message from me to Gordahl."

In a few seconds, Remlishos said, "We're ready to record, sir."

"Ghent, captain of the *Ontrevay*, addressing Gordahl, chief of science fleet. We have experienced communication issues for the past few days. In case our silence has prompted concern, I assure you that the *Ontrevay* and its crew are safe."

Ghent drew a deep breath. "We have discovered much concerning the exotic matter which caused the planetary breakup in SMG76428. That material is present in the nebula and poses substantial risk to ships with gravity fields. No gravity-generating ships should travel near the nebula. I repeat, do not permit ships to approach the nebula while generating artificial gravity. I have much more to report, Gordahl, and look forward to a long conversation with you soon."

Ghent closed the channel, and Kena murmured, "That should get their attention."

Ghent uttered a soft chuckle.

The open bay now filled the screen. Within another minute, they passed between the doors, and the familiar walls surrounded them. The craft jerked as the anchor field engaged it, then the gravity field reactivated.

Hrndl's voice announced, "Ghent, your section is sealed and pressurized."

He reached across the console again to open the hatch.

Kena released her belt and tried to stand. Heavier than expected. She struggled to her feet. Was this the gravity difference, or was she really that weak?

Metchell entered the craft. "Sit down again, Kena, until I check you over."

"I really want to get out now."

His steady gaze flicked over her, then settled on her face. Apparently, he decided to humor her. He gripped her arm and guided her toward the hatch, where Hrndl stood with one foot inside the craft.

"Full support," Metchell said, as Hrndl hooked her hand beneath Kena's other arm. "Remember, she's had a gravity change."

Dhgnr stood just outside and reached in to support her as Metchell let go.

"I'm all right," Kena mumbled, then tripped on the hatch sill.

Their grip was too firm to let her fall. Dhgnr steadied her then wrapped his arm around her waist and picked her up.

Kena startled and couldn't help a bit of ineffective struggling.

"Settle yourself," Dhgnr said.

He was going to be stubborn. She got an arm around his shoulders and straightened her back.

The faint hum of a containment field silenced, then running footsteps echoed across the bay. Kena twisted her neck to see who was coming. Quon dashed to her side. She gripped the hand he extended and squeezed his fingers. His lips moved, but he couldn't seem to find words. That was fine with her. She smiled her thanks, and the strain in his face eased.

"We'll take you to your quarters now," Hrndl said.

Kena looked at Dhgnr. "I can walk."

"Perhaps," he said, "but you don't need to."

Quon placed Kena's hand on Dhgnr's shoulder and stepped back.

Kena looked beseechingly at Hrndl.

The corners of her eyes tilted up. "Don't think I will let you win this argument." She turned and started for the door, Dhgnr falling into step beside her.

The voice of her beloved whispered within. *Why do you resist, my dear one? Accept their gift. Rest.*

Kena exhaled and relaxed. She was with friends, be they ever so unlikely. She was home.

The End

CAST OF CHARACTERS

Major characters – Part 1

Kena — senior navigator (Human)
Ghent — captain of the Ontrevay (Plynteth)
Metchell — chief medical officer (Dantokrellie)
Hrndl — senior navigator (Grfdn)
Krdn — second navigator (Grfdn)
Dhgnr — engineer (Grfdn)

Major PitKreelaundun characters – Part 2

Pernanyen — Young member of the ruling family of Frayunomen.
TarKeen — Commander of the Epri7.
Leonfir — Captain of the Epri7.
VanDar — Primary member of the family of Kell.
Travannesal — Primary member of the ruling family of Frayunomen. Pernanyen's father.

Minor characters – Part 1

Betnorel — scientist (Prednian)
Delatin — chef (Prednian)
Delf — senior navigator (Veet)
Elna — navigator (Meklehon)

Eperia — junior navigator (Meklehon)
Frdn — communications (Grfdn)
Frethan — chief navigation officer (Tenelli)
Giddech — navigator (Chonander)
Gordahl —Interstellar Collaborative's chief of science fleet (Meklehon)
Inewin — chief communications officer (Married to Netlyn.) (Tenelli)
Jorlit — navigator (Tenelli)
Leelee — scientist (Paedutae)
Netlyn — navigator (Married to Inewin.) (Tenelli)
Opyera — communications (Prednian)
Piert — chief science officer (Veet)
Presh — scientist (Jathrepon)
Quon — navigator (Veet)
Remlishos — chief engineering officer (Meklehon)
Rnl — resource management (Grfdn)
Salsheen — scientist (Dantokrellie)
Thrayl — scientist (Tenelli)

Minor PitKreelaundun characters – Part 2

DrenVid — medical assistant
Freltenloe — doctor
Gwillenin — guardian of Jennellee
Jennellee — orphaned child, also called Pearl.
Rialmerray —chief officer of tra-pentazine protection
Shannandi — medical assistant
ShenLee — maintenance technician
YefRon — doctor

THE NEXT ADVENTURE

Want to hear more about Kena and the crew of the *Ontrevay*? Keep an eye out for the next novel in the Diverse Series...

Diverse Demands

A race teeters on the edge of civil war, while another faces extinction. Kena has promised to help one of them, but the other pleads for Antony's aid. Will the conflicting needs of alien races destroy the budding love Kena and Antony have explored during their journey aboard the *Ontrevay*?

Sign up for Sharon's newsletter at SharonRoseAuthor.com and be the first to know when more adventures are released.

MORE FROM SHARON ROSE

NOVELS

Diverse Similarity
Diverse Demands (future)

SHORT STORIES

AGENTS OF RIVELT

Never Blackmail a Thought-Reader
Don't Rescue Me
Orphaned
Trapped Rescuer
Assassin Hunting
Counterfeit Apprentice
Forbidden Spy (future)

More titles are coming in the future. Find them all at Sharon's
website: SharonRoseAuthor.com

ACKNOWLEDGMENTS

As I pondered who and what to mention in the acknowledgements, two things happened. First, gratitude swelled to enormous proportions. Then, this page become a daunting task, for how could I ever express my appreciation to so many?

Some are obvious. My family, for instance, for their encouragement over the years and their patience as I talk about fictitious characters in make-believe worlds. But even as I list Phil, Jason, Raechel, Philip, and Laura, my mind travels to siblings and in-laws, and to friends who feel like family. My gratitude extends to all of you.

My editor, Bridgett Powers, who has become such a dear friend. Without her, this book would never have been published, for not only is she a skillful slayer of evil adverbs, she is also a fabulous encourager. But then I think of so many others. Realm Makers and other conferences come to mind. Whether you are an editor, agent, publisher, cover designer, conference organizer, volunteer, guide in the craft of writing, fellow author, guru of discoverability, or anything in between—some of you have never even met me, but you've had far more impact than you know. My thanks go out to all of you.

And then there are readers: My critique group, Write Now at Living Word Christian Center. My Advance Reader Team. Those readers I've never met who sent me kind words about earlier stories. You are all a blessing and encouragement to me.

To each and every one of you: Thank you! May the help you've given me multiply and flow back to you.

ABOUT THE AUTHOR

Sharon has a life-long fascination with people. Communication, culture, personalities, viewpoints, beliefs...anything that makes each of us beautifully unique.

For over fifteen years, she explored those interests as an Information Technology Business Analyst, acting as a liaison between savvy business customers and brilliant IT geeks. There were days when that job felt much like translating concepts between alien cultures.

In 2016 Sharon waved goodbye to big corporations, to focus on her dream of writing science fiction and fantasy. What better way to dive deep into the complexities of humankind? For, every far-flung adventure starts from the treasures hidden deep within us.

Sharon is the author of the Agents of Rivelt short story series, the novel *Diverse Similarity*, and many more stories still finding their way onto the page. When she's not writing or reading, she may be traveling, enjoying gardens, or searching for unique coffee shops. She lives with her husband in Minnesota, USA.

For more information or to contact Sharon, visit:
SharonRoseAuthor.com

 facebook.com/AuthorSharonRose